TRADING

SECRETS

Thomson Roy

This is a work of fiction. All incidents and dialogue, and all characters with the exception of some well-known historical and public figures, are products of the author's imagination and are not meant to be construed as real. Where real-life historical or public figures appear, the situations, incidents, and dialogues concerning those persons are fictional and are not intended to depict actual events or to change the fictional nature of the work.. In all other respects, any resemblance to persons living or dead is entirely coincidental.

Published by Thomson Roy

ISBN 9781735898414

DEDICATIONS

WITH LOVE AND GRATITUDE FOR

Janeice Wright Roy
Her gift of love and support during all the trials
leading to this work,
And every moment together

IN MEMORY OF
Eleanor Thomson Roy and Charles Thomson Roy
The musician and the engineer
To whom I owe everything

W. Francis Marion
Marine, trial lawyer, leader, mentor

Charlie N. Carter
Investigator, engineer, companion, friend

“Three can keep a secret if two of them are dead.“

-Benjamin Franklin

“If you want to keep a secret, you must also hide it from yourself.”

-George Orwell

PROLOGUE

KYUSHU ISLAND, JAPAN, SEPTEMBER 14, 1978

The roar of the M3H rocket engine shattered the calm of the Kagoshima launch control bunker. Director Kano Asao's body shook and his vision blurred. His engineers held their breath as the noise and vibration receded. Only this trial in space could confirm the success of their invention riding in the nosecone.

Soft clicks from digital readouts filled the emptiness. Tearing away from the flight desk, Kano threaded his way to the blast doors, then broke into bright daylight. The launch facility spread across a rocky plateau jutting into the Pacific. As he strode up the hill to the administration building, Kano felt the sun warm his back. Looking up, he saw the coastal waters quivering like a thousand silver flashes.

Kano pushed into the administrative building and took the stairs two at a time. Entering a sparsely furnished office, he saw the Space Center director's vision riveted on the rocket's trail through a broad window. The director's eyes glistened as he turned and planted his fists on a wooden bench. "Kano-*san*, your new computer will strengthen our nation. This is a triumph—"

A deafening explosion hurled Kano to the floor, his body hit by shards of debris. A metallic taste bloomed in his mouth. He struggled to rise, staring at the smoking rubble littering the room.

As he raised his eyes, Kano's knees buckled. His friend's body was pinned to the bench by an iron rod, like a roast on a spit. The body shuddered and fell still. A jagged hole now filled the wall behind the silent corpse. Down the hill at the bunker, Kano saw clouds of billowing smoke pierced by licking flames that were incinerating his team and any chance for the success of their mission.

Chapter 1
EAST TEXAS, 4:30PM, THURSDAY, NOVEMBER 16, 1978

The office trailer felt like a steam bath. I was a young lawyer stuck in the middle of a sea of pine trees, fighting the owner of the giant paper mill my client was building. Rural Newton County was far from where I thought my career would take me.

Sweat slid down my neck as I finished improvising seals on metal file drawers by scribbling my initials in Whiteout muck: JP for Jake Payne. A wheezing window air-conditioner cranked out nothing but noise. Hot, wet beads soaked my shirt.

The angry owner's rep—Boyden—had bullied our young project manager into submission. I'd had to step in. After flying down from South Carolina and sizing up the situation, my first professional act had been to insult the owner's egomaniacal representative by calling him Bohack—not Boyden. Over and over.

Blood vessels popping from his neck, he'd just kicked us off the job by issuing a hurried letter that breached our contract. Not bad for a half-day's work.

Our scrawny office clerk, Billy, was on lookout through a dirt-streaked window. Our project manager stood dazed. I wiped the white gunk from my hands and picked up the phone receiver to finish a call to my firm. "All set?" I asked.

"Yep," Preston Lawton my mentor and senior partner confirmed. "Git goin'." I hung up, grabbed my black leather bag, and herded our project manager toward the door.

The clerk yelped and his voice broke. "Here they come, swinging some kinda weapons." The office door flew open sending a trash bin crashing across the trailer.

Boyden's mountain sized foreman stuck in the door frame, then shot through followed by three others brandishing iron bars. The foreman's shoulders heaved as he whirled a huge pipe wrench above his head and slammed it onto a metal desk that caved in like a cardboard box.

"Nobody moves. Nothin' leaves this office. Boyden's orders."

Our project manager turned white. I took a couple of deep breaths.

"No need to get excited. Look here." I pointed to my initials in the white splotches. "All our document drawers have seals. Break 'em and you're in for a heap of trouble."

The foreman's face darkened as he tried to square this information with his instructions.

A crackle from his radio split the silence and a guard reported, "The contractor's van left the site a while ago, moving fast." Our file cabinets were empty. I'd told the van driver to switch our job documents to a station wagon off-site, then head home. At least they were safe.

The foreman started around the table toward me. I held up my hand. "You open anything, touch anyone, you'll answer to the law." But which law? On a call that morning I learned the local judge was coming to the site for a visit, due any minute. I had to assume he was in Boyden's pocket, a trick he'd used all over the world. A quick search on Lexis-Nexis back home had said so.

"You'll be up in court," I warned.

The foreman stopped. He turned, pushed his buddies toward the door, and snapped, "Come on. Gotta tell Boyden."

I hefted my document bag, pushed the project manager toward the door, and yelled at the clerk, "Let's go."

Sirens screamed in the distance and we froze. Nothing out there but a million pine trees, the construction site. And us. Our police band radio squawked and a deputy's voice cut through. "Copy. We's headed to the office trailer where they's stealing stuff." Boyden had called *his* sheriff in to haul us up before *his* judge.

I grabbed the job site radio and called our man at the front gate. "You see the sheriff's cars?"

"Two of 'em, both headed outside the site to the back gate." And our trailer.

The contract, the facts, and the law were on our side. I had to get home fast to file suit in Federal Court.

I jabbed a finger at the clerk. "Go start the pickup."

The sirens blared as the sheriff's cars turned the corner on the dirt road and headed straight for us. We sprinted outside to the revving pickup. I said calmly to the clerk, "Head through the site to the front gate."

He just stared at me.

Our project manager screamed, "*Gun it.*" Our clerk stomped on the gas. The lugged tires spit gravel and red dust. The boy's knuckles turned white.

"You like NASCAR, Billy?" I asked.

"Richard Petty. Me an' Momma both."

Our pickup steamed toward the front gate, trailing a billowing red cloud. Another giant iron rod-wielding worker blocked our exit.

"Slow down," I said.

The clerk slammed on the brakes and our pickup bucked to a stop. The sirens stopped, too. The sheriff's deputies must be back at our trailer, out of their cars looking for us.

The worker threw down the rod. In two long strides he filled my open window. "Gonna search you for stolen property."

"No, you aren't. My papers are protected by attorney-client privilege."

The worker started for my bag. I shoved it onto the lap of the project manager wedged between me and the clerk. A hand like a meat hook brushed my chest and grabbed air.

"*Stop.*" I yelled at the man in the hard hat. I was down to my last hope, the one my mentor had just created. "Or you'll be up for assault before a Federal judge. By noon, in Beaumont." Thirty miles away. "You want a criminal record?"

He looked across the site. No help in view, his shoulders collapsed. I shoved his limp arm out the window and shouted, "*Gun it!*"

Billy stomped again. Gravel and red dust flew again. And our pickup shot through the front gate.

DUSK

My client's Beechcraft King-Air twin-engine plane knifed through the cloudless blue sky turning crimson in the west. The motors thrummed a gentle massage through the airframe that relieved the tension from our escape. That should have put me to sleep. But my mind wouldn't shut off.

I'd rescued our project manager, outmaneuvered Boyden, his sheriff, and his judge. A trial in Federal Court would be a winner. I should be happy.

But it was not the kind of win I'd ever imagined back in college when I'd decided against a career in business. I'd looked forward to quiet productive hours in a corner office of a sleek tower in a big city, designing legal strategies for large corporate clients.

My first day at the firm, Preston Lawton, the senior partner I'd never met, stalked into my converted supply-closet office, dropped a stack of files on the desk, and barked, "Read that and come up an' see me." A frenzied hour later I knew that some gudgeons had been misaligned on some trunnions. I needed an engineer's help just to understand the facts.

The fascination of trial work wasn't the legal issues—to me they were simple. Or the use of brilliant intellect—intuition was worth more under pressure. The hook was human nature. People lied. And you could catch them at it. That took what a psych major I knew in college called "regulation of emotion." Preston called it "findin' the other guy's hot buttons, mashin' 'em, and keepin' yours out of it."

"Lightning up ahead," the pilot warned. "Storm's too big to go around. Hold on."

I grabbed the arms of the seat but couldn't get a grip on my thoughts. Working with Preston, I'd learned to bore witnesses to death while they painted themselves into tight corners. During a trial you had to manage the flow of emotion in the courtroom until the jury, the judge, and the public in the gallery all ran smack into the brick wall of a story you'd built while they were distracted. Once you experienced that, you were hooked.

At least for a while. After four years I knew that when you cut through all the drama, you were just rehashing other people's mistakes. Fair fights like the one in Texas were rare. Personal injury cases—torts—were worse. A clever defense could deny a needy quadriplegic victim his insurance money. I hated torts.

The King Air hit an air pocket, dropped sharply, then recovered, something I'd had a hard time doing in personal injury cases. The worst were the dead and mangled bodies in my mind. They set off panic attacks. The first one hit me in law school. I lay on the floor of my apartment clutching my chest, fighting for breath, afraid I was dying.

I hid the attacks from everyone but my doctors to avoid doubts about my professional fitness. The medical experts couldn't say why the panics hit and didn't have a reliable treatment. One suggested distraction. I used classical music, a gift from my mother. Another advised long, exhausting runs. I ran a lot.

I knew what caused the attacks. Horrible visions of tortured bodies, bodies of people I loved. I poured all I had into study and work and avoided relationships with their potential for emotional loss.

They call law a profession, but it's more like a trade. Rules and tight logic create order, like a carpenter's chalk line and T-square. That's the way the book law, the "office" law, works. That's why I got into it: to use my mind, not to lose it.

But trying cases turned out to be more like plumbing a house full of leaks with no blueprint. I needed stability and sanity, not chaos and panic attacks. I was ready to quit.

The gyrations of the plane stopped.

I'd applied for early admission to New York University's master's program: tax, corporate, and securities law. New York City and the biggest law firms in the world. A second chance. Some classes would start in summer school. I would miss them if I got bogged down plowing through documents and depositions, scrapping with carrion-feeding lawyers over the carcass of a paper mill.

If I got into NYU another associate could easily take over this slam-dunk case.

Chapter 2
RAPPONGI DISTRICT, TOKYO, 8:30AM, FRIDAY, NOVEMBER 17

TWELVE HOURS AHEAD OF U. S. EAST COAST TIME

Cotton wicks burning in cut glass oil-filled holders cast flickering shadows across the copper and leather surfaces of the dark room. Kano's knee pistoned up and down beneath the table in the private gentlemen's club as he waited for the old man sitting across from him—Shin, Kano's benefactor—to speak.

Kano remembered his father's words. "Do not interrupt Shin when his eyes are lizard-slits." Shin was dressed in a mouse-gray suit, dull white shirt, and bland dark tie like any anonymous corporate *sararīman*. Except Shin was the wealthiest man in Japan.

Kano's pain from the Kagoshima explosion and shame from Shin's verbal abuse hurt inside, but he could not show it. At least he had brought news of a successful relaunch of his invention.

The lizard eyes snapped open. "*Relaunch*? That admits your failure. *You* are the technical expert. *You* pushed for the test in space to confirm the success of your invention. I provided you with the means to honor the nation . . . . And you *betrayed* that trust."

Kano waited to be sure the old man had finished the verbal beating.

"Yes, Shin-*san*. But now we can report to other scientists how we overcame the disaster with real discoveries and effective solutions."

"You wish to broadcast your failure?"

"No, Shin-*san*, to share our knowledge with the scientific community, to show Japan is a leader, a pioneer, an equal worthy of respect."

Tendrils of ash wreathed up from Shin's gold banded cigarette.

"Here is what you will say." Shin drilled deep into Kano's eyes. "Nothing." The slits reappeared. "Here is what you will reveal . . . *nothing*. You will explain . . . *nothing*."

Kano's eyebrows raised slightly.

"Do not show weakness," the old man hissed. "Japan is new to computers. It is not yet a member of the inner circle of technologically advanced countries. Any flaw will draw notice. Ten great victories could not erase the shame of one failure." Shin seemed lost in the curls of ash curling slowly up from the gold bands. "Report only the success of your recent launch."

Inside, Kano cringed as the haggard gaze of the families of his dead team members focused on him. The grieving families would have to remain silent too.

Chapter 3
EAST 55TH STREET, MANHATTAN, THE SAME DAY

TWELVE HOURS BEHIND TOKYO TIME

Sun-washed frescoes of St. Jean de Luz at the *Côte Basque* encouraged lively dining. Conversation and laughter mixed with the ring of crystal goblets and the clink of Christofle silverware.

But not at one table where talk had dried up like an overdone flan.

Madison Whitmire, distracted by the prospect of her meeting the next morning, ignored her host. In his deep charcoal gray suit, blinding white button-down shirt, and brilliant silk rep tie, he looked like the managing partner of a leading New York law firm, which he was. Austen Swinton of Swinton, Canfield. Madison knew he was only there to fulfill an obligation to her late father.

Other diners might easily mistake Madison for a model talking to her agent, though she wore a dark-blue business suit and severe reading glasses. Blond hair framed her honey-toned skin. Her sparkling cornflower-blue eyes had captivated boys and men since she was a baby. Her parents' friends remarked on how much Madison resembled her beautiful mother.

But Madison had used her brains to overcome those advantages, already at a young age a successful research scientist and executive.

Their table formed a pool of silence in a sea of merriment. Her parents' lawyer managed Madison's trust funds after a tragic accident left her a teenage orphan.

Swinton had been her father's roommate at Harvard and had even dated her mother. Until she met and married his roommate, Madison's father.

Wielding the trust assets like a club, Swinton had constrained Madison's life at every turn until she entered grad school on a grant. No longer dependent on that money, she only came to the annual review of accounts at the law firm and dinner out of a sense of duty.

Madison pushed peas across the plate with her fork. She excelled at Harvard, then rejected this man's plans for her, choosing science over law. She stared at her veal ragout, wondering how the fun-loving father she remembered could have counted this man as a friend.

He broke the silence. "You're subdued. Working hard?"

"My team has been pushing flat out on a big project." Government secrecy kept her reply short. Her team had perfected her invention, an optical computer, in time to meet tomorrow's deadline. All the important NASA decision-makers and government gatekeepers would be there. Any one of them could put a stake through her project. Only this trial in space could confirm her invention's success.

She paused while the waiter cleared the table. "We're at a turning point."

"What's it about?"

She snapped her head up and glared at him.

With a flourish, the waiter placed a meringue and sorbet creation before them. She knew he remembered it was her favorite since she was a little girl. "*Bon anniversaire, Mademoiselle* Whitmire." Madison smiled at the waiter. He blushed and fumbled with his serving napkin.

Madison saw the lawyer wince at the server's bashfulness as he served the *vacherin*.

She escaped before the coffee.

Chapter 4
GREENVILLE, SOUTH CAROLINA, LATE EVENING, THE SAME DAY

After the King Air landed, I drove to the office and drafted the complaint for Texas. We had to file in the morning to get a court order so we could go back on the site before Boyden started messing with it. Another of his tricks confirmed by Lexis-Nexis.

Back in my apartment, I dropped into bed tired but grateful for our escape. Until concern about torts, panics, and my career turned my brain into a whirlpool. I tossed and turned, bathed in sweat, unable to get a grip.

My head flopped sideways as the fuzzy green numbers on the alarm clock rolled to 3:30. I pulled on my running gear, hobbled to the back door, and set off to run on the sodium-vapor lit park trails.

An hour later, exhausted but back in control, I showered, collapsed onto the clammy sheets, and fell asleep.

Sun streamed through the window and hurt my eyes. My body ached. Then I saw the fuzzy numbers roll to 8:30 and jumped out of bed. I'd slept through the alarm.

Pulling on clothes, I hurried to the front hall, and opened the door to pick up the papers. My foot skidded and I cracked my head on the door edge. Rubbing the pain, I looked down.

I'd slipped on the mail that had dropped through the slot while I was away. There on the floor was a white envelope with discreet embossed lettering: New York University School of Law.

Chapter 5
LAWTON LAW FIRM, GREENVILLE, SC, 9AM, FRIDAY, NOVEMBER 17

The letter from NYU was fat, an invitation to New York. As I drove into the firm's parking lot I slapped the steering wheel and howled. My firm's red brick Georgian office building whispered southern gentility while its location across the street from the county courthouse boasted influence.

But that was the past. I needed to accept admission to NYU by January first or risk losing priority to regular applicants.

I climbed the back stairs. Usually I ran, but this morning my head ached and my legs felt like bags of sand. Recounting our success in Texas and receiving Preston's grudging praise would be easy. Then the hard part. Quitting.

Verna, Preston's secretary, nodded me into his office with a finger to her lips. He was on the phone. I slipped into the cracked red leather chair.

"Your expert's from New Jersey. Just proves no one within eight hundred miles believes your client." He turned to me and mouthed, *Gimme a minute.*

Silent in the red chair, the law school admissions clock ticking, faced with rejecting my mentor, my throat went dry. How could I tell this man who'd rescued me, trained me, and turned me loose with his best clients that I was leaving?

"I'll be brutally frank, Heywood. This case ain't worth the powder to blow it up. But if they'd take three-hundred thousand," less than half the authority I knew Preston had, "I got to pass it on." A slight smile contradicted his weary voice. "Okay. I'll tell 'em, but I'm not promising a thing."

As I started to speak, he slammed the receiver down, stared straight at me, and cut me off.

"What the hell happened in the *Newman* case?"

"The what?"

"You don't remember do ya?" He leaned in, wild hairs spiking from his fierce eyebrows, long coppery strands spilling down his forehead. Suddenly he was the adversary his opponents feared. "Some dumb ass forgot to ask for a jury trial." An unforgivable and potentially costly professional error.

I shuddered as his words pulled me back into the whirlpool. Personal injury. Torts. I'd just finished dictating the *Newman* answer when the construction company's president called to demand I rush to bail out his project manager.

I'd told my secretary to give the draft to another associate to review then file with the court, quickly read the Lexis-Nexis news base about the Texas project owner, then rushed to the airport. Texas had sucked up all my attention. And I, the dumb ass, had let it.

"*Newman,*" I struggled. "Client's crane slipped off the new State Bank building, killed the operator." A dead body joined the whirlpool. I clutched at a straw. "Client should be all right. It's a death case." You were better off if you killed a low-paid victim. No damages for pain and suffering.

"Should be all right?" Preston's furious glare deepened. "All right before a jury. This is goddamned Federal Court. You gotta *ask* for a jury."

I knew that. I scrambled to understand what had gone wrong as the panic took hold. Didn't Beau Stoner, the associate who filed my answer, know the difference between state and federal civil procedure?

As Preston highlighted the risks of my error, I lurched between the inquisition in the red chair and the darkness in my mind. The whirlpool spun faster.

"You're off the Texas case."

"*What*?" I started up out of the red chair.

Preston waved me back down. "Beau'll take over. Give him the file and brief him."

"*Beau*?" I'd wanted to hand the case off, but not to Beau, the pampered son of a major firm client. This was my own damn fault. I felt I was inside the crane now, plunging into a full-blown panic attack, barely making out what Preston was saying.

"Listen here and listen good. That screw up in *Newman* is a pure-T disaster." The whirlpool became a whirlwind with pieces of my life flashing into view before being sucked back in.

I could hear myself whispering, "I'm sorry."

"Don't want sorry."

Chapter 6
STILL IN THE RED CHAIR

Sweat soaked my shirt, sticking it to the cracked red leather. Preston's lips moved but I couldn't hear. As I clawed my way back to the outside world, his voice broke through.

"Got something else for you. That Consolidated Technologies theft case. All about some kind a plastic film." He glanced down to look at a yellow pad through half-height reading glasses perched on the end of his nose. "Polyethylene teref . . . tereth . . . hell! P.E.T. film. Part of CT's chemical business." What? "You got a meeting at ten, in forty-five minutes, at their plant out by Cameron."

The tornado disappeared.

Preston had played me like a fiddle. I'd screwed up in *Newman*. Yet he'd just handed me a much tougher assignment. More indebted to him than ever, I couldn't say no.

"You got a deposition coming up in Dallas, some German guy, name a . . ." Preston looked down at a legal pad on his desk, "name a Wy-DELL."

"Consolidated?" I recognized it. A complex intellectual property case for a Fortune 100 client. Cameron was a good twenty-minute drive. Excited over a challenging case unrelated to torts, I had to review the file and get going. I forgot about quitting. Distraction was a double-edged sword.

But Preston wasn't finished. "There's a memo here about the meeting. You got to light a fire down there in Dallas. Your contact, the client's in-house patent attorney, wants some action." He riffled through a stack of papers on the worn chest behind his desk and handed me a CT memo about the ten o'clock meeting. A lot of people copied, with labels like COR/IP, CAM/GM, CAM/PE.

He broke in on my effort to decode the letters. "Here's what you need to know. Technology stolen by an executive. Trade secrets, not patents. Lots of proof issues."

That was an understatement. I would have to find evidence that the client took all measures possible to keep the know-how secret, and that the defendant hadn't learned it or developed it independently. The case could turn on how expert the defendant was and his resources.

"We filed suit here against the CT plant manager named Malinkrodt." Hmm, an individual, so not so hard. "There's another case. One in L.A. run by the Gordon law firm. In the first deposition in our case, Malinkrodt gave up a technology firm out there. CT had the Gordon firm file a separate lawsuit in California." Preston glanced at his yellow pad. "Against that company named, uh . . . InterTech, run by a Swiss guy."

Two law firms and two cases? That seemed like disrespect toward my firm

"The Gordon firm deposed the Swiss guy and he let slip some Japanese company was InterTech's client."

Whoa! "What Japanese company?" That could mean huge resources on the other side.

"Don't know. The Gordon firm added a John Doe defendant to their lawsuit since that's related to InterTech."

Our case was beginning to feel like a sideshow. Maybe getting out of the Texas case wasn't so smart.

"Your contact at CT is Tom O'Hanlon. Deposition's coming up fast, coupla weeks. Any questions?"

They crowded in: legal, factual, personal. This case could drag on for years.

I slumped in the red chair. I had been intent on quitting the firm when I sat down. My mistake in *Newman* had set me back. At least I knew how to take a deposition. If I could ace this one, I could quit and accept NYU by the first of January without a cloud hanging over me.

Preston shouted. "Verna, get Judge Chapin on the line." Then he turned to me and growled, "Gotta fix this *Newman* thing. *Git!*"

Chapter 7
THE WAY TO CAMERON

I left my draft complaint for Texas on Beau's desk, grabbed the CT file summary, and raced out of the firm. Excited about the biggest case I was ever likely to get out of this small-town practice, I jumped in my hand-me-down Chevelle and took off toward Cameron.

As I wove between cars on the Interstate, it was all I could do to glance at the memo. It seemed Weidl was Austrian—not German—but there was nothing about any interview with him. That usually meant a witness who wouldn't talk to you, going into the deposition blind.

There were all those people copied, including two technical people. They should be sharp since they worked for a major corporation. I would need them to identify and value any stolen technology.

And the facts would be complex. Trade secrets, unlike patents, weren't defined before the theft. You had to build them from the client's know how and the defendant's data, if you could get to it. Like that hole in the traffic up ahead. I gunned it and swerved around a delivery truck that was clogging the left lane.

People from Corporate in New York were also copied. Even a John McElwain, PRES/CT. Uh oh. Hierarchy.

Faceless executives. Complications I'd tried to avoid by giving up on a business career after a summer job in college. The guy who hired me promised me a bright future. I went to work one morning to find the marketing floor empty. Our whole department had been fired overnight.

I hit the brakes to avoid a slowdown where the road narrowed, swerved into the left-hand lane to get out of the way of a big Buick, and leaned over to slap the memo to keep it from sliding off the seat. Honking erupted behind me.

There was a phone call scheduled with the L. A. firm. Two cases, same facts. Weidl's deposition was set in our case only. That called for even closer cooperation. I knew about the Gordon firm. All the law review types who wanted a West Coast career interviewed there.

Suddenly I spied the turnoff on the right and cut in front of the big Buick, waving an apology. As I thought back to my performance in the red chair, I felt a hole open in the pit of my stomach.

Panic. Personal issues had set off last night's attack—not torts. Then a professional error had triggered the one in the red chair—not torts. My weakness was seeping into my whole career and into my personal life.

I'd never told anyone, not even my doctors, that the real source of my attacks was images of my mother and sister writhing in pain as they burned to death at home while I was away at law school. Visions of their last moments and the weight of my guilt had cast a pall over my studies and my work.

I pulled up to a traffic light and stopped behind a large tanker loaded with chemicals. As I sat there, my chest tightened and my vision started to blur. I mashed the tape player button. Chopin.

Chapter 8
CONSOLIDATED TECHNOLOGIES, CAMERON, AFTER 10AM

I was already late when I pulled into the visitor's parking lot. No time left to worry.

Low red brick and glass buildings bearing the CT logo spread across manicured grounds. Behind them large metal stacks emitted white vapors. The receptionist handed me a campus map on which she had marked the way.

I raced down a windowless hall. Peering at room numbers bathed in fluorescent light, I dropped the map and bent down to pick it up. A white-shirted man barreled through a door looking back, talking to someone. "Well, he's gotta be here somewheres. Ain't got—"

He hit me full tilt. We sprawled on the floor and looked wide-eyed at each other.

"You okay?" I stood and offered him my hand. "I'm so sorry. That was my fault."

"Dang. No. Sorry. I shoulda been looking where I'as going. I'm all right I reckon. You all right?"

"No problem." That southern accent. CT was making an effort to hire locals. At what cost? I helped him up.

"Would you have any idea where Conference Room 3 of the Engineering Wing is?"

The man peered at me through thick glasses knocked askew. A crooked grin spread across his face and revealed the most amazing tangle of tobacco stained teeth I'd seen this side of a high school hygiene film.

"You're from the Lawton law firm, aint'cha?"

"Yes, sir. Jake Payne."

"Dang. How about that! I'm Charlie Cauthen." One of the technical people from the memo. "Glad ta meet ya." He grabbed my hand and worked it like a rusty pump handle while I tried to hide my surprise. "Been lookin' everwheres to find ya. Welcome to Consolidated Technologies. Tom's down the hall."

Cauthen was thick-set and powerful, not tall, with thinning gray hair. His mouth seemed on the verge of a smile, but his eyes were dark, alert. He had a mottled-reddish complexion. As he turned and set off, I noticed the skin condition rose up from the back of his shirt collar, too. An honest-to-God redneck. Not the image that leapt to mind from the memo's description of Charlie Cauthen, Cameron's Chief Project Engineer.

"Got to get a guide dog for you law fellers." He tossed the words over his shoulder as he gathered steam. "Already lost that Beau. Could get expensive." I stooped down, picked up my briefcase, and broke into a jog to catch up.

Chapter 9
CAMERON R & D COMPLEX, 10:15AM

Madison Whitmire had flown down from New York with Tom O'Hanlon on a CT corporate jet. Seated in her Cameron office, she was uneasy about the imminent Houston launch decision. The head of Mission Control operations security, dead set against putting her invention on the NASA flight, would be there.

There was something else. The dinner the night before had caused her a restless night. Swinton's arrogance and false charm reminded her of other dismissive men, some of them among her academic advisors. She had countered their hostility by working harder and thinking better. She bristled as the memories flooded back.

Darker, more humiliating affronts had almost caused her to give up science. Women were in a strange limbo at Radcliffe-Harvard when she entered college. In her junior year, unpleasant male advances became vicious, fueled by the threat of female competition. She endured puerile double-entendres, disgusting jibes, and filthy propositions. She had barely escaped from a terrifying groping in a bedroom on the third floor of a friend's dorm.

Her unease over last night revived the embers of a fire she thought had burned out when she got into corporate research. Pressure to generate profits from cutting-edge technology demanded teamwork. The snarky sexual innuendos disappeared among the researchers. But not among the business execs.

She shuddered, trying to break the hold of her memories.

Chapter 10
CT MANUFACTURING CONFERENCE ROOM 3, 10:15AM

I followed Cauthen into a room with windows that framed a broad view of the imposing CT campus. A man in his late forties, large in every dimension, levered up from behind a table and waded toward me.

"Hi. I'm Tom O'Hanlon. You must be Jake. Glad to have you on board." Not the up-tight headquarters patent lawyer I had imagined. That was two Consolidated execs, two busted assumptions.

O'Hanlon's crew cut was so short his scalp showed through. A green plaid tie proclaimed his Celtic heritage. His open grin lit up a round face and an open hand offered a greeting.

"Sorry about the delay. Anybody else coming?"

"No harm. Madison, uh, Dr. Whitmire's running late. I'll call John Morgan at the Gordon firm in California." O'Hanlon punched in a number and hit the button on the speakerphone.

A click, then a curt "Morgan here," reverberated through the room from L. A. "My associate, Panatopoulus, is with me."

"John, George. It's Tom O'Hanlon with Charlie Cauthen. Meet Jake Payne from the Lawton firm. He's taking over from Stoner in the case here."

"Gentlemen, it's a pleasure to meet you," I said. "I look forward—"

"O'Hanlon," Morgan ignored me. "Let's make this quick."

Tom reviewed the events that led to a confrontation between CT's plant manager, Edwin Malinkrodt, and his boss, Jack Staley, head of the Cameron site.

"Malinkrodt was in Italy visiting a CT client. Tried to sell his services as a consultant. The Italians smelled a *ratto* and faxed Malinkrodt's private business card to Staley. Malinkrodt was running a secret company on our time, trying to trade our secrets for his personal profit. Staley confronted Malinkrodt and fired him on the spot."

"History of bad blood between them?" I asked.

"Malinkrodt expected to be named general manager but Staley, a marketing guy, got it. After he was let go a document clerk came up short three microfilm rolls Malinkrodt had checked out. He wouldn't return my calls. I phoned Preston Lawton who filed suit here to depose Malinkrodt."

My first confirmed assumption: this case started out as a fishing expedition.

"Why is Weidl only being deposed now?"

Charlie answered. "Buncha luck. Weidl works at Elant in Dallas, one a our clients who puts magnetic coating on our P.E.T. film to make audio, video tape an' such. One a our salesmen met him out there. Over lunch Weidl said he'd worked with Malinkrodt in California. That woulda been while he'as still with us. We got ta find out what they cooked up."

Deep sea fishing. And I had a redneck engineer for a guide. If I was going to impress O'Hanlon now was the time.

"Looks like Malinkrodt revealed the West Coast angle," I started in. "Gave up this InterTech firm and its owner. Hans Mueller? What have you got on them and any Japanese defendants, John?"

"That's when we became lead counsel in these cases," Morgan said, asserting authority and ignoring my question. "The Gordon firm is West Coast and Asian counsel for Consolidated Technologies."

Coordination had been a casualty of Morgan's first words. Now it was just a dream. I shot a glance at O' Hanlon. He hadn't reacted to my attack on the L.A. firm's lack of results. I realized the two-firm approach worked for him as much as it irritated John Morgan. O'Hanlon hadn't talked about merging the two cases. Our firm was still in the game.

It made sense. A senior executive had gone off the reservation and might have sold—hell, could still be selling—Consolidated's technology. That made O'Hanlon, the guardian of the secrets, look bad. He wouldn't mind a fight between outside lawyers if it got things rolling.

"We're pursuing the major defendants out here," Morgan asserted.

I felt a surge of litigation adrenaline. "What do you have on the Japanese?" Morgan didn't respond, but I knew from the file memo. "You got nothing from the InterTech office search. No background on Mueller's contacts in Japan. You've still got a John Doe defendant, no identities, no names. It's been over a year and you have nothing to show for it."

There was a pause on the other end of the line. "Getting that office search order was a win, Payne."

"But nothing turned up in the inspection at InterTech over a year ago. So. What. You just stopped looking?"

"We'll file a motion this week to search Mueller's home," Morgan spat out. A tall order after their office search came up dry. "This deposition could interfere with our proceedings."

The L.A. lawyer was improvising. Badly.

I piled on. "You found nothing at InterTech's offices. Why waste time in California when we've got a live witness in Dallas who could be crucial to the chain of disclosure?"

"You've got to reschedule Payne."

Morgan's firm might be the biggest one in California and Morgan a star litigator, but I was not impressed. I looked over at O'Hanlon to referee our wrestling match. He was grinning.

"We're going ahead with the deposition," I said.

Morgan nearly jumped through the phone. "We have the big defendants out here. Our judges are used to complex international cases. This is where we must concentrate our efforts. Are we about done O'Hanlon? I've got work to do."

He clearly meant *real* work. I couldn't believe Morgan's disrespect for Tom O'Hanlon.

"Okay," Tom said. "The Lawton firm set Weidl's deposition in their case. Jake, why don't you flesh out the questions? We can go over them before we go to Dallas."

"You're going?" A hitch in Morgan's voice revealed his surprise.

"I plan to," O'Hanlon said. "You know our general counsel. He wants to stay informed; this might be a breakthrough." O'Hanlon had mashed a button!

I piled on. "John, are you going to phone this one in, send George, or attend in person?"

Silence, then a mumbled exchange at the other end. "My associate will be there."

I'd garnered support from O'Hanlon. Time to play nicely with others. "I appreciate your cooperation."

"Payne, you copy me on everything," Morgan insisted. "We don't want any screw ups"

"No problem." Unless he was coming, too. "George, look forward to meeting you. See you in Dallas in a couple of weeks."

“Sure thing, Jake.” Amiable sounding at least. With a loud click, they were gone.

I climbed down from my litigation podium and looked at the memo and told myself *focus Jake*.

The next item was the deposition, the reason we were in a hurry.

“Charlie, what about Weidl? You’re listed for him. Will he help us or hurt us?

“Heck if I know. I worked some with Elant Systems debugging production start-ups and such, but don’t really know Wey-dell.”

Chapter 11
R & D BUILDING, CAMERON

Madison slipped into the R & D Conference Room. Her hair was pulled-back by a plain clip and she wore a standard white lab coat. The room was packed with her team and representatives from NASA and DARPA, the Defense Advanced Research Projects Agency. She spied the scowling head of ops security from Houston and nodded to DARPA's lawyer whose presence reminded her that she was supposed to be at a meeting with more lawyers.

Lawyers everywhere. They would have to wait. She was here to receive a verdict on her life's work.

Her project manager was presenting their proposal. Everyone knew it was Madison's research that had unraveled the complex chemistry and physics that could turn laser light signals sent through plastic into computing that was faster and more stable than silicon, It could be particularly effective in the natural vacuum above the Earth's atmosphere. *If* her team was awarded the launch and *if* her invention worked.

Any of the forty or so validators in the room could block her trial with a shaded opinion, a well-timed frown. Government employees were expert at bureaucratic risk-avoidance.

When the presentation ended, the DARPA program director looked left and right, assessing the faces of the program chiefs ranged up and down the head table. Satisfied, he stood to speak. Madison leaned forward.

"Gentleman, and lady, for I see Dr. Whitmire has joined us. Innovation is risky." He paused. Madison knew the near loss of three astronauts on the Apollo 13 mission nine years ago still haunted every NASA program. People craned to get a glimpse of Madison. She held her breath and gripped the table.

"But the logic of your presentation is sound." Her head snapped up.

"Let me drop the procedural jargon. As a scientist, I'm excited. We all are at DARPA and NASA. This flight could mean a new era in computing and space exploration due to Dr. Whitmire's groundbreaking theories."

Madison started to tremble inside.

"The evaluation team has voted. We hereby approve your project for inclusion in the I.M.S. mission launch scheduled for February 2, 1979. Your device will be in the nosecone on that day. We're good to go."

The room erupted. Madison lowered her head and clenched her fists to get control, then jumped up and shot her hands high, knocking the clip from her hair. Her blonde tresses broke free to spin and shine in the light.

She'd been on many victory stands. But this was the best, the absolute best. She turned to acknowledge her team. They mobbed her with shouts of congratulation. She laughed and struggled to keep back tears brimming in her blue eyes.

"Break out the sparkling grape juice, boys," she shouted over the din at Cameron, the center of the buckle on the Bible belt.

Then, late for her meeting with the lawyers, she pushed free of the crowd and headed out.

Chapter 12
MANUFACTURING CONFERENCE ROOM, 10:25AM

The door opened and I turned to meet the research guy. Instead, a lithe blond woman about my age stood in the doorway talking excitedly to someone in the hall.

She was dressed in a charcoal gray suit and an open collared white silk blouse. A classic pearl necklace set off her honey-toned skin. Her business attire couldn't completely hide an attractive figure. As she turned, smiled, and whispered something to Tom O'Hanlon, her hair shimmered in the light.

Then it happened. She turned back to her colleague and pirouetted. It was just a hint, but it reminded me of a ballet dancer I had known well: my sister Ann. And that was enough. It triggered a cascade of blows: a flame-filled hallway, charred bodies. *Panic.*

As Dr. Whitmire walked toward me, the slight arch of one eyebrow and the pleasant curve of a brilliant smile were warm yet professional. She reached out to shake my hand. "You must be the new lawyer. Payne. I'm Doctor Whitmire. Please call me Madison. Welcome to CT."

I stared numbly as a hole opened in my mind and I started to fall in. I took her hand awkwardly, held it too long, then dropped it like a hot coal. Fighting for control, I stammered, "Uh, yes, um . . . Doctor. Whitmire. Of course. Jake. Jake Payne."

Her thousand-watt smile dimmed.

"You look a little surprised, Payne." Her informality evaporated. "Expecting someone else?" *Like a man*, hung in the air.

"Uh, no, no. Not at all." I lowered my head as the pain grew, closed my eyes, and imagined running through a sunlit park, wind rustling through the trees.

I willed my eyes open and the room came into focus: there were no mutilated bodies but Tom O'Hanlon was not smiling, Charlie's eyebrows had shot up, and Dr. Whitmire riveted me with her blue eyes. I gripped the back of a chair and strangled out, "Let's get going."

Her answers to simple questions revealed Dr. Whitmire's impressive résumé and job responsibilities. She ran the Cameron R & D center and several others. That gave me time to calm down. I began to think again.

Given her expertise, I needed her to simplify explanations as she might have to for a jury. "Okay, Doctor. Imagine I'm a fifth grader. What does Consolidated do at this production facility?"

She eyed me coldly. "It makes highly sophisticated film, polyethylene terephthalate, that's P.E.T., plastic film." She moved on at a pace measured to facilitate understanding by an underdeveloped brain.

"It's like making cookies with very fancy, hot dough. You heat raw plastic to a liquid and pump it through a kind of squirt gun with a horizontal slot. As it shoots out, you grab it in mid-air with clamps, like clothespins, stretch it into a sheet without a rolling pin. It speeds up to one-hundred feet per minute as it stretches from nine inches up to ten feet wide while it's heated in a tenter—that's a big oven. Then it's flash-cooled by a curtain of chilled air."

"Different temperatures, dimensions, thicknesses, and speeds give it different textures, like crispy or chewy.

And you can vary the doughs." I caught a gleam in her eye. "You stick bits in it, like chocolate chips and nuts, and you get different performances. Is that simple enough for you?"

"Perfect."

"I thought so. The fourth graders at Hampton Elementary understood it, too."

She'd just demoted me a grade. Her right eyebrow arched again, shooting me to the back row of desks. I had to get her mind off me.

"Doctor, what do you think is of value on the missing microfilms?"

Her blue eyes narrowed slightly. "They were only plant documents. Nothing to do with R & D. Charlie's group made many improvements that create real value. That's not my area of expertise."

As she walled off R & D from my questions her voice developed an edge.

"What else were you working on?" This was fishing, but my fishing. Her eyes opened wide for a split second. She glanced at Tom O'Hanlon before she answered.

"I've just explained our commercial production expertise."

"But what about other innovations, maybe in R&D?"

"Malinkrodt was only responsible for production security. He had no access to my work."

"Look. At the outset of all this no one even knew Malinkrodt was coloring outside the lines, did they? Please answer the question." It came out as hostile, argumentative, unprofessional. With a client for God's sake. I was still way off-balance.

She leaned forward like a pitcher taking a sign, then let fly.

"A fishing expedition without any factual basis is a waste of my time and CT's resources. I've got critical research to manage." Her blue eyes shot bolts of lightning.

I was dying inside but couldn't back down. "Isn't it possible we should think about the unthinkable, Doctor? If somebody else had earlier, we wouldn't be here today." She shifted in her chair. A tic? "By the way, who's responsible for security in the research areas?"

Her nostrils flared and her cheeks reddened. "I am." A tic for sure and I'd just mashed a hot button. I checked the schedule. Time was almost up.

She needed to understand how complicated this case could be. Malinkrodt had been acting as a consultant. Consultants I'd seen in construction cases drew out disclosure of information to maximize fees. I had to get her to see how that same process could disguise proprietary secrets, making our job even more difficult.

"Why do you think your employer identified your knowledge as relevant here?"

She paused before replying. "I know the science and use it to create novelty, not how to scale it in production. Charlie knows those details much better than I do."

"Madison, we all believe Malinkrodt sold valuable CT technology to the Japanese through InterTech. But as a consultant, he'd be motivated not to be too obvious about it.

"That's where it gets thorny, where your overview of the science and the technology would be invaluable to our investigation. Malinkrodt could offer glimpses in writing, add hints in lectures, suggest experiments in the factory. Maybe that's a little like your invention process: there's no clear path when you start out. Is that a fair statement?"

Sure it was, but she wasn't going to agree with anything I said. "It's not unlike trial and error discovery," she acknowledged, barely. That was as close as I was going to get to a yes.

"What kind of resources would it take to follow such a trail through the research and manufacturing records here at Cameron?"

Madison stared at me hard, struggling behind those sparkling blue eyes. She looked out the window and her body went slack like a sail losing wind. To her credit, when she turned to face me she was professional again.

"It would be difficult," she said, deep furrows on her brow. "It would mean reviewing hundreds of documents using knowledge of practice *and* theory . . . ." She jolted. "*In Japanese.*"

I tried to close the sale. "A solid grasp of the underlying science, not just the technology. That's just one perspective you would add to our search. Sounds like we may need you, Charlie, and some Japanese-speaking scientists just to translate."

Charlie's eyebrows shot up again. "And a bunch a specialists." Madison and Tom nodded agreement.

Time was up. I'd wrestled her attention from me onto the case and a significant role for her in it. "I know you have other matters to attend to, Doctor. We'll talk again soon. I want to thank you for—"

She rose and was gone before I could finish.

Chapter 13
10:50AM

Tom and Charlie fixed on me, waiting. I felt like I was about to walk over broken glass. I had to come up with a legal strategy that worked for this big corporate client. Weidl, the first step, was clear. But I would need help.

"Tom, I hope you've got some friendlies around here, because Morgan and Dr. Whitmire don't qualify."

"I'll handle Morgan if he becomes a problem," Tom offered. "But Madison Whitmire is an amazing talent. She's the only female scientist in our entire organization and the youngest head of a divisional research operation, man or woman. Consolidated has invested a lot in her."

"I was impressed by her résumé."

"It's a phenomenal record, Jake. She's strong willed and she has irritated, yet outperformed, most of our best scientists. You'll have to make an effort."

After that mild rebuke, it was time to deliver. "Weidl's the key. He's got to be neutral. On our side would be better. I'd like to interview him as soon as possible."

Tom was eager now. "Agreed."

"Then if any valuable information did get away, prying the facts out of a Japanese defendant will take a lot of resources. Is Consolidated Technologies' top management ready to commit them?"

"Jake, I've pushed hard to get to the bottom of this case. I have the support of our general counsel. Frankly, anything with legal attached to it, especially litigation, is anathema to top executives. So far, we've convinced our president John McElwain that we can't pass on this one. But, sure, the guy at the top can see a lot of downside. If you have a weak case."

I knew how to gain support in construction cases with local owners who were protective of the companies they had built and that bore their names. This was different. "When the time and cost mount up, and they will, what happens?"

"What can I say?" Tom replied. "Results generate support. Dry holes increase pressure to cut and run. What else?"

"I'll need technical expertise to work up this case."

"That's easy. Madison will be available whenever possible, but Charlie's on this full time starting now."

So this redneck and I would be spending a lot of time together. "Ever worked on any legal cases before, Charlie?"

"Well, I spent most a mah Army time in the C.I.D. right after the Korean War."

"C.I.D.?" That was new to me.

Tom chuckled. "Charlie was the only private in the elite U.S. Army Criminal Investigation Division. Ran rings around all the lieutenants."

"Well, I'as dumb enough to apply and they'as dumb enough to take me. Story a mah life. Wouldn't have come out so good without help from a bunch a Asian friends."

"Charlie, what say we take a trip to Texas before the deposition? I don't think Weidl will open up over the phone, but you might strike up a conversation using your contacts at Elant."

"Now you're talkin'."

A secretary wheeled in a cart with lunch. Tom wolfed down a pimento cheese sandwich and left to report to Staley.

"Charlie, you think Weidl will cooperate?"

"That dog might not hunt. He's scairt. Wanted the deposition on a weekend so Elant wouldn't find out."

"I didn't catch that. Who set it up?"

"Beau filed a notice, then somebody from the L.A. firm got it changed."

I frowned. "You sure about that?" It didn't make sense. Morgan had chosen the date for my firm's deposition. Now he was trying to postpone it?

"Pretty dad gummed sure. Tom told Jack Staley that this morning."

"That seem strange to you, Charlie?"

"They's lots about those California fellers seems strange, what they wear, how they comb their hair."

"We have to be sure Weidl will cooperate at the deposition." A curious fact lit up my thoughts. "He's Austrian, right? Wonder if he's a U.S. citizen."

"You want I should check around?"

"What, in Dallas?"

"The Nation's Capital. Not all a my C.I.D. buddies got out."

"Only if it's on the level."

"You're in charge, Jake," Charlie shot me a wide grin, exposing his amazing set of teeth. "Lemme get started. It's been a pleasure." I stood, received another exuberant hand pump, and he was gone.

Worn out, I dropped into a chair. At least O'Hanlon had backed me, a chance to show I could hold my own against John Morgan and the Gordon firm. Yet the risk of failure was growing with each revelation. If I could pull off a win, I could redeem myself to Preston. But not if some corporate political tsunami washed it all away. The stakes, issues, and complex motives of all the players in this case dwarfed my professional experience so far. And January first was coming on fast, like a freight train.

I turned and stared out the large windows. On the far side of the campus, I saw Madison Whitmire in a white lab coat, dark rimmed glasses, her hair pulled back, captivating a swarm of men.

Suddenly her stunning features decayed in my mind's eye, as they had when she walked into the room. The horrible images of my mother and sister as they burned seared my memory for the third time in less than twenty-four hours. I slumped in the chair as my vision started to black out.

Chapter 14
LAWTON FIRM, THE SAME DAY

I sat at the big table in the firm library, staring at the CT case files spread across its polished mahogany surface. The disturbing images of Madison Whitmire were gone for now, thanks to another run and a quick steam bath at the Y.

I wanted some background on Japan, so I'd stopped by the county library. All I knew about East Asia I'd learned in a college history course. I recalled that the Chinese and Japanese sparred for centuries using Korea as a boxing ring. Until the Japanese learned western technology, leapt ahead, and trounced the Chinese in the Sino-Japanese War in 1895. For the next forty years, the Japanese joined Westerners at imperialism's trough to exploit China, the most populous country on earth.

Post-war corporate Japan was an unknown to me. The books said that after Commodore Perry used cannon fire to open Japan for US trade, Japanese elites strove to build entrepreneurial groups into a strong state-capitalist military-industrial complex, expert and proud enough to take on the US with the attack on Pearl Harbor.

The Allies held many Japanese executives in jail at the end of the Pacific War in 1945. General MacArthur, named to head up the Allied Occupation, boasted he'd break up the big state-supported Japanese conglomerates, the *zaibatsu.*

Then, faced with the threat of communist unions and political parties gaining ground in a war-devastated Japan, McArthur let up and released many prisoners who went on to lead the Japanese recovery as the industrial groups morphed into something called *keiretsu,* bigger, stronger, and more influential than ever.

Grainy images of organization charts from microfilm reels of business magazines in the library showed tangled masses of corporate spaghetti. Some as big as General Motors. Maybe that's why even the Gordon firm with all its resources was having trouble.

I created a detailed chronology on a yellow pad. Grunt work, but the only way anomalies would stand out. I picked up the file labeled Client Documents and looked at a page from the CT document archives logbook. It showed the three microfilm rolls checked out, but there were no initials in the place for the recipient. How the hell was I supposed to prove it was Malinkrodt who took them?

Then I started in on the depositions. A close reading of Malinkrodt's didn't add anything. As I turned to the deposition transcript of the head of InterTech, Mueller, the library phone rang.

Chapter 15
LAWTON FIRM LAW LIBRARY, 5:15PM

"Jake, I have a Mr. Cauthen on the line." A click signaled the receptionist's transfer.

"What's up, Charlie?"

"That feller in document storage, Frank Brazeale, came by to see me. I think you need to talk to him right away."

"What about?"

"Not sure. He wanted to know if he could trust you. I said he could."

Word traveled fast on the CT grapevine. My integrity questioned by the document clerk? First Morgan. Then Madison. Was anybody at Consolidated in line on this case?

"How do I get in touch with him?" I dialed the number Charlie gave me.

"'Lo?"

"Mr. Brazeale? Frank Brazeale?"

"Who wants ta know?"

"This is Jake Payne from the Lawton law Firm. Charlie Cauthen asked me to call you about the Malinkrodt case."

"Yep, but don't let's talk about that on the phone."

"Can we meet? The sooner the better."

"I cain't meet tonight. I got the rasslin'."

I realized the blind accordion player would start playing outside the firm when people began crowding into the auditorium, flowing around him on the sidewalk outside our library windows. The crowds gave me an idea.

"The auditorium is right next to us. I'd like to see you before the show tonight. It won't take long. Tell you what. Park in our lot for free. Give the attendant my name, then knock loud on the back door."

"Okay, but just you. No one else."

Mueller's deposition revealed he had worked for over a decade in Japan for well-known hi-tech companies. Then he relocated to L.A. as a 'technology consultant.' The Gordon lawyer asked how InterTech got clients, how it ran and documented its projects, a decent job of staking out Mueller while digging a pit for him to fall in.

When he asked for InterTech's client's name, the fireworks started. Mueller's attorney objected. In South Carolina courts when there was an objection in a deposition, the witness replied, subject to later ruling by a judge. The lawyers must have reached some accommodation in California because Tom O'Hanlon didn't know who InterTech's client was.

Suddenly the blind man's speakers howled. I dropped the deposition, picked it up and started thumbing through it for the questions about InterTech's clients. I found them. Mueller's lawyer was objecting.

"We're going to stop right here and strike that response from the record. You don't have a shred of proof about any wrongdoing and we have contracts to protect . . . ."

I turned back a page to see what was to be struck: there was nothing. No mention of an InterTech client. I checked the page numbers. They went from 150 to 152.

Court reporters base their reputations on reliability. If the court ordered a redaction, there should be a note. It was three hours earlier in California. I could call Morgan, but might as well hit my head against a brick wall. I phoned the number on the front of the deposition.

"Oh, dear," the court reporter said after I explained the problem. "We're the top transcribing firm in Los Angeles County. I hope we didn't make a mistake."

She got her original and reported, "That's a relief. Here it is, page 151. Quote. So, via InterTech, who was Mr. Malinkrodt consulting for? Unquote. Mr. Mueller. Quote. He was doing some lectures on basic production efficiency for Minimura Corporation of Japan. There was no written information involved. Just general stuff. End quote. That ends the page and on the next page the other lawyer objects. Does that help?"

I nearly fell out of my chair. The Japanese defendant already had a name: Minimura. John Morgan should have known that. And through him, Tom O'Hanlon.

I asked her to send me a copy and was thanking her when I heard loud banging at the back of the office.

Chapter 16
ANOTHER REDNECK

I opened the door to find a specimen typical of rural upstate South Carolina, lanky, with a sunken chest, faded jeans, a Richard Petty T-Shirt, and a Howard's Equipment Rentals baseball cap. Frank Brazeale. I led him to my closet-office and moved a stack of depositions off a chair.

"How can I help you, Frank?"

"First off, I gotta trust ya. Which I do, I guess. Charlie Cauthen said you'as a straight shooter."

"I'm glad to hear Charlie thinks so, Frank."

"And Verna," he added.

"You know Verna?" Preston's secretary. Frank had sought a second opinion.

"She's a cousin a my sister's husband, over ta Punkintown."

A southern family tree. I shook my head.

"Verna knows Beau Stoner, too, Frank. You ask her about him?"

"Well," he hesitated, then went ahead. "Verna's pretty high on you." My client referral system lacked class, but it produced results. "What can I do for you?"

"'Fore we get into it, I got one more. Can you perteck my job over this thing?" He stared hard.

"I can go to the top of Consolidated Technologies." But could I? I wondered who in the Consolidated corporate hierarchy I could trust. "If you provide information in support of the company's interests, I'll get you protection or I'll find you the best employment lawyer I can."

"That first part sounds purty good. But that second part sorta lets the air outta the tahrs."

"Tell you what. Give me what you've got. I'll keep it to myself until I find corroboration, uh, supporting evidence. If there is none, I can't use it. If there is, you've got back-up to verify your story." He still hesitated. "I might not even need to call you as a witness." Silence. "You want to call Charlie and talk it over?" I couldn't believe I was saying this, "Or Verna?"

His body released, like a fire hose draining water. "Naw, I'm good. I kinda try to live by the mirra test."

"The mirror test?"

"Come from my Daddy. You get up in the morning, go to shave, and gotta look yourself in the face. If you don't like what you see, you got a problem. If you can help get me to where I can look myself in the mirra again, I'd be obliged."

I winced, recalling the hiding I'd taken from Preston that morning. "I know just what you mean."

"Guess I'm ready, 'cept for one more thing. What I tell you, you don't tell nobody from New York where you got it." This guy had more conditions than a new car warranty. We engaged in a deep discussion about attorney-client privilege. It was amazing what these people picked up in auto wreck cases. The privilege didn't protect Frank, just the company. He didn't like that. This interview could butt up against the wrestling with nothing to show for it.

"What are you so concerned about?"

"I got my reasons." Frank sat low in the chair, thinking. Then he straightened up. "Charlie was right. You're OK. You know about them three rolls a microfilm?"

I straightened up, too. "I just ran across the sign-out sheet in the file. There are no initials for whoever checked them out."

"See, that's just it. Malinkrodt would come down in a big hurry, order 'em up and leave."

"How'd you handle that?"

"That's all spelled out. You go to the head a plant security to report any funny stuff."

"To Malinkrodt?"

"Yessir. I mentioned it to him once. He just walked away. Even sent his secretary a copy for him to sign. Never heard back."

"Wait a minute. You said, 'He would come down.' He did that more than once?"

Frank slumped, head down. "Purty regular 'fore he left."

"But the file only has one sign-out sheet, the one for the three rolls. Where are the others?"

"I know, I know." Frank ducked his head like a schoolboy held after class. "He turned all t'other rolls in, so all those sheets was canned. That sheet you saw was the last one. Just 'fore he left."

"Who else knows about this Frank?"

He stared at the floor, drilling holes. Then he looked up, eyes filled with pain.

"Look here. I was already way up there. Malinkrodt was the head a the plant. Bunch of people between me and him on the ladder you know."

"But why didn't you mention these other reels after Malinkrodt was gone?"

"Should'a . . . . Ditn't."

Here came the one-word replies, like a reluctant car wreck witness on the broken steps of a mobile home. I knew his interview was over. "You understand. I have to ask these things."

"I know. One a your responsibilities, right?"

"Guess we all have them."

"You got that right. I'm responsible to keep them films safe." Frank shook his head from side to side.

"Frank. Do you remember what was on those other rolls?"

"No way I could keep all that in mind. I got more'n twenty check-outs a week."

"That's too bad."

"That's important, hunh?"

"Sure is."

"Yeah. That's what I thought."

I watched Frank wrestle with himself again. He started to speak, then stopped. Finally, he looked me square in the eyes and said softly. "That's why I began to write it down."

"You *what*?"

"After the first time he didn't sign, I began to keep track."

"You still have that?"

"In my truck. I'll go git it."

It was clear I'd passed Frank's final test. Otherwise, I never would have seen the list of over thirty rolls of microfilm Malinkrodt had checked out or learned that someone other than Malinkrodt had rattled Frank badly. Frank headed to the wrestling and I went back to the library.

Anomalies were piling up. Why wasn't O'Hanlon aware of Minimura? What was Morgan's game, interfering with our deposition, then opposing it? Then there were all those tapes. There was much more information missing than anyone knew. And someone had messed with Frank Brazeale when he'd tried to report it.

I looked down at a note the receptionist had left on the table. It was from Charlie.

Chapter 17

SHINJUKU WARD, TOKYO, MONDAY MORNING, NOVEMBER 20

TWELVE HOURS AHEAD OF U. S. EAST COAST TIME

Kano was at a meeting of the Japan Coordinating Committee for the International Magnetosphere Survey—the I.M.S.—on the fortieth floor of a sleek modern skyscraper in a new business district of Tokyo. He was half-listening to the first agenda items, waiting for the last one: the results of the Kagoshima disaster investigation.

His mind filled with the hard face of Shin from their meeting two days before.

The Chairman called for the final topic. Kano's attention snapped back to the meeting and he rose to introduce his young project leader, Sato Itsurō.

Sato was ending his report on the failed KYOKKO satellite launch. Against doctors' advice he had risen from a hospital bed after an operation to investigate the explosion, driven by the memory of his lost colleagues. He had discovered the cause and a solution. The recent satellite relaunch had been successful.

But Sato was ashamed. He should have died with his friends. At least his efforts had proved that they were not at fault: the successful relaunch honored their sacrifice.

He summed up. "Unexpectedly high levels of solar energy in the Earth's magnetosphere led to the explosion. This could not have been anticipated. Solar flares created high energy in the ionosphere that caused the optical device to send an incorrect signal to the ground tracking equipment. That induced overheating and started an electrical fire, the cause of the explosion.

"Improved shielding now protects the optical computer. The relaunch proves it is effective. All future modules will require this."

Sato sat down quickly, thankful for this vindication of his friends and grateful that he had not broken down in front of the committee.

The head of the physics department at Tokyo University, Chairman of the I.M.S. committee, was hostile to Kano's dream. "Isn't it true that the experimental nature of the optical computing module led to the failure?"

Sato was struggling for an answer when his boss rose to speak.

"I have met with the National Computing Board of the Ministry of International Trade and Industry." Kano paused to allow the weight of the all-powerful government agency to sink in and impress the committee. "MITI has determined that it is in the national interest not to publish any information about our advances in this area."

Murmurs filled the room. Sato looked at Kano-*san* in shock. There had been a news blackout since the explosion. The families of his dead colleagues had been ordered not to talk about their loss, forbidden to mourn publicly. Sato had assumed that would end now that he had cleared the team of fault. The raw spot inside him, the one Sato thought was beginning to heal, felt as if it had been scraped by a hot iron.

The chairman glared at Kano. "Your haste has put the reputation of the nation at risk."

Kano turned a cold face to the chairman. Sato was surprised to see his boss's hand shaking as he passed out a memo on I.M.S. stationary with a letter from MITI attached.

"This is the only information that Sato will submit to the I.M.S. Working Group in Hawaii. That is the ruling of MITI, supported at the highest levels."

Sato knew what "highest levels" meant. They all did. The committee had no choice. He looked on in anguish as the members chopped Kano's document, affirming the silence that consigned Sato's lost colleagues to oblivion.

Because someone had ordered it. And MITI had obeyed.

Chapter 18
EASTERN AIRLINES TO NEW YORK, MONDAY MORNING, NOVEMBER 20

TWELVE HOURS BEHIND TOKYO TIME

Charlie's note said we were to meet Tom in his office first thing Monday. We sat together on the flight to Laguardia. Due to Frank's rebuffed effort, I was even more concerned about who I could trust at CT. I needed help with the polymer terminology, but much more with the client's internal politics.

"What was the C.I.D. like, Charlie? Or if you tell me, do you have to shoot me?"

He laughed. "They's another department takes care a that. I kept a bag packed under my bed all the time. They called me ten minutes before a car showed up. I couldn't tell Jaynelle, my wife, where I's going or when I'd be back. Didn't know, neither."

"Where'd you end up?"

"East Asia, breaking up stolen arms and drug rings. Spent a lotta time in Korea and Japan."

As we talked, it became clear that the investigations he had been assigned to and his successes were extraordinary. The U. S. Army had trusted him with major responsibility. And he'd delivered. His answers to my questions were straightforward, thoughtful, and coherent.

I decided to give him some rope and told him about the missing reference to Minimura, Frank Brazeale's list of missing microfilms, and Frank's thwarted attempt to pass that up to management.

"Who do you think we can trust in CT, Charlie?"

"Seems pretty clear some higher up scared the bejezzus outta Frank. Until we put them to the test, I'd say don't trust no one." He grinned. "Cept me, a course."

"How about Tom?"

"That's a tough one. He told me once his granpappy come over from Ireland and got hisself killed digging the foundations for the Brooklyn Bridge. Lotta them sandhogs died trying to make a new life for their families. Tom isn't one to cut and run. But how come he didn't know about Minimura?"

Our taxi emerged from the Midtown Tunnel into the street-level chaos of Manhattan. The energy set me on edge. As we got out of the cab in front of the CT building at Rockefeller Center, the slick CT logo from Cameron gleamed at us from a massive block of spotless chrome. From the lobby to the whisper quiet elevator and the thick carpet of the executive floor, the chaos of the street gave way to the silence, power, and managed control of corporate America. Greenville and the chaos of litigation were a long way away.

We'd just sat down in Tom O'Hanlon's office high above the Avenue of the Americas when there was a rap on his open door. A trim grey man with grey, gleaming, slicked-down hair, steel-rimmed glasses, and a small scar just below his cheekbone stood at the entrance.

"Tom, are you available for lunch today?" He had a slight German accent and his request didn't sound like a question.

"Sure, Felix. Anything in particular? Or just lunch?"

"Lunch, and an update on that Malinkrodt case. Ten minutes, in the executive dining room."

"We'll be there. Felix, this is Jake Payne, the new lawyer on that case. I think you know Charlie Cauthen. Jake, meet Felix Untermeyer, head of International Licensing for CT and special projects for our President, John McElwain."

I got up and extended my hand. Untermeyer looked past it and through me. "Ten minutes." Then he was gone.

Tom started to get up.

I spoke up. "I wanted to talk to you about Weidl's deposition." Frank Brazeale's questions about who my client was were relevant here, too. Tom, though a lawyer, was a CT employee, not the client. Until we had answers to some big questions, Charlie and I had decided to be careful. Tom sat back down.

I pushed ahead. "We don't know what we'll find in Dallas, so we need to get there as soon as we can, since the deposition's coming up fast. Charlie'll talk to Weidl first, to loosen him up. Then, if Weidl's game, I'll try to get a look at any docs and prep him."

"Good. Let's have lunch and then go over it." He stood up.

"Tom, after we met, I reviewed all the files and I have a couple of questions." He sat back down again and looked hard at me, his face a blank mask.

"Like?" O'Hanlon the corporate exec at CT headquarters was much more guarded than at Cameron.

"There's nothing in the file about who Malinkrodt actually consulted with."

"Well, just the names Mueller gave up."

"You mean in the deposition?"

"No. His lawyer objected to that, but Morgan negotiated a solution. Mueller gave up a list of the clients he didn't have non-disclosure agreements with. None had links with any work we do at Cameron."

That was a start, but what about Mueller's other clients? They were the ones that mattered. I was disappointed by Morgan and I caught a warning look from Charlie. He was, too.

"No one mentioned that Friday; I don't have that list. Any reason we were not informed?"

"Jake, I can't say. Have you talked to Stoner?"

Political liability, like excrement, flows downhill. I didn't want my firm, or me, to get covered in it. "I checked. I spent Friday afternoon poring through our entire case file. Nothing ever came in from Morgan or the Gordon firm about a motion to suppress or any agreement. Nothing."

That caught Tom by surprise. "I'll have to look into that."

"Who's on Mueller's list, Tom? Fujimi? Tonika?"

"No. Where'd you come up with those names?"

"I did some research. What about Minimura, Nippon Plastics?" My visit to the Greenville County Library was paying off.

"Good God, no. We would have gone after them."

"Are they big competitors?"

"They both make P.E.T. film, but compete? No. Certainly not Minimura. Overall, they're a huge company with lots of resources. But in that kind of film, they're just a bit player. They've approached us for a license, but we've always turned them down."

I kept at him. "This all started because of the missing microfilm?"

"Right." He was firm.

"Three rolls? Nothing else?"

A sharp stare, then an even firmer. "Yes, three."

"You mentioned potential fall-off in top level support for this thing. Where are we today on that?"

Tom's lips thinned. "You'll see first-hand at lunch, Jake. Then we'll talk more about Dallas." He got up and strode out of his office.

The corporate dining room walls bore soothing beige and cream striped coverings. Each table was set with crisp white linen, silver cutlery, and fresh flowers. The tall windows offered a commanding view of Manhattan. I could get used to this kind of lunchroom once I finished NYU.

A hostess greeted Tom. "Nice to see you, Mr. O'Hanlon. Just the three today?"

"Hi, Annie. No, we're with Felix Untermeyer."

"Oh." Her smile dimmed. Most bosses I knew had an enforcer that everyone tried to steer clear of. Untermeyer seemed to be CT President John McElwain's hammer. "This way."

She placed padded leather-bound menus before us. "The salmon steak is wild from Scotland, in a sage cream sauce. And the veal Oscar is good, if you're hungry. Enjoy."

Felix came in and sat down.

"Veal Oscar," he sniffed. "A bad way to ruin a good schnitzel. Wine?"

His own glass appeared as he spoke. We said no thanks and ordered.

Untermeyer glared at Tom. "Are you ready for the Weidl deposition?" Charlie and I might as well have gone out to a street vendor for a hot dog.

"Closing the last investigative holes as we speak, Felix."

"This has become a bit of a crusade for you, hasn't it, Tom?" Felix let that comment hang in the air. "No one likes the way Malinkrodt acted. Unfortunately, even a non-compete agreement can't stop him from using his expertise. Adding that unnamed Japanese defendant was a mistake. I have to tell you; it's caused a few eyebrows to be raised."

He liked pushing buttons.

"Felix, this is an investigation, not a witch hunt. Those missing microfilm rolls are real. I hope as much as anyone that this is a dead end. But if we're going to protect the fantastic discoveries that pay our salaries, we can't leave any stone unturned."

Our meals arrived but Felix didn't notice. His face tightened in a frown.

"Yes, Tom. Of course . . . if we're effective. But we must be successful, or we lose our usefulness, don't we?" He picked up his silver knife, having just held a verbal one to Tom's throat. "*Bon appetit.*"

I looked at Charlie for a read. His eyebrows had peaked like a mobile home roof in a high wind. Untermeyer's corporate infighting turned the commanding view of Manhattan dark and threatening. Some lunchroom.

This guy was hostile and right next to CT's President McElwain. Tom didn't know about Minimura or the extra microfilm rolls. Or worse, he did. Some higher-up had brushed off Frank Brazeale's attempt to report a security breach. CT's own lawyer in L.A., John Morgan, was obstructive, at least, and possibly linked to a major problem with the deposition. I hadn't helped. I'd angered Madison Whitmire, a key investigation resource.

I felt like I was out on a weak limb in a high wind. I was glad to have Charlie out there with me.

Chapter 19
FAIRMONT HOTEL, DALLAS, TEXAS, TUESDAY AFTERNOON, NOVEMBER 21

After Untermeyer threatened Tom, my unease turned to alarm. Charlie and I had booked the hotel in Dallas under assumed names. At his knock, I opened the door to my room to let Charlie in.

"Did your buddy in Washington call back about Weidl?"

"Last night. He's a naturalized citizen, no immigration problems, but I got us a little useful info."

"What?"

"Weidl worked for InterTech in L. A. Turns out he had a claim for back pay. Got pretty hot about it. But he landed a job offer from Elant and left for Texas. I got an appointment at the plant in a hour. Got to get going. Oh, one other little titbit. Old Stefan spends a lotta time at the Cotton Fields, a high-tone girlie bar."

"They collect that kind of detail? And you can get to it?" My apprehension quickly gave way to an idea. "You think that could be useful?"

"Like maybe he'll loosen up and talk a lot more someplace he's comfortable? If we hit it off, we can take him there tonight."

"You better handle him. He might clam up with a lawyer." As many odd places as I'd interviewed witnesses, I didn't think a strip club was the right place to prepare for a deposition. "You and I can debrief later tonight and decide if there's a chance I could talk to him tomorrow, okay?"

"Right. I'll call you after I get back."

I was anxious to know how their meeting would go and had an idea. "I'll go out to eat. Just call the hotel and leave me a message before you go with Weidl to the club."

"Gotcha," Charlie said and took off.

Chapter 20
DALLAS, AROUND 8PM, THE SAME DAY

Charlie's message said they were going to the Cotton Fields. I'd asked the concierge for a good Tex-Mex place near there, downed great enchiladas at the restaurant, and got to the nightclub before Charlie.

As I came through the door, throbbing music set my chest pounding. A wide bowl with intimate, dimly lit tables flowed down to a stage bathed in warm lights where college-age girls undulated. Alcoves with privacy curtains ranged along the sides of the bowl. I worked my way to the hostess whose skimpy costume fit right in with the whole set up.

"Welcome to the Cotton Fields, hon." She placed a warm palm on my chest and cooed, "What can I do to make your day go away?"

"I'll take one of those alcoves, down front. But," I hurried to add, "I don't want to be disturbed. And I'd like you to steer a Mr. Cauthen to a table by the stage where I can see him when he gets here." Charlie would be using his real name with Weidl. I described Charlie and palmed the hostess a twenty. She signaled to a cute brunette with bright green eyes—young enough and with a body tight enough to be a cheerleader—who came over and pressed my hand against her warm lower back. She began to lead me when I saw Charlie come in the front door. I stopped and turned to listen.

Charlie gave his name and told the hostess a Mr. Weidl would join him. I saw her perk up. "Got a special place for ya'll." He slipped her a bill and she called over another young stunner. I nodded for my cheerleader to head to the alcove.

Charlie jumped when the girl brushed against him.

"Well, all right, hon! Party of two, ready to party! You come with me."

She held Charlie's hand against her bare lower back as she glided to a table down front. He wondered what a fifty would get you in a place like this.

Two girls on the stage flirted aggressively with the ties to their halter-tops until they came undone. Another girl came up behind Charlie and leaned over. Her breasts massaged his shoulders as her long hair fell across his cheek. She smelled like some kind of flower. He could die right there. Then he realized he'd die for sure if Jaynelle caught him in a place like this.

The girl handed Charlie a note and whispered breathily in his ear. "From a friend, hon." He opened it, wondering how explicit a proposition it would be.

Don't look for me. I can see you. If we need to talk, head to the men's room. I'll meet you there. Jake

Explicit, all right. Not what Charlie had expected, but he appreciated the teamwork.

Weidl came through the front door. Six-four with a large frame, a brushed-up haircut, sporting a dark blue silk shirt under a yellow linen jacket, he stood out even among big Texans. Charlie waved and caught Weidl's eye.

Stefan pushed through the crowd to the hostess and handed her something. She motioned and two tall, buxom, blond girls flowed up to Stefan, attached to him like lampreys, and whispered in his ears. His face lit up like a Christmas tree. There you go, Charlie realized. A fifty.

Stefan sat down at Charlie's table. "Isn't this great?"

"I'm adjusting to it, Stefan."

The two girls asked in unison, "What can we get you to help your day go away?" Charlie recognized good quality control behind the consistent processes. He'd try to point that out to Jaynelle before she lowered the axe.

"Up to you, Stefan."

"Double bourbon in a tall glass. Lots of ice." He grinned at Charlie like a possum with a sweet potato. "That's better than that damned iced tea!"

"Vodka and tonic and a pitcher a water," Charlie requested. He'd learned to dilute *saké* in Japan and *soju* in Korea during *geisha* and *keisung* parties. He figured it would work with vodka at a strip club in the US. This could be a long night.

Nursing his drink, Charlie managed one to Stefan's three. The music sped up and pumped out energy that increased the heat of the room and the crowd. Stefan's accent thickened. If Charlie didn't get somewhere soon, he could end up with nothing. Then Stefan sagged and leaned over.

"Charlie. I'm glad you came to town. The Consolidated people aren't all as nice as you."

Charlie had to lean over to keep Stefan upright. "Aw, Stefan, what's that mean?"

"Well, dey cause me problems."

"Anything I can do?"

"It's a special case." Stefan looked hazily around the room and leaned even closer to confide, "Dey're making me a witness in a lawsuit. I could get in trouble with Elant."

"Somethin' to do with Malinkrodt? I'd heard you knew him."

"Yeah."

"I know the people working on that. Maybe I can help. What's the problem?"

"Elant has been good to me. I was working in L. A. when dey called and moved me here with a bonus and everyting. It's a real good job, Charlie."

"I can see that, Stefan. You're right talented. They appreciate that."

Another young dancer, drawn like a bee to honey, sidled toward the table until Charlie caught her eye and warned her off.

Stefan stared into his bourbon and shook his head. "I got dese papers."

Charlie turned and locked his gaze on Stefan.

"I should have got rid of dem. But now dere's dis court ting coming up. Elant doesn't know about it. I don't know what to do."

"What kind of papers, Stefan?"

"From my last job."

"The one with Malinkrodt?"

"Yeah."

"What's in'em?"

"Working papers, industrial drawings, reports. It was my job. Malinkrodt gave me information and I wrote it up for my boss to present."

"Present to who, Stefan?"

"To de Japanese we were working for. To Minimura."

Charlie spilled some of his drink on his shirt. He needed to talk to Jake, after one more question.

Stefan looked up, bleary eyes drooping. "Maybe dose papers should just go away. Elant could fire me."

Alarmed, Charlie said, "They don't hire people they haven't checked out, Stefan. You're a real good engineer." Time to finish up. "How come you still have the papers, anyway?"

"My boss, Hans Mueller, told me to get dat stuff out of de office. People were coming to look at de files. I tought I could use de papers to get him to pay me, so I made copies. But den, I got dat Elant offer. Dey shipped everyting." He shook his head. "I should have gotten rid of dose papers."

"Stefan, getting rid a stuff a judge is lookin' for can get you in a heap a trouble. Maybe I can help you out with Elant."

Stefan, looking beat down, perked up. "You would do dat, Charlie?"

"I've got some ideas that could help, sure. But I'd need to look at the stuff you've got."

Stefan's head dropped again. "I don't have dem."

"What d'ya mean?" Charlie had to keep from shaking Stefan. "You just said you have 'em. Do you or doncha?"

"Not at home. Dey're in storage, at another place."

After Stefan received the subpoena, he said he had moved them and stored them under another name.

"I have de key on me all de time."

Stefan was worried, cautious, and unpredictable. It was late and he was drunk. Charlie motioned to another dancer who was about to go on stage and pointed to Stefan. She came over, put her hand on his chin, lifted his face, and sat down in his lap. Stefan's focus shifted to the girl's breasts an inch from his nose.

"'Scuse me a sec." Charlie got up and headed for the men's room.

I met Charlie in the back hall. He described the papers for Minimura. "Jackpot, Charlie. How'd he get them?"

"Had 'em copied outside the office."

"Did he say why?"

"His boss told him they had to get them out of the office before some search."

"My God. Charlie, Morgan sent U. S. Marshalls to search InterTech. Someone must have tipped off Mueller. There had to be a leak. Try to find out how Mueller knew. Then we need to see those papers before the deposition. You think Stefan will let us?"

"Well, right now, he's loaded like a freight train an' getting hard ta handle."

"So no shape to drive . . . . Offer to take him home. Then get him to show you the documents."

"He's not interested in talking about papers. Besides, he don't keep 'em at home. He's got 'em in one a them mini-warehouses."

"It's either convince him to let us see them or go to court to prevent him getting rid of them. You'd have to sign an affidavit."

Charlie figured the documents wouldn't be around by the time the lawyers got to court. And how would it look if Charlie had to swear that he got Stefan drunk in a titty bar? Jaynelle would pitch a fit.

Chapter 21

Heading back to his table, Charlie saw Weidl pawing the lap dancer. She stood up and tried to leave but Stefan grabbed her arm. Charlie walked over to the hostess.

"I'm real sorry about my friend, ma'am." He pointed to Weidl. "What do you do with a customer like that?"

"Stefan? He's a regular. It happens all the time. No problem. We call him a cab and send his car home with a valet who takes the cab back. A couple of the boys will help you." She turned and motioned to two muscular types in dark T-shirts and light-colored sport coats lounging at the bar.

Charlie wondered how to get rid of the girl. Then she bent down and thrust her breasts close to Stefan's face. His dream suddenly fulfilled, he let go. She danced away.

Charlie sat down next to the disappointed Austrian, now swaying like a sapling in a storm. "Stefan, those papers you copied . . ." Charlie caught Stefan as he started to tip.

"Oh, forget dat."

"Well, how come your boss was so nervous?"

"*No!* I could get in trouble."

Charlie backed off. "It's almost eleven. Let's get you home. They'll get your car to you. Just give me the keys."

"Dat's a good idea, Charlie. I can't see too good." He fumbled in his jacket pocket and handed Charlie a bunch of keys.

Charlie glanced down and saw a bright red plastic disc. As he tried to help Stefan up, the muscle from the bar appeared.

"Hold on one minute, fellers. I gotta run to the men's room."

As Charlie headed to the back hall, he saw a man get up from the bar and fall in behind him. His C.I.D. instincts kicked in so he stopped and turned like he was going to sneeze. The man turned his back and hid his face. Charlie had seen that move in the back alleys of Asia. He spied Jake coming down the hall and put his hand on the key with the tag in his pocket.

This late there was a lot of traffic to and from the men's room. Jake started toward Charlie who warned him off with his eyes. Charlie turned to one side to hide his hand and palmed the key. With the other hand he made a scene of pulling out a handkerchief.

The man from the bar watched closely. Charlie gave a few false starts, buried his nose in his handkerchief, bent over double, and exploded with a massive faked sneeze. At the same time, he bumped into Jake, dropped the key into Jake's coat pocket, and whispered, "I'm being followered. *Git away*."

Chapter 22
FAIRMONT HOTEL, AFTER 11PM

The man who'd been tracking Weidl followed Charlie's car as it turned into the Fairmont garage and pulled into a space. The tail drove on by, went outside, and parked on the street. He hurried into the lobby in time to see Charlie pick up his room key and get in an elevator. The man looked at the hotel event board, then went to the front desk as the elevator doors closed on Charlie, alone.

"Say, I thought I saw that fella at the seminar this afternoon and it just came to me. I haven't seen him in years. Isn't he Bill Spence with Chevron?"

As she looked at the guest's registration info, Charlie's tail eyed the elevator floor indicator as it stopped at eighteen.

"No, sir. He's with Consolidated Technologies."

"What's his name?"

She looked up and gave him a cold stare. "It's not Mr. Spence. I can't give you any other information."

He had to phone in but he could wait a while to see if he could find out anything else.

Chapter 23
FAIRMONT HOTEL, LATE THAT NIGHT

Back in my hotel room, I called Charlie to come up. As I emptied my pockets onto the top of the desk, I noticed a strange key with a red tag. Then I remembered Charlie brushing up against me in the hall. Picking up the key, I read the engraving. "U-Stor-It." Under it there was a number: B11. I turned the tag over, saw a name on the back, and smiled.

There was a knock on the door. I put the key down, looked through the peephole, saw Charlie's mangled teeth, and let him in. "What was that all about at the club?"

"Like you said, I got him to give me his keys. I was gonna talk to you about how to handle it. But some feller at the bar started after me and I got concerned. So, I passed the key to you."

"Jeez. I wasn't sure I heard you right in the hall. Someone followed you?"

"Following Weidl I reckon at first, now me. At least back at the club. Don't know about after, but could be."

Charlie's C.I.D. training was paying off. If someone was following Weidl, were they with Malinkrodt? More likely Mueller. "Does Weidl think Mueller knows he made copies?"

"Well, I don't know about that but old Stefan's nervous as a cat in a kennel a hunting dogs. He's thinking about trashing the papers."

"That would be a disaster. I understand better now what you did in the C.I.D., Charlie, great work. Now you have his confidence." I picked up the key with the red tag.

Charlie fidgeted and looked up. "Well, he gave me his keys, but he sorta didn't give me that key."

"What do you mean, sorta?"

"Well, see, he gave me his key ring and this one was tangled up in it."

"But he agreed to let you see the documents, right?"

"Not 'xactly, not yet."

I'd begun trusting Charlie, but this was like questioning Frank Brazeale. "He doesn't know you took this key and he hasn't agreed to show you the docs?"

"That's about it."

"What exactly were you thinking, Charlie?"

"I'as thinking I'd better put that key in a safe place before that guy tried to get hold a me."

"So, at the latest, when Weidl wakes up tomorrow morning to drive to work, he's going to discover it's gone."

"Hmm, good chance a that."

"Where's this storage place?"

"Don't know."

I found the Dallas Yellow Pages in the bedside table drawer and dropped it on the desk. "Storage . . . storage." I ran down the listings until I found "U-Stor-It".

Charlie peered over my shoulder. "Dang. Double dang. They's four of 'em."

"They're franchises. See?" I showed him the back of the tag with the name on it.

"Here 'tis. Geiger's U-Stor-It." Charlie picked up a hotel pen and wrote the address on the note pad by the phone.

"Let's see if I've got this right, Charlie. We've got a stolen key in the wrongful possession of an officer of the court. The key might lead to incriminating documents in this case, if we knew where they were, which we think we do, because just maybe they're in this "U-Stor-It" here in Dallas."

Suddenly, I realized there was another complication. "If they are, there's got to be controlled access of some kind, probably a coded gate. If we had the code, and the owner's permission, which we don't, we could get access to the lock this key fits. And maybe find some documents that don't belong to us and that we have no right to have."

"Well, now, wait a minute, counselor. Don't seem that old Stefan has any right to those documents, neither, if they came from InterTech."

I eyed Charlie and recalled Frank expounding on the intricacies of attorney-client privilege. "But they're in *his* storage, Charlie. They're not sitting on a table in the lobby of the Fairmont for anyone passing by to pick up. And someone, we don't know who, may try to prevent us from getting at them or try to get rid of them." I looked at my watch. "It's past midnight and we've got, say, three or four hours to figure a way out of this mess."

Charlie's head sagged. "I'as just gonna mention that."

Chapter 24
11:40PM

After our trip to Manhattan, I'd been glad to have Charlie's help in the political maze at CT. Now in Dallas, I'd seen how the C.I.D. would handle a tough situation under pressure and I was grateful for his experience. But this was heading off the rails. I needed to write down the events, sort them out, think about them, and plan our next step. While I worked on my notes, Charlie deflated into a chair. I got up to go to the john. When I came back, he was standing up.

"Looky here. I got us into this mess. I'll get us out."

I looked up. "What do you mean?"

"I took the key then dumped it on you. You got perfessional rules and such."

"We're in this one together, Charlie." I hope he understood we were a team, but I also wanted him to know we had to keep this on track. For all his expertise, I was the lawyer, for God's sake. "We'll sort it out and find a solution."

"I could call Weidl first thing in the morning, tell him I got the key. Just like it happened. Then I ask to meet him to give it back. Then I'll try to talk him into going with me to look at them right then."

Charlie's idea was practical, legal, and reassuring. He put the key in his pocket.

"Sounds like a plan. Do you think he'd agree?" I asked.

"They's a purty good chance. We hit it off all right." Charlie looked down.

"What?"

"Well, we got the key. I could try to get a look at what the papers is. Right now. You wouldn't be involved. May be the only way to pin Minimura to Malinkrodt. Someone's working hard to stop that from happening." He looked up, hopeful.

"Look, I want to get to the bottom of this as much as you do, but if we try to steal Stefan's papers, we run big risks. Consolidated's trying to stop illegal acts, not commit new ones. I can't do it, I can't let you do it, and you know it. The only way out of this is for you to call Weidl first thing in the morning, like you said."

"Sounds like good legal advice."

"All right. Let's get some sleep."

Chapter 25
11:50PM

Weidl's tail was still in the lobby. He'd seen no sign of the guy from Consolidated. It was late. He couldn't cover them both. He went over to the bank of pay phones to call in his report.

"It's Driscoll. I'm still in Dallas."

"It's late there. Did he go to the club and pass out again?"

"He went, but he wasn't alone."

"Who was with him? Another girl?"

"No, a guy I haven't seen before." Driscoll described the incident in the hallway. "I can't be sure, but he may have brush passed something to a third guy. If he did, he's good. I couldn't get a look at the other guy's face. But the pass? That's a hunch."

"I don't pay for hunches. Two more guys? You know who they are?"

"I tailed the first one to the Fairmont. I'm there now. He's with Consolidated Technologies."

"Who the hell at Consolidated makes brush passes?" He paused. "Could be corporate security. You get his name?"

"I only know his floor, but they won't give out his name or his room number. I'll need help. There's two, maybe three guys to watch."

Driscoll got approval to hire another private eye, then an order to report back in the morning. He called a P.I. he'd tag teamed with once on a surveillance in Dallas and told him to meet him first thing in the morning near Weidl's apartment. Driscoll hung up, looked around, and saw a different clerk at the front desk. He walked over.

"Say. I forgot my friend's room number. He's with Consolidated Technologies, on the eighteenth floor?"

"Sir, I can't give out room numbers."

"Aw, that's too bad. We need to set a time to meet for breakfast and prepare for a session we've been asked to lead."

"Sorry, sir."

Dead end. Driscoll walked toward the front entrance.

The clerk called out. "I could call Mr. Black for you, if you think it's okay this late." Driscoll grinned and nodded approval. "There's a house phone on the desk over there. I'll connect you."

He let it ring ten times. Nobody sleeps that hard. If he lost Black, he'd catch hell. He went to the elevator for the parking garage to check for Black's car. The elevator was slow. He saw the door to the garage stairs and raced down them two at a time.

Chapter 26

AFTER MIDNIGHT, THE NEXT DAY, WEDNESDAY, NOVEMBER 22

After Charlie left, I noticed the key was gone. I figured he had taken it to give back to Weidl. Then I noticed Geiger's address was gone. I called Charlie's room. It rang without an answer. Charlie was gone too.

Charlie turned the car's overhead light on to see the map he got from the front desk. As he neared the end of the route, he slowed down.

He didn't like going behind Jake's back, but this thing felt like an investigation back in Asia. The dog fights he'd been in had no rules, except last man standing won. The lawyers could argue all they wanted to, once the cards were face up, but in Charlie's C.I.D. world, you never made it that far if you didn't keep moving ahead.

He spotted the sign, "Geiger's U-Stor-It," and pulled over. It was in a strip mall near warehouses and freight truck yards next to the Interstate, with a fence, a gate, and a road to the storage sheds down a hill behind the office, all lit by bright lights on tall polls. Charlie checked his watch. It was nearing one o'clock. There were no lights in the "U-Stor-It" office. He looked back up the street and didn't see any cars.

Jake had mentioned a code. Charlie saw the gate was hitched to an automated opener. On the office side, there was a box with a keypad. Barbed wire coiled all along the top of the fence.

The lot dropped off to the right behind the strip mall to an area of bare concrete pads. On that side, a chain link fence ran behind the strip mall.

He walked along the fence toward the new construction, ducked behind a row of tall bushes, and came to where the original fence stopped. The construction company had added a temporary one and chained them together but not well. He gave the new fence a shove, then pried the bottom of the fence ends until they spread apart. Dropping to his hands and knees, he wriggled through.

Charlie started sidestepping down a steep, newly graded dirt slope. His feet shot out from under him and he began to slide on his butt. Trying to slow down, he reached out with both hands. His left hand hit something sharp and pain shot through it.

He hit the bottom of the hill with a thud, covered with dirt. By the light from the poles, he could see blood oozing from a deep cut in his left palm. He pulled out his handkerchief, wrapped it around the wound and closed his fist to try to stop the bleeding. It hurt like fire. Then he took off across the construction and started up toward the sheds.

Stepping into the alley between the "A" and "B" sheds, he heard a sound come from the construction area. He spun around, waited, and listened. All he could hear was a truck shifting gears as it labored up the grade on the Interstate.

The second door on the right was marked B11-20. He tried the handle. Locked. He took out the key with the red tag. It fit and the door creaked open. The sheds and the door blocked the light from the poles.

As he moved into the dark bay, the door started to swing shut. Charlie jumped, stopped it with his left hand, and stifled a yell. Pain radiated from the cut and he bent over double.

Sticking his foot in the doorway to keep the door from closing and locking him in, he felt along the wall for a light switch and flicked it. Nothing. He looked outside the door and saw a length of pipe on the ground, grabbed it, and propped the door open.

He could barely make out the “B11” on the first locker down and to the right. He felt for the locker handle. It had a small padlock. He tried the door key. It didn’t even fit in the slot. That key must’ve been loose in Stefan’s pocket.

Charlie muttered and looked around, measuring by sight. He lay down, stuck one foot out to keep the door open, took the pipe in his good hand, and propped himself up with his cut hand to get some leverage.

He gasped as pain shot through his arm like he’d leaned on a hot stove. Gritting his teeth, he held himself up, and raised the pipe with his good hand to take a whack at the padlock.

Chapter 27
TRIP TO GEIGER'S

When Charlie didn't answer his phone, I knew why and I didn't like it. We'd agreed to wait until morning. Then I recalled he'd only acknowledged my plan was "good legal advice." The guy from the Cotton Fields might be on Charlie's tail. I was mad, but I couldn't leave him alone at night in a deserted part of town with someone after him. He could lead the tail right to the documents, crucial evidence that we had to preserve.

I hurried to the front desk and got a map from the clerk. When I asked for the best route to Geiger's she said that sure was a popular spot this late, confirming where Charlie had gone.. The closer I got to Geiger's, the madder I got.

Down the street, I could see the 'U-Stor-It' lot, daytime-bright from lights on tall poles. I spotted a car parked across from the entrance and another one behind it. I pulled over and got out, scurried across the street, and ran into the shadow of the office. Edging closer to the fence, I froze.

There was a leg sticking out of an open door in Building "B". That had to be Charlie. In front of this end of the same building, I could see another man crouching. A sharp report rang out and a pained “Gol dang!” echoed through the buildings. The stalker pulled something out of his belt and started toward the door to the lockers. I cupped my hands and shouted, “Charlie. Look out behind you.”

Despite the pain, Charlie was poised to give the padlock another hit when he heard the warning. His left hand burned but he scrabbled around to face the door and kept it open with his throbbing hand. With the other one, he grabbed the pipe and raised it.

A shoe appeared and he whirled the pipe low. It cracked hard on a shin. Someone fell forward, hands and head crashing into the pavement. A blackjack skittered across the asphalt.

Charlie recognized the tail from the Cotton Fields. The man began to push up on his arms. The iron pipe was heavy, so Charlie swung it at the right arm, not the head. The arm crumpled and the face crashed into the blacktop again. Charlie scrambled forward on the ground. Pain seared his left hand and he saw stars.

The man groaned and started to move. Charlie started to lunge for the blackjack. A hand gripped his leg. Charlie ground his good hand into the pavement, drew his left leg forward, then kicked hard. He caught his attacker in the neck. The assailant lost his grip and Charlie sprang forward and grabbed the blackjack.

I saw Charlie’s hand come down on the man’s head. The guy slumped and lay still. “It’s Jake, Charlie. I’m up at the gate. You all right?”

I heard a muffled reply, “Better than t’other one, counselor. ‘Preciate that warning. You wanna come down here and gimme a hand?”

“How the hell do I do that?”

I stood beside Charlie as we looked at the man out cold on the asphalt. A slow trickle of blood seeped onto the pavement from a gash in his head.

Blood. A mangled body. I fought to keep control, but this was live, worse than torts. I was running on empty. Charlie, the criminal investigation expert, had gotten us into this mess.

"What do we do now?"

"Like any good plan, Jake. Impervise."

He knelt and put an ear to the side of the man's face. "His breathing's okay. Should be out fifteen, twenty minutes." Charlie stood up, stashed the blackjack in his waistband, and bent down to check the man's coat pockets. He pulled out a flashlight and a small bag, like a schoolboy's pencil case, and handed them to me. Then he searched the man's pants pockets and fished out a wallet. He took out a driver's license and put the wallet back.

"Hope he gets pulled over."

I turned away from the sight of the blood . "We've got to get out of here. What do we do about him?"

"Keep that door open." Charlie switched on the flashlight, gave it to me to hold, motioned to point it at his hands, took the case from me, and unzipped it. "Well, aint that thoughty. He brung his burgling kit."

"Charlie. We've got to go!"

"Just a sec, pardner." He pulled two long, thin metal objects out and knelt before the door of locker B11. My head swiveled back and forth between the unconscious man and what Charlie was up to. Blood from the man's head was congealing on the asphalt. Starting to lose it again, I breathed deeply. Busy fighting panic, I could only watch.

"What'd you take out of his pencil case?"

"Hold that light on this locker door."

Panting, eyes wide, I watched as Charlie held the padlock on B11 and cupped one of the metal sticks in the same hand. With the other hand, he pushed something into the lock, then flicked his wrist. The padlock sprang open. "Shine that light in here . . . . Well, ain't that purty."

I looked in the locker and saw four big bags full of papers. Charlie pulled one from the nearest bag. "Gimme a little more light, counselor." He scanned one page, then pulled another from the second bag and looked at it. He did the same with bags three and four, "InterTech and Minimura. This is it." He pulled all four bags out of the locker. "Here. Take two a these."

"What?"

"We gotta take this stuff back to the hotel."

"Steal these, too?" I hissed. "No way, Charlie. What about him?"

"He'll either wake up and hightail it or he's in for a lot of explaining come morning." He looked up. "Which ain't too far off." Charlie closed the locker door and re-locked the padlock. He grabbed two bags, turned, rolled the guy out of the way with his foot, then started jogging.

My feet felt nailed to the ground and my mind was stuck, too. Charlie was half-way to the dirt embankment. He turned back, stared at me, yelled, "Let's go," and took off.

Chapter 28
FIGHT OR FLIGHT

I was shocked by Charlie's betrayal. We could still put the documents back. The attacker would not squeal on us. He was trespassing, too. We could approach Weidl in the morning and confront him like we'd planned. Charlie's way was a dead end. My way was the legal way, the safe way, the right way. So what if someone was playing by different rules, or no rules? We'd find a way to trip them up, just like Boyden at the paper mill. But if Charlie and I got caught with documents that we really had stolen, we were in trouble.

I started to call out to Charlie to stop him, when the leg of the man on the ground twitched. The man was still out, but that couldn't last. I started breathing hard.

If we put the documents back in the locker and he came to, there'd be a fight. This guy looked fit, maybe an ex-cop or military. If he woke up after we left, he might break in, destroy the documents and our only chance of a physical link between Cameron, Malinkrodt, InterTech, and Minimura.

Without that, the case was lost, but to who? We didn't know, but someone willing to doctor a deposition, thwart a Federal court ordered inspection, tail a witness, and assault Charlie. Yet Charlie and I had stolen a key, physically assaulted someone, and broken into the locker. Now we were stealing property that was subject to my own subpoena.

In the middle of this debate, a thought emerged and stood out: someone was playing us for chumps. I couldn't blame them. Beau would not exactly have set off any alarms. It felt like I was back on the paper mill site with the sirens headed for us for "stealin' stuff" from our own trailer.

I didn't know who was after us now, or where they'd stop. But we were out of time and Charlie was already scrambling up the dirt slope with two bags of stolen documents. Weidl's documents were our only chance to move the case forward. Without them, it was over.

My legs started churning and I ran after Charlie one more time, the two bags of evidence banging against my thighs.

Chapter 29
FAIRMONT HOTEL, 5:00AM, THE SAME DAY

"Okay, Charlie. What have we got?" While I had wrangled the four bags up to my room, Charlie had picked up a first aid kit from the front desk. I cleaned and bandaged the cut in his palm.

The driver's license Charlie had taken was for a James Radnor from California. We had to figure out what we had so we'd split the papers into technical and non-technical piles, listed them, and wrote brief descriptions.

Charlie looked up and let out a whistle. "The link 'tween these InterTech drawings and Cameron is dead on. I'd like to have Frank Brazeale go over 'em with the originals, but most of the drawings looks like perfect copies of Cameron's except for the name on the title blocks. Look here, on this site plan. See this little number here, on this drawing marked InterTech?"

"Yeah, 957. What's that?"

"It's the 'xact number of feet the foundations of the Cameron factory is above sea level. This thing is a copy by a dumb ass, most likely Stefan Weidl."

"Dumb ass" reminded me of sitting in the red chair in Preston's office. But this was a screw up by the other side. If this drawing ever went before a jury, 957 would be a clincher on liability. "Anything else?"

"Lots. There's one note that ain't a copy. It covers five or six things, one I can't place."

"Like you said, we'll have to get the experts involved."

"What about the legal side, Jake? Have I got us in a mess, or what?" Now was not the time to argue with Charlie about criminal law.

"That guy at Geiger's isn't going to call the cops. But we have other problems. First one is how to handle Weidl. If he gets mad at us and balks, he can make the deposition difficult. You need to sort it out with him first thing this morning. And we've got to get the documents back to him in a way that he can't deny having had them. The guy who attacked you will try to stop that."

We were both dog tired and Charlie's hand must've been hurting like a sonovabitch.

"One more thing," I said. "With all the heat around these documents, we need to get them on the record as soon as possible. We should move up the deposition."

"Can we do that?"

"Weidl would have to agree, another reason we've got to win him over. And Malinkrodt has to agree, too. It's his right as a party to the suit.. That could be a problem. I'll let Tom O'Hanlon take care of Morgan. It's my deposition anyway. Once we're over those hurdles, and the deposition's in the can, these documents should get us to Minimura's files in Japan."

"If we can get to their records, we can break this case open. But they'll put up a fight. And we've already got a bunch of determined people working against us."

"We got an expensive corporate security group. They oughta be good for something."

"I hate to remind you, but Tom O'Hanlon was out of the loop. Remember how worried Frank was? We don't know who knows what up the line at Consolidated. We better keep this to ourselves for a while longer."

There I was, an officer of the court, staring at four bags of stolen documents I had subpoenaed. Our unknown opponents' attack and our response created issues way beyond Weidl's deposition. At this rate, I might never get to NYU.

Chapter 30
6:15AM, THE SAME DAY

We had to get the documents back in Weidl's locker. But Charlie had said Weidl wanted to destroy them. At least one thing was clear. We needed a copy. I grabbed the hotel services book.

Charlie was asleep in the chair when I got back from the business center, lugging a full set of documents with me.

"Charlie. Wake up."

He groaned. "Wha . . . wha'zit? Where . . . ."

"We've got work to do."

He sat up, rubbing his eyes.

"Come on, Charlie. I need you to teach me one of your C.I.D. tricks. Then you can sleep until you have to make a phone call."

I left Charlie in my room and went back to Geiger's with copies of Weidl's originals in the trunk. The office opened at six. It smelled of stale cigarette smoke and fried bacon. A frowsy woman leaned on the counter, her head drooped over the newspaper. She swatted at the ashes that fell from a lit cigarette dangling from her mouth. Through a door behind the woman, I could see an old man in a sitting room watching TV with the volume blaring. That wasn't good. The building doubled as a residence.

"Excuse me, ma'am."

The woman looked up and said something I couldn't hear over the TV. I shrugged. She turned and yelled at the old man. "Fred, cut that thang off. Got a customer. Can't hear a thang."

"What?" he shouted.

"I said . . . . Oh, for goodness sakes. Sorry, mister. He's deaf as a post. Can't say I'm much better. Hold on a minute."

She stormed into the back room and snapped off the TV.

"You cain't do that," the old man complained. "I's watching my program."

"What?"

We'd been lucky. I wanted to rent a box so I could get the gate code and replace the documents in Weidl's storage. While the couple argued, I looked around the office. On top of a cabinet behind the counter, I saw some electronics, including a video recorder.

I stared at the machine, then walked outside and looked up. A surveillance camera on a light was aimed at the sheds. My plan was worthless. Last night's events were on tape.

The old couple were still going at it. I stared at the recorder, but staring wouldn't make the tape disappear.

Chapter 31
OAKDALE APARTMENTS, DALLAS, EARLY MORNING, THE SAME DAY

Driscoll came to on the asphalt at the storage place. His head rang, blood caked his hair, and raw, painful scrapes covered his face and hands. He tried to get up and collapsed from the pain in his shin. He checked his coat pockets. Empty.

"God damn it!" He patted his pants pocket and felt his wallet with relief, then noticed his jacket and trousers were torn. Light was creeping up in the east. He'd clean up at a gas station on the way to meet Madden, the other P. I.

Driscoll staggered as he got out of his car into the early morning chill. He tried not to limp as he walked over to Madden's Chevy. Madden buzzed down his window. Hot air from inside hit Driscoll's scraped face like a blow torch, causing him to groan.

Madden gave Driscoll a long look. "It's freezing out here. You don't have coats in L. A.?" He saw Driscoll's scrapes and stopped. "What happened to your face?"

Driscoll glared at the other P. I. "You need to focus on the job."

"Tail him, right? Who else is involved? How'd you get banged up?"

"I tripped!" Driscoll was getting angry.

Madden looked down at Driscoll's torn pants then back at the raw red marks on his face. "And fell off a building?"

This P. I. needed to focus. "You got to make this guy nervous. He's talking to the wrong people."

Madden's face turned grim. "Double time for the risk."

Driscoll wanted to punch the guy, but he had no choice. "If I'm gonna pay you that much, you got to put the fear of God into him. Understand? And make it stick. I'll only pay extra if he shuts up."

Driscoll drove to his hotel, showered, changed, and doctored his face. When he pulled out his wallet at the newsstand in the lobby to buy a pack of cigarettes, he noticed his driver's license was gone.

"Bastards!" He rushed back to his room, picked up another fake ID, and headed to the Fairmont.

After he parked, he went into the lobby and over to a writing desk, picked up the house phone, and asked for Mr. Black's room. No answer. He called the front desk. Black was still registered.

He stopped by the pay phone and went over the story he'd come up with. Then he called in to report. It was early Central Standard time, but his call was answered.

"It's Driscoll."

"Yeah?"

"This Consolidated guy's definitely got someone else with him. They went to a storage facility last night and probably took something that Weidl had stashed there."

"They took something? Who's the other guy? Where are they now? What the hell am I paying you for?"

"They had access to the storage lot. I couldn't go in." An excuse came to him, but it raised new problems. "I'd a risked showing up on the surveillance cameras. A patrol car cruised by and I had to duck out of the way. When it was clear, they were gone. I couldn't see what they took."

"Okay, okay." There was a pause on the line. "It's possible Weidl has some papers we need. If these guys from Consolidated are still there, you do what it takes to get whatever they got."

"Papers?" Driscoll was glad to have something he could complain about for a change. "God damn it. That would have been good to know the last time I was here. You just told me to toss the apartment. What kind of papers? How many?"

"I'll tell you what you need to know when you need to know it. Could be a couple of arms full. Some, big blueprint size. Got it? Call me back as soon as you've done your job."

Driscoll hung up and kicked the wall. That made his shin hurt worse. He limped over to a chair. His contact paid well, but the guy had a reputation for getting nasty. If the men from Consolidated had the papers, they could be in one of their rooms or in the trunk of one of their cars. His contact was not happy and that was bad for Driscoll. He sat down to give his wounds a rest and think.

If he had something hot and knew he was being tailed, what would he do? Take precautions. Hide them. Or copy them. At the business center. He got up and limped across the lobby.

Chapter 32
GEIGER'S OFFICE

I still had to put the documents back in Stefan's locker, then get back to the hotel. The old lady came back to the front desk shaking her head. "Sorry, mister. What can I do you for?"

She didn't ask for an ID, so I filled in the paperwork in the name of James Radnor and got the code and a key to a locker I didn't need. When I got to the B building, the light was still out, but the iron pipe was sitting there. I wedged the door open.

Taking the spring lever and small pick Charlie had given me, I fiddled with the padlock on the door of locker B11. It took a few tries, but the lock finally popped open. I put the four bags back, got back in my car, and drove to the front gate.

I went into the office. The couple were arguing in the back room. I got what I wanted, rang the bell, called out, "Thanks." And jumped in my car

The couple came into the front office. I waved, but they bent down to the VCR, then stood up arguing again, both gesturing at the VCR. I couldn't help smiling as I looked down at the seat next to me.

We were back on the straight and narrow, except for the video tape I'd stolen.

Chapter 33
OAKDALE APARTMENTS, 7:00AM, THE SAME DAY

Stefan Weidl was agitated. His first thought when he woke up was to see if Charlie could really help him. He got dressed, put his wallet in his pocket, and reached for his keys.

The one with the red tag was gone. He tried to think about last night, but it was a haze. Jimmy drove him home and gave him back his key ring. But the red tagged one was missing. Those damn papers were giving him a headache, on top of the one from the bourbon.

He started tearing up the apartment to look for the key when he saw a note slipped under his door. He picked it up and unfolded the paper that looked like it was torn from a notepad.

> *We're watching you. The men you're talking to can only make things worse. Keep quiet or you may get hurt.*

Stefan dropped the note like it was on fire and shuddered. He ransacked the apartment until he had to leave for work. No key. All he could think about as he drove to work was he had to get rid of those papers, as soon as he could.

Chapter 34
FAIRMONT HOTEL, 8AM, THE SAME DAY

When the Elant offices opened, Charlie called their switchboard and had them put him through to the general manager, then to Weidl.

"Stefan. It's Charlie Cauthen. How're you feelin'? That was some place you took me to. Hope you got home all right." Charlie talked fast to get his story out. "You had a loose key you handed to me with your car keys. In all the rush to leave, it got left in my pocket when I gave your keys to the valet. I want to get it right back to you."

Stefan's voice rose an octave, "Dat's good!"

"I can come by your office and drop it off. Say, you mentioned some papers you have for your deposition. When I bring you your key, you can show me the papers and we can have dinner. How's about that?"

"*No! No!* Look, I'm real busy Charlie. Don't come here. Just leave da key for me at da front desk at da Fairmont. As soon as you can. I'll pick it up, maybe dis morning."

Charlie said he would and was hanging up the phone when Jake came in, gloating.

"I got mine, Charlie. How about you?"

"Just finished talking with Mr. Stefan Wey-DELL. He's nervous as a cat in a room full a rocking chairs. Sure don't want to meet me. No way he'll talk to you. Oh, and I called information in L.A. for a James Radnor, the name on that driver's license? No luck at that address or any other one in the whole city. Either he's unlisted or it's a fake. What's that?"

"I got a little present for you." I put the video cassette on the desk. "Home movies from the surveillance camera at 'U-Stor-It'. You, your nemesis, and yours truly engaged in trespass, assault and battery, and theft."

Charlie stared at the tape. "God Ahmighty, Jake. I never thought a looking for a camera, I'as so juiced." He looked hard at Jake. "You're the lawyer! How'd you do that?"

I shrugged

"I screwed up," Charlie said. "I'm sorry I put you in a tough spot. You saved my butt." Then a grin stole back across his face. "We're getting the hang a this working together. You got potential, Jake. You just might make a good investigator yet." Jake pulled his fist back to deck Charlie who, cackling, piled on Jake and held his arms to his side. "Then you could give up that lawyering and make some real money."

Driscoll's contact would be pleased. It had been easy to find the copies at the Business Center made for a Mr. J. Randolph, Room 2012. Driscoll had seen the name InterTech in the papers. With them in the trunk of his car, he felt much better as he pulled into the parking space at Geiger's. Except for one thing.

He looked up and saw the surveillance camera on a pole. Just what he was afraid of.

A buzzer rang in the back as he opened the front door. The VCR was behind the counter. No one was there. He walked over and looked in the back room. Still no one.

He went over to the VCR, pushed eject, and a cassette popped out. Someone opened a door into the back room. Driscoll grabbed the tape and took off. He'd find a vacant lot on the way back to burn the papers and the tape, then pick up tailing Mr. Black again.

I left Charlie watching the stolen tape and went to the Business Center to pick up the copies they were making. The attendant came out of the storeroom shaking her head.

"Nothing there, Mr. Randolph. You sure they weren't delivered to your room?"

"I'm sure, Miss."

She looked at a sheet on the counter. "Here it is. That's a relief. Your colleague, Mr. Wilson, picked the packages up earlier this morning."

"Wilson? From South Carolina?" I was bewildered.

"Uh, no. From Los Angeles."

Chapter 35
8:45AM, THE SAME DAY

After Charlie finished the video, he put the key in an envelope with Stefan's name on it, and took it down to the front desk. Then he went back to Jake's room. He had dozed off when the phone rang. He answered and listened. No one. He hung up.

Radnor might have found out Jake's room number. He was probably downstairs, trying to see if he could pick up tailing Charlie again. Charlie'd had enough. He headed toward the elevator to catch the guy and confront him.

When the elevator door opened, Charlie peered out and saw Stefan pick up the key at the desk, then hurry toward the front entrance. Charlie started to leave the elevator to go after him when he saw Radnor get out of a chair and follow Stefan. Charlie stepped out of the elevator after Radnor cleared the front door, and saw Radnor stop to talk to another guy in a car waiting out front who must have followed Stefan from work. Across the lobby, Jake walked out of the business center. Charlie hurried over to him.

I smiled after Charlie warned me, but it was a weary smile. "We're done here. Let's head home. We have to compare the docs to Frank's tapes."

"Nunh uh, Jake. Old Stefan's fit to be tied. I bet he's going ta get rid a the documents." He explained Radner's movements and the addition of another tail.

"What are you thinking?"

"Might as well join the parade."

I stood there. But not frozen, like on the asphalt at Geiger's. If Weidl did trash the documents I'd put back, he'd swear they were gone, and we'd have a big problem explaining how we had a set.

Unless we could use it. On the ride back from Geiger's before dawn, I'd thought over our predicament. I'd never been outside the law like this but Charlie had kept rock steady after he was attacked. While his C.I.D. instincts had gotten us into trouble, they had also gotten us out of it, at least part of the way. I couldn't have done that.

We were the target of criminals and had no idea how far they were ready to go. Now I had to listen to Charlie's suggestions and add them to legal considerations as one set of criteria before we chose a course of action. It might be useful to see what Stefan was up to.

"Okay but listen. I'm calling the shots and we won't take any more risks." It didn't hurt to at least say it. I wasn't ready to admit that his schemes, whatever they turned out to be, might be the best path through this shifting landscape.

Chapter 36
ON THE WAY TO GEIGER'S

Charlie drove my car. Radner knew Charlie's. We had to push it to beat Stefan. If one of us was going to get pinched in a traffic stop, better if it wasn't the lawyer. Charlie drove fast and ran two red lights.

When we got to Geiger's there was no sign of Weidl. We looked up carefully. There was only one surveillance camera, the one I had spotted earlier that morning. The camera covered the aisles between the A, B, and C buildings. The old couple were arguing in the office by the VCR. The old man threw up his hands as his wife slid a new tape into the machine.

"Looks like Geiger's skimped a little on security cameras," Charlie said.

"It was in the right place last night," I replied. "And it covers all the way down to the dumpsters at the back of the lot."

Charlie snuck behind the bushes and took off to watch Stefan's locker. I had warned him to keep out of camera range but find a place where he could observe Stefan. I drove the car into the lot of the strip mall to the right of Geiger's, parked where I could see all the way to the dumpsters, and settled in to wait.

Weidl pulled up to the security keypad and punched in his code, then drove down to the bay for B11.

I saw Radnor drive up and park across the street. I collapsed down low. He got out, looked up and down the street, walked over to the gate, and slipped behind the bushes to get a good view of Stefan's shed. His partner must be back at the Fairmont, watching Charlie's car.

Charlie saw Weidl park his car in front of his storage bay. Weidl got the four bags and loaded them in his trunk. Then he drove to the dumpsters at the back of the lot. Charlie followed, weaving around the sheds, and saw Stefan throw all the bags into the first dumpster, then pour fluid from a can over them. After a final look around, he lit a match and threw it in.

With a *whoosh,* a ball of fire and a cloud of black smoke erupted. When the flames settled down, the only thing visible was a heat jet. Stefan got in his car and drove to the front gate, slapping the steering wheel and rocking along with the radio like a teenager who'd had a hot date.

I watched Radnor as he watched Weidl. By the time Weidl pulled up to the front gate, Radnor had disappeared. I got out and saw Charlie headed toward the dirt bank. I had an eyewitness now, but I wanted more.

"He burned 'em, Jake. I saw him do it."

"He's making it hard on us, Charlie. We'll have to overcome his sense of relief."

Charlie waited until the office was empty, then performed what I hoped was our last illegal act.

As we pulled out of the parking lot, the couple stood by the VCR in the office and argued, again. They'd already had a bad day. I thought of another benefit from stealing two video tapes. Maybe they were on CT P.E.T. film

Chapter 37
NEAR WEIDL'S OFFICE

Driscoll felt confident as he called his contact from a phone booth.

"It's Driscoll."

"What have you got?"

"The second guy is Randolph. J. Randolph. Can you check him out?"

"Doesn't ring a bell. What about the papers?"

"I found them at the Business Center and got them out from under Randolph's nose. They're InterTech documents all right. Randolph or the other guy put the originals back in Weidl's locker, but I put pressure on Weidl not to play along with them. It worked like a charm. He went out to the storage and burned the papers. They're gone. We're clean."

"You're sure?"

"Dead certain."

"Did you get 'em all?

Driscoll was banged up and hadn't slept. He was close to the edge. He didn't need any second guessing. "I was in the Business Center and carried them out myself, dammit. I made sure I got both bundles they'd put in bags."

"What have you done with them?"

“*Burned ‘em.* We don’t want any of them around loose.”

“Did you count them and check them against the log before lighting a bonfire?” This guy was never satisfied. No way Driscoll was going to mention the video tape he’d stolen and burned to cover his assault on, then humiliation by, Black. He’d seen Weidl burn the documents with his own eyes. That was enough.

Chapter 38
RAPPONGI DISTRICT, TOKYO, 3:30PM, THURSDAY, NOVEMBER 23

TWELVE HOURS LATER THAN U. S. EAST COAST TIME

Shin Isaki sat on a banquette in the gentlemen's club he used for clandestine meetings with members of the Diet. It was just far enough from the national legislature to be convenient without attracting reporters covering politics. The club's owner, a former prostitute Shin had set up in business, made sure no one disturbed him. It suited his schedule that Kano, who had requested an urgent meeting, meet Shin here again.

In his late 70s, Shin looked younger. Slight, inconspicuous in his gray off the rack suit from *Takashimaya*, the big department store on the Ginza. His fortune had come from Japan's unofficial colonization of northern China before 1941. Gold he had stolen in the chaos of occupation and received from extortion and illicit activities on behalf of the Japanese occupiers.

Shin's grandfather had been *samurai*, an elite warrior subject to the disciplinary code, *bushido*. Then the Americans threatened Japan in the 1850s to force it to open to the West after centuries of isolation. Even the sharpest *samurai* swords were no match for the cannons of Commodore Perry's gunboats. They flattened the entire city of Yokohama in minutes.

Radical reform was imperative to preserve the island nation. Most of the strong *daimyo*, the regional lords, responded and imposed the *Meiji* Reforms on a puppet Emperor. The reforms took away Shin's grandfather's privileges and status in exchange for dwindling allotments of rice. Shin's grandfather protested honorably by taking his life.

But Shin's father died a drunk leaving Shin to grow up waiting on tables of rough men at his aunt's brothel. When Japan became an aggressor in northern China, Shin worked for the secret police. The puppet province the Japanese named Manchukuo was the perfect grindstone on which to hone his skills and serve the nation to overcome his father's shame. His exploits had earned him the name *kitsune*, the magical fox.

Shin watched the haze rising from his cigarette resting in an indentation of a copper ashtray. As it rose, the column of ash split into strands that twisted, separated, and merged again, part of one languorous plume. He had learned much while studying smoke, tracing the intricate wisps while his mind wandered, seeking connections.

Kano entered the room and bowed deeply. Shin gestured for Kano to join him.

"How is your father?"

The style of address, without an honorific, was a sign of familial warmth. "Thank you for inquiring, Shin-*san*. He is resting as comfortably as possible. Many kind hands are there to help him."

"You honor your duty to him, a patriot and a worthy man in those difficult days. He was a great help to my activities in the north."

Kano nodded with deference and caution.

"What have you come to tell me?"

"There is a development." Shin saw Kano try to keep his knee from twitching. "Some Consolidated people found papers hidden by the Austrian engineer. They could link the Cameron facility technology to InterTech."

Shin stared into Kano's eyes. "What will happen now?"

"The engineer will testify under oath soon."

Shin gazed at the strands of smoke drifting up from his gold banded Gallery Treasurer cigarette. He started, as if waking from a dream. "If the witness does not testify, the link is not proved. You have employed expensive lawyers, have you not?"

Kano struggled to reply. "The Consolidated lawyers have sent people to talk with the witness. They have the right to do so and our lawyers say we cannot prevent it. We cannot be sure what he will say." Shin watched as Kano shifted and sat up straight. "But under pressure from operatives of our lawyers, the witness burned the documents."

The wisps of ash rose, separated, wandered, but stayed within a column of air. "This witness could still speak in this questioning?"

"Yes, Shin-*san*. But he seems unwilling to do so. He destroyed evidence. He risks sanction by the court. Our lawyers say he has broken under pressure."

Lawyers and their games, Shin thought. How could anyone trust men who sold their loyalty for a fee? Shin's eyes turned to slits, his vision focused on the wisps that separated, twisted, wandered, regathered. He waited for a pattern to emerge.

He sat up, crushed the unspent portion of the most expensive cigarette in the world into the gleaming copper, and leaned forward. The small coals burning in his eyes locked onto Kano. "Go tend to your father."

Chapter 39
LAWTON LAW FIRM, SOUTH CAROLINA, THANKSGIVING EVE

TWELVE HOURS EARLIER THAN TOKYO TIME

On the flight home from Dallas, I settled into a first-class seat that felt like an armchair. My mind drifted, aided by the low whisper of air slipping past the plane and Charlie's rhythmic breathing as he slept. I wandered through the startling events of the past thirty-six hours. Our set up of Weidl at the Cotton Fields, though unconventional, was good zealous lawyering. Until Charlie shifted into C.I.D. mode and punched back hard against an unknown threat. He had juked, twisted, and scrabbled to thwart an attack and secure Weidl's documents. On the pavement at Geiger's, I cut through a fog of analysis to run after him, as I'd been doing since our collision at Cameron.

We were partners now, combining my knowledge of rules and Charlie's instincts from Asia to protect our case. Part of my brain was sharpened by the non-stop action between the Fairmont and Geiger's since midnight, which yielded more adrenaline rush than any litigation fight I'd known. But the rational lawyerly part threw up its hands in dismay and shouted *you dumb ass*, this isn't litigation. It's a chaotic, bare-knuckled brawl with no rules. *You've got to get out.* I didn't sleep well.

I arrived at the firm the next day. Charlie and I had agreed we had to move fast and work on Thanksgiving. In my closet, I found a package from the business center at the Fairmont on my desk: the original documents from Weidl's locker at Geiger's. Charlie and Frank were lugging a reader to our office to uncover connections between them and the thirty rolls of microfilm on Frank's handwritten list. We still needed to get Weidl on our side but we felt we had to move the depo up, so we were short on time.

Preston was in the office before Thanksgiving dinner to prepare for a trial. Sitting in his cracked red leather chair again, I felt I held a better hand this time. He leaned back into his thinking position: sideways to his desk, the heels of his scuffed shoes resting on his worn credenza, looking at the ceiling, hands steepled, his fingertips brushed against his lips as if in prayer.

"So, the original documents are sitting on my desk downstairs," I concluded.

He turned his head towards me, peered over the half-height reading glasses perched on his nose, and cast a baleful look. "You mean the *stolen* documents."

"Yes, sir." He sat up, turned toward me, and leaned forward.

"What you gonna do now?" he asked. Softly, but with Preston that could easily precede a withering blizzard.

"Link them to Malinkrodt and Japan. We've got a witness out at Cameron, Frank Brazeale, supported by his contemporaneous handwritten notes, who can tie Malinkrodt to the contents of thirty rolls of microfilm, data from which showed up in Los Angeles. He'll be here shortly to tighten up the links Charlie already made in Dallas."

"Anything of value?"

"It's all of great benefit to Consolidated and O'Hanlon confirmed to me that Minimura was far behind in P.E.T. film production. We could stop them using it. But we'll need access to Minimura's files to prove monetary damages."

"Go on."

"Second, we have an independent witness, Weidl, who will identify physical evidence tying Consolidated Technologies' property, Malinkrodt, InterTech, and Minimura together."

"You got no evidence of delivery beyond InterTech yet, do ya? No final reports, nothing sent, no proof they got it."

"Parts of drafts. No full ones, names or dates." I'd pushed the facts. Preston had jumped on it. "But as soon as all these papers are identified in Weidl's deposition, we go to Minimura and threaten a lawsuit unless they cooperate. That's how we'll get to damages."

"A witness who's afraid to talk 'cause he's being stalked and scared to death by God knows who, a witness you subpoenaed for papers that you just took without permission. Even if he cooperates, which is a long shot, you don't know whether he can testify anything was really delivered to the Japs." Preston spat out that last word with venom only a Marine wounded in the Pacific could muster. "Is he ready to testify?"

Weidl had confirmed verbally to Charlie that it was all done for Minimura, but we needed him to say it on the record. I sidestepped Preston's question, because I didn't know the answer. I did have a way to get there, though.

"We got Weidl on video tape attempting to destroy documents under subpoena by a Federal court and direct testimony from Cauthen confirming that Weidl did it. Charlie was just twenty-five feet away." I wasn't going to add that we couldn't use the video cassette at trial because I had Charlie steal that, too. Or how we'd explain Charlie was watching. I was counting on not having to.

"If I hear you right, what that German fella burned was photocopies. Hard to explain how you know. And you got yourself in the chain of custody of the originals, not to mention abetting theft and assault. There's the possibility of Jake Payne being removed as counsel from the case. We lose a client. And you lose your license to practice law."

I knew all that, except Weidl was Austrian. I was deep in Preston's red leather chair, but I had one card left to play.

"Weidl will testify. He'll be concerned about what a Federal judge would do."

Preston almost whispered now. "Listen here to what I'm saying, son. He didn't destroy the evidence, *by your own testimony*."

"You're absolutely right. But there's one thing we've got going for us."

"What's that?"

"Weidl still thinks he burned the originals. We have him on tape." Just because we couldn't use the tape at trial, didn't mean it was useless.

Preston peered at me.

"A bluff?" In one move, he reared back in his chair and threw his arms out wide. "Good God Ahmighty." He sat back up and leaned in again. "You gone stark, raving mad?" The glower and the spiked eyebrows were back again. But I thought I saw him suppress a smile.

The office intercom crackled. "Yeah?"

"Jake's people are here, Mr. Lawton." Preston looked at me and threw his hands up in mock surrender.

"*Git!*"

Chapter 40
LAWTON LAW FIRM

Charlie and Frank spent all day in the conference room. At five when I came back in, stacks of microfilm rolls rested next to the reader. Weidl's documents were set in squared-off piles, topped by yellow pad pages filled with notes in Frank's neat draftsman's handwriting. Each note linked a technical issue from a document to the microfilms on the list he'd given me when we first met, as Charlie had predicted. Only one sheet of paper lay off to the side with no notes. Four P.E.T. related items were not on Frank's roles and the last item was new. And a puzzle.

"What about that, Charlie? Do you have to go back through the films?"

"We tried ever which way," he said. "We need to run it by some a the technical guys at the plant."

"I don't think we have time to do that if we move the deposition up. We've got enough for now and can work on that later. Make sense?" I asked.

"Yessir. You ready to call Tom?"

"Let me talk to Frank a minute." He caught on and left the room.

"How you want to play this, Frank? You want to be here when we talk to Tom O'Hanlon?" Frank had not said much to me all day, but he'd been less nervous than the last time we'd met.

"No way. You kept your word real good. You got that *corrabalation* and I'm out of it. Appreciate it."

"How's that mirror test working out?"

He looked up sharply. "I'm gettin' by Jake. Gettin' by."

"I need something else, Frank. Who did you tell about the other microfilm rolls?"

"Jake, I never showed that list to nobody but you."

"I believe that, Frank. I do. But that's not what I asked."

"Hunh?"

"I think you *tried* to show someone the list but got shut down. Isn't that right?"

Frank's jaw went slack. "How'd you know that?"

"You just told me." His eyes opened wide. "Now who was it?"

The name was a surprise: Jack Staley, Malinkrodt's boss and a fast-rising executive favored by John McElwain, the Consolidated president. This could go all the way to the top of Consolidated.

Chapter 41
LAWTON LAW FIRM, 11:15AM, THE NEXT DAY

Tom, Charlie, and I were in the conference room with Weidl's documents. When I called Tom at home the night before, I told him we needed him here right away, no questions asked. He wasn't happy to be disturbed during football on Thanksgiving night, but I held firm and told him these documents could pave our way to Tokyo.

Before Charlie started, I said, "We'd like you to hold any questions until Charlie's gone through the links." Tom nodded assent.

Like a good demolition man Charlie had timed the explosions from the documents to go in a precise order for maximum effect.

I summed up. "What we're saying, Tom, is, you've got a case now and we think we can get to the Japanese, to Minimura. Is this enough for you to keep the executive floor off your back?"

Tom looked at the squared off stacks of microfilm, the yellow pages of notes scattered on the table, and Charlie's expectant face.

"Guys, this is one helluva job. Now I understand why you wanted me here to see this." Then he trained his questioning green eyes on me. "But why all the cloak and dagger?"

Charlie and I exchanged a glance. He nodded, *okay, your turn.*

"You've only heard what's in the documents. That's the good news."

Tom's face hardened. "What do you mean?"

"We think someone's fighting this lawsuit with the gloves off, outside the ring. We don't know who. Minimura, maybe, given the resources, or InterTech and Mueller. Whoever they are, they may have a connection within the Gordon firm in L.A."

Tom started and leaned in, his palms pressing on the table, "What the hell are you talking about?"

The explosions started up again: the missing page from Mueller's deposition by the Gordon firm in California, Mueller's knowing he had to get the documents out of the InterTech office before the Federal marshall's visit, the tail on Weidl, then Charlie's fight at Geiger's, Radnor's theft of the extra copies from the business center, and, finally, Weidl's bonfire while Radnor watched.

"We've got a VCR set up so you can see the tapes."

Tom tapped his pencil softly on the conference room table.

"What you're talking about is . . . is some kind of conspiracy. It's absurd." His eyes narrowed and he turned aside, then, after a moment alone, said quietly, "I can't explain these incidents. We've got to call Bob Langston and tell him about your suspicions." Tom's boss, the CT general counsel.

"Hear me out," I said. Charlie and I had anticipated his reaction and had to cut it off. "We understand your point. These suppositions raise a bunch of tough issues. But we have two concerns. First, Weidl's documents are explosive. We have to get this deposition done as soon as possible to preempt any more interference and put pressure on Minimura. We think we should move the depo up to this Sunday. We should keep that between us and put off notifying anyone else until Weidl's testimony is on the record. Even inside CT."

Tom sat up. "You can't—"

"Second," I rushed on, "We have another investigation to consider: finding out exactly who is with us and who is against us. Without tipping our hand. The fewer questions within CT while we do that, the better."

I stopped to gauge Tom's reaction. He'd let me cut him off, but I couldn't read his face.

"This is a bizarre situation," I said. "It points to Minimura or Mueller, people outside the company." Time for another detonation.

"One more thing. John Morgan is Consolidated's own counsel, yet he could be out of control. Or he could have thought he had cover inside. He should report everything to you, right?" Tom's eyes went wide at the idea Morgan might have a cut out within CT. "You've been getting a lot of pushback internally. Is that just corporate weathervanes lining up with John McElwain's reservations, or is someone inside at work to derail this case for other reasons? It could be either. It could be both."

Tom's eyes drilled into me. Had we gone too far, too fast? We didn't have any more time. Charlie thought Tom could take it. I wasn't sure.

Finally, Tom spoke. "You're accusing a senior partner of a nationally recognized law firm of malpractice and worse. And you're implying that the top management of Consolidated is compromised, too."

I was way beyond baiting Boyden in a mobile office trailer in rural Texas. "Could be, Tom. We're putting that on the table. That might be why they're piling on you so hard in New York."

He looked down, maybe recalling his strained conversation in the executive dining room. "Sure, I've been getting God awful pressure: from Staley, from

Langston, from Untermeyer, all coming from John McElwain himself, no doubt."

He stopped. I saw no sign that he was convinced. He needed to feel the risk in his bones, like we had in Dallas.

"What if you still get internal resistance after the deposition? We'll have to figure out why. But that would be the easy part. Look. We were able to implicate Minimura, but we know we were damned lucky. Whoever is behind this knows we're not pushovers. We have to be on guard against more intense sabotage efforts. I don't want to have to rescue Charlie in any more back alleys."

"Jake." Tom shifted in his chair. "It's a lot to take on board. Suppose you're just being paranoid?" He had to say it, but there was no conviction in his voice.

"I may be wrong. Hell, Tom, I'll be delighted if I am. All I'm saying is, we've come across a trail here that needs to be followed. The risk of ignoring it is too great." I recalled Tom punching back at Untermeyer's effort to squelch the case over the sole *meunière*.

"If after you see our videos, you still believe in your heart that this is all going away, I've got a bridge to Brooklyn I want to sell you."

He let out a laugh and the tension evaporated.

"My granddad died building that bridge." Tom's brow knit as he stared at the splayed-out documents and squared stacks of microfilm that wouldn't go away. "I'm not saying yes to your theories. But with all you've put together, I'm not saying no. Not a word about this to anyone until you finish the deposition."

"We'll get Weidl on paper, under oath. You agree, Charlie?"

"Hunnert percent, Jake. Hunnert and fifty."

"And Tom. With all these doubts floating around, we're moving the deposition up, to this coming Sunday, if we can. You may need to handle Morgan."

"That's a smart move. I'll get Morgan in line. You've got until Monday, right after Weidl's deposition."

"I'll go get Preston to call Malinkrodt's lawyer and reschedule. Charlie, you're headed to Dallas this afternoon. My secretary's got your ticket. And Charlie? Not a word to Jaynelle!"

Charlie grinned for the first time all day. "Ah'm gone."

Tom got up to go look at the videos.

"Hold on, Tom. We're not quite done yet. I need to show you something."

He sat back down. I picked up the single sheet of wrinkled paper next to the piles of documents and handed it to him.

"What's this?"

"It's one of Weidl's documents. A handwritten list. These items don't match any of the stuff on Frank's reels. Neither Charlie nor Frank have any idea what that last item means. Do you?"

Tom sat down and scanned the list. He shot me a concerned glance but didn't say anything.

I left him with it and went upstairs to get Preston to put pressure on Malinkrodt's lawyer to move up the deposition.

Chapter 42
DALLAS, LATE THAT AFTERNOON

Charlie drove his rental straight to Elant's office. He slowed as he drove past the front entrance, looked, then sped up, turned a corner, and pulled into the delivery entrance. Thirty minutes later he knocked on Stefan's door, the big man jerked up and turned white as a *weißwurst* sausage.

"Hey there, Stefan. Told ya I'd see ya soon. Let's get a bite to eat. Then I'm gonna take you to a picture show. And you're the star. Come on. My car's out back."

"Charlie! Out back? Is dis about dose documents?"

"Yep. Elant knows all about it, Stefan. It's okay. They're glad you're helping us. Let's go." Charlie started to leave.

"But Charlie." Stefan stood, his eyes wide open. "I've done a terrible thing. I burned dem."

"I know." Charlie started walking. Stefan grabbed his arm and spun him around like a rag doll.

"You know? You *can't* know!"

"Got it all on video tape, Stefan. You look a little peaked."

"Are you gonna put me in jail?"

"Last thing on my mind, Stefan. You're gonna do the right thing. Your boss thinks it's the right thing. I just talked to him. Consolidated thinks it's the right thing. You're home clear. All you gotta do is identify your documents."

"But what documents? *I burned dem*!"

"Not your originals. I got 'em with me at the hotel. In the safe. Come on. We gotta go."

Stefan staggered after him.

"Charlie, I don't know what's going on. You got it all worked out and I'm not in trouble? Dat note warned me to be afraid of you."

"What note?"

I went back to the conference room after Preston worked the phone with Bailey Tinsdale, Malinkrodt's lawyer. That was easy. Preston had something to trade in another case.

As the door swung wide, I saw Tom was gone.

"Jake," my secretary said, "he watched the videos then booked a flight to New York.

He had left without a word to me, but I had other business. I grabbed a yellow pad from the stack and went to work on notes for Weidl's deposition.

Later Charlie called in from Dallas.

"You sure you weren't followed?"

"I saw Radnor in his car, staring at the front gate at Elant. Stefan and I slipped out the back way." Charlie chuckled, "Radnor was still there."

"What'd your boy think of the tape?"

"He like ta died. Told him he could wipe the slate clean or spend a lotta time with real mean lawyers. And he'd get to stick one up old Mueller's backside. He's on board now. His boss at Elant was great. I'll be on Stefan like a tick on a hound dog 'til you and Frank get here. Got him staying at the hotel with me tonight."

“Our flight leaves at six in the morning. Lands at 7:15 in Dallas. Anything else?”

“One thing. I’m calling from Stefan’s apartment. We got ourselves a little sitiation.”

I gave him instructions on how to handle it. And Stefan: no Cotton Fields.

Charlie rang off and the switchboard put Tom through. He’d been holding and said he was checking to confirm that Tinsdale had agreed to move the depo up. He didn’t say why he left in such a hurry. Later he called again to tell me he’d talked to Morgan who went ballistic but promised to put George Panatopoulus on a flight to arrive in Dallas the next day.

Chapter 43
FAIRMONT HOTEL, LATE AFTERNOON, SATURDAY, NOVEMBER 25

Frank and I joined Charlie Saturday morning and spent the rest of the day with Weidl and his documents. Tom O'Hanlon called to say he couldn't make it. By five, we'd been through three hundred and four documents.

"Okay, guys, that's it. Charlie, would you and Frank make sure the docs are in this order?" I handed Charlie my revised list. "I want you to double check and make sure we don't mess up tomorrow."

"We got it." He joined Frank in the connecting room.

I picked up the last document, the one I'd showed to Tom O'Hanlon. I put it on the table in front of Weidl. "Stefan, do you recognize this?"

He peered at the wrinkled sheet and smoothed it out so he could read it better. The writing was in pencil, smudged, and hard to read. "I . . . let me see." He picked it up to get even closer.

"I don't remember working with this one, but it's not Malinkrodt's writing. It's Mueller's. I heard him and Malinkrodt talk about topics, but I never saw this list." I asked a few more questions. It was clear Stefan didn't know anything about the items. We were done, and he took off.

I turned back to my yellow pad full of notes and began to add the last few questions, when there was a knock on the door.

Chapter 44
GEORGE

The door opened. I looked up and stared in amazement at a huge man filling the door frame. Charlie and Frank peered in from the other room.

"Hi, guys. George Panatopoulus. Glad to be here."

Morgan's associate was as big as Stefan. He had that same kind of California haircut, an open silk shirt, and a gold neck chain. They could be twin brothers. I'd never seen a corporate attorney dressed like that. I got up to greet him.

"Glad to meet you, George. Jake Payne. We're going to need a bigger room unless you and Stefan hold your breath."

He smiled. "I just said hello to him in the hall. He said you guys are almost done?"

I introduced Charlie and Frank, then filled George in. We finished quickly and decided to all meet in the lobby at six-thirty to go to the Border Crossing for dinner.

"How about a drink, George? We can talk shop."

George laughed. "The drink part sounds fine, Jake."

The Saturday evening crowd in the Fairmont's lobby bar vibrated, ready for a good time. So was I, but I had to hold off. George relaxed. He told me he'd been a tight end at Stanford, an All-American, before law school and law review.

"You're an examiner for the California State Bar exam, too? Quite an honor." We seemed to hit it off. He was friendly, open, easy going, a total contrast to Morgan.

"Nice break from practice. I do a little teaching, too."

"How can you keep up with big firm billing requirements?"

"Well, between you and me, I'm looking for a life-style change."

"That must be a California thing."

George laughed. "Yeah, maybe. I'm moving to Beverly Hills. Boutique entertainment law firm: no big firm bullshit."

I realized my heading to NYU was the same thing, without the West Coast slang. He checked his watch and stood up. "I have to call the office. See you back here at six-forty-five."

I gazed out over the lobby, happy to catch a breather. Today had been excellent. Stefan explained in detail how Malinkrodt shuttled documents to L. A. He placed Mueller's instruction to remove papers from InterTech just before the Federal Marshalls' visit. Mueller had to have been tipped off. It made a complete, thoroughly credible story, even boring. Great testimony at trial: no chinks for a defense lawyer to exploit.

It should go smoothly tomorrow, if no one asked Stefan if he'd had the copies in his possession ever since he'd made them in California. There was only a little testimony I needed on the InterTech evidence chain, then monotonous document I.D. three-hundred and five times. Make that three-hundred and four. The last one could get interesting.

I saw Charlie and Frank come out of the elevator. Frank was gawking at the lobby and furnishings as they came over. "Gollee! This place beats the Holiday Inn at Cameron all hollow."

"Time for a quick drink, guys?"

"Jake." Charlie had something on his mind. "What about that last document, the little scribbled paper?"

"What about it?"

"Couldn't help but notice that you took Stefan aside to talk about it."

I couldn't go there in front of Frank. Tom O'Hanlon had called me with specific instructions.

"That's a list a things to give Minimura, right?" Frank offered. "Sorta Malinkrodt's shopping list for Consolidated technology, near's I can tell. But I still can't tie them no way to any of the microfilms."

"Guys, you've done great. But on this one I can't go any further, for now."

"How come, Jake?" Charlie said with a grim look. "We ain't in this together after all?"

It would be a real cheap shot to dress Charlie down for his actions at Geiger's. "We sure are. You've got to trust me on this one." I tried to give Charlie a reassuring look. "We'll talk about it later, okay?"

A bellboy walked by ringing a chime and holding a small chalk board that read, "Message for Mr. Cauthen."

"Now what?" I asked. As Charlie headed off towards the front desk, Stefan and George stepped off the elevator chatting amiably, looking like two long-lost California brothers on a Texas holiday.

"You good about that, Frank?"

"Yeah, Jake. I'm good. You kept me outta this and kept your word."

"It's not over yet, Frank."

Chapter 45
THE BORDER CROSSING, DALLAS, EVENING, THE SAME DAY

Frank drove Stefan and George in Charlie's car to the restaurant. I drove Charlie so I could fill him in on my conversation with Weidl. Charlie told me what the message in the lobby was about. We called Tom O'Hanlon as soon as we got to the restaurant.

The Border Crossing was jammed and noisy. Our group was in high spirits, even Frank. At first, he stared in horror when his plate arrived, "What's that green stuff?" Now he was eagerly spooning guacamole on everything. Charlie was keeping close to Stefan as planned. I was on Stefan's other side, so I could hear them. George was on my right. He seemed more subdued than at the hotel.

Charlie warmed Stefan up. "I wanna thank ya for helping out today. Ya got a great memory for all those documents."

"I spent a lot of time on them with Malinkrodt, Charlie."

"We don't have the final reports, just drafts. Did you ever see the final ones, see them sent to Minimura?

"No. I'm sure they were, but I didn't do that."

"Was they just about the production and product issues we went over today?"

"What do you mean?"

"This is industrial stuff, nothing about development or new products in the works, was there?"

"Naw, Malinkrodt was firm about that. He and Mueller had a fight about it. Mueller is a good one for fighting."

"What about?"

"At first, Malinkrodt had a lot of ideas about information. Pretty quick, he cut back. Mueller got excited. He may have made some promises to Minimura and thought Malinkrodt had backed out on what they had agreed. But Malinkrodt insisted. That caused a problem about fees. Mueller said Malinkrodt was stupid about negotiating. Malinkrodt didn't like that."

"Stupid?"

"The Japanese wanted to see the factory, see the lines operating. Malinkrodt took them on a tour."

"Of the Cameron factory?"

"Yeah. He said they didn't have to sign in because he was the plant manager. After, they went up to his lake house to finish the contract. The Japanese told him, 'We don't need the technology guarantee. Please cut your price twenty-five per cent.' That surprised Malinkrodt, but he agreed. Mueller was upset. But when he tried to argue the guarantee was important, the Japanese said, 'We have seen the factory. We know it works!'"

I was taking a sip and spewed margarita all over my plate. Charlie guffawed and slapped Stefan on the back. This plant visit was going in the deposition for sure. While it was hearsay, it was fuel for second depositions of Mueller and Malinkrodt.

Charlie picked up a fresh pitcher. "Here, Stefan, have some more a these mara-garitas."

I turned to George. "You probably get much better Mexican food in California."

"The food's fine, Jake." He stared down at his plate.

"Anything else you need?"

George looked up at me, his amiable smile replaced by a grim scowl. "How'd you get these docs?"

George was a nice guy, but he was Morgan's nice guy, and an experienced litigator. He had most likely talked to his partner back at the hotel. This could be Morgan's opening shot. At me.

"Stefan had them. You see any problem? We're both here for Consolidated."

"I'm going to level with you, Jake. John has a bug up his ass about these documents. Wants me to dig into the chain of custody."

"Well, sure. It's a key point. Anything in particular?"

"Morgan thinks Stefan lost possession of the docs and you had something to do with that. He says he's got a copy of a mail receipt and wants you disqualified for being a witness in the chain of custody."

I turned to George, ready to play. "Is this some kind of law firm hissy fit? Morgan wants my firm out so he can hog the billings?"

"Jake, hold on. All this testimony is worthless if anyone can blow a hole in the chain of custody. You know that."

Of course I did. Preston had, too, right off.

George stared straight at me. I got an inkling of what a defensive back might have felt with two hundred twenty pounds of pure muscle racing straight toward him.

"Morgan has instructed me to tell you to stop the deposition until this is worked out. He's got a judge in L.A., ready to back him up." George leaned in, close. "Tonight."

Chapter 46
TURNING THE TABLE

Morgan had pulled off the gloves. Based on Driscoll's sleuthing, no doubt, he'd had someone check with the Fairmont's business center. George watched my reaction closely. "What about it?"

"Of course there was a receipt. We mailed a copy." There it was. The last white lie if, as I expected, Stefan played ball with us tomorrow.

George sat back, done with Morgan's dirty work.

"I told John we could work this out, but he just kept pushing. He's angry about your firm even being in the case. I don't want to be a part of that. I better call John to stop the judge."

That wouldn't happen and I had to let George know why.

"I couldn't agree more, George. A pissing contest between co-counsel? No way, unless there's cause." I let that sink in. "Unless there's cause, George."

"Don't get all defensive about this, Jake. I'm playing straight with you."

"And I'm going to play straight with you. Morgan is way over the line. I've got facts that go far beyond hardball. They point to criminal activity by and on behalf of John Morgan."

George dropped his fork. The clatter got lost in the hubbub of the Saturday night crowd. "What the—"

"Morgan thinks Stefan didn't have the originals. And I did. Why would he suspect that?" George's eyebrows raised. "He hired private investigators to shadow Stefan, then Charlie. But the guys he used were incompetent. Charlie snuck Stefan out from under the nose of one of them yesterday."

George's eyes widened. He fell back in his chair like he'd been knocked flat at the line of scrimmage. His face turned angry and his body seemed to blow up like a steel balloon. "How the hell do you know all that?"

Charlie and I had called Tom as soon as we got to the restaurant. We'd told him about the note slipped under Weidl's apartment door. I'd had Charlie turn it over to the Dallas police. He had received their response when he'd returned that phone call in the lobby of the Fairmont.

Tom said he couldn't wait until Monday. He had to call his boss Bob Langston right away and bring him up to speed. Weidl was staying with us at the Fairmont and we'd have him on record the next day. Charlie and I agreed it was under control now so it was okay to inform Langston, and okay for us to lay it out for George. But Tom had called us back and informed us of a critical development that changed everything.

Chapter 47
THE OTHER SHOE

"George, Morgan hired a P.I. from Los Angeles named Driscoll. Driscoll needed help so he took on a local private investigator named Madden, who he instructed to threaten Stefan. Stupid thing to do. Last night the police lifted Madden's prints off a nasty note he stuffed under Weidl's apartment door. The prints matched Madden's P. I. registration. They sweated Madden this afternoon and he gave up Driscoll."

"Turns out Madden didn't want to get physical with Stefan, so he thought up the idea of the note on his own. The cops arrested Driscoll at the airport, trying to leave for L.A. He gave up Morgan, for trespass at Stefan's, assault on Charlie, and intimidation of a witness, the note to Stefan."

I waited for George to process a charge of criminal activity by a senior partner at a major international law firm, his direct boss. Then I dropped the other shoe. "The L. A. police are picking up Morgan as we speak."

George went rigid.

"Look, George, I believe you don't have anything to do with this. I just learned about Morgan's arrest after we got to the restaurant. I wasn't going to say anything. But with what Morgan's tried? Look, I'm sure you're clean, but Morgan may have been setting you up."

George stared, his mouth open. Then it started working. "If what you say is true, I'm quitting the firm Monday."

Tom and I had settled on how to handle the Gordon firm.

"Tom O'Hanlon knows all this. He's authorized me to decide about your firm's participation in the deposition. It's noticed in our case, after all. Your firm has a conflict, or worse. You're welcome to attend as an observer, if Malinkrodt agrees, but not to speak."

I actually felt sorry for George and gave a little advice, as a colleague. 'The cops may try to interview you tomorrow, but it's probably not in your interest, without representation. It might become a suspect interview."

My warning hit George, with more force this time like an angry defensive back at full speed. "You do what you have to do, Jake. I'm sick of this. I'll quit tonight."

He looked troubled. Then he smiled. He knew how to take a hit.

"I'm just going to sit back and enjoy the evening. Say, you heard about the Cotton Fields? Stefan loves it. I'm ready to celebrate my new career."

It was late. Diners spilled out onto the pavement in front of the Border Crossing. The margaritas had long since taken effect. Frank was wearing a kid-sized sombrero. George draped a massive arm around him, teaching Frank a Spanish song and grabbing at the sombrero at the same time. Stefan was in the men's room. I was concerned he might be throwing up. I took Charlie aside.

"I spelled it out for George. I don't think he knew. He was mad, but he's taking it standing up." I looked over at George weaving back and forth on the sidewalk. "But maybe not for long. He's leaving his law firm and wants to hit the Cotton Fields tonight. You better keep Stefan away from there."

"I'll go head Stefan off and get him back to the hotel. I'll take Frank, too. You going with George?"

I looked around the strip mall. "Don't want to. There's no sign of a taxi. I may have to drop him off. Meet you back at the hotel."

Charlie got his car keys from Frank and went to find Stefan.

I asked inside. It took forty minutes to get a taxi, if you were lucky. As I walked outside, a low-slung red Camaro with blacked out windows cruised into the parking lot and drove slowly toward the restaurant.

"So, George, you still headed for the Cotton Fields?"

He released Frank from a bear hug and crushed the child's sombrero on his own head. "Ready to go. I'll drive. Whoa! Look out."

He staggered and started to fall in the path of the Camaro. It braked suddenly. The horn blasted. George saved himself with a spectacular whirling gymnastic round-off with one hand on the ground. Even drunk, his reflexes and body control were award-winning. He stumbled a few steps, recovered his balance, and ended up standing next to the Camaro, still weaving. The driver gunned the Camaro, burning rubber as it peeled off.

"Easy, George. Look, you can't get a taxi here. I'll drop you off at the club. Or maybe take you back to the hotel?"

George leaned on me and I almost crumpled under the weight. He put his head down until our foreheads touched. "That bastard Morgan played me for a sucker, Jake. I'm mad, mad as hell."

A few hours ago and fifty pounds lighter, that could have been me. I backed away from George and turned to go get my car when the red Camaro that had circled around the parking lot made another pass in front of the restaurant.

The car slowed. The front window started down. George lurched toward it, arms wind milling, and yelled, "Hey, cowboys. You assholes wanna wrestle?"

George pulled his fist back and let fly. He hit the passenger whose head snapped back. The window post whipped George's forearm as the Camaro tore away. George yelled in pain.

I ran over. "Jeez, George. You all right?"

"Stupid redneck shits. I wouldn't mind a little fight tonight."

"You sure you don't want a ride back to the hotel?" George was big, but he'd drunk at least a pitcher of margaritas on his own. The cosmopolitan veneer was wearing thin. His tight-end aggression was showing through.

He started singing and batting the air with vicious jabs. "'In them old Cotton Fields back home.' Let's go."

Chapter 48
FAIRMONT HOTEL, DALLAS, SUNDAY, THE NEXT DAY

Tom O'Hanlon and I had updated each other in a late-night phone call. I described George's reactions to news of Morgan's perfidy and Tom gave me final instructions on how to handle the handwritten note from Weidl's documents. They were very precise and limited, but he said he couldn't tell me what it was all about. He didn't say when, or if, he could.

For the deposition, I'd booked a larger meeting room and an extra table where Frank had set up the documents. Tom's boss, Bob Langston, had blistered him for not warning about Driscoll and Morgan. I was sorry for Tom, but the note, the police, and Morgan's arrest weren't our fault. The managing partner of the Gordon firm, called out of a big charity dinner in L. A., assured Tom that Panatopoulus was not involved and could attend the deposition.

George hadn't showed yet. Maybe he'd already quit, at least in his own mind.

Bailey Tinsdale was there with Malinkrodt. The engineer was short, with a round midsection. He was in his late fifties with thinning gray hair and rimless glasses. Dressed up with a beard and a wig, and smiling, he could have passed for Santa Claus. But his eyes were smoldering, and his red face looked like he was on the verge of a heart attack.

The introductions were short and painful. Malinkrodt sat, arms folded, fists clenched and avoided any eye contact. Charlie was on the phone. Frank stood ready to shuffle the exhibits to me for Stefan to identify on the record. We were just waiting for George.

Charlie put down the phone. “Still no answer in his room.”

Malinkrodt leaned over to Bailey, who listened, then said. “Jake, you called this. Let’s get on with it.”

I had dropped George off at the Cotton Fields. He must be sleeping it off. I turned to the court reporter. “Miss Altgeld, please swear in Mr. Weidl.”

By dusk that afternoon, it was time to wind up. Weidl had been a star. Between his natural bent for precise detail and his anger at Hans Mueller, he laid his story out like a carpet. Malinkrodt, through it all, looked ready to jump over the table and strangle Stefan.

Frank handed me the last exhibit. I would follow Tom’s instructions to the letter, but he had a lot of explaining to do.

“Mr. Weidl, can you identify this document marked SW Deposition Exhibit 305?”

“It’s a hand-written list. That’s Hans Mueller’s handwriting.” I handed it to Bailey, who showed it to Malinkrodt. His eyes opened wide. He stared at the paper as if it could bite. I had to pull it from his grip so I could hand it back to Stefan.

To my question, he said, “This is not one I copied. It got caught up in the others when I took them from the office.”

“How is this document related to the others we have seen?”

“They were either copies of prints from the microfilm rolls Mr. Malinkrodt gave me or draft reports. But I overheard Mr. Mueller and Mr. Malinkrodt discussing topics like this at the beginning of the project."

"What did they say?"

"They talked about what should be in the proposals to Minimura."

"Thank you, Mr. Weidl. No further questions. Mr. Tinsdale?"

Malinkrodt seized Bailey's coat sleeve, yanked it so hard they almost butted heads, and whispered fiercely in Bailey's ear. Under questioning, Stefan repeated that the list was not in Malinkrodt's handwriting and he'd resisted efforts to disclose more.

I saw Malinkrodt's facial muscles and hands relax. He almost smiled.

Chapter 49
5:25PM, THE SAME DAY

All my effort since Cameron aimed at this moment. I couldn't have gotten there alone. In the worst moments when all hell had broken loose, Charlie had known what to do to keep the case alive. Since then, we had been forced into some tight corners. And we'd cut a few. But we weren't in jail, and John Morgan was. What a team: law and disorder.

All the key P.E.T. items from Frank's microfilm reels were on record under oath. The only loose end was that handwritten list. The deposition would cause an explosion when it hit Tokyo. CT should be pleased and I could begin packing for NYU.

"No more questions." I turned to the stenographer, "Miss Altgeld, thank you so much—"

A knock at the door interrupted. I got up and opened it. A man in a dark suit with a name tag stood there with another man in a suit and two uniformed policemen. "Can I help you?"

The name tag spoke. "I'm Alfred Edwards, the Fairmont's weekend manager. I'm sorry to disturb you. Are you Mr. Payne?" I nodded. "This officer would like to speak to you." I turned to Charlie and motioned for him to join us in the hall.

The other suit spoke. “Mr. Payne, I’m Lieutenant Malcolm Boyd, detective with the Dallas Police Department.”

“I’m Jake Payne an attorney here to take a deposition. This is my client’s representative, Mr. Cauthen. What’s this about?”

Detective Boyd said, “Hi, Charlie.” What the hell?

“Hey, Malcolm.” Charlie pumped the detective’s hand like an old friend. Ah, I realized: Madden’s fingerprints.

The detective continued, “Mr. Payne, I believe you have some connection with a Mr. George Panatopoulus from Los Angeles. Your company booked his room here. Do you know him well?”

“No, not really. He’s a lawyer from another firm. I just met him yesterday. We were expecting him here this morning. Why?”

“I’m sorry to tell you this. He was found dead in an alley across town early this morning.”

I turned to look at Charlie and saw Tom O’Hanlon striding down the hall.

Chapter 50
6:00PM, THE SAME DAY

The police were treating George's death as a homicide with good reason. He had two bullet holes in his chest and one in his head. I told them how the news about Morgan upped George's margarita consumption. Our description of the incident with the red Camaro unleashed a storm of questions.

After the detective left, Charlie and I gave Tom a summary of the deposition.

"That's excellent. Just what you promised." Then he paused. "The Gordon firm was notified three hours ago about George and called me. We're all working on the final arrangements. But neither of those things is why I came. I booked a corporate jet before I knew George was dead. That's a terrible coincidence. Come with me. I need to introduce you to someone."

We went to another floor and walked into a small meeting room. A guy, four or five years older than me, dark eyes, dark hair with flecks of gray on the sides, and square, black framed glasses, sat at the table. His cheeks were clean shaven, but you could only tell that up close. They were dark as three days' growth. He looked vaguely familiar, but he didn't say anything or get up.

"This is Nico Amalfitano, the lawyer for DARPA, The Defense Advanced Research Projects Agency. We've been working with him for some time under government funded research contracts. In fact, he was at Cameron the day you joined the case, Jake, working on what I need to tell you about."

Amalfitano nodded but remained silent.

Tom continued, "The reference none of you could figure out in the note, 'OC-X', is the name of a top-secret R&D program at Cameron involving optics, the O; computing, C; with an X research project designation. The technology has major commercial and national security implications."

I looked at Charlie. His eyebrows peaked again, in surprise this time. "You think Malinkrodt gave that away, too?"

"Jake," Tom said. "OC-X is based on Madison Whitmire's discoveries. It's separate from P.E.T. film. We have no idea what this reference means, but we must check it out, carefully. We don't want to create a problem if there is none." My words from Friday at the firm now coming out of Tom's mouth.

Amalfitano finally spoke. "Tracking it down is critical. The main thing is that's the government's business. They paid for the research."

That sounded simple, but it wasn't. "If this is so secret, why are you telling us? We don't have security clearances."

"Charlie's was updated," Amalfitano replied. "You have one, too."

I was used to detonating verbal explosives. Now Amalfitano had just lit a fuse. Was Preston in on this? Tom O'Hanlon obviously had been. Did Beau have a secret security clearance, too? "Since when?"

The bomb went off under my feet. "You were checked out as a precaution and cleared as soon as we knew you were going to be assigned to work with CT and Madison

Whitmire. Your P.E.T. case and the OC-X reference are now inextricably linked," Amalfitano said.

That didn't answer my question.

"And what? We work on both? Neither, because you guys are taking over? What?" Amalfitano was good at ignoring what I found extremely important.

Tom jumped in. "If there's something to this, we can't tip our hand. You were right to be suspicious Friday, Jake. I was shocked by your hypotheticals, but when you showed me the OC-X reference, I knew you were on to something. I couldn't tell you until I got Nico's OK. That's why I left abruptly. I called him from the airport. So now, except for us—the four of us—and whoever Nico activates in the government, nothing changes."

I needed to hear plainly what this development meant, for the case, now cases, and for me.

"Tom, am I off our case?"

"No, Jake. You've done a fantastic job." His enthusiasm could be reassuring; it seemed genuine, but I realized they were stuck with me. Switching lawyers now could raise suspicions and interfere with their inquiry. And that meant I was stuck with them.

"Let me get this straight. We use our P.E.T. investigation of Minimura as cover for your OC-X investigation. We try to find out if someone stole OC-X without disclosing what we're really after. And if we find it, what, you shoot us?" I'd been kidding when I'd asked Charlie that.

"Not bad," Amalfitano said. "Except the last part. Won't happen."

"Not by you, maybe."

"Hot damn!" Charlie was clearly excited to be back in the military intelligence game.

I was alarmed that I was being asked, hell, told, to sign on to a sensitive international investigation with God knows who running it.

My legal brain shifted into overdrive. "Do I have two clients, CT and DARPA, or just one with a parallel DOD investigation? Are Malinkrodt and Minimura suspects? Who else? We're civil investigators subject to legal rules. Now it seems we've been going up against sensitive government technology thieves who play by no rules. If this is international, shouldn't the CIA get involved? No one ever accused *them* of playing by the rules."

"I seen this before with the C.I.D.," Charlie explained. "This thing is military. They don't want any civilians gumming it up. Even civilian spies. They'll run this as far as they can, and they'll get their way."

My shoulders tightened in anger. "Last time I checked *I* was a civilian. I don't know about you guys, but that seems like uneven teams. Charlie and me against national security technology thieves? Maybe even the Japanese government. Spies. What about all the agencies that should investigate this: NASA, DARPA—DOD—the FBI?"

"Charlie's right," Amalfitano said. "It's Department of Defense only, for now."

"What about the CIA," I insisted.

"They will be interested if we turn anything up. Right now, all we have is questions," Amalfitano replied.

Nico wasn't the only one with questions. "What does that mean? If they do get involved, will they protect us?" George's recent death was on my mind, even though that seemed linked to the rednecks in the Camaro.

"Would they cooperate with us? Why would they? Will they get in our way? What's to stop them?" And would they become interested only when we were in over our heads, or worse, would they use us as bait to flush the thieves?

"They could help, Payne, but I can't promise anything."

I was asking for clarity, not promises, but this was all turning murky. Government involvement also posed a thorny professional ethics question for me: who was my client now, or clients?

"Can I tell Preston about this?"

Amalfitano's expression hardened. "Four means just us, not five."

"And Dr. Whitmire?" I asked. "She has a top-secret clearance for sure." She was defensive when I had asked her about R & D my first day on the case back when I was just reacting to her and fishing. This made me look prescient. But now, I realized, her reaction that day might make her look guilty.

Amalfitano spoke. "She has a clearance, but she's not on the team for now."

I turned to Tom. "She's a suspect?"

This was her invention, her life's work. She had just seemed upset, not guilty of anything. I already had a stiff barrier to overcome to gain her trust. Tom's words to me at the end of her interview at Cameron came back. *You'll have to make an effort.* We needed her on our team.

Amalfitano finally offered some information. "And anyone else at Cameron related to her project is suspect."

"Jeez," Charlie said. "That's a lotta folks, everyone in R and D, then there's suppliers."

"And CT headquarters," I said. "And Jack Staley." Tom stared at me. "Remember Frank Brazeale tried to approach higher-ups with Malinkrodt's strange behavior? I just learned he tried to talk to Jack Staley. That fits our suspicions of Friday, too."

Tom's naturally upturned lips went flat.

I was shocked by the involvement of OC-X, frustrated by Amalfitano's silences and by his responses, the ones that were ambiguous and the ones that weren't. If I had to keep on the case because of this new development, that would interfere with my career plans.

I'd put them on hold to prove myself to Preston and I had. This case could take years to resolve. I'd seen complex cases like the asbestos defense work take over whole careers for trial lawyers, good ones.

It was worse. If I had to stay in, for whatever reason, I'd just lost control of what I'd worked hard to make *my* investigation. I'd gotten rid of Morgan. Now I had Amalfitano and the whole U.S. government on my back. "So, we're the infantry grunts in a national security offensive?"

"The P.E.T. case can go ahead," Nico explained. "But any discovery of OC-X information becomes part of the government's case. And Charlie's got it right. That takes priority. I have authority under Federal law and our contractual agreements with CT and their employees to conduct confidential inquiries. We will, without notifying anyone else: not Mr. Lawton, not Dr. Whitmire, no one, Jake."

There was no doubt now. He'd just assumed control and warned me about screwing up. It felt like our phone call with Morgan all over again, minus the disdain. Maybe.

Tom stood up. "Sorry, guys. I've got to check on arrangements for George."

He reached into his inside coat pocket. "Charlie, Jake, here are tickets for a flight to New York tonight. See you in my office tomorrow morning at 8."

I was going to New York, but not to NYU. We started to leave. Amalfitano motioned for me to stay. He stared at Charlie who got the hint and left.

Chapter 51
HISTORY

"Payne, have you got a minute?" As if I had a choice. I'd decided I preferred Amalfitano when he wasn't talking.

"We've met." His voice suddenly sounded cordial, almost friendly.

"I thought you looked familiar. Where was it?"

"I was a couple of years ahead of you at U. Va. law"

"Sorry I didn't remember."

"Not surprising. We try not to stand out."

"We?"

"CIA, Jake. I was in the CIA before law school." This was not cordial. It was business, spy business. Was Nico with the CIA during law school? If so, he probably still was. And he knew exactly how they would play this. Hell, how *he* was playing it. DARPA could just be a cover.

"I was sorry about your family." Most of the law school knew, but why was Nico bringing it up? Then it hit me: my security check, my medical records. He knew about the panic attacks. My professional fitness was under suspicion. This wasn't scapegoating. It was cause for them to worry. Or maybe, the way they operated, something they could hold over me.

"Yeah, well. It was tough for a while. I managed." In fact, it destroyed my first year. My exams were bad. I didn't make law review, I didn't land a summer legal job, and I didn't end up in New York.

Chapter 52
KITA CITY, TOKYO, JAPAN, SUNDAY, NOVEMBER 26,

TWELVE HOURS AHEAD OF EAST COAST TIME

For years Shin had searched in Tokyo for a secure place to live and, more importantly, be at peace amid the urban sprawl. With unlimited financial resources, he had bought *kyu-Furukawa,* an English manor house built by a Japanese nobleman in the heart of Tokyo. This had been an area of quiet villages with only a rail link to the city when it was built in 1917. Now it was part of the capital north of the Palace, yet totally isolated from the noise and distraction by the manor's vast, restful gardens.

Shin needed the calm to restore him before he met Kano. The executive had brought his problem to Shin. Because of his debt to the boy's father, and the benefit for the nation, Shin, had solved it. Then when Kano told Shin in Rappongi that Minimura might become involved in the U. S. courts, Shin had intervened again. But he had failed. That could not happen under his control.

But it had. Shin had used another network, not his own, to address Kano's legal problem. Shin's own American assets had been tied up, so he had turned to his *yakuza* connections. Shin had known the gang leaders as young men after the war and had used them many times in Japan with excellent results.

But while they were strong on the American West Coast, they had to use mafia contacts in Texas. And those idiots had eliminated the wrong person, a lawyer, not the Austrian engineer. They had "killed the bull by trying to straighten its horns."

But the responsibility, and the shame, were Shin's. And, deep in his own heart, he knew, not for the first time. Shin's mind hurtled back to the one major failure of his life.

It was 1928. Shin was based in the ancient Manchurian capital of Mukden, working for the Japanese occupation military force, the Kwantung Army. He built and headed paramilitary gangs that used violence to protect and strengthen Japanese interests.

The sun was hot near the embankment where Shin's team had parked a civilian truck. The hill supported part of the Japanese-controlled train-track that passed over the Chinese railroad line from Beijing. Shin and his men had kidnapped three Chinese, members of a warlord gang from the province to the north who now lay in the truck bed, trussed, gagged, and scared. With reason. Shin knew they wouldn't live long.

That morning Colonel Komoto exhorted his men, including Shin, with an ancient *samurai* poem:

> *If the gods are in your way,*
> *do not be afraid to deny them.*
> *Do not hesitate to forsake them,*
> *for* bushido *is madness,*
> *and no great deeds will be accomplished*
> *without madness.*

Shin had been chosen to assassinate the Mukden Tiger, Marshall Zhang, a Chinese warlord, and thorn in the side of the Japanese army in China. As the Marshall's train approached, Shin ordered his men to throw the Chinese to the ground, beat them to death, and leave them by the tracks. Then they drove the truck away to watch the event that would crown their success.

Marshal Zhang's train thundered under the upper track. Shin looked up and saw Japanese soldiers on the overpass. The blast knocked Shin and his men to the ground. The derailed train killed the Marshall. And the Japanese soldiers. Their bodies fixed the blame on the Japanese, not the Chinese. Shin could have been shot for not knowing the soldiers were still on the overpass. But Colonel Komoto needed his special skills. Forty years later, Shin still bore the inward shame.

This time he had "reviewed the past to know the future." So he would use his own assets and plan a thorough operation that would leave nothing to chance.

In the 1960s, with the growth of Japanese global trading power, Shin obtained the services of a talented American, a former operative of OSS in Japan, who had been let go when he skimmed money from smuggling he had been ordered to do.

He held great anger towards his country and was reliable, for an American. Most of them did not understand loyalty and obligation. They were driven by personal gain: power, glory, money. His man was, too, but there was more: hatred for his country.

Movements of Shin's men in front of the manor house signaled Kano's arrival. Shin knew Kano's scientific and business learning was exceptional but he was skilled in the white sphere, not the black sphere where Shin's genius excelled. Shin's wisdom came from the guts of real life. It was "stronger than the shell of a turtle." He had failed Kano. He would not do so again.

Shin bowed to Kano as he arrived, who was visibly stunned by the gesture. Silently in his shame Shin vowed that nothing would stop *kitsune,* the magical fox.

Chapter 53
CT CORPORATE OFFICE, MANHATTAN, 8AM, MONDAY, NOVEMBER 27,

TWELVE HOURS BEHIND TOKYO TIME

Charlie and I caught the late-night flight to New York. We pulled up to the gate at 1:15 Monday morning. Hitching a ride on the CT corporate jet would have been nice, but we weren't invited. I assumed Amalfitano wanted to talk to Tom alone about the investigation, confirmation of my loss of control in the case.

Up until Stefan's deposition, I was glad to be outside the CT executive loop. Now I was outside Amalfitano's loop, with apparent, but no real, authority.

I tried to shake off George's death as we met with Tom, Felix Untermeyer, and Tom's boss, the CT General Counsel in his big corner office. Untermeyer, it turned out, was a lawyer, too. He'd had Tom O'Hanlon's job before he became head of international technology licensing.

I was finishing my verbal report. "The deposition and its exhibits will put pressure on Minimura to permit a proper investigation in Japan. That is the only way to document any damages."

Tom completed the logic. "We propose we send the deposition to Minimura and negotiate a consent discovery."

The CT general counsel shifted in his chair and turned to Untermeyer. "Felix?"

"Malinkrodt's actions were wrong, of course. But is there any shred of evidence other than hearsay that CT information was in fact sent to Minimura? If we accuse them and fail, word will spread across the international business community, Consolidated will be a pariah to potential licensing partners."

The general counsel turned to Charlie and me. "You guys have done an amazing job on this case so far."

Untermeyer cut in. "But now we have to consider corporate policy and reputation. I have us on John McElwain's agenda." The three of them, without Charlie and me, went to see the CT president.

Tom seemed to slink into his own office. He'd lost. McElwain chose a watered-down letter to Minimura, proposed, and being drafted by Untermeyer. That made no sense. The Japanese would stonewall a weak letter and CT would give up. I was sure Minimura was already strengthening their defenses.

I said, "While we wait, we should retake Mueller and Malinkrodt's depositions and get the records from Mueller of the final reports delivered to Minimura. We've got time before the results of Nico's investigation and Minimura's reply."

Tom was out of the corporate loop, too. He shrugged, still smarting from the meeting with McElwain. Something seemed wrong.

We couldn't let up. "Amalfitano has to prioritize clearing Madison Whitmire. While she's a suspect, she can't work full bore on the P.E.T. case much less OC-X. That would hamstring both investigations. As soon as she's cleared, she's back on both tracks."

Tom detoured and raised another roadblock. "When she's cleared, you'll have to mend your fences with her, too, Jake. It wasn't just the R & D that set her off in your interview." We were getting nowhere.

As we got up to leave, I took Tom aside. "I don't get it. Can't CT's president see the impact of Weidl's deposition?"

"There's an untouchable issue," Tom sighed. "CT's president has been joining public policy committees in Washington. Smart money says he's gunning for a high-level position in government after he cashes out of Consolidated. Untermeyer has been bringing up CT's reputation ever since we filed suit in California and added a Japanese defendant."

The chickens of my early fears were coming home to roost: corporate politics, litigation by personal interest, not the company's or the shareholders'.

"Well, at least we can move on the further discovery."

"Hold on, Jake. We can't take other steps until my boss approves."

I was stunned. "I guess that really means Untermeyer, with McElwain's blessing." Untermeyer was a bastard, but an attentive-to-detail bastard.

Tom winced and tried to toss me a bone. It felt more like slop as it hit. "Give me drafts of your discovery proposals. I'll run them by my boss." Another layer of sludge Charlie and I would have to wade through.

Chapter 54
LAWTON LAW FIRM, TUESDAY, THE NEXT DAY

I dropped into my hand-me-down office chair, dismayed over executive incompetence at the highest levels of CT. No, it was worse. A jumped-up head of a local trash hauler with a high school education, or not even, might be incompetent. I'd seen owners of small contracting companies do stupid things. But John McElwain was a product of Andover, Yale, Harvard, a top consulting firm, and head of a Fortune 100 company for God's sake. Top of the heap of American education and industry. Bucking for a position of leadership in government. And a self-serving bastard.

But I was, too. My own plans would disappear into limbo unless I could find a way to get off the case. Until then, I was still CT's lawyer, responsible for the outcome. I had to calm down and find a way around the ego of the CT president.

Was this what I could expect of executives I would work for in a New York corporate law practice? Preston had introduced me to the owners who ran his best construction company clients, entrepreneurs. Quirky? Sure. Brash? Yes. Principled? Maybe. But willing to give up what they had built without a fight? Never. They took decisions and responsibility. And gave me free rein to run their cases. In comparison, New York was a tar pit.

Unless . . . unless what? Had I learned anything from my epiphany on the asphalt at Geiger's? Something about Charlie's refusal to give in to chaos, to keep going against the odds.

"Stop wallowing," I said to the only guy in my office. I stood and swiped the leavings of the lawyer's trade off my desk. Case reporter volumes hit the floor, their tissue-paper thin pages crumpled and bent over. Yellow pads with scribbled, half-formed legal arguments lay jumbled on the floor.

I stared at a clear expanse of worn oak. Still too usual, where I did my legal thinking. "This is not a legal problem," I told myself. "It's a political problem, an ego problem, an emotional problem." What had I asked Charlie back in Dallas, "How would the CID handle this?" The question became; how would a lawyer caught in a web of corporate self-dealing handle this and come out with his professional and personal self-respect intact? My mind cycled through possible avenues of a way out. Politics. Law. Law. Politics.

I grabbed a fresh yellow legal pad from a desk drawer and headed to find a different perspective, to the one place in the firm where anything was discussed, where every morning free association held sway, where one wild story triggered another: the basement coffee room.

Staring at the cheap pressboard paneled walls, I wondered *What if Charlie were a lawyer*? The image of Charlie's mangled grin atop a three-piece, chalk-stripe, charcoal gray suit caught me off guard. And it helped. He faced everything with a grin. And then he *impervised*.

I began scribbling down whatever came to mind, list of factors, thickets of words that gave rise to other words, curved lines connecting elements, then, on reflection, struck through and rerouted, looking for a way out.

I kept at it until my eyes glazed over. Then I grabbed a coke from the fridge and went at it again, until I ended up with everything crossed out except two disparate ideas and a line between them: misprision of felony and Blake Patterson.

The first was an ancient common law crime for failing to report a crime. It sounded kind of circular, like Catch 22. I liked it. In the library, I found that there was an old, seldom used statute making it a Federal offense.

Blake was a friend in college. His father had been up for Secretary of Commerce until favors he had done for some Russians in Switzerland came to light.

I called Blake to check the facts. He remembered, vividly, "My dad was bitter. Some of his best friends dropped him from consideration for a Cabinet position faster than you could say "*do svidaniya*."

Even if Tom couldn't reveal the OC-X problem yet, he could explain to McElwain a duty for CT to report interstate theft of trade secrets. It wasn't collusion with Russians, but it could be a black mark if it came up in a Senate appointment hearing.

I finished the unsolicited memo. As I dropped it in the out tray in the mailroom, I felt better. I'd been haunted by a vision of CT corporate lackeys piling logs on a fire in the path of our attack on Japan while a CT executive dithered. Even if the memo did no good, the distraction might keep my anxiety and frustration from spinning out of control.

Chapter 55
LITIGATION CONFERENCE ROOM, SWINTON LAW FIRM, MANHATTAN

Evan Garrett was a sixth-year associate on the fast track to make partner the next year. Yale undergrad and Harvard law, editor of the law review, clerk for a Second Circuit Federal Appeals Court Judge, then a US Supreme Court Justice, his ticket had all the right punches. He was one of ten lawyers, eight crack litigation associates and two highly regarded junior partners, waiting for Austen Swinton who had called this meeting on short notice without explanation

Garrett had only worked for the managing partner once. His work had been professional, competent, but the matter had been settled, preventing Garrett from showing Swinton what he could do in the heat of battle.

Swinton burst into the conference room filling it with crackling energy. He stopped and stood silent, commanding their attention, pumping up the suspense.

"You're here because you're the best we have. Our main client in the Far East, the linchpin of our successful expansion strategy, Minimura, has just retained us on a major case of trade secrets litigation."

Heads turned and murmurs spread. Swinton wasn't an intellectual property firm, but it had built a reputation over decades as a bruising competitor in every area of practice, pouring the brightest associates into no-holds-barred conduct of any business fight: mergers, acquisitions, SEC investigations, in the US and Europe. Now Austen Swinton was leading the firm into East Asia, capturing Japanese clients on business matters. But this was the first outright business litigation any of them had heard of, a sign of extreme confidence by litigation-shy Japanese. And Minimura was a leader in the all-powerful association of Japanese companies, the *keidanren*. Other companies would follow their lead. A make or break opportunity for the firm, and for their careers.

"Minimura knows we're the best, but we will astound them. You will not only win, you will impose a crushing defeat, demolish the opposition, whoever they are." He turned to catch the eye of every associate in the room. "Anything less is not acceptable. The future of our Asian strategy is at stake." Ten pairs of eyes shone eagerly.

"Evan Garrett will lead the defense in Japan and coordinate with Minimura's lead corporate firm in Tokyo."

Chapter 56
HONOLULU, HAWAII, 11:30AM, THE SAME DAY, TUESDAY, NOVEMBER 28

SIX HOURS BEHIND U. S. EAST COAST TIME

Sato craned his neck to see over the crowd in the lobby of the Royal Hawaiian Hotel on Waikiki Beach. The final breakfast and speeches of the International Magnetosphere Survey—the I.M.S.— Honolulu conference were over. The breeze from the ocean was cool but sweat from his hands started to stain the manila envelope he held. He could not focus on the spectacular view of the Pacific Ocean surf, only on his racing heart and the dangerous cliff he was about to jump off.

As planned, Kano had sent Sato, Kano's best man and best English speaker, to this meeting of the I.M.S. Special Study Group. Kano forcefully repeated his instructions to Sato before he left Japan. "You must maintain MITI's order of silence. Absolutely no hint of the Kagoshima disaster can escape during your trip."

In Japan, a superior's decision is unquestionable. That ethic was part of the air Sato breathed growing up. Like water to a fish, a young man needed it to survive but he didn't know it was there.

Obedience was drilled in from birth by family, schools, institutions, and society. No schoolboy, or schoolgirl, could vary his or her appearance from the norm. A thick book of regulations defined the measurements and condition of school uniforms, haircuts, and what one does outside school. The slightest deviation caused a report to parents, who would be disgraced.

The obligation never ended. No employee would think of leaving for home while his section head was still in the lab, no matter how late or how little work one had left. The fear of shame, exposure of failure before others, led one to strive to comply with the rules and orders you were given. No other action was conceivable.

Sato had turned this over in his mind many times since the meeting with the I.M.S. committee in the office tower in Shinjuku. He knew his studies at Cal Tech had affected his scientific attitudes, improved them in fact; the emphasis on thinking for himself had helped him produce more insights and better work than his colleagues, winning him more responsibility. But he realized now that was not the only change.

Until the I.M.S. committee bowed to MITI's order to keep his friends' deaths secret, Sato was unaware that his will had changed, too.

The Americans had recently announced the February launch of an optical computing module on the US I.M.S. satellite, like Minimura's computer that had caused the disaster. Sato's investigation of the explosion confirmed that silence by Kano, his team, and the Japanese authorities would condemn many Americans to death.

Since that news, Sato's sleep had been even more troubled. As he worried about his role in hiding the blast at Kagoshima, he realized that his will had in fact been strengthened overseas, but in ways that were not acceptable in Japan. It was his individual will, now linked to what he believed, in this case not the same as the belief imposed on and accepted by those around him.

He knew the decision "at the highest levels" that Kano was enforcing was wrong. And murderous.

Before he left Minimura's office in Tsukuba Science City to travel to Hawaii, Sato had written English summaries of the evidence explaining the reasons for the explosion at Kagoshima. The documents made a small package. But written in the dense language of physics and mathematics, the story of the looming disaster would be clear to the top optical computing scientist in the world. He had put it all in the manila envelope.

During the conference, Sato had tried without success to deliver the package to Professor Vyseliunis from MIT. As a member of the I.M.S. steering committee, the professor was constantly in demand by others more senior than a young Japanese delegate.

Sato had written on the envelope: "DO NOT OPEN. Please deliver to Dr. Madison Whitmire." Professor Vyseliunis had been on her Ph.D. review committee. Sato had seen this on Dr. Whitmire's dissertation, a bible for him and his team. In his turmoil, Sato believed this was his only chance to get crucial information to Dr. Whitmire without alerting powerful people in Japan.

Conference attendees filled the lobby, waiting for a sightseeing cruise. Sato knew the professor was not going. The reception desk attendant told Sato the professor had booked a flight for Boston. Sato peered over the crowd and saw the professor exit the elevator in deep conversation with a fellow committee member.

As Sato tried to make his way through the crowd, a short, powerfully built Hawaiian in chauffeur's livery rushed up to the professor yelling.

"Come. *Aiii*, already late."

Heads in the lobby spun around as the man in the dark uniform grabbed the professor's suitcase in one hand and pulled him with the other toward the hotel entrance. The crowd tightened to see the cause of the disturbance. Even pushing with the force of a commuter boarding his train to Tokyo, Sato would not reach the professor in time. The chauffeur, distressed and yelling now, dragged the professor toward the exit. "*Loa hopena o*. Very late."

Sato held up the manila envelope and yelled to make himself heard. "Professor. Professor. Please take this with you."

The professor called to him over the noise of the curious crowd, "I'm in quite a hurry here. Send it to me."

Then he disappeared and with him, Sato's chance to warn Dr. Whitmire.

Chapter 57
DALLAS, WEDNESDAY, NOVEMBER 29

Stefan looked both ways before entering the street, then edged his car out of his apartment parking lot and headed for work. He was more careful now, even in small things. And he didn't go to the Cotton Fields anymore, not after what happened to poor George. Stefan stopped fully at the red light before going ahead. A few hundred yards further he would cross over Interstate 30 on the route he took to work each morning.

Traffic was light, but he still used his turn signal and looked intently in the side mirror as he moved to the righthand lane. Things at work were back to normal and the nagging fears he had over Mueller's documents were behind him now. Almost forgotten. He even hummed a favorite song, looking forward to helping start up the new production line today.

A car pulled up beside him in the left-hand lane, too close, and then slowed to his speed. Dallas was becoming more like Los Angeles. Stefan didn't like being near other cars. He accelerated, but the other car kept pace. He checked his rear-view mirror, hoping to slow down. There was another car behind him, hanging on his bumper.

Stefan sped up again. Both cars kept pace. He looked ahead for a place to pull over, but he was starting up the overpass. The shoulder narrowed and the ground began to slope off steeply to the right. Stefan decided to slow down and let the two cars go by. As he took his foot off the gas, he felt a strong jolt from behind. The car had hit him! At the same time, the car to his left swerved, pushing Stefan's car out of its lane.

Stefan felt another, more violent hit from behind again and lost control. His car, corralled and pushed relentlessly by the other two, veered sharply right, crashed through the railing, and hurtled down the steep embankment. Its momentum propelled it through a safety rail onto Interstate 30 and into the path of oncoming traffic.

The driver of an eighteen-wheeler, running hot, tried uselessly to slam on the brakes. The trailer loaded with industrial fittings swung forward, a massive wall of iron parts gaining speed as it headed right toward Stefan.

Stefan screamed and raised his arms as if that would protect him. White scrolling lettering touting the strength of heavy gauge Arnhardt steel fittings was the last thing Stefan ever saw.

Chapter 58
JOHNSON SPACE CENTER, HOUSTON, 9AM, THE SAME DAY,

Madison was plagued by men bent on interrupting her launch preparation. Tom O'Hanlon and the DARPA lawyer, Amalfitano, had insisted on meeting with her about some government contract issues before she left New York for Houston. It had been a waste of her time—she had almost missed her flight—and an unwelcome reminder of that lawyer at Cameron, Payne. The problem she was in Houston to resolve only made her mood worse: politics in the person of another insensitive man, Norman "Bull" Halsey.

NASA's selection of Madison's OC-X project for the I.M.S. launch capped her efforts of more than a decade. She'd begun thinking about optical computing in a physics class at prep school. A woman physicist was a contradiction in terms, even at Harvard and MIT pursuing a joint doctorate. The careless insinuations about R & D leaks that Payne had made were a threat to her career in ways the man couldn't understand. Rumors start easily but are impossible to root out. Detractors looking for an excuse would jump on them to block her career.

With preparations for the I.M.S. launch in February steaming ahead, she didn't need the time demands of the Malinkrodt case, the flippant curiosity of Jake Payne, or avoidable problems like the one that had complicated this trip: Halsey's intemperate nature. She waited in a conference room for Grover Walker, her OC-X group manager, to wrap up the visit.

Bull's massive frame dominated as he charged into the room, trailed by Grover, breathing hard. "Look, Bull," Grover tried to explain. "the results are all within spec and they cover all the mission critical requirements. Your additional tests could take months and delay lift off, unless we pull the OC-X from the . . . ."

Grover was a talented researcher, but a babe in the woods in organizational infighting. He had just stumbled over Halsey's real objective. Bull's nickname was due to his physique and his temperament. He turned and leaned into Grover, his powerful torso rigid with anger as he stabbed a blunt finger in Grover's face.

"Mission integrity, Walker. Mission integrity. They can tell me to put your damned contraption in this satellite, but I'm responsible for the success of this flight. And I'm telling you we need these tests to confirm reliability. You're not in your ivory tower lab here, bub. This is the real world."

Grover turned to Madison and threw up his hands.

"Norman." She lowered the volume and softened the tone. Halsey bridled at her use of his given name, but Madison was not going to play the old boy game. "Everyone wants this mission to succeed. That means bringing it off on time with the OC-X module on board."

She knew Halsey's arguments and they were specious. He was insisting an experiment on the ground to demonstrate capabilities only a successful space flight could confirm. Perhaps Grover hadn't handled this in the most diplomatic way. His retiring manner had given Halsey an opening to exploit.

Madison continued quietly, corralling Bull. "These performance standards were worked out over months of cooperation between Grover's team, DARPA, and NASA in Washington. We've met and surpassed them all. If you can't accept that, we'll have to take it directly to the steering committee in D.C. Are we done, or should we get on the next flight to Washington?"

He glared at her. Madison knew that for years agencies were in awe of his spotless record for launch security. But as technology advanced, his absolute rule was eroding in favor of technical expertise. They both knew that Madison had the knowledge, the connections, and the results to get him overruled in Washington.

He stood over her, struggled to regain control, then fumed, "I'm putting this in writing. The flight will only go off over my objection if these tests are not run." He turned and stalked out of the room.

Jim Cernak, the head of operations at Mission Control Houston, trailed after Halsey and gave Madison a sympathetic look and, she would swear, a thumbs up.

Chapter 59
LAWTON LAW FIRM, 10:40AM, THE SAME DAY

Charlie and I were working on additional detailed discovery requests and deposition questions for Mueller and Malinkrodt, when Tom O'Hanlon called. I hadn't talked to him since I'd sent my memo and our earlier discovery recommendations that were still moldering in CT corporate limbo.

"Are you guys sitting down?"

"Good news?"

"No. It's horrible news. Stefan Weidl was just killed in a traffic accident in Dallas."

My mind reeled. The shocking news launched visions of the big Austrian tormented by fear at the Cotton Fields; steadfast as he blew the case open in his deposition, and laughing stepping out of the Fairmont elevator with his twin George. Now they had both been cut down. If George had been murdered by mistake, as Charlie and I had surmised, someone had just corrected the error. There had to be some malevolent force, more dangerous than Driscoll, circling around our expanded mission.

Charlie was on the same wavelength. "A accident? No way."

"I just got a call from Detective Boyd in Dallas,' Tom said. "They have nothing to indicate it was other than a horrendous hit and run traffic mishap. Stefan lost control on his way to work. He crashed through a railing onto an Interstate. Got hit by an eighteen-wheeler doing seventy."

I said, "Tom, you don't believe this was a coincidence, do you?"

Charlie was quick with a more useful question.

"What good is Stefan's deposition now?"

"The facts are out there," I said. "Tom can send the deposition and threaten the lawsuit. It's admissible as evidence under some conditions, but that leaves a lot of room for defendants to make trouble. We need to get to Mueller for corroboration of Weidl's testimony. You agree, Tom?"

As soon as I said that, I felt another punch to the gut. "Hold on, Tom. We have a call to make. We'll get right back to you."

I leaped to the door and yelled down the hall. "Georgia. Get me the number for Hans Mueller with InterTech in L.A."

As she called it out, I scrambled to mash the buttons on the phone and said to Charlie, "To hell with going through his lawyer. We need to know whether he's still alive."

Charlie turned on the speakerphone. We heard three loud rings, then a crackle followed by a recording, "The number you have reached is not in service at this time. Please dial again or consult directory assistance—"

I slammed down the receiver.

"Yeah," Charlie moaned, "Directory assistance for Rio de Ja-*ner-i-o* or that movie star cemetery out there. He's flown the coop or he's dead."

Chapter 60

WEST SIDE OF LOS ANGELES, 2PM, THE SAME DAY

John Morgan paced across the living room of his majestic Pacific Palisades home, ignoring the coveted ocean view outside his bay window. For the first time in his life, Morgan knew what it felt like to be a loser. Stuck under house arrest, he spent his time raging and plotting.

The L.A. police had hauled him away in front of his partners and staff. Gordon firm investigators were turning his office inside out. But he knew they wouldn't find anything.

He had spread files across a gleaming glass and chrome coffee table, but they held no interest. His only real client now? Himself. Those damned P.I.s had screwed him. Now he worked full time on how to retain his bar license and protect his assets. His strategies had little to do with the law and everything to do with power and influence.

The doorbell caused him to jump. His nerves had never failed him before. Now they did regularly. He'd been called tightly wound, high strung, imperious, and much worse. He had always been the one that made other people nervous. Who would dare come to his house unannounced?

He ripped open the front door and saw a tall, thin man in a conservative dark gray business suit standing on his front step.

"Who the hell are you? Get off my property before I call the police."

The man returned John's fierce glare with studied calm. "John, I think you've had enough of the police."

"Who the fuck do you think you are?"

"I'm an answer to your prayers. Tony sent me." In fact, Tony Alzeda, Morgan's criminal attorney, had only supplied the address. Only one person sent this man. And that man was outside Morgan' panoramic window on the other side of the Pacific.

"The hell you are. Where's Tony? I'm calling him."

"I'll wait." The heavy oak door thundered shut.

On the phone Morgan was put right through to Alzeda. "Who the hell is this guy, Tony?"

"I don't know. I only know someone who's dealt with him—a very big player, John, and this guy makes *him* nervous. This guy doesn't even have a name. He carries around a coupla carrots and a big fucking stick. You need to talk to him."

Morgan wrenched the door open again. He gestured the man in with a swat of his hand and pointed to a straight-backed chair in a corner. The man sat down and casually draped one well-dressed leg over the other.

"So? Tony says I outta listen. Prove it."

The visitor wasted no time explaining what Morgan had to do and how he would be compensated.

"You see, John. You will come out of prison in particularly good financial shape."

Morgan strained to keep from wrestling the guy to the front door and kicking him down the rough flagstone steps.

"That's chump change. Forget it. Every lawyer in the D.A.'s office owes me. Hell, the D.A. owes me." And was afraid of what Morgan knew. "I'll beat this and be back practicing law without any help from you."

"Not if they learn about the files hidden at your storage locker down the road in Venice. And about the assets in your account at Credit Suisse. In Zurich."

Morgan paled and staggered. No one else knew about those bank accounts. No one knew about those files. No associate, no paralegal, no secretary. No one except this guy. Those files had never seen the inside of Morgan's office at the firm. Their exposure would anger a lot of powerful people, people with long memories, deep pockets, and violent associates.

Morgan's knees buckled and he fell back onto the sofa.

The man picked some lint from his sharply creased trousers and watched it sift down to the thick carpet.

"John, you need to be a bit more . . . realistic. You're finished with that side of the law. If you cooperate with the D. A., disclose any contacts, or indicate in any way that you were not acting alone, you will suffer. Prison is a dangerous place." The man paused and fixed his icy black eyes on Morgan.

Then he turned cordial, newsy. "By the way, did you hear Stefan Weidl just passed away?" He uncrossed his legs and ground the speck of lint into the carpet with the sole of his custom-made oxford.

Chapter 61
LAWTON LAW FIRM, GREENVILLE, MONDAY, DECEMBER 18

Tom O'Hanlon had been sitting on my memo for almost three weeks. I was sitting on my closet-office chair, my case strategy in tatters. The extensive further investigation demands that Charlie and I had sent to Tom for presentation to his boss were moot. Stefan was dead, Mueller was missing, and Morgan was silent as a grave, no doubt having been threatened with one if he talked. The case was on life support, suffocating, dying on the vine.

Preston had noted my slack time and put me on helping Beau prepare the paper mill case for arbitration, help he shouldn't have needed. So I turned to the chaos we had left behind as we shot through the front gate of the construction site in Newton County, Texas. It didn't take long. Using the chalk-line and T-square of the law, we turned the chaos into a slam dunk win.

That was satisfying on one level, as a distraction from the sludge factory at CT in New York. But deeply troubling on another. It was repetition of work I'd done before and would do again for thirty-five years. Unless I got away.

McElwain's passive resistance was infuriating, professionally and personally. I had a decision to make. The January first deadline for NYU was closing fast, creating a narrowing window. I had to shoot through it, but I had no idea how.

My phone rang. It was Tom O'Hanlon, his voice full of energy this time.

"We're good to go."

"Go where?"

"Nico has cleared Madison and John McElwain approved release of the deposition to Minimura."

I was stunned. "McElwain had a change of heart? He's going to church? Giving alms to the poor?"

"Let's just say John can now see the downside to his future if we don't pursue this more aggressively."

My excitement couldn't totally erase my disgust that the head of a major corporation would place his own interests above his obligations to his organization, its shareholders, and employees.

"We have an agreement with Minimura for consent discovery in Japan, They insist it start January second."

"That's too fast." And it would kill NYU. Unless for some reason Tom, and Nico, would let me out of the case. He'd said "we", but it had taken time to negotiate with Minimura. And I'd been sidelined while Tom took over. That was a bad sign. Or a good sign. While my head was halfway into summer school, my heart felt adrenaline kicking in over the prospect of a fight in Tokyo, if I was still on the team. I needed clarity. I had to feel Tom out.

"No wonder they've pushed to hurry us up. We gave them weeks to get ready. And we're just getting started, heading into the holidays. I don't think that's a coincidence. How'd that happen?"

When McElwain backed down, Tom couriered Stefan's depo to Minimura the same day. Weidl's testimony and the over three hundred exhibits took their toll. Minimura agreed to talk and Tom worked it all out. He gave me a quick summary of the deal. Some of the terms were too restrictive but he hadn't asked my opinion. Yet there he was, treating me as if I was still CT's lawyer. So I acted like it.

"Translation will be a problem. And why can't we get documents and interrogatory answers before we go?"

"It's not perfect, Jake. But it's more than I ever thought we'd get. Besides, we retain the right to sue in a U.S. court if we aren't satisfied by their responses. Consent to jurisdiction. No preconditions."

"No bar to a jury trial?"

"Not if we sue in Federal Court and ask for one."

I knew that. *Newman*, again. But my mind was bouncing between NYU and Tokyo. I had to hear it. "Am I still involved, Tom?".

"Of course. Word from the top, CT's General Counsel, and its President. Bob Langston wants you on the case and John McElwain agreed." Somehow my memo had hit home. If the client wanted me, I was obligated. I couldn't quit. I wondered how Nico felt about that. I'd have to confront him. For now, I had to focus on Japan. That got my adrenaline pumping.

"You realize what eleven days ago was, Tom, don't you?"

"Uh . . . Thursday?"

"December 7th. Pearl Harbor." He laughed. The confident, competitive Tom O'Hanlon from Cameron was back.

"Minimura's digging in. They've retained two law firms: a major international firm in New York, Swinton, Canfield, and the top international law firm in Tokyo, Nakashima and Ômi. You'll meet our investigation team tomorrow at Cameron. Our own march across the Pacific is about to get underway."

I envisioned squads of Minimura lawyers burning midnight oil and heating up transpacific phone cables to foil the investigation Tom's agreement had just authorized. They had a big head start. I started to ask him how Madison was taking it, but he had hung up.

Chapter 62
NEW YORK, THE SAME DAY

Madison listened to a voice mail on the new phone system in her office at the CT research headquarters in White Plains. Her boss, the head of CT Research, was ordering her to go see Tom O'Hanlon about a trip to Japan. She bridled at the command barked through her handset. He knew she wouldn't like the extra work, so he'd deflected her anticipated pushback in O'Hanlon's direction.

It had to be the Malinkrodt case. The timing couldn't be worse. As she'd done with resistant males for over a decade, she had easily taken care of Bull Halsey. That was part of the job. But now she was going to have to spend weeks on production technology irrelevant to OC-X, tied to the insufferable lawyer from Cameron.

She called for a car to take her to Manhattan.

Madison blew into O'Hanlon's office like a tornado. "I just heard. You want me to go to Japan to head up the team on the Malinkrodt case?"

Tom stood and offered his hand. She ignored it. If he was waiting for calm to settle in, she would make sure that was a waste of his time. O'Hanlon sat back down in his desk chair and said, "You and Charlie will head up the technical matters. Jake Payne will lead the team."

"That's your decision?"

"Mine and Bob Langston's, approved by John McElwain."

She knew she couldn't buck them all, but if she was going to be involved, she could fight for better odds. "It's bad enough that I have to do double duty when I have the biggest project of my career in full swing."

"I need to expl—"

"Minimura will pour incredible resources into this case." She leaned forward, planted one hand on Tom's desk, and jabbed at him with the index finger of the other. "I don't want our efforts or the company's interests compromised by less than a first-rate team."

She struggled to remain professional, but the energy of righteous anger filled her voice. "What about the Gordon firm? Aren't they counsel on one of the Malinkrodt cases? Why aren't they leading this?"

"Please, Madison. Sit down. This is going to take a while."

As he talked, she interrupted with sharp, hectoring questions. But as the shocking tale unwound, her anger turned to bewilderment.

Tom revealed the complex maneuvering culminating in the deposition that entered the documents into the case. Then he explained the scope of the trip to Japan and the many expert technical personnel CT was ready to commit to it.

She had to admit Payne's last questions from their interview at Cameron had described the difficulty accurately. And CT had truly stepped up. It occurred to her, now that Tom had her attention, that Payne had understood the case well from his first day on the job. That undercut her concern about his legal competence. But it didn't excuse his attitude towards women or his reckless questions about her management of research.

As her heart slowed down, she opened her mind to consider the new reality. "Thank you for the explanation. I'll look at this assignment differently as a result." But her emotions continued to carom from the complexity of investigating the case to her simmering anger over Payne's behavior.

She started to stand when Tom said. "There are a couple of other things you have to know." She lowered slowly back down.

He told her about the deaths of the lawyer from L. A. and the Austrian witness from the deposition. Her cheeks turned pale.

"Tom. You can't think that's related to this case."

He shifted in his chair and straightened a legal pad on his desk. "The police have no leads and no motive. But Jake and Charlie think they must be connected. They believe the death of Panatopoulus, the Gordon associate, may have been a mistake. And that Stefan Weidl's was not."

For ten years she had been cloistered in academia and industrial research labs. There was conflict, of course, but it was kept in check by the discipline of corporate policies.

What civilized people could operate in the roiling morass Tom had described? She had to admit that Payne and Cauthen had.

"You've got to have absolute confidence in Jake Payne on this trip. We have no idea what might come up in Japan."

She conceded, "If he is the person you just described in tough circumstances, I'll make it work." She had no choice. She had to go to Tokyo. But she didn't have to like it. "I may have misjudged his legal skills. But part of that was his fault. He was unprofessional."

Tom started to talk. She cut him off to brand her final position on his mind.

"I'm ready to let that go if he will. The question is, will Payne accept to work with a woman and keep his idle speculation in bounds?"

She watched as O'Hanlon studied her, started to speak, then seemed to think better of it. He raised his hands, palms up, and shrugged. “That’s up to you and Jake to sort out. I’m asking that you make the effort. Both of you. We need to go to Cameron tomorrow to meet the rest of the team.”

Chapter 63
CT MANUFACTURING OFFICES, CAMERON, 1PM, THE NEXT DAY

I pulled into the CT parking lot at Cameron a month to the day after my first visit. Tom and Charlie met me in the lobby.

"What have we got, guys?"

"Damnedest thing I ever seen," Charlie crowed. "Old Tom has outdid hisself. We got Madison and five top engineers, plus two Japanese Ph.Ds. to translate, all headed for Tokyo. Twelve others from the plant and R an' D for back-up stateside. We got horses. A whole herd. Come on."

Tom said, "We need to talk first." He led us into a small room off the lobby. "I need to update you. Nico will join us later. You know we've cleared Madison. I've met with Jack Staley, too."

Alarmed, I said, "You didn't mention Frank?" I'd promised him anonymity.

"No, no. It was part of a regular intellectual property update. I didn't want to spook him. I began with production, then touched on R & D since Madison reports to him for security."

"How'd he react?" I asked.

"It should have been straightforward. Company policy requires anyone to report suspicious criminal activity to legal. Frank's attempt to talk to him would qualify."

"What did he say?"

"He didn't mention an incident, just kept saying he'd followed company procedure. I checked with Bob Langston. Nothing. If Jack passed something along, it wasn't through Bob's office or me."

"Who the hell could that be?" Charlie wondered. "Ain't nobody up at that level but you lawyers and McElwain hisself."

"Or Untermeyer," I said. I already knew he was McElwain's hammer. Staley could easily rely on that. "He's a lawyer, just not in the legal department. He reports directly to McElwain for special projects. He's qualified to be Jack Staley's back-up."

And Untermeyer had threatened Tom in front of us. But was Untermeyer just executing orders from McElwain, interpreting them on his own, or something else?

"Nico's still investigating Untermeyer," Tom explained.

"How did Madison take the news about OC-X?" I was about to meet her again.

"She doesn't know."

"*What?*"

"She reacted badly to your leading the team, Jake. She's convinced you're a Neanderthal. And she was smarting over your questions about R & D. It was too much to lay OC-X on her then. Nico will join us later and we'll explain OC-X to her."

"Four men lined up against her, who've kept her in the dark about OC-X while she's the target in a national security investigation? I hope you brought flak jackets."

We entered the conference room. Three tables were piled with documents, a team of engineers working at each one. At a larger one, Madison talked to another group in lab coats.

I met each team member and learned their expertise: polymers, film drawing, slitting, rolling, the whole production process. One, Jerry Suddeth, spoke with a thick Southern accent and fractured grammar like Charlie. The only Japanese there, Hara Ichiro, was about fifty years old, with bristly salt and pepper hair. He was short, stocky, very fit, and spoke slowly, with concentration and precision.

"My family name is Hara, but please call me Harry. It is simpler. I left Japan after undergraduate degree to study at Cal Tech and received a Ph.D. in production instrumentation." His speech became more difficult. "Since I joined the company after university, I have not been back to Japan."

Shaking hands with Madison sparked an emotional jolt. My brain handled it better this time but my gut didn't. At least I looked her in the eye. I could see she had problems, too. Dark crescents underlined her sparkling eyes and her golden hair had lost some of its sheen.

"Congratulations on the NASA project," I said. "I'm sorry this comes at such a bad time for you."

"I hope I can help, Payne. You'll have my full cooperation."

Tom ran through the case history to date, concluding, "You'll arrive in Tokyo on January first and begin work with Minimura the next day." Madison had to be back in Houston well before February second, the date of the OC-X launch. She had insisted on it.

I outlined the terms of the agreement with Minimura. We could send them written questions and a list of types of documents to receive when we arrived. We had the right to tour their film factory in Nagahama. At the end, we could interview an executive under oath at the US consulate to use against Malinkrodt.

Tom was responsible for the limitations in the agreement and explained, “We can’t use outside people because of secrecy and expertise. The translation will require proprietary technical knowledge. Harry and the other Japanese speaking employee, who will join us in Tokyo, will have to handle all that. Harry has already worked up a glossary of technical terms with Japanese characters that will help you sort documents.”

I wanted them to know what they were signing on for. “This is being done by agreement. That doesn’t mean it will be friendly. Minimura’s people will be resistant. They have top notch US and Japanese legal counsel, so all their people will be well coached. You should expect them to be polite but not give an inch. CT must try to reach a settlement, but as a last resort, we are still free to file a lawsuit.”

Tom suggested that Charlie, Madison, and I plan the team’s work until we left for Tokyo, just two weeks away, including Christmas. The rest of the team went back to work. In a little over an hour, the three of us had fleshed out a first take on trade secrets based on Weidl’s document and a work plan through our departure, good cooperation that boded well for Tokyo.

Everyone was ready for a break. Madison left to check on her OC-X team. Tom pulled Charlie and me aside. “Come on.” He led us to another room. Nico Amalfitano had arrived.

"We’ve used our contract rights to check out the list of people we’ve compiled,” he said. “We’ve found nothing to implicate any of them in removal of information, untoward financial gain, or ideological animus to the United States.” Lawyer-speak for drilling a dry hole.

“There’s nothing to it after all?” I asked. “What about Malinkrodt? What about national security?”

“This is a limited search based on CT’s agreements and Federal contracting law. We haven’t found anything suspicious. We haven't opened a national security investigation yet." That raised legal questions I needed to put to him.

"What about Morgan?" I asked.

"He hasn't given up anything on your case," Nico admitted. "There are rumors about problems in other matters, but nothing solid. We don't know who Morgan was really working for. The cops have nothing more on the two deaths in Dallas, either."

"And Mueller?"

"He booked a one-way ticket to Rio from L. A. but never boarded. No sign of him since." We were all silent.

"That's not much progress," I said.

Nico and Tom nodded slowly.

Tom asked, "Nico, we've kept the OC-X matter between us so far. Can we tell McElwain or Bob Langston now?"

"Or Preston?" I added.

"I'm asking you to hold off."

I muttered to Charlie, "Does this qualify as a pure-T disaster yet?"

He shook his head and headed for the door. "I gotta get back to the fellers."

"So," I said to Nico, "the ball's back in our court on this issue? Charlie, me, and Madison, snooping around in Japan for Consolidated, and the US government?"

Tom tried to ease the tension. "Look at the team we've got now, Jake. I'll get Madison. We'll put all the cards on the table with her." He went to find her, leaving me alone with Nico.

Chapter 64
JAKE AND NICO

I needed answers. "This new FISA law. How bad is it?"

Nico looked as if he'd just lost his best friend because he had: authority to conduct an aggressive national security inquiry into espionage by Americans on American soil.

I knew that such inquiries without judicial oversight had ended recently. The Senate had been on a CIA witch-hunt since Watergate and Senator Church had piled on with a Senate inquiry. Teddy Kennedy had ramrodded a bill through Congress imposing restrictions on intelligence agencies' activities in the U.S.: the Foreign Intelligence Surveillance Act, FISA. President Carter had just signed it into law at the end of October.

"Charlie and I think George Panatopoulus and Stefan Weidl were murdered because of this case. Now maybe Mueller, too. Doesn't that justify getting the FBI involved, at least down in Dallas, since the local police haven't found anything? This is national security. We're civilians with another job to do."

Of course, that would mean more turf battles. Nico's mouth twitched from neutral to a scowl.

"The black letter provisions of FISA are clear. But no one knows how it's going to work in practice, so it's having a chilling effect." Another euphemism, understating the problem no doubt. Nico was genuinely shaken, and more open than in Dallas.

"But I've talked to O'Hanlon. We have attorneys in firms in D.C. that we work with regularly. Large firms with many capable people. If you need help, they have resources and can step in right now."

There it was. Nico's opening gambit to get me off the case. It might be against a spy's nature but I wanted plain, straight talk. "You want me off the case? Just say so."

"I'm offering you assistance."

I'd spent a lot of energy chewing over my predicament. I'd even plotted out scenarios of how I could leverage this into a somewhat graceful exit from the case. But, like my decision to follow Charlie in the storage lot at Geiger's, my thoughts of quitting were nailed to the floor.

I wanted a chance to punch back against the vicious opposition that had surfaced. And I wanted to win this thing. It also happened to be true that there was no good alternative to Charlie and me.

"I can handle my end, Nico. I'm not quitting. You'll have to fire me. I'm worried about your end."

He sighed, stuck with me. "You've convinced Bob Langston you're up to it. That's a big deal. More help was my idea. This has turned dangerous, Jake. If you have any concerns, I want you to get out now, free and clear." Not exactly a ringing endorsement of my professional skills. My turn to not talk straight.

"Nico, I know you mean well." I still thought he could be concerned about my panic attacks. "My answer's easy. I want to do this. And frankly, in the time we have to get ready for Tokyo, I don't think anyone else can do it as well as Charlie and I can."

"Are you sure you couldn't use some muscle from another firm?"

I'd thought about that, too. I'd craved more support when Tom announced the agreement, but not just any kind. A CIA ops team would be nice. "Tom has limited us on translators. Other than that, I need two kinds of muscle: technical experts, and bodyguards. The room out there is full of experts. Can you promise me real muscle? FISA only affects investigations in the U.S. Can't the CIA get involved in Japan?"

He looked away. Clearly, DOD wasn't going to let go of this thing yet. First, corporate politics, now so-called "intelligence" politics. I'd have to settle for what I could get. "At least tell me that you're busting your tail in Washington for us."

"I am. And since you're hell-bent to go to Tokyo without any backup, I'm going to give you something." He pulled a card out of his suit coat and wrote on the back. "Here are my office contacts and my home number on the back. Use them if you get in a bind."

"Thanks." I guess he thought it was a big deal on the part of a CIA operative. I placed it, conspicuously and respectfully, for him to take note, in the inner pocket of my wallet.

The door opened and Charlie came in. "Those guys is fired up out there."

"That's good because we have a tougher job than ever," I said.

Charlie grinned again. " Nico, can you pass out them little badges and decoder rings now?"

Chapter 65
CAMERON, 4:45PM

Madison had finished talking with Grover Walker and was going through her mail. Grover was working well with the NASA ops manager from Mission Control in Houston, Cernak. That was good because she'd burned all her bridges with Halsey whose letter she had just read. He had objected, to NASA, DARPA, and a few other defense agencies, to the inclusion of OC-X in the I.M.S. launch.

Sorting through the rest of her mail, she discovered a flimsy blue international airmail letter addressed by hand, postmarked from Japan with no return address. She opened it and read:

> *Dr. Whitmire, I have vital information about your work. I must get it to you before February. I cannot send by mail. You will know it is me by the word kagami.*
>
> *A friend*

She was staring at the letter when Tom appeared at her door and said, "We need to talk."

Tom and Madison entered the conference room where we waited. I watched Madison carefully.

Tom began. "We have to update you, Madison. There are some things you need to know before you go to Tokyo."

Realizing he was only addressing her, Madison cast a wondering glance at Nico, Charlie, and me. Tom picked up the case where Stefan's deposition left off and revealed the note listing OC-X. Madison didn't say a word, but the color slowly drained from her face.

"We only have a scrap of paper with OC-X scribbled on it. Nothing else refers to optical computing."

Still no comment from Madison, but her arms began to lift off the armrests of her chair, as is she was falling.

I had to make sure she knew how bad it was. "We have physical attacks and two, maybe three, suspicious deaths."

She was glaring at Tom. Then Amalfitano set out the investigation of all the CT people. Madison's arms were back on her chair, a scowl etching her face as he talked.

She shifted. I'd seen her do it at Cameron. The calm before the storm was over. She stood up, eyes flashing, body coiled like a spring. Then she let go with a furious rush.

"Why have you taken this long to tell me? You've known this for *weeks*." We looked at each other and hesitated. "You were investigating me, too, weren't you?"

Madison had weathered arrogant and dismissive colleagues, vicious attacks on her science, rumors about bias in favor of a female, degrading harassment. Nothing had surprised and shaken her as hard as the realization that people she had to work with closely could imagine that she would betray her company, her country, and herself. Then investigate her behind her back. Now they'd ganged up to challenge her integrity.

She'd been cleared. They hadn't screwed that up. But she was boiling mad. O'Hanlon must have known about OC-X when she'd talked to him in his office, after her boss told her to go see him. They were both cowards.

She was still staring straight at Tom. "You knew yesterday I'd been cleared, or I'd never have been told about Japan. You didn't say a word. How could you do that?" She dropped into her chair, head bowed. She sensed the others shifting awkwardly.

It all flooded back to her. The years of sacrifice, isolation, opposition, effort, and success. The launch approval had crowned it all. Suddenly she felt like a rug had been pulled out from under her only to reveal a trap door swinging wide beneath her. She tensed her whole body, gripped the chair, and fought to grab hold of her emotions.

Finally, she stood up again and looked down on them, her voice shaky. "I have always . . . ." She stopped speaking, but felt she was slipping, then falling again. She hit bottom with a jolt, as she had so often since she lost her parents . . . through massive shocks, demeaning humiliations. Yet she'd survived and learned how to stop energy bleeding away in self-pity and channel it into righteous, focused anger. She started again, steadier, poised for action.

"This is a blow and it hurts. To think that some of my colleagues could have had doubts about me and my team, to learn that people were rummaging through our lives behind our backs . . . ."

Tom frowned. "Madison, you have to—"

"Wait, Tom. Let me finish. I can't help feeling the way I do. But I can understand the position you were in. I assure you unequivocally that I had no idea OC-X might be compromised. I am a victim here." She stopped, again.

The room fell deathly still. “I do not take this personally, with any of you.” She looked directly at Jake. “Not any of you.”

In fact, she realized, she owed Jake an apology. What she had seen as offensive meddling turned out to be insightful exploration. At least he wasn’t part of the government-corporate hierarchy calling the shots on the OC-X investigation.

“I’m angry, outraged, that someone may have stolen what my team and I have worked so hard on for so long. If they did, I want to know everything, confront them, and bring them to account for this, more than anyone in this room.”

“You’ve hit me with some big surprises. Now I have one for you.” She pulled out a flimsy blue sheet. “I think we have a mole in Japan. And I think he knows I’m headed there.”

Chapter 66
EVENING, THE SAME DAY

By the time we finished with the team, it was after seven and pitch-black outside. The engineers and scientists were gone. Tom and Nico had to catch flights. Charlie would drive them to the airport.

I knew Madison had to be running on empty, but she managed to lean forward as if her batteries had been recharged.

"Let's go get these bastards."

We packed up and headed out. I walked beside her and slowed to let the others go ahead. There was no time left. I had to make the effort, to explain my behavior back when we met. At least we had worked together uneventfully all afternoon.

"There's something I need to tell you, and it's. . . well, it's personal. Can we talk over dinner?"

She eyed me and sighed. "Jake, I'm exhausted. We'd better get this over with now."

No reprieve. "It's about our first meeting, here at Cameron. I—"

"Look." She cut me off. "I said I'd put that behind me. I know you were only raising questions because you had to. I admit I didn't like it then, but . . . you were right to be suspicious. I owe you an apology, okay? You have it." The anger in her voice overwhelmed her words. "Let's move on."

This was as bad as I'd feared. I moved in front of her. She stopped. Her eyes burning into me, her mouth a thin, cold line.

"That's gracious of you, Madison. But that wasn't the only issue between us that day." I had to get all the way through this. "I'm sure you recall."

She arched an eyebrow and started to leave again. Without thinking, I reached out and lightly put my hand on her arm. She pulled away and whirled to face me. "*Don't touch me!*"

I froze. "I'm sorry." The horrible visions began to force their way into my mind. "You reminded me of someone."

Chapter 67
IN THE DARK

Madison was incensed. He was impossible. Back when they met, he'd been startled to see a woman scientist. Now he was admitting that she reminded him of some other woman, probably some old lover.

She closed her eyes. All the slights, the humiliation, the strain of closing herself off from such distractions for a decade, her anger over the OC-X revelation and the invasive review of her life it had provoked. Her rage piled up into an unstoppable wave that crested and broke with violent fury. She slammed her hands against Jake's chest. She had to put an end to this day that had become a nightmare.

He staggered back, but spoke again. "It was my sister, Ann. You look alike. She was a dancer."

"What are you talking about, Payne?" What the hell was that? Certainly, no excuse for his behavior. "A *dancer*?"

"I'm not doing this . . . ." He stopped, then went on. "Please listen to me, Madison. I saw you enter the room, excited about something. Then you pirouetted, with joy it seemed. I didn't know why. All I could see was my sister, who loved ballet." He looked aside and his voice became a whisper. "But not as she danced. . . ." His face turned red, his eyes moistened, and he rasped, “I saw her as she died.”

Madison’s body went cold. She shrank back and stood still, trying to absorb yet another shock. She struggled to say, “How?”

He cleared his throat, seemed to be looking inward, and held his hands in the air as if he were shielding himself from something. “She and my mother burned to death . . . cringing . . . in a fire, at night, at home . . . . “ He started to cover his face, and caught himself. “The coroner’s report . . . . I wish I’d never read it.”

Her mouth opened wide. Her body uncoiled for what seemed like forever as she struggled to understand his admission. She stared at him, searching, seeing him for the first time. What she saw was bleak, lonely, bereft.

“I, uh, it set off attacks, bad attacks . . . “ He started to back up and turn away. Then he stopped, and faced her full on, doubt clouding his face. Then suddenly it was gone. And his secret came stumbling out.

“Panic attacks. One hit me when you made that move. . . . Like a dancer. I’ve learned to calm them, sometimes. But not . . . not . . . .” He stopped again, looked down, then whispered, “They still hit me in personal injury cases . . . . the bodies . . . .“ He couldn’t go on. He covered his eyes with his hands.

She stared at the floor, embarrassed for him. Then she hunched her shoulders and wrapped her arms around her torso to keep from shaking as the impact of his confession coursed through her and laid waste her certainty, and something else.

He looked up, his face clearing as if some storm had passed.

“I haven’t told you this out of a need to bare my soul. It’s not to reassure you that I’m not a wacko misogynist, though I’m not.” He seemed to search for words, then, composed, continued,

“It’s so you can understand that I respect your talent, your achievements. . . . I can’t imagine the shock you received back in that room today. I need to put the past behind us, so I can do everything I can to help you get to the bottom of it. And so you know I'm doing everything I can to keep my own problems in check."

He offered her a seat in a chair.

She dropped into it and hunched over, her hands threaded wildly through her hair, then cradled her head.

Chapter 68
CT LOBBY, CAMERON

Jake's explanation left her speechless, contending with unbidden feelings from obscure origins. Finally, a startling discovery crept over her. She had been wrong. Recklessly wrong. Blindingly, self-centeredly, egotistically wrong.

A horrific loss had left him with a serious affliction. Not at all what she had imagined. He had shared his secret, but with so much difficulty that she had seen pain consume him until he was spent. In doing so, he had exposed a weakness that others could exploit to undermine him. A power she thought she would never give to another person. Because she knew deep inside what it felt like to bear such a secret.

She lived with the effort it took to always be on guard, to maintain vigilance against others, to outfight and outwit the power they tried to exert over her, to hold her emotions in check every waking moment, like lions in a cage, struggling but never allowed to roam free.

As she realized the secret inner life they shared, she began to shake. Her mind turned on itself, confronting a gaping chasm in her own life. A forgotten wound inside her began to open and a deep pain began to grow. She recalled the raw emotion she had seen in his eyes, consuming him, and feared pain could consume her, too.

Then she looked into his eyes again— composed now, steady, calm—and realized he had walked through the fire and survived. She could too.

Now she could see him as he was, his pain gone, without the blinders of her false conviction. She knew what she should do.

“You’ve done it, again.”

His eyebrows shot up in surprise.

She had been stunned by the revelations about OC-X. Now she was shocked by his honesty, but in a vastly different way. Slowly, inside, she felt a warmth she had not felt since . . . a very long time. She too spoke softly.

“You’ve been honest, Jake and . . . and thoughtful, both times we’ve met. You were worried about doing the right thing for your family then. Now you’re trying to do the right thing for me.” Her sudden emotion stirred insight, too. “You were right to question me about R & D back in November and you’re right to share this with me now.”

He sat down.

She saw now that he had risked his fate with her, in full knowledge of what she could do to him: tell O’Hanlon and Amalfitano about his condition and get him kicked off the case. Yesterday in O’Hanlon’s office, she would have. No question. But she had been put in check when O’Hanlon told her how tough Jake had been in a chaotic, threatening situation. Now there was another, more compelling reason that she wouldn’t betray his secret.

She recognized a decency that, in her self-absorbed state, she might never have discovered. That was a shock. The unspoken issues could have become a fatal weakness under the extreme stress they would face in Japan. As he addressed her doubts, they disappeared, erased by his candor. Yesterday, her reservations about working with him abated because O’Hanlon had asked her to put them aside. Now they disappeared because she chose to let them go.

"You put my understanding ahead of your self-interest. I'm not sure anyone has done that for me since my parents died."

His eyes opened wide. "I didn't know. We've both lost our parents . . . . Madison, we'll face tough situations over there. We'll need to rely on each other."

Competition and mistrust had dogged every step of her life for over a decade. She had pushed anyone, everyone, away and intimidated them to protect herself. No one had reached out. Always working alone and wary, her anger fueled personal accomplishment. She discovered now how much that had cost her.

His story not only removed an obstacle from their work. The warmth she felt was like finding a precious keepsake that you had lost and forgotten, only to realize on holding it again how much it meant to you.

"You are right, Jake, we will need to," she replied, "and we can. We both can now."

They got up, walked across the lobby together, and out the door.

Chapter 69
KYU FURUKAWA, THE SAME DAY, TUESDAY, DECEMBER 19

TWELVE HOURS AHEAD OF U. S. EAST COAST TIME

Shin paced in the dark paneled library of his manor retreat. Even here he could not escape. Yesterday his nation was master of its fate, playing with the all-powerful Americans like children. Today, a threat loomed on its doorstep.

He had known for months that the Carter administration had been courting the Chinese to open formal diplomatic relations, stupidly, treacherously, thoughtlessly, but with determination. At least six years ago Nixon had wanted something in return, playing the Chinese off against the Russians over Vietnam.

President Carter was opening to China out of a naive view of human nature. Shin knew the Japanese would pay the price for American idealism and weakness. He had not anticipated how quickly the bill would come due.

The day before, the seven-member Politburo of the Standing Committee of the Chinese Communist Party, the real center of power, had in a single session given Deng Xiaoping a majority and approved his audacious economic plan, the Four Modernizations: agriculture, industry, national defense, and science. If it had just been another turn of the wheel, temporarily putting Deng's clique on top in the thousands of years old cycling of Chinese dynasties, it would not have merited notice.

But Japan had shown it was possible to break the death grip of its own history a hundred years ago and had grown to become a world economic powerhouse. If the Chinese applied modern science and economics to their vast population with their inherent cultural arrogance, the consequences would be disastrous for Japan and the rest of the world.

Deng's ascent to supreme power signaled a break in the cycle. It was a rejection of decades of destructive, radical excess. Zhou Enlai, only Premier of the People's Republic since 1949, seated at the right hand of Mao until his death three years earlier, had proposed the same Four Modernizations in 1963. Deng and Zhou had known each other as study workers, then Communists, in France after the First World War and at the top of the Chinese Communist Party ever since. They agreed: Mao Zedong had been a genius in civil war, but in the final fifteen years of his rule, a disaster for their nation.

Stung by Zhou's reforming zeal, Mao unleashed the Great Cultural Revolution. It plunged China into chaos and caused economic free-fall for a decade. Deng himself was demoted and shamed. His son was crippled during the infighting. Even after Mao's death, the battle between ideologues and pragmatists raged on.

Finally, two mindless years after his death, Mao's wife, and the other power-crazed radicals in the Gang of Four had been destroyed. Deng, the indomitable phoenix, was back, ready to lead a bold resurgence of Chinese power.

Shin sat down at his desk. He lit and took a deep drag from a gold banded cigarette, placed it in the carved stone ashtray, and watched the tendrils of smoke ascend.

Four modernizations. A cryptic program, but a message as the Chinese liked to deliver them, through numerological slogans; four wide-ranging, vague goals. But this time they were real. Deng's ascendancy signaled that the fight between conservatives and reformers, the war that could have kept China weak indefinitely, was over.

Shin needed more information about Deng's moves and he was about to receive it.

An attendant opened the door and ushered in Shin's political protégé, the Minister of Planning. With Shin's support, he would be the next Prime Minister.

"Your message said it was urgent, Shin-*sensei*."

"A problem has arisen."

The minister's face fell. Shin groaned inside. The politician's first thought would be for his future, not the nation's. Shin almost lashed out but checked his anger and held up his hand.

"No, not that. The election will take place as planned. This is about the Chinese."

"Ah. The restoration of diplomatic relations. Just the other day, the American's quietly extended an invitation to Deng to visit the US. The Americans are abandoning Taiwan, another ally. You think we will be next?"

"It is inevitable. Deng has total control. He has packed the Politburo. It has approved his program for Chinese resurrection."

"His program will take time, even for Deng, who moves fast. We hear he accepted their invitation the day he received it."

"When he visits America, will they sign agreements?"

"Empty promises of friendship and economic ties, with few specifics, I hear. They are spending more time negotiating the stops on his U.S. tour in February, as they did here in October."

"Where will he go?"

"Mostly industrial sites: an auto plant. Ford, I think. Boeing. He insisted on one site in particular: NASA in Houston. He has asked to be present at the launch of their I.M.S. satellite in February. They have some new computer technology that will be inaugurated with this mission."

"What kind of technology?"

"Optical computing, according to the NASA press account."

Shin looked at the smoke rising from his gold ringed cigarette perched on the edge of the intricately carved stone tray. The confluence of rising wisps set off a flash of insight. He had to talk to Kano at once, but he was sure that would only confirm what he already felt.

"This could be extraordinary," he said, "like *kamikaze*. Another divine wind!"

"The one that saved us from the Chinese invasion from Korea?" The Minister was puzzled. Every schoolboy knew the tale of the failed Mongol Chinese emperor's fleet's attempted invasion of Japan in the thirteenth century, blown off course and destroyed by a providential typhoon. The story had been trumpeted incessantly, used as a pillar to support State Shinto during the Meiji Restoration in the mid-nineteenth century. "That's hard to believe. In what way?"

"I think the Americans, without knowing it, are going to kill Deng Xiaoping."

Chapter 70
OVER THE PACIFIC OCEAN, SUNDAY, DECEMBER 31

The CT team and I were flying to Tokyo on a Japan Air Lines 747. The first-class cabin was luxurious, but I couldn't sleep. Charlie and I were the only ones awake. I had gone over my meeting tomorrow with Minimura's lawyer from New York. Now I was trying to relax by reading James Clavell's novel, *Shōgun*.

"Listen to this, Charlie. The Japanese almost boiled in oil an Englishman who tried to crack open Japan four centuries ago. You bring any herbs with you for flavoring or is soy sauce okay?"

"No, but I'm starving. They got a lounge on these big planes. Let's go upstairs and check it out."

We navigated the tight circular staircase to the upper deck. The steward at the bar was pouring a bubbly liquid into a tall stemmed glass of orange juice for a passenger I'd noticed in the first-class waiting area in San Francisco.

"Whatcha got there?" Charlie asked.

"It's called a mimosa," the man replied. "Champagne and orange juice. Breakfast with a kick. Would you care for one?"

"Sure. Not gonna get much chance to have a drink anytime soon. Bartender, gimme one a them things. And some peanuts. Jake?"

"Soda water, lime, and some ice, please." I turned to our neighbor. "Hi, I'm Jake Payne. This is my colleague Charlie Cauthen."

Charlie grabbed the man's hand and got the pump handle going, almost spilling the man's drink. "Pleased ta meet ya. We're headed for Tokyo. How about you?"

"Clyde Auchincloss. I'll be at the US Embassy there for a month or so. Why will you be there?"

"Well, we're on sort of a group tour, here," Charlie offered, "We got another bunch out cold down there in First Class. Be in Tokyo for a coupla weeks."

The diplomat raised an eyebrow. "Business or pleasure?"

"We hope it's both," I said. "But mostly business. I'm a lawyer. My friends are with my client." It could be useful to have a contact at the embassy. I'd already notified the consular section about a deposition. "We're investigating a dispute between an American and a Japanese manufacturer. What takes you to Japan?"

"I'm really a business guy, but I signed on for a term as a special advisor to the Secretary of Commerce. You may have heard we're establishing relations with China soon. I'll check out the reactions in the Japanese business community."

Charlie took a sip of his drink. "Say, this thing is good. Whadja call it?"

"Mimosa," Clyde repeated. "Two parts orange juice, three parts champagne.

"Ain't that a tree?"

"Yes. It was imported to the U.S. from Japan in the 18th century, for its beauty. But it's also dangerous to some U.S. species."

"Sounds like Japanese electronics."

Auchincloss looked appraisingly at Charlie. "You're absolutely right. Your situation sounds unusual. I read in some embassy traffic that there's an interview scheduled at the consulate in a couple of weeks. You know anything about that?"

I liked the fact that this diplomat understood business. "That's us. We have an agreement to take testimony."

"How'd you get access to a Japanese witness in Tokyo? That's rare." He paused, looking more closely at me now. "Actually, it's unprecedented."

Charlie started to speak but shot me a questioning glance. I gave him a warning look and mouthed, *no names*.

"Learned there mighta been some industrial information that got to where it shouldn't. I guess the Japanese would rather sort this out in private than wash their dirty linen in public."

"Could I get your card?" I asked. "We might need some help cutting through red tape."

"Sure." He fished a silver card case out of his coat. "You need a lot of these in Japan. I'd be glad to help in any way. Really. You have an opportunity to make a point here on behalf of American business. I'd hate to see bureaucratic fumbling get in your way." He turned the card over, wrote something, and handed it to me. "Here's a personal number in case you need any help." I took it and put it in my wallet, next to Nico's.

Charlie pulled out his wallet and handed Auchincloss his card.

"Sorry I don't have one," I said. "It's still an ethics violation for lawyers in South Carolina to carry a business card. Advertising ban. Thanks for offering. We'll definitely be in touch in a few weeks."

"No advertising? That might be the only activity that's out of bounds for lawyers." I smiled to humor him. "I used to deal with plaintiff's lawyers when I was a corporate executive. Products liability and everything else."

Madison came up the stairs and joined us at the bar. She declined a mimosa but asked for soda water. I introduced her to Auchincloss. "Will you excuse us Clyde? We've got some things to discuss before we land."

"Of course. But please. I mean it. Contact me if there's anything you need." He finished the last sip of his drink and headed down the spiral staircase.

Except for us, the lounge was empty. We sat on a curved bench surrounding a small table, both bolted to the floor, and talked over our plans for tomorrow. I was meeting Evan Garrett, an associate from the Swinton firm, Minimura's New York lawyers. Charlie had a visit planned with a friend. He invited us for an early morning walk.

Madison passed. "I need all the sleep I can get right now."

My meeting wasn't until one. We would meet for dinner at seven the next evening. Madison and Charlie headed back downstairs, leaving me noodling on a cocktail napkin over ideas for my meeting with Garrett.

Chapter 71
FIRST-CLASS LOUNGE, JAL 747

"May I join you?" I looked up to see Harry, the Japanese scientist from our group, standing quietly.

"Please sit down. Can I get you a drink?"

"No thank you, Mr. Payne."

"Harry, call me Jake." I remembered the emotion that came over him when we met at Cameron. "This must be quite an experience for you, returning home after so long.".

"It will be very strange, yes. Even now I am unsure how I will act."

"Act? What do you mean?"

"In Japan, you must consider your status relative to each person you are in contact with. You must choose the correct relationship in order to determine how you stand, how you bow, even the grammar you use."

I had no idea it could be that complicated. "The grammar?"

"There is one kind of speech for a man to use, another for a woman. And there are different words, endings of words, for the many levels of honorific speech depending on your position and that of the other person."

"That sounds exhausting. English must seem simple."

"In America, the language is not simple for me, but getting along with people is much easier." He went silent for a while. "I am not sure I will recall the proper ways to act." Then he added softly, with some difficulty, "Or that I want to."

"Why is that?"

"Coming to the States changed me. The sense of freedom was frightening at first. As time went on, it was like I could breathe for the first time." He was talking very quietly in his careful, precise way. "I could focus on what was real, what mattered, not on what I was afraid someone else might think of my behavior. It allowed me to think new things, to do new things." He looked surprised at what he was saying. "It changed the way I studied, how I learned. It was as if a large weight was lifted from my shoulders and a cloud removed from my brain."

He still wrestled with something.

"Are you concerned the cloud might return?"

He looked up suddenly, startled. "Yes . . . yes. I think that is it!"

I watched. He sat up straight, suddenly hopeful, bold.

"You know, Harry, we're grateful for what you are doing. Not just for Consolidated, but for the team, for each of us. We need all the assistance you can give us. We are in this together. If there's anything I can do to make this easier for you, please take me aside, any time."

His shoulders relaxed a little. We needed him in top form in Tokyo. "Going back to Japan does not mean you have to give up what you have gained. If you feel it's helpful to be, well, Japanese, you can be. But if you want to be free, you can be that, too. You can choose whenever you want to." We sat for a long while in silence.

"I believe you are right, Mr. . . . uh, Jake." He smiled with relief. "Yes, that is what I was trying to understand." He looked at me directly for the first time. "I could not imagine having this conversation with a Japanese person, especially with a boss." His smile broadened into a grin. "And never with such a young boss. You have helped me. I must thank you."

Harry stood up, bowed slightly, and went back down the circular staircase.

As I stared at my scratchings on a cocktail napkin, images of scores of Swinton and Nakashima lawyers plotting against us leapt to mind again. I had a lot more back-up going into this fight than I'd had back in Texas, fighting that owner's rep, Boyden. Charlie, Madison, Harry, and all the CT experts. Corporate support from the top.

But the tip of the spear, the fight to win the legal case, would be between Evan Garrett and me. We were on Minimura's home ground. He had legal resources like the one's I had rejected from Nico . . . though I was sure they would not have done me any good.

Chapter 72
TOKYO, MONDAY, JANUARY 1, 1979

Charlie and I left the hotel early the next morning and followed the hotel map for a brisk walk to Tsukiji, the Tokyo fish market. There we saw tons of every marine species imaginable unloaded, auctioned, and carted off. The cold morning air bore the sharp tang of saltwater. Flashing scales and odd wet creatures poured from trucks that had rushed their contents from the nearby port.

"I love Tokyo this time a morning," Charlie said. "Not so crowded."

We watched workers at a food stall slurping down hearty bowls of seafood soup full of seaweed, eyeballs, and tentacles. "Not after a twelve-hour flight," Charlie warned.

As we walked, he pointed out old haunts that hadn't been razed for post-war development. There seemed to be building height restrictions in the center of Tokyo like in Washington, probably due to the frequent earthquakes in Japan. Massive undifferentiated office blocks marched in rows down the streets of Marunouchi, the business district near our hotel, the Imperial.

"I'm meeting a friend at the Dunkin' Donuts, under the railroad."

"I'll find my way back."

"Naw. Come on. You'll like Nakamura. Ever'one calls him K, just K. He's a Buddhist monk." Charlie steamed ahead and, as usual, I had to catch up.

"How do you know him?

"Work. C.I.D. He'as young then, like me, but learning to be a Buddhist priest. Studied English as a boy. Translators was in short supply during the Occupation. They'd put ever'one from bigwigs to street thugs in prison. He got a whole lotta experience in a hurry. When I got here, he helped me a bunch. Met lotsa interesting people through him. Got me outta a lotta jams."

I could see the Dunkin' Donuts sign ahead. "What does he do now?"

"Wife's family owns a temple. More like a business, I'd say. Big fees for ceremonies. But he's got a regular job during the week with some kinda trade association."

"Ah, Charlie. It is very good to see you." A soft, low voice interrupted our chatter.

We both started and turned to see wide-open eyes set in a curious brown face, peering from behind thick lenses.

"K," Charlie slapped the man on the back, "you old horse trader. He loves westerns, Jake. Moves silent, like a snake. Nearly scared me ta death."

Charlie introduced me as his lawyer. K's voice was mild, somehow soothing. I had to strain to hear him. He called me "*sensei*". Charlie explained that meant an honorable person, like a teacher. I wasn't sure lawyers qualified. K seemed about Charlie's age, dark skinned, thin, bald, as, well, as a Buddhist monk.

"How's business?

"It is, ah, always most interesting and, ah, very curious. Many people, you see, mistake business for reality. As we know, Charlie, reality is something deeper on which business is just, ah, floating, like a lotus on a pond."

"Still talking in them Zen riddles," Charlie grinned. "You keep up with any of the old crowd? What about Goat Boy, or Slim Yi? And that nice kid in Korea, Baik?"

"Goat Boy. He met an unfortunate end. He irritated some . . . , ah, I think you could say, powerful people."

"Sounds about right. I never trusted that *yakuza*. And he smelled bad, too. *Whooee*!"

"Slim Yi is different, Charlie. Married beautiful Filipina, very nice trading company in Manila. Very easy for a Chinese man, if he has bodyguards. Very rich. Very respectable. His son is senator."

"That sounds about right, too, K. He knew the price a everything down to the last *sen*. How about Baik? I liked that boy. He sure had it tough."

"Yes. Henry Baik never found his family. He now works in US Embassy in Seoul."

"No kidding. I thought he was purchasing stuff for the PXs?"

"That, too, but through other people. That powerful air base commander, General Davis. Henry saved him many headaches in Korea. Henry wanted job in Embassy. Wrote to General. Got job. Still there. We have, ah, some business together."

"This could go on for a while, K. I'm hungry."

"Should we eat here, Charlie?"

I looked up at the massive rusted metal and soot-stained concrete railroad superstructures hugging the small donut and breakfast shop.

"I don't think so, K. This is just the only place I knew would still be standing. Let's go somewheres we won't get sick."

"I know a place you will like. Many crazy people there. They will have a *bonenkai* party. You are welcome too, Payne-*sensei*."

"Jake," Charlie explained, "January the first's called *shogatsu* in Japan, a national holiday. Ever'one gets together for a big party to put the worries of the old year behind."

"Sounds like the Cotton Fields, Charlie."

I thanked them but declined. Charlie pointed me back to the hotel and they took off, leaving me alone to meet Evan Garrett.

Chapter 73
LOBBY, IMPERIAL HOTEL, TOKYO, 1PM, THE SAME DAY

The New York lawyer was easy to spot. Tall, lean, impatient, wearing a tailored dark gray suit.

"Evan? Evan Garrett?"

"Payne."

"Jake Payne." I reached out to shake hands. No response. "Why don't we talk in the coffee shop?"

He had blondish hair—just long enough to say prep school, Ivy League, Upper East Side Manhattan—and clear ice-blue eyes.

"I'd like to go over our requests and the delivery logistics," I said.

He reached into a soft top-grain black leather document bag and pulled out some papers.

"Here's how it's going to work, Payne." The temperature of the conversation started dropping from its chilly start. "The first documents will be handed over Thursday."

"That's in three days!" I objected.

"Minimura has questions about the others."

My irritation grew, as Garrett intended. "The first docs should be handed over tomorrow morning, with your questions," I said, "which could have been sent two weeks ago, after you got our requests." Tom's agreement said nothing about delays.

Ignoring my complaints, Garrett said, "We will have the leaders from each side meet tomorrow at Minimura headquarters, then have lunch in the executive dining room." That was also in the agreement. These guys had thought out every possible delay beforehand.

"In the afternoon we will provide you with our questions. If your answers are satisfactory, the first documents will be available at Minimura on Thursday." He was holding the first docs hostage, no quarter given.

He plowed on. "We will assign a Minimura employee to each member of your team. It will facilitate communication." Within Minimura only, I was sure, They would monitor every movement, each document, every discussion, or minor chat, and, if they could, our thoughts.

Their plan was thorough, dilatory, suffocating and there was no contract mechanism I could invoke to fight back

Chapter 74
NEAR THE IMPERIAL PALACE GROUNDS, TOKYO, 1:30PM, THE SAME DAY

With the arrival of the Americans, Shin had taken rooms at the Kudan Kaikan Hotel not far from the Imperial Palace. Before the war, the hotel had been the military club from which the Young Officer's clique had launched their abortive coup on the passive civilian government in 1934. The staff of the hotel still revered the young rebels as national heroes and were eager to provide any service to Shin, head of the War-Bereaved Families Association.

Since he connected Deng's US visit to the launch of the American's version of Kano's optical computing technology, Shin had pushed his organization incessantly. They made thorough surveillance arrangements that he could monitor from the hotel. The management installed phone lines, radio antennae, whatever Shin required.

The first report was coming in from Shin's men parked outside the Imperial Hotel. They had sighted Hara. Shin listened over the speaker.

"He is leaving the hotel. It is the older Japanese from the book." Shin's network had obtained the names of the

CT group from Kano and had researched each one. Hara, as a Japanese, was of primary interest.

Thirty minutes later Shin's team reported that Hara, still on foot, was nearing the tourist café on the esplanade in front of the Imperial Palace.

"He is approaching a Japanese, a younger man. They are going inside and sitting down."

Shin motioned to the leader of the surveillance details. "Have them go in and try to listen."

They could not hear the conversation. After about forty minutes, their target stood up and offered his hand. The other man started to reach for it, then bowed and left in a hurry.

Shin issued orders. "We know where Hara is going. Follow the other one. Find out who he is."

Chapter 75
CAFE, IMPERIAL PALACE ESPLANADE

Hara, Sato's uncle, had written him to say he was coming to Japan and suggested they meet. Sato was a boy when his uncle left Japan to study in the US. The younger man had arrived in Tokyo by train earlier from Tsukuba City, a new science and innovation hub where he lived and worked. From Tokyo Station, he had called the Imperial Hotel to leave directions, eager to meet his uncle.

Sato bowed but his uncle offered his hand. Sato shook it. His uncle insisted Sato call him Harry. They went inside. It was awkward at first. They covered work and shared scientific interests. Gradually they relaxed, exchanging family news and some good stories, and talked about life in Japan and the US. Sato liked Harry very much. He reminded Sato of his friends in the U.S., quick, open, curious. But speaking Japanese.

After he returned from Hawaii, Sato learned from a friend in the Minimura P.E.T. department that they were preparing for a visit by CT. He'd observed Kano's office closely and searched it whenever he could. That's how he'd come across the names of the CT delegation to

Minimura, emboldening him to send his anonymous letter to Dr. Whitmire.

Sato viewed the CT visit as an extraordinary *zenshō yusho*, a surprise victory, that raised his hope to explore the possibility of meeting Dr. Whitmire before he had to leave to catch his train back to Tsukuba City.

"Uncle, what is it that you are doing in Japan?"

"I'm here for my company." Harry said, without more.

"Consolidated Technologies, you wrote. I have heard about their famous polymer division."

"Do you work with them?"

"No, Uncle. But I have some interest in the work of a person of the research there. Do you know anyone in that division?"

"Very few. Who would that be?"

"A Dr. Whitmire,"

"But I came here with her!" Harry blurted out. The surprise on his face turned quickly to a frown.

For Sato, the chance to warn her was suddenly real and immediate, but he did not know what to do. His uncle was staring at Sato, ill at ease, his open friendliness suspended.

"I read a report on her research in a journal. If you were not too busy, perhaps . . . perhaps I could meet her."

His uncle said nothing. Sato was disappointed. He had to leave before he said something that would offend or could get his uncle in trouble. Abruptly, he stood up.

"My last train is leaving soon. Thank you for meeting, uncle." His uncle offered his hand. Sato's palms were sweating like in Hawaii. He had to bow instead.

Chapter 76
TOKYO, FRIDAY EVENING, JANUARY 19

We'd been working flat out for eighteen days straight, twenty hours or more each day. Every night I called Tom O'Hanlon to give him updates. They weren't good.

Garrett's responses to our requests were exasperating. The first week had been bad, the second, worse. Written replies from Minimura were systematically late. Instead of scorched earth, Garrett's firm had chosen the blizzard defense: provide everything possible, but nothing useful. Our team altered their review process several times, working with our two tireless translators and Harry's glossary to try to process documents more quickly, but we were drowning. That and hopeless optimism, not any revealing discoveries, was why we'd extended into a third week. My anomaly-spotting methods only worked if had enough time. But we didn't.

Most of the team was getting by on five or six hours of sleep a night. Me, a little less. I had to debrief Madison and Charlie, summarize the results, and call Tom O'Hanlon to catch him in the morning in New York. I could feel the pressure from the executive suite in his voice, shooting down the international cable. Each question hit me like a hammer. My tepid answers left me depressed.

At the end of our last day of document review in Tokyo, I sat up front with the taxi driver as we headed to our hotel. Jerry, Charlie, and another engineer were stuffed in back. I looked at a poorly written note in my file and said, “Charlie, what did your tenter expert say about the last Minimura production report . . . . Charlie . . . . Jerry?” I turned to see why they weren’t answering. All three were fast asleep. During a ten-minute ride.

Madison and Charlie were in my room for our evening recap before I called Tom. It felt like the walls were closing in. Our final document request had been perfunctory, the response useless. All the team had left to do was the plant visit.

Madison summed up her areas. “We have some references in the research, development and marketing monthly summaries to topics Malinkrodt talked about, but so few that they could just be random. And nothing we can tie directly to significant giveaways.”

“How about the production records, Charlie?”

“Nothing so far. And this is all they say they got. I hated this part in the army. You knew it was there, but you couldn’t prove it. We ain’t got no smoking gun. We ain’t got no gun. We just got a bunch a smoke and it’s blowin’ away fast.”

In an hour, we would leave to catch the bullet train to Nagahama and the factory audit with damned few leads. The only real evidence we’d added confirmed that Malinkrodt had worked directly with Minimura while still an employee of Consolidated. But we had no proof he handed over anything of value to Minimura.

After the factory visit Saturday, we’d decided everyone needed a break. We’d visit the ancient capital of Nara Sunday morning, then stay in Kyoto at a nice hotel, and return to Tokyo Monday morning to interview Kano at the Consulate and draft the final report for Tom O'Hanlon.

Chapter 77

WASHINGTON, D.C., FRIDAY NOON, THE SAME DAY

TWELVE HOURS AHEAD OF TOKYO TIME

Nico was waiting for Tom at the Old Ebbitt Grill near the White House. Since it opened in 1856, pictures, beer steins, and political memorabilia had spread abundantly over every vertical surface. The DARPA investigation results, in contrast, had been meager. Since the team meeting at Cameron, two executives were Nico's only remaining targets.

To go any further, he had to request court ordered wiretaps and surveillance. The new FISA procedures were a problem. DOJ lawyers were nervous. No one wanted to set a bad precedent.

Tom settled into the booth. He'd been at the U. S. Patent Office in Alexandria and had stayed over to meet Nico. "Any news?"

"No unusual money showed up in any of Staley's or Untermeyer's known accounts."

"Jake was convinced Staley was reporting to Untermeyer. Can we get more about him?"

"I have to go through the DOJ and the courts for more aggressive action." Nico and his boss had been arguing for weeks. "I don't think I'll get approval to go that route."

Nico didn't have anything else to offer. "How's it going in Tokyo?"

"Not great," Tom admitted. "Minimura has dumped a massive number of documents, but nothing incriminating has turned up. They're headed for the factory visit with almost nothing in hand. I saw Untermeyer at a meeting and he almost laughed in my face. Jake was right. By waiting to send Weidl's deposition, we gave them time to prepare for the visit. The team is burnt out. They're going to take a break for the weekend before they pack up."

Nico felt trapped. The violence after Weidl's deposition and the strange OC-X reference were compelling. He had joined the CIA while there were still some of the original hands present, before they were hounded out of the Agency. He'd experienced the pall the Senate investigation had cast over those who remained: the excessive caution, the circumspect analysis, the endless meetings with no decisions taken. Now there was FISA. The political risks for audacious intelligence work were compounded by criminal legal risks.

This might be Nico's last chance to make a difference. He didn't want to give up without a fight. Jake had made a courageous, if foolhardy, decision to stick it out and give it his best shot. Nico had promised to do whatever he could. He needed more than his boss at DARPA, Dave Stancill, was willing to support, which was almost nothing.

Chapter 78
NAGAHAMA, JAPAN, SATURDAY, JANUARY 20

We had arrived late Friday evening at the town of Hikone after taking the *shinkansen* bullet train from Tokyo. It was the dead of winter, not the summer tourist season. The skeleton staff at our cheap, dreary hotel spoke almost no English. Even Harry had a hard time with the local accent to get my call through to Tom. My report had been short and painful.

The next morning, we took taxis to the factory in the nearby town of Nagahama. The road ran along the shore of Lake Biwa, the biggest lake in Japan. It was cold and rainy in the pre-dawn dark. Spray from wind whipping off the lake buffeted our cars, coating the road with a treacherous sheet of ice.

As we turned away from the lakeshore, we passed between towering rocks and entered the town. Black-streaked concrete houses and dimly lit storefronts squatted along the roadside. They looked captive, trussed behind power cables and telephone lines hanging from grimy concrete poles. The view was depressing. The results of the day's work were worse.

It was early evening, already dark outside the Minimura plant. The lights throughout the factory site were dim. It was damp and cold even in the offices. All of Japan, except the Ginza shopping area in Tokyo, seemed driven to save electricity. The team had inspected the factory and was comparing notes to what they had filtered out of the Minimura documents. Groups of Consolidated and Minimura engineers huddled around the large conference tables, exchanging comments. The conditions were raw and so were tempers.

Charlie had been a dervish. He'd gone through the plant three times with each different CT process team, prodding, crawling over equipment, questioning line operators through interpreters. Madison kept up the same furious pace. She would review the documents with Harry and the tech team, huddle with Charlie, then try to tie it all together. No one from CT was quitting.

At first, the Japanese engineers had been courteous. But Charlie, Madison, and I all noticed that as the questions about the factory continued, the engineers became more defiant in their replies. Two of the younger Japanese in particular became aggressive. Madison and Charlie had to intervene to keep emotions in check and to keep the team focused on technical issues.

We were nearly done when an argument broke out between Charlie and one of the two young engineers. I walked over as Charlie was pointing to a drawing.

"What's on Line Two, at the entrance to the tenter on the left side, ain't the way it's shown on the plant drawing. Somebody done changed it. And looky here."

Charlie pulled out a copy of one of the documents from Weidl's deposition.

"See this here guide at the side of the tenter?" He reached for a copy of one of the handwritten notebooks from Malinkrodt's lectures and pointed to Harry's handwritten translation of a passage. "Here, on this little sketch, right there? See it? That's a drawing of this here thingamabob that's on a CT machine. What you put on your Line 2 does what this thing does at Cameron. It's just built a bit different. But it wasn't there before Malinkrodt's lectures and now it is. We got the before and after drawings. How come?"

"No, no, no," the young engineer objected in English. "Is not same. Is not doing same thing. Look." He started to write something on the plant drawing copy. I was impressed once more at how fast the Japanese could write their complex characters. Then I looked closer. The engineer was writing an explanation. In printed English. Upside down. So Charlie could read it. No one from Minimura was quitting, either.

Charlie stared at the young man, then broke out into a wide grin and laughed. "I got ta hand it to ya Mikimoto. You're fast on our feet. But you're wrong."

"Name is Minamoto, not Mikimoto," the engineer shot back.

"Well, they's both mice," Charlie said to the dumbfounded engineer. "And these two things is doing the same thing, one in our plant in Cameron, one out there on Line Two. Just like Malinkrodt told ya."

Minamoto started to object but one of the minders who accompanied them everywhere put a hand on the young man's shoulder and frowned slightly. I remembered this patent lawyer had claimed that he had never been to Nagahama. I doubted it then and I didn't believe it now. The young engineer stood up and walked away.

"You okay with that, Charlie?"

"I got all I can get."

"What was that about?"

"It ain't a smoking gun, Jake. But it ain't nothing. We worked nigh on to six months to get that tenter guide worked out. It solved a wrinkle problem and let us run up the tenter speed a good bit. Malinkrodt didn't know why, but he knowed enough to get 'em fooling around with it. We got four or five other things like that we seen today. And they's in the documents we been pawing through ever since we got to Japan."

"You want to go further tonight?"

"No sense. That's it. We's done."

Back at the hotel, Charlie, Madison, and I sat at a table in the cold hotel dining room. Cheap plastic plants covered with dust cast gloom over the area, the opposite of the faint cheer that they were meant to provide. In a far corner, Japanese factory workers we'd seen arrive on a tourist bus warmed up with beer and *saké* after finishing their dinner. Harry said they were on a winter holiday and must have lost the vacation schedule lottery.

After a long exchange between Harry and the headwaiter, the kitchen had come up with some pan-fried spam, canned corn, and more rice, plus three Sapporo beers. We'd turned down the offer of Tora beer on principle. It was made by Minimura. After what passed for dinner, the rest of our team had gone across the road to a Pachinko parlor. Charlie said the game was like slot machines but more mind numbing. This was the first chance the three of us had to talk now that the factory visit was over.

"Madison, overall, what do you think about what we saw today?" I asked.

"I agree with Charlie, Jake. For the first time since we got here, we have some things we can argue about. It's not one-for-one copying, but we can put them on the table."

"Charlie, has any of that led to performance and quality improvements that could prove damages?"

"Well, that's the tough part. You can see they's trying hard but on this equipment it doesn't do much for 'em. They'd need a whole new line to really ramp it up."

Madison said, "It goes back to what you explained in our first meeting, Jake. How Malinkrodt could mask knowledge and lead them to something? From all we've seen today, either he did a good job of that, or he didn't really understand what the improvements meant, and couldn't explain their full impact. Either way, there's not a lot of value we can identify. After all the effort and expense, our findings aren't worth much."

This was the most candid, gloomy appraisal I'd heard. Our month-long effort was limping to a bleak, disappointing end. "That's all? We're done?"

"That's about it, pardners." Charlie added a warning. "If we's not careful, we'll finish what Malinkrodt began just by asking more questions, and neither CT nor none of us'll get paid for it, except the lawyer here." Charlie grinned and faked a sharp right to my jaw. Then he leaned back. "I'm plumb tuckered out, ya'll. I'm heading up."

Madison and I lingered over our beers, grabbing a welcome moment of peace. During the non-stop work ever since our deep conversation at Cameron, a close bond of cooperation had grown between us, and Charlie.

"Should we go to Nara and Kyoto tomorrow or is that just too much?" she asked.

"We could split into groups, those that want a tour and those that want more rest."

"Well, I doubt Harry and Yoshi will be coming along. They're totally exhausted. Without translators, we have to stick together so we don't lose anyone."

"All together then." I smiled. "'Innocents Abroad.'"

We sat in silence. It was a calm, easy moment, until my mind jumped to a topic we'd covered each night in Tokyo.

"I wouldn't expect anything to show up here, Madison. But I have to ask. Any clues about OC-X?"

"Not a hint."

"Well, that's good then, right?"

"In a way, yes. I guess. Everything we've seen on the technical side from Weidl through today is only about plastic film, not optics or data transmission through polymers, except for the sole reference in Mueller's handwritten note."

"But it's like we've said about production, Jake. Proving a negative is impossible. Would it be better to catch them red handed with OC-X materials or data? Of course not. But we may never know what that note meant. That leaves a big hole in our investigation and a cloud over my work. I'm left with questions that will stick with me for . . . well, for a long time."

Her shoulders sagged as she stared at the foam sliding down the side of her glass of beer. She was the inventor, responsible for research security, in on the investigation. And she would probably never know what was behind that one maddening reference.

"Madison." She turned her head and I looked into her worried eyes. "You've done all you can. You've got Houston to look forward to. That will be a success and you can put all of this behind you."

A warm but tired smile spread across her lovely face.

"Thanks, Jake." She took my hand and gave it a grateful squeeze.

Chapter 79
TOKYO, THE SAME EVENING

Shin and Kano were in the Veteran's Bar on the top floor of the Kudan Kaikan Hotel. All the other men in the bar were of Shin's generation and had no doubt served in some capacity for the Emperor, military or civilian, before and during the war.

The hotel was public, managed under a grant from the government. Many of the old soldiers stayed there when they came to visit the *Yasukuni-Jinja,* the nearby shrine honoring those who had served the Emperor in the eleven major military conflicts since 1867. Even at this time of year, some would go upstairs to the closed rooftop beer garden that overlooked the Imperial Palace moat and gaze silently at the shrine, remembering.

In the distance, they could see the massive red metal *torii,* the traditional Japanese gate separating the mundane from the sacred, at the entrance to the *Yasukuni* shrine. In spring, the rooftop provided a magnificent view of *sakura,* the Japanese cherry blossoms that covered the far hill leading down to the Imperial moat during their short lives.

The flowers were a symbol to all Japanese of the beauty and fragility of life. They had been used in poetry to evoke the lives of *kamikaze* pilots.

Shin had grilled Kano each evening about the work of the CT team. "Are your defenses still holding strong?"

Watanabe, the patent lawyer, had called Kano from Nagahama to give the report Kano was passing on to Shin. "They finished their inspection of the factory this evening and have almost nothing to show for their visit to Japan."

"Almost?" Shin fixed his gaze on Kano. "Did they find something? With all the effort and expense of your preparations how could that happen?"

"They have only uncovered a handful of minor experiments that our patent lawyers meant for them to discover. If they went home empty-handed after so much effort, they would be humiliated and angry. They might try to create mischief for us with their unpredictable legal system."

Kano was clever, like his father. When Shin had caught errors in the old man's reports, the wily accountant had pointed out that they were of no consequence. They had been left in on purpose to distract the auditors from much larger and harder to find monetary diversions.

"Do you have reason to believe that they are satisfied with the result?" Shin demanded.

"They are vexed, of course, but these planned 'discoveries' create a release of tension and some comfort that their trip was not in vain. They leave Nagahama tomorrow morning to visit Nara, then the rest of the day in Kyoto, to relax."

Shin sniffed. Such soft, unworthy opponents. "Then you will be rid of them?"

"We will meet next week in Tokyo. By our agreement, I must give sworn testimony at their embassy. They will use it against Malinkrodt. I have rehearsed with our lawyers for the past week."

Kano was thorough, but Shin bridled at the shame of a Japanese citizen submitting to the badgering trickery of a foreigner in his own country.

Kano was quick to reassure Shin. "I will reveal nothing except to confirm that Malinkrodt was here and talked about readily known production information."

"What about Sato?" After the meeting in front of the Imperial Palace, Shin's researchers had uncovered the traitor Hara's application for a Fulbright Scholarship and found his home village. That led them to the link to Sato, Hara's nephew.

"I have added a great deal of work on top of his regular duties. And your men have kept up their surveillance. He is overwhelmed. That has blocked him from further contact with his uncle."

Shin knew things were going well in Japan. That was a good omen for his ultimate objective. It was less than two weeks until the American rocket launch at Houston in Deng's presence. Now was not the time to lessen vigilance. The contact between Sato and his uncle caused Shin concern. Sato had identified the cause of the failure at Kagoshima. And the American woman expert was here in Japan. Shin would keep the traitor Japanese Hara and the woman under surveillance until they left Japan.

Since he had learned of the link between Sato and his uncle from America, Shin had given more detailed instruction to his man in the US to give to the lawyers, the one inside Consolidated, and the one at the New York law firm. All was ready.

"We must drink to the success of our final thrust."

Shin motioned to an attendant who left and returned carrying a tray laden with a graceful porcelain flask, two small rough-finished cups, and a finely grained irregular wooden box grown dark with age. The vessels represented the imperfection of nature wrought by the seasoned hand of a master craftsman and worn by use.

The contrasting elegance and rustic simplicity merged in a pleasing harmony.

The flask contained a measure of rare *daiginjō-shu*, prized alcohol made with *Yamada nishiki* and *Miyamizu*, the finest rice and water from the *Nada* region. This rice wine had been a favorite of the *shōgun* and of the nobility of the Edo period for over three-hundred years.

Shin took the *masu*, an antique box that once graced the palace of the *shōgun* and placed one of the *choku* cups inside it. Then he poured the wine from the *tokkuri* flask into the cup in front of Kano. Shin let the clear liquid flow down the *choku* and pool in the *masu*.

The apparent waste was in fact a careful gesture of generosity. He held the brimming *choku* in both hands and presented it to Kano to show trust and harmony. In turn, Kano took up the flask, filled the remaining cup to overflowing, and presented it in the same way to Shin. They raised their offerings in anticipation of the final ordeal and savored the complex flavors as the alcohol warmed them.

It was a ritual cleansing, a ceremonial act. The intricate plans Shin had developed to assure Deng's death had invigorated him as only extreme danger and violence had when he was young. Now his arrows were drawn in their bows, ready to be sent on their way toward their intended targets. With his guidance, they would find their marks over the next few short weeks.

Chapter 80
ARLINGTON, VIRGINIA, SATURDAY AFTERNOON, THE SAME DAY

TWELVE HOURS AHEAD OF TOKYO TIME

Nico stared out the window of the DARPA suite in the new office tower in Crystal City, watching the icy Potomac River slide by. Dave Stancill had called him in on a Saturday when he knew no one else would be around. Stancill refused to let Nico go to the Department of Justice to seek FISA authority for domestic surveillance.

"No way, Amalfitano. I will not stick my neck out for some CIA inspired stunt. The Senate Intelligence Committee is primed for any monkeying around with FISA. I'm not going to let you put my pension at risk."

As a son of Italian immigrants, Nico had a rough time growing up in a rundown Irish neighborhood in Massachusetts. He'd pushed back, hard, and earned grudging respect during no-holds-barred ice hockey games in the Pit, on a frozen lake inside an abandoned quarry.

The CIA had been a way for Nico to give back for his parents' sacrifice in coming to America and promoting his education. It had taken an effort to make his way. Even in law school, where his grades were excellent and he was invited into the inner sanctum of a secret society and onto the prestigious Jefferson Lecture organizing committee, he was often given the grunt work. It had only confirmed his resolve after he'd returned to the CIA.

He had earned recognition for his tenacious investigation of foreign espionage. His DARPA assignment was intended to broaden his business experience before he returned to counter-intelligence.

Yet here he was, stymied in a potentially explosive espionage case. Despite his promises, he was unable officially to help Jake and the team in Tokyo working to uncover the truth behind the OC-X reference. So Nico had put his pension on the block.

An old friend from the clandestine section owed him. When Nico explained the context, his colleague was eager to help. He had access to the latest surveillance equipment that even the FBI had not received. Nico told him to stick like flypaper to Felix Untermeyer and report every detail to Nico, outside the office.

Nico had viewed the first product, a video tape, in his basement at home last night.

In the surveillance film, Untermeyer took a circuitous route from his CT office, watching his back carefully. Nico could see him enter the Shamrock Bar on 47th Street near Rockefeller Center and join a well-dressed man sitting at a table towards the rear. The picture fuzzed up, then resolved as the camera adjusted to the low-light conditions.

The sound cut in at this point as the hypersensitive directional microphone was switched on.

"Well?" Untermeyer demanded.

"It's a go. We're working on the material. It will take some time, a week, perhaps less, but it will be exactly what you need. Are you sure you will get access undetected?"

"That is no problem," Untermeyer snapped. "You know I convinced John McElwain to put me in charge."

"Yes, but you have always been alone before," the other man pointed out. He seemed displeased.

"I have explained how that will be handled." Despite his outward calm, Nico saw Untermeyer was fidgeting with his hands and his voice had turned slightly shrill. "You have nothing to be concerned about."

Untermeyer got up and left and the tape ended.

Nico had made the right decision. The investigation had hit pay dirt. His man had let Untermeyer go back to the office and had followed the contact instead.

Chapter 81
KYOTO, JAPAN, SUNDAY AFTERNOON, JANUARY 21

We left Nagahama early on the train to the hoary capital of Nara as planned. On the ancient grounds, a giant bronze Buddha was enclosed in a massive wooden building, the biggest in the world. It was surrounded by mossy trails flanked by ancient stone lanterns and thickets of ferns. Deer roamed unchecked through the silent park. It was difficult for an American to understand the seeming jumble of images carefully preserved over eleven centuries.

The guidebook contained vague references to Chinese influences, adding to the complexity and obscurity of the site. It was as disorienting and unfathomable as everything else we had confronted since we landed in Tokyo.

We got back on the train, arrived in Kyoto, and got to the Miyako Princess Hotel by one o'clock.

The alarm woke me in a totally dark room. I'd crashed as soon as we'd arrived and set the alarm so I wouldn't miss my appointment, then I had closed the curtains. At first I didn't know where I was. Then I remembered it was still Sunday afternoon.

I shook my head and got up. I heard the door of Madison's room next to mine click shut. She said she might walk into the city. I intended to spend the afternoon letting the staff in the spa help me unwind. The knots in my shoulders, neck, and everywhere else needed professional attention.

The spa was not far from my room. The attendant showed me to a locker. I folded my clothes, put the large towel around my waist, and followed a sign to the shower. There were individual stations. I hung my towel on a peg and sat down buck-naked on a squat wooden stool. There was a shower head low on the wall with a flexible plastic hose and a tray on the floor with an array of soaps and lotions.

Following another man's example, I washed slowly, lathering up and rinsing several times, enjoying the foaming soap and the hot water washing away unruly thoughts of the unhelpful mass of Minimura documents and the maddening half-clues from the factory. I turned the temperature higher with each rinse. Finally, I wrapped my towel and headed to the communal bath.

Built on top of the floor, with steps and a railing to help climb up and enter, it was large, three by four meters, about one meter deep. It was covered inside and out in ceramic tile, with a bench around the inside. Several men sat immersed to their necks, basking in the heat with their eyes mere slits as steam rose off the water. The attendant came up, grunted, took my towel, and left. I stepped on the edge of the bath, held the rail, and put my foot in the water.

Owwwwhhaaa! It was scalding hot. I thought my toes had exploded as pain shot up my leg. I bit my tongue and yanked my foot out of the water.

I looked around. No one seemed to notice my discomfort and loss of dignity. I tried again. As I eased in, the submerged parts adjusted quickly, leaving a ring of pain at the water line. My anxiety spiked as my groin approached the surface of the steaming water.

Once the searing pain subsided, wisps of steam rose from the water, moistening my face. As the heat penetrated, my muscles abandoned their resistance. I was slowly roasting but didn't care. I could die here like the frog in boiling water: scalded, dumb, and happy.

The attendant appeared with a fresh towel, grunted, and motioned. As I stepped out of the bath, he wrapped me up tight, like a mummy. Then he led me to an alcove off another room of the spa. To my surprise a tiny woman in blindingly white shorts and shirt, and knee socks, but no shoes, bowed and indicated that I was to lie down on a pad covered with an equally sparkling sheet.

I started to comply when she gently touched my arm and signaled me to remove my towel. I lay down as fast as I could on my stomach and waited for a soothing rub down, while she covered her amused laugh with her hand and bowed in apology for my discomfort.

Suddenly the dainty figure slammed my back with her forearms. With hands like steel mallets, she pummeled my shoulders. Then with fingers like iron vises, she systematically assaulted every muscle in my body, pinching, pressing, and squeezing, finding every knot, and bearing down on them until the pain was excruciating. Then it went away and the muscles unwound. As with the bath, after the initial shock, warmth spread slowly, melting all tension away.

Just when I started to fall asleep, the woman climbed on my back and began another assault with her knees, legs, feet, and her full body weight. She stretched my head back and pulled it from side to side, twisted my hands and fingers, my arms, legs, and torso. My joints were cracking like pine knots in a fire.

By the time she climbed off and bowed deeply, I felt like a puddle on the table. She offered me a thick white robe and I had to summon up the will to put it on. The male attendant came up and handed me a cloth bag with my belongings in it, showed me a pair of yellowed plastic pre-war looking sandals, handed me a richly embossed envelope, and pointed me out the door of the spa. Too weak to object at wearing a robe down the hall, I took the bag and shuffled toward my room.

As I walked, I took a stiff card engraved in English and Japanese out of the envelope:

> *Dear Spa Guest, as a token of our appreciation a gift*
> *is being delivered to your room. We hope you enjoy it.*

Suddenly another door opened. Still staring at the note, I bumped into someone.

"Sorry," I said, looking up from the note.

"Jake!" It was Madison. She was also wrapped in a fluffy white robe with her own cloth bag and sandals.

"Madison! I thought you were going for a walk." My senses came alert as, all guile deactivated by the bath and massage, I gazed at her in wonder. Her blond hair tumbled in damp tresses to her shoulders. Her skin was soft and shining. We were so close I could feel the warmth streaming from her through my robe.

"I was, but then I thought you had a good idea. Wasn't it fantastic? I never thought I'd be this relaxed again. Maybe I never have been!" Her smile danced. She seemed oblivious to the strong impact her glowing appearance, sparkling enthusiasm, and closeness were having on me. I lowered the envelope to cover the evidence now growing under my robe. That only attracted her attention and a giggle.

I struggled for something to say, anything. "Did you have a masseur or a masseuse?"

"What a woman," Madison gushed. "I never knew the human body had so many instruments of torture. But the result is wonderful, isn't it? How was your masseur?"

"Well, to tell you the truth, he was a woman." I felt my face reddening.

"Jake, you *prude*!" Madison punched my arm, turned her head away slightly, and cut a mischievous glance at me as she laughed. "You're blushing!" Then she pirouetted gracefully, linked her arm in mine, and hugged it close to her as we started walking towards our rooms.

She turned again and raised an eyebrow. "Are you sure they only give massages in there? I've heard what happens in Asian spas for men."

I could feel her body moving under the thick terrycloth. "Madison, I forgot to ask about the full range of services." I tried not to stare at her lovely face, but I couldn't take my eyes off her. "Should I have?"

"That depends," she squeezed my arm and laughed again, "On how the whole thing affected your inhibitions."

"Well, if I had any going in, they've all been steamed and prodded into oblivion."

We arrived at our rooms. The door to mine opened and a bellboy stood there in surprise.

"So sorry, sir. I was just delivering warmed *saké*, a gift from the management." He bowed deeply and scurried off down the hall.

I turned to gaze at Madison. She was beautiful. We were warm, relaxed yet stimulated by the spa treatment. It was . . . . I should invite her in to share the *saké*. Maybe then . . . .

What the hell was I thinking?

"I'll call the management and see they deliver some *saké* to your room," I babbled. "See you at seven for dinner."

I nearly dove into my room, leaving Madison standing there, agape.

Chapter 82
TOKYO, LATE AFTERNOON, TUESDAY, JANUARY 23

Two days later, I was interviewing Kano at Minimura headquarters the day before his formal deposition. Garrett was there, on full alert. We only had a few items to claim damages for and we knew Minimura would fight them to the end. I didn't want that clogging up this testimony that would be read into the record at Malinkrodt's trial, my real focus. Kano was proud of his fluent English, so we weren't using an interpreter.

"Mr. Kano, did you and your team have access to the film production lines at Cameron during this visit?"

"Yes."

"And how did you get access?"

"Mr. Malinkrodt."

"Did he take you to the security checkpoint?"

"Yes."

"Did you and your team sign the entry log?"

"No."

"Why not?"

"Mr. Malinkrodt signed for us." That should pin Malinkrodt to the wall in a jury trial.

Madison and Harry were finishing up in the unheated basement of CT headquarters. On the train back from Kyoto, neither she nor Jake mentioned their encounter in the hotel, though she felt it hung in the air between them. She had not been that close to a man in years. Or that playful. While Jake interviewed Kano on the top floor, she and Harry checked document references for the team's final report.

Suzuki, the employee assigned to monitor Harry, stood breathing over Harry's shoulder, rubbing Harry's nerves raw. Harry spoke English to irritate Suzuki.

I had one more topic for Kano before I ended the interview. *Now he would give up OC-X.* Right. The spa at Kyoto had softened my brain, but I had to try for CT, for Nico, and for Madison.

"When you and Mr. Mueller first discussed the scope of Malinkrodt's lectures, who suggested the topics to be covered?"

"Mr. Mueller and Mr. Malinkrodt."

"You didn't request any?"

Kano looked at me with a hint of pity, and then said, "We always let the other side talk first."

"Did you add anything?"

"There was no need."

"Mr. Kano, was there anything they proposed that wasn't related to P.E.T. film?"

"No. Nothing." He didn't change his tone or pace. There was no indication he knew anything about OC-X. I had no basis for going further.

In the basement, Madison put down the last document from her stack. The team had little to show for a month of intense work. Was anything noteworthy? Her mind drifted unbidden back to the hotel in Kyoto with Jake. It could have been fun. The spa had put them both in the mood. But he had pulled back. Enjoying the easy friendship they had developed was probably right. It was certainly simpler. Still, she had to smile at his embarrassed arousal.

Harry chatted idly with Suzuki in Japanese for the first time since they'd arrived. Madison could tell by their body language that they were relaxing, having an animated but friendly discussion. They smiled and nodded in that synchronous way she'd seen between Japanese, encouraging each other to share.

Then Harry flinched. He recovered quickly, but he had been thrown off balance by something Suzuki said. Harry asked for some water and Suzuki left the room. Harry rushed over.

"This is incredible, Dr. Whitmire. We were discussing a fishing village we both know."

She smiled at his enthusiasm. "Is that important?"

"No, no. That's just a coincidence. But he said he couldn't vacation there this summer."

"Harry, what's the point?" Maybe there was some Japanese relationship thing she was missing.

"How many production lines are there at Nagahama?"

"Three. They have no expansion plans. We asked every way possible. Only three."

"You are right. But Suzuki cannot go fishing this summer because he and the whole central engineering department will be in Nagahama to accelerate installation of Line Four. A whole new production line!"

They grabbed Charlie from the room next to theirs. His face lit up at their news. "There ya go. A smoking gun."

I was about to finish up with Kano when Charlie stuck his head in the door and motioned me into the hall. I called for a break.

He leaned in as Madison explained the Line Four bomb.

"Charlie, how long does it take to plan one of these things?"

"Eighteen friggin' months."

This was too good to be true. And it was. "All you have is Suzuki's slip up?"

Charlie grinned. "Your turn, counselor. Work some a yer lawyer magic."

"Madison, go back and occupy Suzuki. Charlie, come with me. Let's go fishing."

"Now Mr. Kano." I looked down at a random document in the folder I held, then closed the cover and placed it on the table. "In the answer to interrogatory thirty from set two, Minimura says there are no plans to expand capacity at Nagahama, right?"

"That is correct."

"What do you have to do to plan a new film line?"

"What?" The first question that surprised Kano and finally something technical that I knew about: critical path scheduling, same as any construction project.

"We have a process."

I walked Kano through a rehearsal of the production line design process, looking at Charlie as my gaffe meter and keeping it as boring as I could. Kano was bewildered, then disengaged and indifferent. Garrett interrupted once, then gave up and let me drone on.

Finally Kano began to shift in his chair. His eyebrows knit a few times, the muscles around his mouth tightened. His boredom became impatience, then irritation.

"So, all together, we're talking about, uh . . . " I looked at my notes, "say, fifteen to eighteen months before you begin the installation?"

Kano rolled his eyes towards the ceiling. "Yes, yes. At least eighteen months. Some of the equipment will come from Germany."

An admission. My trap banged shut. I leaned in over the table and let loose, snapping words off like breaking dry twigs to start a fire.

"Then how can Minimura begin installation of a brand-new production Line Four at Nagahama in four months?"

Kano's gaze turned to stone and his jaws clenched shut. His cheek muscles spasmed like a landed fish. Garrett's face contorted and he grabbed the edge of the table. They'd just hit my brick wall, my story of the case. I had to keep cool and use the heat of my frustration that had piled up over the last month. I jumped to my feet and punched the air.

"Wait, a minute, Payne, you can't—"

"I can and I am, Garrett." I spit out the accusation. "Minimura kept back critical documents, lied in its answers to our interrogatories, and concealed development and design work at the factory, all in violation of our agreement."

"What documents?" Garrett demanded, recovering, trying to slow things down.

"Nothing you intended for us to see, I'm sure." A bluff, but I kept on mashing every button in sight. I stuck my finger in Kano's face. That had to be an unforgiveable insult in Japan. "I'm through being lied to by you, Mr. Kano."

Garrett's breathing rasped like a file dragged across iron. I turned on him, jamming my finger into his chest.

"I hope you're through being lied to." His face turned pasty-white. The bottom had just dropped out of his case. He knew about the deception. He had to. He'd orchestrated it.

Kano's stare swiveled between me and Garrett. I plowed on, amping up the volume.

"Mr. Kano, when did you decide to hide Minimura's theft of Consolidated Technologies' property and who helped you do it? *Tell me. **Right now.***"

Garrett jumped up and careened around the table.

"Hold on. You can't talk to him like that."

I planted my feet, sensing the chaos boiling up in Garrett's mind. His defense was in tatters, his client was on the ropes, there was a leak but he had no idea where or how he had missed it. I knew the primordial part of his brain had begun worrying about his career.

"Payne, stop. We have to talk."

He grabbed my arm.

"Watch it, Garrett." I yanked his arm away, shoved him hard, and moved to block Kano's view of his lawyer.

Garrett yelled at his client, "*Do not say another word. Payne, outside.*"

I barked, "Charlie, keep an eye on Mr. Kano. Call if he tries to leave."

We entered the hall. I could see fear and cunning fighting across Garrett's face while he sought to find a way to slow down the train wreck his case had just become.

"You don't understand Japanese culture, Payne. Things don't happen like in the West. No one man makes a decision. You cannot confront them like that. They cannot even understand what you are asking because it's a collective society." His uptown Manhattan accent dripped with condescension. He was beginning to recover from the blows I had landed. "They go to lunch. Everyone looks at the menu. Someone says, 'The hamburger would be nice.' Another says, 'The ham and cheese is good.'"

Fear was eating his cunning for lunch. It was pathetic.

"They go around the table, everyone with a different idea. At some point, and no one knows when or why, they all agree on the tuna salad."

His irrational overconfidence was good. Time to punch right through it..

"Garrett, save your bullshit. I know when I'm being lied to and you don't want to be involved. The last lawyer that tried that with me is under arrest in California." He had to know about Morgan.

Garrett started to speak. I stuck my palm in his face and growled, "Cut the crap. Kano and everyone at Minimura has been lying through their teeth to us since day one. And you and your law firm are under suspicion unless you all come clean."

A climax to our fight loomed like an oncoming train.

That was it. A train.

"We're suspending this interview. You choose, right now. Either we're on the bullet train for Nagahama tonight and Minimura coughs up all the information on Line Four. Or my team is on the next plane for New York and we'll see you in Federal Court in forty-eight hours."

Tom O'Hanlon would agree. I didn't know about the higher ups. Too bad. This was a Carolina cat fight, not a New York corporate tea dance. "Your choice. Five minutes."

"Payne. I must talk to my client."

"Talk all you want, Garrett." Time was our enemy. More delaying tactics like the blizzard of documents Garrett had thrown at us, could be fatal. So I had to put him in a vise and turned the screw on his decision time. "If you don't order the *shinkansen* tickets within the next five minutes, we're out of here and ordering our plane tickets home. Decide. Now. Your train or my plane. I'm not waiting."

We stepped back into the room. Garrett conferred animatedly with Kano, in Japanese, trying to eat up time.

I turned to Charlie and said in a loud, clear voice, "Go pack up. Hail four taxis." I headed toward the door, with Charlie scurrying to keep up with me this time.

We were halfway down the hall when Garrett yelled, "Wait!"

Chapter 83
SWINTON LAW FIRM, NEW YORK, 9AM,THE SAME DAY

TWELVE HOURS AHEAD OF TOKYO TIME

In Manhattan, Shin's man had received the call. He had been waiting in the lobby of a sleek midtown tower. Now he was parked in the corner office of the founding partner of Minimura's American litigation law firm, Austen Swinton. The lawyer was on the phone with Garrett and the Japanese lawyer, Nakashima, in Tokyo. A throbbing red vein split Swinton's forehead in two.

"Garrett, you fool. How did they find out about Line Four? No way you will cough up the design—"

"Shut up, Swinton," Shin's man interrupted. "Tell him to turn over all the Line Four documents and get off the phone."

Swinton hesitated. No one told a senior partner what to do. His name was on the door. But this relationship was unique.

The man leaned over Swinton's desk, amping up the volume of his orders. "*Get off the phone! **Now!***"

Swinton relayed the instructions, hung up, and started to talk. "We need to—"

"I told you. You need to focus on one thing, and one thing only. Keep CT and its whole Japan investigating team distracted by the P.E.T. case for two weeks." That was Mr. Shin's command, but Swinton would only know it as this man's order to him. That was enough. All official measures in the US would be activated. They'd had an extra month to prepare.

"Now let's go over the contingency plans to be sure you're ready to act." As they checked off the American agencies to put on alert, the man was pleased.

Shin's trap had close on Swinton who would now exercise his influence to close the net in the US as Shin would in Japan. Shin's man's experience was also an asset. He bore into the details of Swinton's plan using his knowledge of, and hatred for, US intelligence and law enforcement networks.

Chapter 84
NAGAHAMA AND TOKYO, JAPAN, THURSDAY, JANUARY 25

That night, after the explosion over Line Four at the end of Kano's interview, we rode the bullet train in stony silence back to the factory. The next morning, fourteen volumes of Line Four specs, drawings, and studies covered the main table in the same workroom we'd used before. Nearby, we found boxes of notes from a second series of lectures that Malinkrodt had negotiated directly with Kano, cutting Mueller out.

Malinkrodt had photocopied other, more confidential reports, not on Frank's microfilms. He had seeded that key technical information from Cameron throughout short memos and elaborated on them in lectures. The threat of discovering that trove must have been what had excited Malinkrodt over Mueller's handwritten note at the end of Weidl's deposition back in Dallas.

Madison and Charlie estimated the total P.E.T. damages at over thirteen million dollars. But there was nothing about OC-X.

Thursday night, before the team was to leave Friday morning, I had a revolt on my hands. They had a right to blow off steam. They were elated with the victory over CT, but they were sick of Japanese food. My answer: the Ribera Steakhouse about fifteen minutes from our hotel, a place frequented by American professional wrestlers touring Japan. Sapporo beer flowed freely.

In celebration, I'd urged everyone to order the best on the menu. Jerry Suddeth, the engineer who worked for Charlie, had taken on the *"Taihō* Eating Challenge", named after the *sumo* champion with the most wins. Jerry ate almost three pounds of grilled steak, plus sides, in thirty minutes, and won ten thousand yen. He even got to wear a Ribera Steakhouse jacket with a raging bull sewn on the chest, for a picture to pin on the restaurant wall. Somehow, it seemed a fitting celebration after all they'd been through.

Jerry stood up and addressed the team. "I learned a lotta things here in *Ja*-pan. One is, never turn down a Japanese meal." The whole table guffawed. Jerry, performing as Frank Brazeale in the role of a foreign food critic, had been suspicious of everything he had been served since he landed in Tokyo, surviving mostly on rice and an occasional bowl of noodles. No wonder he'd met "The Challenge".

"An' be very respeckful to all Japanese." He bowed awkwardly to Harry and the other CT translator. "Unless you find 'em sneakin' 'round your factory *without a badge on*!"

Loud applause and gales of laughter erupted. The exhaustion effervesced into euphoria.

I rose and proposed a final toast. "Here's to your dedication and hard work. You never gave up. You overcame every obstacle. *Kanpai*." They all stood, cheered loudly, clinked their glasses of beer and *saké* and drained them, one Japanese custom they'd readily adopted.

The bill was big enough to buy a small car. The engineers would fly back tomorrow. Charlie had prevailed on Jerry to go in on Saturday after he got back and check references to back up the final report.

Back at the lobby in the Imperial Hotel, I shook hands with each member of the team and wished them a safe trip home. I made a special point of thanking the Japanese for the exhausting work they had performed. Then I took Harry aside.

"I remember our conversation on the plane. On top of all the hard work, I know it was especially difficult for you."

"Thank you, Jake. What you said to me on the plane was a very great help. I am now back in touch with my family and am staying a few extra days."

"I'm glad. Consolidated Technologies and all of us owe you a debt of gratitude, Harry. You cracked the case." I bowed to him, managing not to lose my balance completely.

After the good-byes, Charlie, Madison, and I headed up to our rooms. Jerry rode up with us on the elevator. He, Charlie, and Madison talked about the documents Charlie wanted him to find at Cameron.

I took stock. We'd prepared the questions for Kano's deposition tomorrow. I'd called Auchincloss, the guy from the embassy we'd met on the flight over, and left a message with my hotel room number, asking him to meet me at the Consular Section of the Embassy before the deposition to make sure everything went smoothly. There was nothing left to do. Our triumph set off thoughts of NYU for the first time in weeks.

I'd called the NYU dean of admissions in late December to explain my predicament. We'd argued. He agreed to hold my place for a month but financial aid was already being doled out. I might need a bigger loan, or a bonus, after what we'd accomplished. Right. Not after quitting the firm.

My mind took off. But the canyons of Wall Street weren't where it ended up. It drifted to Madison's predicament and considered what it had been like for her in Japan. The Line Four discovery had eased her pain. Then the memory of her warm body and high spirits at the hotel in Kyoto intruded, causing a spike in my, uh, interest. We were in the elevator, next to each other in an enclosed space, again. I began to blush, again.

"Jake? Hello. Jake?" Madison was staring at me.

"Sorry."

"I was telling Charlie. I need to talk to you both right now."

After the discovery of Line Four, we suspected our rooms had been bugged. We should have assumed that from the beginning. If they had been, they still would be, so we went to the executive lounge. It took up a whole floor. Madison chose a table in the middle of the deserted room and wasted no time.

"Harry had a message for me from his nephew. He called tonight and insisted Harry pass on one word: *kagami*."

Charlie and I stared at her, drawing blanks.

"That's the password from the letter from Japan I got at Cameron. With the mission over, Harry's nephew wants to meet me before we leave. He insists."

"What the heck's a '*kagami*'?" Charlie asked.

"Harry says it means mirror," Madison continued. "It evokes the reflective principles involved in optical computing." She explained Sato's interest in her work. "It also has something to do with Imperial relics, symbols of the Emperor as the source of Japan's spiritual power. One is a jeweled mirror."

She stopped to watch us, then continued excitedly. "Harry's going to call Sato tomorrow and try to set up a meeting this weekend."

Charlie leaned forward. "Whoa, lady. This ain't Cameron. If this guy's got something on Minimura and OC-X, it's a lot stickier than P.E.T. We know how nasty somebody already got about that." No one could forget Dallas, George, and Stefan. "We gotta turn this one over to Nico, right Jake?"

"That would make sense." Nico had promised he would help. "And this is Japan: the CIA can use all its tricks and resources." FISA didn't apply here. "I'll try to get a message to Nico tonight."

"There is no time to wait," Madison protested. "My flight's Sunday. I've got to be at the launch in Houston next Friday. I can meet Harry's nephew Saturday. I'm not going to miss this." The implacable Whitmire will Tom had warned me about was now on display once more. But we were alone, in Tokyo.

I was in my hotel room finishing my nightly call to Tom.

". . . and Madison leaves Sunday for Houston. Charlie and I have booked a Monday flight for New York."

"Great job. Bob Langston will be impressed. They all will, even McElwain." Thirteen million dollars bought a lot of enthusiasm, even from the top CT executives. "Tomorrow night go to dinner at the *Toh-Ka-Lin* Restaurant at the Okura Hotel. Tell the chef you're celebrating. It's the best Chinese restaurant in the world. You've had enough Japanese for a while." I didn't mention Ribera. He'd get the bill soon enough.

"I wish you could be here to join us, Tom."

I paused, hoping he would notice the shift in tone. I couldn't risk calling Nico directly, so I was counting on Tom to pass Madison's news on to him.

“Say, Madison has a message for her office. You remember that problem she had back in November, the day we all met at Cameron, with her mail?”

“What? I don’t—"

“That strange letter. It was the right address after all. She’s anxious for you to know all about it. You should let your friend know, too. Good night, Tom.”

Chapter 85
TSUKUBA SCIENCE CITY, JAPAN, EARLY FRIDAY MORNING, JANUARY 26

Tsukuba was quiet in the early morning. Sato had taken a long walk before work to a public telephone, trying to make sure he wasn't followed. It was different than the phone from which he had called his uncle to propose the meeting. This was the phone with the number Sato had given his uncle to call with Dr. Whitmire's reply. Sato continued to survey the street but saw no one lingering. But how could he know? The phone rang.

"*Mushi-mushi.*"

It was Harry. "Your question was a good one and so is my answer." He was careful, but that meant Dr. Whitmire had agreed to meet Sato on Saturday.

"That is good news, Uncle. In the evening would be nice." Sato would have time to take precautions. "Do you recall viewing the cherry blossoms with the whole family?" There were many popular viewing sites, but their families had made a special trip into Tokyo to view the famous pink and white blossoms surrounding the lake behind the Imperial Palace. Sato was referring to a spot high on a bank across from the Imperial Palace, overlooking the *Chidorigafuchi* moat.

“We had the best view right from the restaurant, didn’t we?” Harry was proposing the location.

“Yes. That was good. But we had to eat late. Do you recall?” They had eaten at seven, because of the crowds. Sato hoped that would stand out in his uncle’s memory.

“Yes, nephew. I remember it well. It would be nice to eat there again, at the same time. Everything the same.”

Sato was elated. Harry and Dr. Whitmire would be at the Egmont Hotel at seven in the evening on Saturday. He would be there waiting for them.

Hara continued speaking.

“Ueno Park was the best viewing place. Do you remember, nephew?”

“Your father always chose the best place.” But it wasn’t Ueno Park.

Shin’s watchers had followed Sato. They noted the time and place of the call and radioed the Kudan Kaikan to report the suspicious activity.

Chapter 86
TOKYO, MID-MORNING, THE SAME DAY

It was five minutes until ten. Madison, Charlie, and I sat in a conference room in the consular section of the American Embassy. We were with an interpreter and a court reporter, waiting for Kano and Garrett to arrive.

Clyde Auchincloss stuck his head in the door. "Mr. Payne? Got your phone message. Sorry I was out. Is everything in order?"

No, but this was no place to talk about Harry's nephew. I still thought a meeting with Madison was unwise.

We shook hands. "Please. It's Jake. Thanks for coming by. We're all set. I hope it wasn't too much trouble for you to check on the arrangements."

"No trouble. Your mission interests me." He lowered his voice. "How has it gone?"

I shrugged. "Less than we might have hoped for, but more than we expected." I glanced around the room and said, "Can I talk to you in private for just a minute?"

"Sure. There's an interview room next door."

He led me into the hall and we ducked into a small cubicle. I had to hurry.

"Clyde, this case has been a series of surprises. Each time we got stonewalled, we caught a break. And the cover up effort on the other side has been immense. When we first cracked this thing open back in Dallas, our chief witness had an unfortunate accident. A lawyer on our side was shot and killed, and his boss was arrested for criminal activity against his client's interest."

"Good God, man. What have you run into?"

"Since we arrived? Three weeks of utter obfuscation, dissembling, and withholding of evidence, until we broke it open. They hid a major expansion project based on data from our research delivered by a former plant manager. We have the drawings and plans to prove it."

"Has your defendant admitted all of this?"

"The facts, yes. That they knew the info was stolen or valuable, no. This deposition will not address that, only our executive's role. I guess that's why I wanted to fill you in. It's not over and we don't know just what the next surprise will bring. All we know is there are some big ones still out there."

"When do you leave Japan?"

"We're scheduled for Monday," I said. "But if anything sensitive comes up, at least two of us might have to stay over. We might need your help." I hoped that was enough to keep him willing to lend a hand until Nico came through.

"Do you have any reason to think you might?"

There was only one thing I could say for now. "Yes."

"What kind of help?"

"Can't say."

He nodded, we shook hands and he took off.

Chapter 87
TOKYO, EVENING, THE SAME DAY

Kano's deposition went well, but only for the case against Malinkrodt. He did not give any ground on the value of the Line Four changes or admit that they were in any way related to Malinkrodt's visits. But after the second factory discoveries, I had all we needed for the P.E.T. case against Malinkrodt and negotiations with Minimura. Madison, Charlie, and I followed Tom's advice and went to the *Toh-Ka-Lin* restaurant in the Okura Hotel for our final celebration. The décor was subtle except for a central area with clever mirrored panels that spread images of an exuberant flower arrangement throughout the room.

I followed Tom's instructions and informed the *maitre d'* that we'd like to see the chef." With a broad smile, he led us to a table in the center of the room next to that arrangement, the focal point of the restaurant. We sat down with spectacular bird of paradise flowers hovering over us. The *maitre d'* whispered urgent instructions to the captain, who scurried off to the kitchen.

Dish after amazing dish arrived in a nearly endless stream. All were delicious. I lost count at fifteen. Each course had just enough for a modest portion that a server placed on a small plate in front of each diner. These were changed with every course. For only three of us, the bill was still bigger than the one at Ribera's. Enough to buy a Lincoln.

I raised my wine glass. "Here's to Stefan Weidl. None of this would have been possible without his cooperation."

"And poor old George," Charlie added. "May all them other buggers rot in hell!

In the taxi, Madison had told us she planned to meet Sato. The waiter removed the last plates and withdrew. Madison leaned forward and, in a low voice, said, "It's tomorrow night at seven, near the Imperial Palace."

I didn't like it and explained about my efforts with Auchincloss and Nico. "We can get professional help. You don't have to take this risk."

"I have to hear what he has to say in person and evaluate it. There's no time left. I must be in Houston before the launch next Friday. Harry needs be at this meeting with his nephew for translation, but he knows nothing about OC-X. I'm the only one who can question Sato."

"If we have to do this, Charlie, how can we manage the risks? You're the Asian expert."

"We done this kinda thing in the Army. White guy, er, girl always sticks out in public, so you need a native to front it. I reckon Harry could meet Sato in the hotel lobby. Then if the coast is clear, he can take Sato to meet Madison in a room inside. But things was way different back then. We was professionals working with the all-powerful U.S. Army. I been up against Driscoll on a dark night and, if it weren't for Jake, I'd still be lying on the ground. Or under it. Good backup's real important."

I couldn't order Madison to do anything. Any hope for support from Nico arriving in time was flowing away faster than rainwater down a storm drain. Auchincloss might provide some administrative support, but not physical protection. Then I recalled our meeting with K Nakamura near the Dunkin' Donuts.

"Charlie, I can't be sure Tom understood my reference to the mole's letter. We have to assume we can't get help from Nico by tomorrow evening. Would your friends be able to help?"

"My friends?"

"Yeah. Mr. K and those guys you mentioned. The *yakuza* and the Chinese guy."

"Slim Ah's in the Philippines, Baik's in Korea, an' Goat Boy's missin' in action."

"Can you and I at least talk to K tonight?"

"He goes home way west a Tokyo for the weekend. But he gave me his phone number."

Chapter 88
LOWER MANHATTAN, 12:30PM, THE SAME DAY
TWELVE HOURS AHEAD OF TOKYO TIME

Untermeyer looked up at the white sign, its impertinent red neon letters marring the view of the towers of the financial district in southern Manhattan and shouting: DINER. The Pearl Diner was famous for its meatball parmigiana sandwich and the low-class smell of hot oil and bubbling fat exuding from the kitchen. It drew well-heeled lunchtime crowds, but Felix seemed to gag as he moved toward the back of the room.

His contact was there. Since the call from Staley a week ago about his talk with O'Hanlon and the government lawyer, Untermeyer had worried non-stop. His contact made him wait all week for a reply to his request for help, when there was no time to waste.

Untermeyer approached the table and pulled out a chrome-backed chair that scraped across the cracked linoleum floor. His dependence caused a wave of fear to wash over him.

The man pointed to a black leather document bag on the floor. "It's all in there."

Untermeyer took a set of papers from the bag and spent time scanning them in silence.

"You're clear on the instructions?" the man concluded.

"Of course. It's my plan."

"I meant the logistics. Take the case and leave this evening. Here is your ticket. Your plane's at 7:40 from LaGuardia. There's a stop. You'll be met there by two technicians. They'll stay with you until the job's done."

"When will that be?" He sounded nervous again.

"During the weekend or not at all. We'll keep you updated. Your rooms are booked at the place you indicated." He handed Felix an envelope.

"And the other matter?"

"One half of the funds were transferred this morning. The balance will be in your account in Zurich after you complete the mission."

Nico's friend's video equipment worked as well as before, but the sound cut in and out. It did, however, catch a reference to a bank in Zurich. He had also taken photos of Untermeyer as he left the Pearl with the document bag. The photos were time stamped and compared unfavorably for Untermeyer to the ones of him entering the restaurant twenty minutes earlier, empty-handed.

Nico had instructed his friend to follow Untermeyer in Manhattan and report if he tried to leave. Untermeyer took a cab to Laguardia and the man followed him, then called Nico at home from a pay phone across the gate from a flight to Atlanta.

"Untermeyer has checked in. He has to be headed for Cameron."

That raised problems. Nico now had proof of some kind of illegal activity planned by Untermeyer and a lead on an undeclared Swiss bank account. Tax fraud was probably a snap if he could use the evidence. But he didn't have a clear idea about how to accomplish that because it was all obtained illegally.

This trip was yet another problem. Manhattan offered cover to tail someone. A plane, with a change to Greenville and very few people around, was much riskier. Nico had already overdrawn his account with DARPA. He couldn't take a chance on Untermeyer discovering a tail on the way to or in South Carolina.

Tom had called to tell Nico about a curious message from Jake. It might refer to a contact from the mole Madison had talked about at Cameron, the handwritten letter, and the code word, but it wasn't clear.

Things were heating up, but Nico couldn't expect any more help.

"Okay. It's too dangerous to follow him on the plane. But keep checking flights from Greenville and pick him back up when he returns."

Chapter 89
TOKYO REGION, SATURDAY, JANUARY 27

Some major *keiretsu* like Minimura had used their increasing success to allow employees to work only a half day on Saturdays. It was time for Sato to leave Tsukuba to meet Dr. Whitmire, but events had caused his anxiety to spike.

Since early December, the news had been full of the trip of Deng Xiaoping to the U.S. Sato had learned with horror from a news story about NASA that Deng was to be in Mission Control in Houston when Dr. Whitmire's invention was launched.

Attempting to pass the envelope to the professor in Hawaii had been frightening, but there had been no other Japanese around. Sending an anonymous letter had been easier. Now every fiber of his nerves was fighting against his need to go into Tokyo.

A well-known phrase—*the nail that sticks up must be hammered down*—had been running through his mind. Since he had called his uncle Harry, it had become a waking nightmare: Sato cringing as a huge iron mallet blotted out the light just before it crushed his skull. He tried repeating an anchoring syllable to empty his mind, but his hands were shaking. Then he recalled the vision of his friends burning to death. He must do this.

Opening his eyes, he checked the papers he had put in his knapsack a final time and left his apartment. He went for noodles at a *ramen-ya* shop and a long, ostensibly aimless walk.

But, as he had planned, he ended up on the platform at the Tsukuba train station, waiting for the 14:12 express train to Tokyo. He held the red backpack straps tightly with both hands as he surveyed the platform.

On a Saturday afternoon, there were not many people: a few families, an older couple, two men, one reading a paper, the other smoking idly. One of them glanced at Sato and his heart leapt. It might be nothing, but he could take no chances.

The train entered the station, slowed, and stopped. The heavy pneumatic doors slid open with a sigh. Sato stepped just inside the door and waited. Everyone else on the platform boarded the train. As the doors closed, Sato jumped back onto the platform. The doors locked shut with a hiss and the train began to roll. He was alone on the platform, more utterly alone than he had ever been.

Sato hurried down the stairs and headed for the bus station to take the shuttle to Tsuchiura station on the JR Joban Line, an alternate route. At Tsuchiura, he would take a local train to Tokyo and get off at the busy Akihabara Station, and wade into the afternoon crowds streaming through the subway tunnels seeking the latest electronic gadgets in the crowded shopping area. Then he would head for the Kudanshita stop, a short walk from the Egmont Hotel across from the Imperial Palace and gardens.

Sato would need all the time between now and seven o'clock to get there in time to meet Harry and Dr. Whitmire, and all the courage he could summon.

Chapter 90
TOKYO, 2:31PM, THE SAME DAY

For many years, Shin had been a member of the board that administered the *Yasukuni-Jinja* precincts. He and his fellow members were seated on tatami mats in the *Kaiko Bunko* Archive Building on the shrine grounds.

The Meiji Emperor had decreed the creation of this shrine in 1869 as a resting place for the *kami*—the spirits—of all those who died in his defense. This was another part of the creation of State Shinto by the architects of modern Japan. Nearly two and a half million souls were honored here. These memorials honored the Emperor and the nation, keeping anger at the nation's subservience to the Americans burning like a white-hot flame.

The board was responsible for the site and thus for the memory of the nation. This year, the timing was propitious. On February second, the anniversary of the ill-fated Young Officer's attempted coup, the explosion in Houston would kill Deng Xiaoping.

Conveniently, Shin and the Board were gathered to confirm the plans for the *Kenkoku Kinensai* ceremonies in two weeks, the anniversary of the day on which Japan's first Emperor founded the nation.

Shin had provided additional funding to assure that this ceremony would be the finest ever. When the explosion took place in Houston, it would strike a massive blow for Japan's independence from foreign powers. To capitalize on the outcome in Tokyo on National Foundation Day, fleets of blaring sound trucks, financed by Shin, would explode with the first onslaught in a campaign to revoke Article Nine, inserted by the Americans in the Japanese constitution, that outlawed war by Japan.

With most of the Americans from CT on flights to the U.S. and just a few days left, Shin had focused his vigilance on the remaining foreigners, including the Japanese from America. His men were also watching Sato until all the CT investigators left the country. One surveillance team had last reported Sato on the platform at the Tsukuba train station, shouldering a red knapsack.

A shrine attendant entered the room and came over to him. "Shin-*sensei*, your driver has asked to speak with you." Shin rose to leave the meeting.

He took the call in the *Kaiko Bunko* hall on the radio handset his driver carried.

"Shin-*sensei*, we are incompetent. We have lost Sato."

It indicated a high level of cunning by Sato, but it was not of major concern to Shin if his other arrangements were executed as ordered.

"There are too many options to be sure of picking up his trail. Remind the team at the Imperial Hotel that they must follow all moves by any of the targets, especially Hara. They could not lose him. And they should watch for Sato, too. He may try to contact his uncle there. No one goes in or out of the hotel that they do not observe."

Chapter 91
TOKYO, LATE THAT AFTERNOON

"He should be here by now." I knew K was coming from his home, far to the west near Mount Fujiyama, but the wait was difficult.

I was running a number of scenarios through my mind, but they lacked any grounding in knowledge of Tokyo or in the real threats that could arise. They served only to pass the time and gin up even more extreme possible horribles.

Madison looked resolute, eager. "I'm sure he'll be here."

The night before on the phone, Charlie and I had explained to K the need for support for her when she met Sato. He had proposed several options and we all agreed the Koreans would be the best.

It was almost five, only two hours to go until Madison was to meet Sato. I'd sent Charlie to check on Harry, who wasn't in his room, and had left no message.

There was a knock on the door. I opened it to find K with his enigmatic smile and a large satchel.

As the Shrine Protection Board was finishing its work, Shin was called away again. This time it was the team watching the Imperial Hotel.

"We see Hara coming out of the hotel. But tour busses have pulled up. Many old people are clogging the entrance. We cannot see for the crowd. They all have white hats and red jackets and shoulder bags. There are some tall young tour guides, holding up small pennants on cane poles. Is that . . . no, that's a guide. Over there. Yes. We see him. We will follow Hara."

He must be heading to meet Sato, Shin realized. "Do not lose him!" This time Shin waited to hear where the target was going.

The followers reported. "Hara walked down Hibiya Dori. At the corner, he went down the stairs of the Hibiya A5 Metro entrance. He is moving fast among the crowd." The transmission began to break up and then was lost.

Shin envisaged the vast underground Hibaya Metro Plaza beneath the Ginza. The Saturday afternoon crowds shopping and seeking entertainment would be dense. There were also many train and metro links. There was little risk Hara could spot Shin's men in the crush of people but every risk that his men could lose Hara.

Chapter 92
TOKYO, 6:10PM

K presented his plan. He had a map and indicated our intended location and the movements of the Koreans. We asked a few questions but could find no gaps. Our planning and our nerves were at their limits.

K ordered *ocha,* green tea. As we sipped it and discussed, the Japanese national beverage calmed our nerves. K went to make some calls. When he returned, he picked up the satchel and placed it on the table. "We must leave now. Please put these on."

Wearing K's garb, we descended a back stairway and came out in a hall near the teashop. K went over to a tall young man herding a large group of senior citizens, all with white hats and red shoulder bags.

"Jake, this is my wife's nephew, Hajima." He had on the same white hat and red jacket K had given each of us. He handed us cane poles with red pennants on them. K said, "We will replace the guides."

Hajima gave a signal and he and the three other guides melted away. An ancient lady in the group came up to K. She smiled as she took his arm and patted his hand and talked to him in Japanese.

"This is my mother. She is thanking you for arranging this outing for her friends in our temple's Spiritual Nurturing Society." She bowed to us, hummed the first few bars of "My Country 'Tis of Thee", and smiled.

Shin was still outside the shrine when another call came in. “This is Blue Team at the hotel. The crowd of old people are leaving. We see no signs of the Westerners, only a tour group and their guides. Should we wait longer?”

“You are not with Hara?” The overpass in Liaoning Province burned in his mind’s eye.

“Shin-*san*. The Red team is following him,” the operative explained.

“Call them! Aid them! Sato will go to him. They must not meet!”

Chapter 93
6:25PM

It was over four hours since Sato had left Tsukuba. In his excitement, his carefully laid plans had given way to feverish improvisation. After getting off the local train at Ueno Station, he had shifted metro lines three times and walked above ground between stations once, his head swiveling to survey his surroundings.

He hadn't detected anyone following him, but his fear continued to grow as he trudged up the stairs from the Hanzoman Subway Station and checked his watch again. It was 18:25, an eternity of thirty-five minutes left.

As he entered the small lane leading to the hotel from the west, above the *Chidorigafuchi* moat, he stared at each of the people on the pedestrian path. The path was dimly lit by cast iron streetlamps. Each person was moving purposefully in the evening dark. He could detect no one loitering.

He arrived in front of the small hotel and cautiously lowered himself onto a bench across the lane. From there, the wide glass windows offered a clear view of the well-lit lobby and reception desk.

Sato's chest tightened. He felt exposed sitting on the bench. Fear surged in his heart. He leapt up, hurried across the lane, and entered the hotel lobby. He asked for a luggage tag and gave his backpack to the clerk after attaching a note: “Hold for Hara Ichiro from the United States.” Then he went back outside to the cold iron bench and took up his distressed watch.

The tour bus we had boarded, following K’s instructions, wound around the extensive precincts of the Imperial Palace, ending up in front of the Grand Palace Hotel where it pulled to a stop. K, Charlie, Madison, and I, minus our tourist guide outfits, descended the steep stairs, and the bus pulled away. Charlie slapped his friend on the back. “That’s pretty slick, K. Just like old times.”

A nondescript gray van eased out of a parking space in the hotel courtyard. It halted in front of the entrance and its sliding door rumbled back. Two exceptionally large, muscular men dressed in sport coats, white dress shirts, and ties clambered out and greeted K. I was on edge but was impressed by the precision of K’s organizational skills and the size of his friends.

While K discussed with the men in Japanese, Charlie said, in a low voice, “These guys may look like *sumo* wrestlers, but they’s Korean all right.”

K finished and came over. “Ah, Jake,” his voice, as always, was soft and soothing. “These are the gentlemen who will provide protection for Harry and Madison. We can observe them from this van. Please make yourselves comfortable. Our destination is only a few minutes away.”

Our van snuck into a tree-lined lane across from the Imperial Palace grounds. It stopped and the beefy guard K called Park got out. He walked down the sidewalk on our left, toward the Egmont Hotel. About thirty yards further, the van stopped again and let the second guard out. He headed across the lane to our right, toward the path through the winter-bare cherry trees that cascaded down a hill to the Imperial Palace moat.

The van continued down the short lane. As it approached the hotel, a man in work clothes appeared and removed two striped traffic cones from a space on the same side of the lane as the hotel. K's driver pulled into it. The workman disappeared as silently as he had come.

K spoke. "Dr. Whitmire, you may go."

Madison was bundled up against the weather and prying eyes. She had tucked her blond hair under a knit cap and wound a thick scarf around her neck and mouth. She got out of the van, gave us a thumbs up, and walked toward the hotel.

"Gentlemen," K said, "Now we wait."

"Looky there." Charlie pointed. "Could that be Sato?" A young man was sitting on a bench across the lane from the hotel. He watched Madison intently as she approached the hotel. We could see his left knee bobbing up and down like a sewing machine. He started to stand, then sat back down.

Madison stepped into the hotel lobby. The first Korean, Park, who had gone beyond the hotel, was coming back. The young man on the iron bench stiffened, but the Korean passed in front of the hotel on the far side of the lane from Sato. The young man relaxed. Then the Korean turned back and went into the hotel lobby. He bowed to Madison and they disappeared into the back of the hotel.

After a few minutes, we saw the other large Korean moving warily along the pedestrian path on the same side of the lane as Sato. The young man's knee went supersonic until the Korean passed by.

Chapter 94
6:45PM

Shin's meeting at the Shrine was over. He met his driver outside the Archive Building. The sky was dark and the air smelled of ozone, threatening rain. They walked down the long path toward the entrance to the shrine, framed by the giant red metal *torii*, toward the secular world.

The driver's radio crackled. "*Ichiban,* this is Red Team.

"*Ichiban* here," the driver replied.

"We have just come out of the Kudanshita Metro stop. Hara, is right in front of us."

The news hit Shin like an electric charge. The Kudanshita metro stop was a few hundred meters away. He grabbed the radio from the driver. "Which way is he headed?"

"Up the hill, toward the Yasukuni Shrine." Directly toward Shin. "Where has he been?" The man described the meandering walks and rides Hara had taken since leaving the hotel.

"Has he seen you?"

"We have no sign of that."

"Is the Blue Team with you?"

"They are caught in traffic, still twenty minutes away."

Shin struggled to control his rage. "Keep me advised of his every move." He handed the radio to his driver. Shin had no idea where the meeting was planned, if at all. But he could not let it happen if it was. He wanted to strangle the traitor Sato himself. His suite at the Kudan Kaikan was only a few blocks away. Hara was so close; Shin could feel his presence. His personal vigilance would overcome any failings of his network. "We will wait here until we get the next call."

Park ushered Madison into the back hall of the Egmont Hotel where he pointed to a chair and signaled for her to sit down. The lobby was hot to pamper foreign guests in winter. She took off her coat, hat, and scarf to wait for Harry and Sato. Park was standing where he could see Madison and, through the lobby windows, survey the lane in front of the hotel. He looked at his watch, then held his hand up to Madison, a sign to stay put. He turned and went into the front lobby.

Shin was still at the shrine, waiting for another report on Hara's movements, when the radio crackled again. "Red Team to *Ichiban*. Target One is going down the pedestrian underpass towards the Imperial Palace. We are following."

Hara would cross under the street, away from the shrine. "Now we can go." Shin, trailed by his driver, strode towards his car parked in a reserved place near the street.

"Red Team to *Ichiban*. Target One has stopped in front of the pedestrian path above the *Chidorigafuchi* that leads to_*Uchibori Dori* and the Hanzoman Metro stop."

Now Shin knew their plan. The lane through the park was different from the other areas the false Japanese had travelled through since he left the Imperial Hotel. It was dark, secluded, with few people. There was a small hotel on the lane where a meeting could take place.

His senses hummed. He grabbed the radio from the driver. "Get closer. Watch out for the younger one. He may be nearby. Be ready to stop them if they try to meet."

Shin would move closer to the small hotel on foot. He felt energy coursing through his body, as if he were back in Manchukuo. *Kitsune*—the magic fox, the name Shin's men had given him— would sow the madness himself.

From inside the van we saw Harry arrive at the entrance to the park on the other side of the hotel. He stopped and stood about forty yards away by a stone pillar and iron gate. Before entering the darkened grove, he looked around slowly.

Park came to the door of the hotel, checked his watch, and looked down the lane. He didn't seem to see Harry by the stone pillar. Park turned and went back into the hotel lobby. I looked at my watch. It was seven o'clock.

Harry crossed over the lane to the hotel side, his head swiveling now like a weathervane in a high wind. The other big Korean was on the Palace side of the lane, across from our van. He saw Harry and slowed his pace.

Harry had gone only a few yards on the lane when he turned to look behind him. A man was entering the grove, picking up his pace. We saw another man emerge from behind the stone entrance pillar.

"We have to get out now and break this up," I urged.

"No way, Jake," Charlie warned. "Let K's men do their job. We ain't in Dallas, this ain't Geiger's, and I bet those guys following Harry is a lot smarter and tougher than Driscoll."

Harry wasn't far from the hotel now, walking faster.

We saw the two men start to hurry after him on either side of the lane. Harry turned back again. Both men sped up. Harry broke into a run. The men did, too. Harry was in good shape, but middle aged. His pursuers were faster. It would be close.

Suddenly, the Korean outside the hotel veered into the lane, moving with surprising speed toward Harry, who whipped his head toward the Korean and almost fell. We heard a deep voice rumble.

"He's telling Harry to run into the hotel," K translated.

The big man stopped and turned to face the two men running after Harry, who ran into the hotel lobby.

Shin's man was breathing hard through the radio as he reported. "Someone is helping Hara who is . . . running towards a hotel. The man has turned to . . . *to stop us.*"

Shin shouted into the radio clutched in his fist. "*Cut him down.* Do not let Hara get to Sato."

Shin heard his man shout to his comrade. "Look, there on the bench, the young one. Seize him. I will get the old one."

I saw there was only one Korean against two attackers, one of which was headed right for Sato. Park was nowhere to be seen. I started to open the van door.

"No, Jake. Stop," Charlie warned. "Ain't no use."

The first assailant pulled what looked like a long baton from inside his jacket as he neared the big Korean. He pushed a button and a vicious blade shot from the handle. The big Korean suddenly dropped low with amazing agility and swung his huge leg in a wide arc.

The assailant's knees crumpled at it met the ham hock of Park's thigh. The pursuer tried to break his fall but banged his hand on the sidewalk, losing his grip on the knife. Immediately the big man leapt up and delivered a massive kick to the downed man's kidneys, then leaned down and hit him with the edge of his huge hand on the back of the neck. We could see the assailant go limp.

I turned to look at Sato. He stood up and froze, transfixed by the violence across the street. The second assailant had stopped, torn between defending his comrade and reaching Sato. He saw Sato's face lit by a streetlamp and started to move toward him. The big Korean turned from the fallen attacker and sped up to block the second assailant's path to Sato.

The second assailant pulled a wicked-bladed knife from his jacket and threw it with deadly aim into the chest of the onrushing Korean, just a few meters away. The man's momentum carried him one more step, then he pitched forward, face down on the path, motionless.

The assailant, now a killer, turned quickly to see K's second big man, Park, come out of the hotel lobby, and watch his friend's corpse fall to the ground. Park moved toward the killer.

Sato started toward the hotel. The blade-thrower ran up to Sato and grabbed him, pulling a second knife from his coat. Park, knees bent and arms wide, edged towards the man with the knife. The man holding Sato spun him around to face Park. The hulking Korean, bobbing and weaving slowly, anticipating any move, continued slowly toward his friend's killer and the hostage.

The attacker threw his knife. We could see Park look down. A dark stain spread around the knife buried in his gut. Then he fell to the ground. I yanked open the van door and started towards the hotel and Madison. Charlie yelled after me, but I wasn't going to stop.

The remaining attacker pulled out a shorter knife and brandished it at Sato's throat. Harry shot out of the hotel, saw the knife at his nephew's throat, me starting to run, and yelled, "Stop!"

The others had piled out of the van after me. Madison appeared behind Harry in the doorway of the hotel. Harry's blood curdling warning hit us like a blow and brought us to a halt.

There was no one left to protect them but us.

Over the radio, Shin could hear running and muffled shouts. Suddenly all was silent except for labored breathing. "Red Team this is *Ichiban*. What has happened?" Shin's man was a trained killer. Surely, he was alive.

"My colleague is down. He may be dead. I killed both his attacker and a second attacker just in front of me. They look like Koreans. Sato is in my grip with my last knife at his throat. Hara and a *gaijin* woman are standing a few yards in front of me. There are four other men standing by a van ten meters to my left, two *gaijin*, one young, one older, and two Japanese, one young, and one very old. Bald, like a *bonze*."

"Has Sato made contact with his uncle?"

"No. As you ordered."

Shin did not know who the *bonze* and the Japanese with him might be, but they must have come with the Koreans. He could identify the other two from Kano's detailed descriptions. Shin's man's report was clear, unemotional, which would have been remarkable under the circumstances, except that Shin had chosen him for his background and his training. His family had been *samurai*. Shin regained his calm. Success was a hair's breadth away.

"Listen. You must be steel. Sharp, strong, and deadly. But cold, young warrior, calm." Suddenly it all came together, like the shards from a breaking mirror in reverse. "Here is what you must do."

Shin motioned to his driver to follow him on foot.

I was stopped next to the young van driver who had a better view. "What is happening to Sato?" I whispered.

"The man holding him has a radio in his left hand. It looks like he's talking into it. The knife in his other hand is still at Sato's throat."

I prayed the radio would distract him. I began to creep forward and signaled Charlie to follow me. K and the driver did the same.

Shin stood at the stone entrance to the park now, watching the scene unfold. Over his radio, he heard his man call out to Sato as he had instructed him. "Where is the knapsack you had with you when you left Tsukuba this afternoon?" There was no response from Sato. "Now. There is no time. Tell me or I will kill you, your uncle, and Dr. Whitmire. Now."

"I gave it to the hotel clerk to keep for my uncle."

Anchored to the sidewalk, we heard the attacker yell in heavily accented but clear English to Harry and Madison, "Go inside and get a red knapsack from the clerk. Do it now."

They stood stock still, bewildered.

"This man left if for you. Go get the knapsack." The attacker whispered something in Sato's ear, and he nodded to his uncle and Madison.

They turned and staggered into the lobby. The knife holder pushed Sato forward. While he focused on the hotel door, I started to inch toward the hotel entrance.

"You, by the van. Stop or he dies." He made another movement with the knife at Sato's throat. "They all die."

Charlie muttered, "They's all dead no matter what, unless we git to that one." I started forward again.

The assailant made a shallow slice in Sato's throat, enough to draw a bright stream of blood. Sato screamed. His captor yelled, a controlled shriek, designed to terrorize. "Not another move, or you kill him."

Harry and Madison edged out of the doorway, Harry gripping Sato's red backpack tightly in his hands.

"Step toward me, both of you," the assailant commanded in the same frightening voice as he inched Sato towards them, sidestepping to avoid tripping as he passed by Park's body lying still on the ground. Madison and Harry were almost within the killer's reach.

Charlie was right. Sato, Harry, and Madison would all die if we didn't do something. We might not save them, but we had to try. I whispered desperately. "We have no choice. Let's go. *Now*!"

All four of us rushed toward the killer.

His blade effortlessly sliced Sato's throat, blood pumping from his arteries, spraying Harry and, behind him, reaching Madison. Then the assassin lunged at Harry, reoriented his arm, and with a backhand swipe, dispatched Harry like he had Sato. Madison was screaming now, her feet frozen to the pavement, blood dripping from her face and dress. Harry's body had fallen behind her. She back peddled, raised her hands to shield her face, and tripped over Harry's corpse.

That saved her life as the assassin's next swipe missed her. I broke from the pack, sprinting towards her. The assassin recovered from her unexpected fall and stood over a defenseless Madison. I wouldn't make it in time.

Suddenly the assassin stopped, a look of deep surprise contorting his face. The tip of a long blade punched through the front of his throat, spitting flesh, cartilage, and blood. Park had risen to his feet. Grisly in his red-soaked shirt, he had pulled the throwing knife from his stomach and, with super-human strength, thrust it through the back of the assassin's neck.

Park and the killer pitched forward onto Madison. She was lying between Harry and the quivering bodies of the knife-wielder and Park, screaming, and writhing to get free. Blood from three corpses soaked her clothes.

I reached her. Afraid that one of the knives might have cut her, or worse, I frantically tore the bodies away.

Harry, his nephew, both Koreans, and their attackers were all dead. Madison appeared unharmed but stunned. I lifted her up and cradled her trembling body in my arms. Steering her away from the crimson scene, I supported her as we edged slowly toward the van. She clung to me, wracked now by sobs. I heard shrill whistles coming from the other side of the park.

K said. "We must get away. That's the police. Someone is still after us."

We reached the van. I looked back at the carnage and saw the red knapsack. It was smeared with blood. Harry's dead hand still gripped a shoulder strap. "Charlie, get the knapsack. Let's go." K stared toward the far entrance to the lane. I could see forms stumbling toward us, lit from behind by the bright light from Kudanshita.

I pushed Madison into the middle seat of the van, climbed in, and held her close. The driver and Charlie, knapsack in hand, crowded into the front seat. K was standing in the street, staring at the bloody scene. The driver had to maneuver the van out of its tight space to turn it around. K stood rooted in the lane, still facing back.

I yelled out the open door. "*K, we have to go. We're leaving. Jump in the van.*" He waited until the last possible moment, then, with a speed and ease I couldn't have imagined he possessed, he leapt in the van, and slid the door shut.

The driver sped down the lane in the opposite direction from the shrieking whistles. In his hurry, he corrected too much. The van fishtailed, knocked over a trash bin and ran up a curb, crushing some low bushes. Then it veered back and overshot to the other side of the lane, scraping two cars. The driver reduced the width of the swerve but didn't seem fully in control.

Ten yards further, at the end of the lane, we shot out into a wide, crowded intersection, crossing against a red light. Cars whizzed wildly around us. K yelled and gestured for the driver to turn left. The driver spun the wheel and the van tipped dangerously.

I slammed into Madison, pushing her against the side of the van. She groaned as I knocked the breath out of her. Brakes squealed. Two loud bangs erupted from the street.

I turned and looked out the windshield. We were turning too late, in the middle of the intersection, against oncoming traffic. There was a car headed straight for us. Our driver pumped the gas and we shot forward as the car skidded past us and crashed into a traffic signal pole. The van finally righted as we careened raggedly down a wide thoroughfare.

Chapter 95
7:10PM

Two old *keikan* from the neighborhood police box, prodded by Shin's driver, huffed up to the bodies on the pavement in front of the hotel and stopped, unsure. Shin stood right behind them. He saw a van maneuvering in the lane to head in the other direction.

A Japanese man, the *bonze,* was in the street staring at Shin. Then the man jumped in the open door of the van and it sped off, whipsawing crazily. In a few seconds, it would come to *Uchibori Dori* at the end of the lane. There they could connect to major traffic arteries. They could be anywhere in Tokyo in minutes. Shin had to act quickly.

The *keiken* were auxiliary police but the only ones close by. Unused to anything more complicated than lost tourists who asked questions in languages they could not understand. Shin's driver had rousted them from the warm comfort of their post and forced them up to the hotel by yelling at them that a foreigner was murdering people in the park.

Shin surveyed the area and confirmed that Sato, Hara, the two Koreans, and his two men were all dead. He didn't see Sato's knapsack anywhere. Shin told the driver to search for it before the real police arrived to take over from the bumbling *keikan*, then he swept toward the entrance to the park, trailing a wave of energy, and turned toward the Kudan Kaikan.

Chapter 96
CENTRAL TOKYO, 7:15PM

Poised on the middle seat of the van, I held Madison tightly. She hadn't said a word. A steady rain began to fall as we raced through the heart of Tokyo to get away from the massacre and the police. The driver, finally in control, threaded our van through the thick Saturday evening traffic, driving fast, swerving, and accelerating, shooting gaps in the stream of cars.

"I never seen anything like it, K," Charlie said. "That feller was a killing machine. How many knives did he have? Where'd he come from?"

"*What were you doing, K*?" I thundered. "*We almost left you.*"

"The killers came from the man behind this. I recognized him, standing over the bodies. He is ruthless."

"Who the hell is he?" I demanded. "Why would he want to kill Sato or Harry or Madison?"

"I met him when he was in prison after the war. He was a big fish in Manchuria. He became a hero to some. Now he is perhaps the most powerful man in Japan, but few know his face. His name is Shin. I do not know his reasons."

"What're we gonna do now, Jake?"

I looked up from Madison's blood-soaked form. "Madison's got to see what's in Sato's bag. That's why everyone died. It's got to have something to do with OC-X."

K spoke again. "There is no way to beat Shin in Japan. He is connected at the top, but in the shadows. You must leave Japan. The hotel will not be safe."

"K we can't run," Charlie objected. "We ain't done nothing wrong. They probably stole Madison's invention. It's all part a Minimura and we got proof they's thieves."

I understood Charlie's point of view. After all, he was making a legal argument. But there were other problems. "Sato's dead. There's no one to validate whatever is in his knapsack. Let's get somewhere safe and have Madison see what's in it." I felt her cringing on the seat next to me, my arms still wrapped around her. I had no idea when she would be able to do that.

K nodded agreement. "You are in Japan. The power you can see is not the power that controls events. Shin can make it seem that Madison is in the wrong. Nothing else will matter."

Charlie looked back at Madison and me, both now covered in blood. "We can't take you into the hotel like that, Jake. If you're right K, we can't stay there, neither. Should we even go there?"

"She may be in shock, but we have to get my documents from my room. Then we have to hurry to the Embassy. Thank God for Auchincloss."

K decided. "First, we'll go to the private entrance of the Imperial. We are only five minutes away. Then to the American Embassy."

Charlie hurried out of the hotel's private entrance pulling a luggage cart with my document bags and two suitcases. He had raced directly from the VIP entrance to Madison's room, stuffed her clothes in a bag, and run next door to my room.

"Jake, while I'as in your room the phone rang. I didn't dare pick it up. I waited 'til it stopped, and the red light blinked. Your mimosa drinking buddy from the Embassy left you a message."

"I knew he'd come through."

"Call him at home. You got his number?"

I'd transferred his business card to the bag with my documents."

Charlie groaned. "It don't sound good. He said to keep away from the Embassy."

K nodded. "That is Shin. He is working very fast."

As we pulled out of the Imperial Hotel grounds, three police cars sped past us and spread out to cover every entrance.

Chapter 97
SHINJUKU DISTRICT, TOKYO, 8:15PM

K opened the door to his apartment and turned on the light. "It is small, but it is the best place for a few hours. It is held in my employer's name, not mine."

I entered carrying Madison who was still dazed. After Charlie's warning, we'd rerouted to *Shinjuku,* a large business area in western Tokyo, away from the Embassy, our hotel, and the parks around the Imperial Palace.

"You may take Madison into the bedroom," K advised.

She slid from my arms, stood up and said in a rocky whisper, "I'm all right." The first words she had uttered since the attack. "I need to look at what Sato brought."

"Madison," I urged. "You need to rest."

"*No.*" She tried to straighten up but lost her balance. I grabbed her to keep her from falling.

"I have to know what I've caused." She righted herself, took Sato's bag from Charlie, stepped over to the sofa, and dumped the contents out. She stood swaying dangerously, looking at several lab notebooks, a thick binder, and a sheaf of thin gridded papers covered with handwritten sketches and graphs.

"There is no way this is your fault." I stood beside her, ready to catch her. Dried blood caked her clothes, hands, and face. I had it smeared all over me, too. "Charlie, get a hot washcloth."

Madison sat down and picked up the handwritten papers. Occasionally she leafed through the notebook or the binder to check a reference, then went back to the sketches and graphs. She brushed aside Charlie's offer of the washcloth. Once she started to collapse. I caught her again. She refused all other help.

The binder in her hands dropped to the floor. She slumped back against the sofa, closed her eyes, and covered her face with her hands. Dried blood flaked off, but she was too disturbed to notice. She took a deep breath, uncovered her face, and spoke in a whisper that sent a chill down my spine.

"My God. It all makes sense. Minimura stole the OC-X information, used it to build an optical computing machine, and put it on a rocket. But there's a serious unforeseeable electrical problem when the optical computer is activated in space. It caused the Japanese space control center to blow up last September, killing over forty people. They covered it up and corrected the problem for a later flight. The same accident will happen in Houston next Friday if we don't stop it. If it does, we'll kill Deng Xiaoping, the Chinese leader, who will be in Mission Control."

Chapter 98
SHIN'S LIVING ROOM, SHINJUKU

All we could hear for a long minute was our uneven breathing. Then I ventured, "You should be able to prevent that, now that you know the problem, right?"

"I don't know. There's a complication. Sato says after he met Harry that first day we were in Tokyo, Kano increased his workload. Sato wrote that he saw people following him a few times. They were taking precautions."

"Surely we can get someone to call it off." I said. "The Chinese leader could be killed."

Madison replied, "Sato thinks that's the point. If we don't stop the launch next Friday, the U.S.
and China will be at each other's throats. That suits Japan."

"How do we stop it?" Charlie asked.

She held up one hand and counted shakily on her fingers. "You scrub the mission. Lots of people must be convinced before that will happen. Or you remove the computer from the capsule. There are other experiments on board. But that would take time they don't have. Or," she held a third finger with her other hand, "If it gets launched, you must prevent the OC-X operator at mission control from throwing the switch that activates it. That occurs in flight when it reaches the critical altitude. If you don't stop activation before then, my invention kills Deng Xiaoping along with everyone else there."

K slowly nodded his head. "This is Shin's plan. He wants the U.S. to be blamed for the death of the Chinese leader. This is why he will convince the police you are criminals. You must all get out of Japan as quickly as possible for your own safety. If he must kill you to stop you, he will."

Madison started to stand, saying, "I've got to . . . I've . . ."

I caught her as she fell, unconscious.

"Charlie, get the bedroom door."

I carried her and laid her down on K's Western-style bed. I couldn't leave her sprawled on the covers like this; she shouldn't wake up with blood all around her. I hoped she would understand.

Trying not to wake her, I got her out of the disgusting blood-soaked dress. Her underclothes had some blood on them, but they would do for sleeping. I gently sponged all traces of blood and dirt from her face, neck, and hands, then toweled her dry and maneuvered her under the sheet and coverlet. She looked peaceful. I leaned over to brush her hair out of her face. She adjusted comfortably under the covers. I kissed her on the cheek, pulled the blanket up, and headed back to the living room.

I searched my document bag, found Auchincloss's card with the private number he'd written on it, and called him.

"'*Mushi-mushi,*"

"Clyde, its Jake Payne. You called me earlier and asked me to call back. Sorry it's so late."

"Jake," Auchincloss said worriedly, "Are you at the hotel?"

"No. I got your message. We've found a safe place. This is a private line."

"The embassy received an urgent call from the Tokyo Metropolitan Police warning us to report your whereabouts."

"Did they say why?"

There was a long silence. Then one bad piece of news after another tumbled from the volunteer diplomat.

"What if I ask for your help in getting us all inside the Embassy?"

"They already have police stationed in front of it to stop you. You can't get by them. If you're picked up on a local criminal charge, we can't intervene. Jake, no one's ever gotten as far incriminating a Japanese company as you have. The reaction shows it. You can't come here. I can't protect you outside the embassy. I'm sorry. I won't turn you in, but I can't help you now. This call never took place."

The line went dead.

"So, what's the good news?" Charlie said, jolting me out of my stupor.

"Isn't any. First, Madison, and probably you and me, are wanted for murder and stealing Japanese national security secrets. Second, the Embassy's out, surrounded by Japanese police. Third, if the local prosecutor and a judge accept the police accusations, which they absolutely will, they can hold us in a cell for up to three weeks without bail before they even charge us or we can see anyone, lawyer or diplomat."

I looked pointedly at Charlie. "By tomorrow morning, every authority in Japan will be hunting us down as criminals." I slumped onto the sofa. "We possess evidence of a conspiracy to frame the U.S. for the death of the Chinese leader, but we have no one with firsthand knowledge to convince anyone it's true."

"K, you said this Shin guy'd use his contacts to ruin us. Seems like it's already started. They ain't limited to Japan, neither. We're thinking he got to George, Stefan and probably that Mueller guy, in Texas and California, damned fast."

K nodded slowly. "He is the wealthiest and most powerful man in Japan, Charlie. He will certainly urge the Japanese authorities to convince their American contacts to accept the Japanese charges against you and to act accordingly. The unfortunate deaths you mention mean he must have an illegal American network, too."

I wasn't a criminal defense lawyer, but some aspects of our predicament were clear.

"I think K's right. It will be hard for the Americans to ignore the Japanese claims. They'll only have the story Shin has fed the Japanese authorities, unless we can get them Sato's papers and convince them they're real."

Charlie kept at it. "How about scientists? If the authorities ain't available, we got to get to someone who can understand the physics and call it all off, or they have to convince someone else to," he said. "By Friday morning. In Houston. Before the launch."

"We can try a lot of things," I said, "but nothing, I think, that would jeopardize our last hope in case all else fails: getting to Mission Control on Friday. Does that make sense?" K and Charlie nodded agreement.

"We have to protect Madison. She's the key to stopping a disaster in Houston," I continued. "We should get some rest and when she wakes up, we'll figure out how to get out of Japan, to Houston, and into Mission Control."

Charlie grinned. "We gotta travel, say, seven-thousand miles and avoid a bunch a cops every step a the way? We just been in training so far, Jake."

There was one other resource I hoped would come through: Nico. He was trying to work with DOJ and the FBI, and, as long as we were outside the U.S., with the CIA. That opened up all kinds of unconventional methods, maybe clandestine, to get us out of Japan. If we could reach him.

But if the Japanese authorities were as alert as K insisted, it was even more dangerous than we had feared for us to try to contact Nico from Japan. They could learn our location. I could only hope that Tom had understood my message about the mole, and had passed it on to Nico.

Chapter 99
EASTERN UNITED STATES, SATURDAY, JANUARY 27

Untermeyer was in his room at the Holiday Inn near Cameron. It was Saturday morning. The phone rang.

"Felix, you need to proceed with the plan now. Are you ready?"

"Of course. Everything is set."

He knocked on the doors of the two experts. They got in the rental car and headed for the R & D complex at Cameron.

Austen Swinton was in a conference room at his firm, listening to an argument between two associates over the best strategy to avoid reporting a client's fraudulent accounting to the Securities and Exchange Commission when the phone rang.

"What?" It was his contact.

"You need to get on the phones and put your network on high alert. The CT team is being hunted by the Metropolitan Police in Tokyo and the National Police Agency across Japan. They will be contacting the FBI. And the Foreign Minister will be contacting the State Department. The U. S. Embassy in Tokyo has already been warned not to allow them on Embassy grounds. Got it?"

"You forget. This is my plan."

"I don't forget how much you owe us or anything else. Call me when you've done your job."

Austen slammed down the phone. The associates stared at the fit of temper from the normally unflappable head of the firm.

This was Madison Whitmire's fault. She was just like her mother. If she had listened to his advice, she would not be in this predicament now. And he would not be forced into taking risks that might expose enormous under-the-table funds he had received from one source to help him build the firm's Asian law practice. That had caused the firms billings to soar over the last ten years.

He turned to the associates. "We'll follow Wilson's line. Prepare the necessary SEC filings." The associates stared at each other, astounded at their debate cut short just as it began.

Austen headed toward his office to call former colleagues and friends in the Department of Justice and the State Department. They in turn would pass the new message to the FBI and immigration authorities. Then he had another call to make to the Director of the CIA, a classmate from Harvard.

Nico was watching the Bruins and the Blackhawks on TV and worrying about Jake and Madison when the phone rang.

"Nico. It's Dwight. I just got word. Your friends at Consolidated Technologies have screwed up. They're wanted by the police in Tokyo."

Why was Stancill calling them Nico's friends now? "That's ridiculous. They're investigating a civil case against a Japanese company. They have the goods on them, caught them red handed."

"Seems they were doing a little extracurricular spying."

That was exactly what Nico had wanted them to do, but in secret. "Who says?"

"They're wanted by the Tokyo police for murder and espionage. And every law enforcement and governmental agency in Japan and the US wants to find them. My phone's been ringing off the hook."

The team's safety and maybe their lives were in jeopardy. This had to be about OC-X. If so, it was an espionage operation with a great deal at stake, unprecedented for the Japanese to engage in, particularly on American soil. It was a dangerous game, and Nico had put Jake and his team in the middle of it.

"I've got to talk to Tom O'Hanlon."

"You won't be talking to O'Hanlon or anyone else at Consolidated Technologies. You're off the case."

Nico almost dropped the phone and did drop into the front hall chair, trying to make sense of what he'd been told. "That's absurd. I'm the only one who really knows this case." He couldn't disclose just how well. "What's this all about, Dwight?"

"You know one of the fugitives from law school. This comes from the top. You sit this one out. Report any attempt to contact you about this case to me immediately or you're done." Something was wrong. Stancill was an obedient bureaucrat, not one to take initiative. Someone was applying extraordinary pressure on him from the top.

Nico barely knew Payne in law school. He had been on a list of possible CIA recruits that Nico had been copied on. That was all, but someone had dug that up, an extraordinary effort to cut Jake off from any help. The final shock was how fast and thorough the net had descended over Jake and his friends. It had to have been prepared in advance. But how, and by who? The cancer went deep.

Dwight interrupted his train of thought. "Have you already had any?"

"What? Oh. Contacts?" Tom's heads up Thursday didn't count in Nico's book, not until he knew more about what was going on. "No."

"That's it then. Have a good weekend."

The bastard. There was nothing remotely good about any of this. If Jake and his hunted team made it to the U.S., with Nico and DARPA shut out, it would become a domestic criminal investigation and be kicked to the FBI. That was bad for Cauthen, Madison, and Jake. The CIA treated intelligence operations data skeptically, but there was no moral judgment, just constant digging below the surface until you got as close to the truth as you could. But the FBI could be heavy handed in intelligence matters. They hated turncoats and it could cloud their judgment. If whoever was after the team wanted to diminish the value of what Jake and the others had learned, this was the way to do it.

Nico knew he could count on Jake. But he'd led Jake to believe he could count on Nico. Now Jake and his team were cut loose, on their own, fugitives in Japan.

Chapter 100
SHINJUKU, LATE SATURDAY, JANUARY 27

Madison was out cold so we decided to get some work done. After two hours in K's living room, we had a rough plan to escape Japan, but it all depended on arrangements K had to make. He said we could sleep in the living room on the sofas. I stood up and stretched. I needed to clean the blood off first.

I peered into the bedroom. Madison was perfectly still, her breathing slow and deep. I took off my shoes, went in, and tiptoed quietly across the tiny room to the miniscule bathroom. There was barely enough room to turn around. I slid back the curved plastic shower doors, ducked into the stall, and turned the water on to get hot as I stripped off my bloodstained clothes.

I raised the temperature as high as I could stand, letting the water pour down. Steam filled the room and began to work the tension out. Not as good as the spa in Kyoto, but I didn't have to take a beating.

The bathroom door opened, and a blast of cold air hit the steam. "Charlie, I'll be done in a minute."

To my surprise, the shower doors slid aside. Madison was standing there, alert, and warm, looking me in the eyes. She had stripped off what was left of her soiled clothes. I started to speak, but she put a hand to my mouth, then held a finger to her lips. They began to curve into a weary but mischievous smile.

She seemed fine and she looked beautiful. It was clear she wasn't going to let me miss this opportunity.

My eyes slipped irresistibly from her gaze to her body. She stepped into the shower and held me close as time stopped. In that small space, she rested her head on my shoulder and we held each other as the hot water and steam washed over us, carrying away the grime, the tension, and the worry.

I gently raised her head off my shoulder and kissed her. She kissed me back and we began a journey of discovery while the world outside disappeared, leaving us in our private haven.

My old dog Gavin was scratching hard at the door. Time to feed him. But it was dark, and the bed was warm. My dog pawed at the door, louder and louder. Then I realized Charlie was rapping on the bedroom door. "Jake. Time to get up. We gotta get a move on."

"Okay," I somehow managed to reply.

It was not yet light. I fumbled around until I found the switch on the bedside table lamp. We'd had two hours of sleep. Madison stirred. We were cupped like two spoons in the narrow bed. I kissed her on her shoulder and whispered in her ear, "Wake up. Time to go skiing."

She rolled towards me, took me in a warm embrace, and kissed me slowly and longingly. Then she opened her eyes and tousled my hair as a brilliant smile lit up her face.

"You're crazy. I have a much better sport in mind."

Chapter 101
SHINAGAWA STATION, TOKYO, EARLY SUNDAY, JANUARY 28

I have no idea how K was able to make all the arrangements our escape in the dead of night. He was whatever the Japanese called a magician. The gray van and driver from the massacre had picked us up at the apartment in Shinjuku before dawn and driven to a store that opened early for us. After we were outfitted, we'd hurried to the Shinagawa subway station. We knew the main Tokyo station would be closely guarded. Even here, a few police holding flyers were already eyeing all foreigners entering the station.

We had to catch the bullet train westbound across Japan on the *Tōkaidō* route. There had been no time to talk about Houston with Madison, much less call Tom O'Hanlon or Nico. But traumatized by the attack in front of the Egmont Hotel and the speed and breadth of the manhunt coordinated against us, no one thought international phone calls were a good idea.

Here, three stops west from central Tokyo Station, we mixed in with a group of college students and pressed through the ticket turnstile. The crowd overwhelmed the attendants who were punching tickets..

Charlie, stuffed into a lime green jacket a size too small and topped with an oversized blue stocking cap covered with white snowflakes, wriggled as he tried to keep a pair of skis together over his shoulder. I peered through the smoked goggles covering half his face. "You like the bunny trails or the black diamonds, Charlie?"

"God Ahmighty," he fumed, nearly cracking his skis on Madison's head behind him. "Don't know how people get anywheres in this gear without killing someone."

"Normally you have a mountain under you," Madison teased. She seemed fully recovered from last evening's massacre, and last night's activities. "You look cute, Charlie. Watch out for the girls."

"If Jaynelle saw me in this get up, she'd die laughing."

K, in the lead, was also dressed for the slopes, his baldness covered by a brown knit cap. He turned back to Charlie and said, "This way, please."

"How long is the trip?" Madison asked.

"Five hours," K replied. "Our train makes only major stops, but there are still over a dozen before we get there. Please give me your passports."

Chapter 102
10:45AM, THE SAME DAY

Shin had stayed all night in the suite at the Kudan Kaikan, but he had not slept much. First, he had made all the important calls, then issued orders and listened as his lieutenants reported on the actions the authorities were taking to locate the foreigners and their accomplices. The fugitives had proven resourceful yet again, no doubt due to the efforts of the Japanese Shin's men were calling the *bonze*. They needed to know who he was.

As time slipped by, it was increasingly possible that the fugitives had escaped from Tokyo. That complicated the search. Shin's main objective now was to keep them from leaving Japan. If the police could get some idea of how they intended to do that, the options narrowed and the chances of catching the criminals increased.

An aide put down the telephone and turned to give a report.

"Shin-*san*, the Immigration police at all international airports and seaports outside Tokyo have now been supplied with drawings of the Americans and descriptions of their crimes."

Shin nodded. If they left Tokyo, they would have to go west. There were no international airports east of Tokyo.

They needed a plane. They had to get to the U. S. in time to stop the launch. A boat to the closest point in Korea would take thirteen or fourteen hours, losing precious time, but that could not be excluded. Covering all the possible launch points would require more resources.

Another assistant entered the room. "Shin-*san,* the Interior Ministry has identified the *bonze.* His name is Nakamura, an executive with a large trade association in Tokyo where he uses their apartment in Shinjuku. He lives west of the city in Kanagawa Prefecture and owns a temple there. The police are going to both locations to search now."

Details Shin would leave to the police.

"Sir," the man continued. "As a young man, he was a translator for the Allied occupiers after the war."

Shin stood up. He had been in prison after the war until all charges against him had been dropped. He searched his memory. Translator? He recalled a skinny young Japanese with big glasses. He was one of the few Japanese that spoke English well. He had been close to the US Army interrogators.

"A courier just delivered this photo." Shin's gaze drilled into the image. It was the man he had seen staring from the lane in front of the Egmont Hotel. Now he recognized him as an older version of the young man who burrowed among the loyal heroes of Japan confined to jail cells, gathering information for the foreign occupiers. This Nakamura was a traitor then and he was a traitor now.

"This is the man." Shin's staff knew that tone and snapped to attention. "All of you. Find out everything about this Nakamura. Report any discoveries to me immediately."

After a short nap, Shin emerged from the bedroom. His lieutenants were at work in the living room.

"What have you learned about the *bonze*?"

"There were signs people had stayed in his apartment last night and traces of blood."

"Where is he now?" His anger was rising.

"No one knows. The dead bodyguards belonged to a Korean gang."

The *bonze* had worked with all types of foreigners against Japan. Maybe he was still involved in other illegal activity. For now, his Korean connections pointed to the probable escape route closest to Korea. Fukuoka.

Shin gave an order. "Connect me to the head of the *kōanchōsa-chō*." The Public Security Intelligence Agency was responsible for all internal national security and espionage matters. They operated under the authority of the Ministry of Justice. They trained and coordinated closely with the FBI. Most Japanese did not even know they existed. To prevent abuse, any investigation required approval from the Public Security Examination Commission. In theory.

Director Akeda, with whom Shin had worked after the war busting socialist heads, came on the line and asked how he could help his old friend. There was no mention of the complex formalities required. Shin explained what he wanted.

"*Hai.* Shin-*dono.*" The director agreed at once, using the highest level of honorific possible, just below the royal family. They may have busted heads together, but the director was acutely aware that Shin could destroy his career with the wave of a hand.

"We have an excellent team in Fukuoka that tracks smugglers. I will personally have them take over the search. We know all the coastal hideouts. You can rest assured we will find the culprits."

"I am counting on you."

But not entirely. Shin signaled to an underling he had called in precisely for this eventuality, a second-generation North Korean who ran Shin's vast pachinko parlor network.

"Contact your friends. They will be incensed and highly useful. When you do, I will give you instructions." *Kistune* was activating every relevant asset of his extensive network.

Chapter 103
FUKUOKA, JAPAN, 12:30PM, THE SAME DAY

Our *shinkansen* pulled into the Japan Railways Hirata station with the whole team aboard, but no skiers. We were well past the Japanese Alps. K had provided us with a change of clothes from a suitcase delivered to him by yet another contact during a brief stop at Nagoya. Lots of Christians traveled to western Japan and I remembered why. It was the last stronghold of converts when they were massacred after evil Westernizing Christianity was outlawed in the early 17th century.

That's why Charlie and I were dressed in dark suits and wearing priests' collars. Madison was demure without make-up in a plain gray suit, a habit, and a collar. A wimple hid her blond hair. I supposed there were beautiful nuns, but after the night we had spent together, I had a hard time adjusting to Madison in that disguise.

K peered out the bullet train window. "Ah. Those are not normal policemen at the entrance turnstiles. Shin continues to press. Please stay close to me."

A tweed cap covered his head since Nagoya. K had arranged for another van here to take us to catch a boat. We were never alone on the train to discuss Houston. I'd given up on trying to call Nico until we were out of Japan.

As we stepped onto the platform, I saw a large contingent of men in dark uniforms standing in rapt attention before a superior barking orders. The crowd would soon disperse, exposing us. K stood in the train doorway, focusing on a man watching the platform and whispered to Charlie and me. "The man in the blue windbreaker by the vending machines is your contact. Use my name. Go with him quickly. I will try to meet you before you leave Japan."

"K, you done so—"

"There is no time, Charlie. Baik will take you to Korea. Go."

K shooed us away and faded back into the car.

As we started to leave the train and go to K's contact, the dark clad officials began to fan out, scanning the platform, and inspecting everyone leaving through the turnstiles. An official gave directions to another group that then streamed through a gate next to the turnstile and onto the platform, looking intently at everyone. The police were closing in on us.

We might run for it if they approached us, but to what end? We depended on K's contact for a way to escape. As the dark-clad officers fanned out, getting nearer, I looked over and saw a new crowd of men streaming up the station stairs and through the turnstile. They spread onto the platform in every direction. A particularly dense group surrounded the police, talking and holding up flyers, blocking the policemen's view. I turned to look at the train car we had just left. Many more men were now milling around the door to the train.

They were all monks in Buddhist raiment, all with heads shaved as bald as bowling balls, and all wearing heavy black framed glasses. I thought I saw a man dressed identically slip from the car into the crowd. It had to be K. The police were now blockaded by a thick crowd of demanding monks. Charlie and I hurried up to the man in the windbreaker, who seemed bewildered as he watched the monks spread all over the platform.

"Mr. Nakamura, uh, K, sent us," I said. The contact nodded, then led us down a corridor to yet another waiting van.

Chapter 104
NEAR HAKATA PORT, JAPAN, 3:30PM, THE SAME DAY

We watched from the deck of the small coastal ferry as it pulled into a simple harbor. Our driver had called this Genkaishima. It was a sleepy fishing village, set on a remote island in the mouth of the channel to Hakata, the busy port of Fukuoka city. Almost all the few boats berthed there were modest fishing trawlers, but a sharp-bowed ship, maybe seventy feet long, dominated the largest dock. It was dirty, with a rust-stained hull. A fast-moving speed boat roared into the harbor, cut its power, and glided to a stop near the big wreck of a boat.

"I hope that speedster is ours," Madison said.

I guessed from the few houses spread up a hill from the harbor that there couldn't be more than a hundred inhabitants of the village. I hoped Shin's network had not yet reached such an out of the way place. In the van, we had driven from the *Shinkansen* station to the small port of Miyanoura where our contact left us. There we boarded this ferry for the ride to Genkaishima.

There was no sign of K. We were without a local guide. Madison peppered Charlie with questions. "K said we'd meet a Mr. Baik. Do you know him, Charlie?"

"Knew him in the fifties. Trust him with my life."

"Why?" she pressed.

"Worked with him in the Army. He'as a young boy then, seven, eight years younger'n me. Quite a story. Grew up north a Seoul at In-chon. Daddy worked for the railroad so got him in a special high school in Seoul. Baik comes home one day and the whole city's empty. No family. He starts walking to his cousin's place outside a town and coming down the road's a buncha strange soldiers. He'd run smack dab into the North Korean invasion of South Korea."

"Then how in the world did you get to know him?" she demanded. I was enjoying someone else doing the interrogating for a change.

"Well, now that'as later. He'as working for the Northerners when one day he's walking out to the beach and the air's full a jet fighters strafing the road. Old Baik dives in a ditch. Now he'as smack dab in the middle a McArthur's invasion. He ends up working on most of the American bases in South Korea. That's where I knew him. Bought everything for all the Air Force PXs. Made a lotta brass happy."

"And him a lot of money," Madison concluded. "When did you see him last?"

"Must of been '52 or '53. Helped me round up a gang a GIs running Army guns back into the US."

"Sounds resourceful," I said trying to allay Madison's concern. "Like K."

"He sounds untrustworthy," Madison worried. "Like for sale to the highest bidder."

"Baik? Resourceful?" Charlie chortled, dismissing Madison's skepticism. "He made K look like a Sunday school teacher. He may grab a chance if he sees one, Madison, but I'd stake my life on him."

The ferry pulled up to the dock and we got off. A short, bow legged Asian man in a well-tailored, loud glen plaid suit crushed a cigarette under a shiny black wing tip and ran up to Charlie, shook his hand vigorously, then enfolded him in a fierce bear hug.

"I never think I see you again, Charlie. I so glad."

Charlie grinned and said to us, "The Koreans got the Japanese beat all-hollow for showing affection. Baik, this is my little tourist group, Madison Whitmire, Jake Payne. Fellers, this here's Henry Baik."

The man turned to us, dabbing the corners of his eyes with a sparkling white handkerchief.

"How you do? No time to waste. Please bring bags." He led us towards the rusting hulk.

"Is that what we're going on, Mr. Baik?" Madison was clearly miffed. "Can this boat even make it to Korea?"

Baik's old tub was picking up speed as she cleared the harbor heading into Fukuoka Bay. The curious Korean was in the boat's control room talking to the captain. Madison and I were enjoying the sun and breeze, after the tense trip from Tokyo. Charlie, who had been busily inspecting the boat, came up to us.

"They's something strange about this boat."

"Charlie," I sighed. "Of course, it's strange. It belongs to someone you know. What else would you expect? After all we've been through, it'd be strange if it weren't strange."

"Well, yeah. I mean no. Not that kinda strange. Looky here. All that rust we saw on the hull?" Charlie was leaning dangerously over the edge of the boat. "It's a mess, but it ain't rust."

"You're worried because smugglers aren't tidy?" Madison was incredulous.

"Not you too, Madison. Jake's enough of a handful. I been all over this deck. It looks like a mess, but it's really in A-One condition. All that paint on the hull is made to look like rust. See?"

As Charlie turned to look down again, I spied a multi-decked boat headed directly towards us from the port of Hirata. The channel was still narrow.

Charlie saw it, too. "Uh oh, fellers. I believe we got company."

The ferry was bearing down on us. Baik joined us as someone on the approaching boat broadcast over a powerful bullhorn.

Baik translated. "They say is Japan *kōanchōsa-chō* aboard commandeered JR Ferry *Nishima*. They demand we stop, prepare for boarding."

"What the heck's the *concha show,*" Charlie asked.

"Like secret police. Big trouble. Very mean." Baik looked spooked. "Never get near them."

The ferry chasing us started to pick up speed and rise out of the water.

"Police commandeered coastal vessel. Is commercial hydrofoil, latest Supramar PT 150 Mark II, Swiss copy of German wartime project. Very fast, thirty-five knots in open water."

We stared in dismay as the giant ferry sped towards us. Our boat made no effort to stop. Suddenly there were popping sounds. Two flares arced over our ship. Then there were rifle shots that kicked up geysers on either side of our wake.

"Very mean," Baik repeated. "Hold on tight to railing. Boat maybe rock."

"You're going to try to outrun them?" Madison shouted in disbelief. "In this tub?"

A deafening roar welled up from the guts of our craft. Water spewed from behind our stern at a furious rate. We all grabbed the railing as our feet began to slip. The acceleration was brutal. Our boat, too, began to rise.

Charlie turned in amazement. "Baik, whatcha got here?"

"American Navy surplus, Charlie. *USS Tucumari*. Boeing's best hydrofoil. Two Allison turbine engines, two Rocketdyne water jet pumps. I serve on her in Vietnam. US Navy want to scrap her."

"And you just up and bought a US Navy ship?" Charlie regarded his old friend askance.

"Well," Baik admitted. "Officially scrapped, not in US Navy records now. Some old friends and I work a deal." He smiled and patted the boat's railing. "She too young to retire."

"Look," Madison pointed back towards Hakata Port. Baik's boat was pulling away from the jetfoil ferry. Several men in uniform on the upper deck were jumping up and down and waving their arms, but we couldn't hear a thing.

"How fast didja say they go, Henry?"

"Thirty-five knots."

"And us?" I asked.

"Fifty-five," Baik smiled. "World fastest hydrofoil. We in Busan in three hours. Most time she go to China."

Madison couldn't resist. "Just what line of work are you in, Mr. Baik?"

"Used to be Korean Marine. Now most time, Miss Whitmire," he grinned, "I work for US Embassy in Seoul."

He turned and winked at Charlie. "But not all time."

Chapter 105
BUSAN, REPUBLIC OF KOREA, 6:25PM, THE SAME DAY

Henry Baik told us we were passing the civilian marine terminal in Busan Harbor, the largest port in South Korea. It was dark but above the glow from the port lights, a bright dome of stars cast an illusion of unchanging calm. At slow speed, the reflection of our night running lights danced in the water. All seemed beautiful and peaceful as we slipped slowly by the terminal. Baik pointed to the dock area.

"See group of big men inside gate over there?"

"Do you know them?" I asked.

"About them. They belong to *Singsangsapa*, one of two big Korean gangs. Big role in Japanese *pachinko* parlors. *Pa* means tattoo. They asked harbormaster to meet us when we dock."

"Can they help us?"

"Never. Men who helped you in Tokyo? They members of *Beomhonampa,* other big Korean gang. Like rice wine and chili oil: do not mix so good." We watched the gang move toward the quay. But as they spread out to greet us, we slid smoothly past.

"We cain't land here?"

“Harbor master a good friend. He directed gang there. We land up bay, U.S. Navy base. No gangs there.”

As we cruised on, we watched the gang members gesturing until they disappeared in the evening haze.

As soon as we had set foot on the dock at the Busan Navy Yard, Baik had glad-handed and backslapped everyone, and we had been whisked onto the giant U.S. Navy Sikorsky transport helicopter. It covered the 150 miles to Kunsan Air Force Base in western Korea in an hour. It was noisy and rough, but the three of us slept the whole way.

Baik, Charlie, Madison, and I stepped off the helicopter at Kunsan. As we walked to a waiting staff car, I heard Charlie talk quietly to Henry Baik. “We can’t thank you enough, Henry. But we gotta get to the U. S.. , all the way to the east coast, and we’s already imposing on you. In Tokyo, we figured we’d get to Seoul and catch a commercial flight to the US. Risky, but we got a deadline.”

“I talk with K,” Baik said. “He call from Nagoya stop on way to Fukuoka. You can’t take commercial flight. Too dangerous. Today you all defense contractors. You leave on Military Air Command to Tacoma right now.”

“You can do that?”

“A little risky.” His connections with the general were apparently still strong. “We have some U.S. driver’s licenses and Air Force contractor passes for you. K sent your passports. Arrived by speedy boat just before we left Japan. They there, too. You take this MAC flight to West Coast. Contractor passes get you through base security in the US. But then you on your own, Charlie. Is all I can do.”

“Gotta thank ya, Baik,” Charlie said. “Can’t say more, but you’re helping us clean up a mess much bigger than anything you and K and me handled back in the old days."

"I very glad to help." Baik gave Charlie another bear hug and passed him a thick envelope. Charlie opened it and showed me the contents: a sheaf of hundred-dollar bills big enough to choke a *sumo* wrestler. Madison and I thanked Baik, piled into the staff car with Charlie, and we headed for the tarmac.

Chapter 106
TOKYO, 8:57PM, THE SAME DAY

It was late Sunday evening, the day after the incident at the Egmont Hotel. Shin was still in his suite at the Kudan Kaikan. His North Korean put the phone down and, trembling, said, "The Koreans have lost them. They disappeared into the US Navy yard. What do we do now, Shin-*san*?"

Another surprise. The bonze had disappeared at Fukuoka. He and the Americans were proving troublesome. Shin's strategy of trading industrial secrets to protect optical computer secrets was now at risk. He would have to exert even more influence and pressure. Shin would have preferred to dispose of the Americans in Japan. From Korea, they could go east or west to get to the U. S. But in the end, it would not change the outcome. *Kitsune* would see to that.

He had learned his lesson a long time ago. Influence in the U.S. was like China. And the streets of the poor neighborhood where Shin first developed his black skills. Except it was easier at the highest levels in the U. S. If the Americans had briefly developed a national spirit during the war, it was dying now, choked out by money, power, and personal ambition. The lawyer Swinton and the turncoat Untermeyer were typical. The

Whitmire woman and her companions would find no one to help them, even in their own country.

Chapter 107
OVER THE PACIFIC, MAC FLIGHT, SUNDAY, JANUARY 28

During the long flight from Korea to McCord Air Force Base in Tacoma, Washington Charlie and I explained our thinking from K's living room to Madison. NASA Mission Control in Houston was new to her, but she told us what she had seen there during her recent trip. She asked us a lot of questions and recounted her conflict there. It was clear she had strong support in DARPA and NASA. After all, at her request, they had overruled the operations security officer, "Bull" Halsey, who had tried to kick OC-X off the flight.

"Wouldn't he be interested in gettin' it bumped now? Can't we get ta him?" Charlie asked.

"He took a beating from Washington over that letter he sent me at Cameron. He won't be anxious to buck the higher ups. He'll head up security for Deng's visit to Mission Control, so now he's heavily invested in the success of the launch. A cancellation would be a PR nightmare for the U.S. I think he'd be suspicious of anything non-standard."

"What about your allies at DARPA and NASA? Wouldn't they believe you?"

"If I can get to them in time, they would understand. But we'll have to find out how to do that when we land."

"Just supposing we can't get to 'em, who then?" Charlie asked.

"There's Grover Walker, my project manager. He'd understand the physics, no problem. He's fine leading a technical team, but he doesn't handle conflict or stress very well outside that bubble. Halsey bullied him at Mission Control until I intervened. With all the corporate and diplomatic prestige at stake here, and so little time . . . it has to be me."

Sato, Harry, K, Madison, so much riding on individuals. How could it come down to that? It started with Stefan the man Shin had killed to destroy his testimony. If we hadn't gotten to him and his documents, the forces working against us could have preserved their version of reality. K had known that. What had he said while we were escaping in the van, in Tokyo? *Shin can make it seem that Madison is in the wrong. Nothing else will matter.* Suddenly I understood in a new way what Shin was trying to do. It's what I did in a courtroom, without the violence. Discredit the other side, win over an audience to your version of the truth, but now for unimaginable stakes. The more pieces of the story you fit together, the stronger the brick wall you built for people to slam into. But in this case, we were doing the slamming. What were the bricks Shin was working with? Industrial property ownership, computing superiority, innovation, geopolitical mastery: all to strengthen Japan.

"This is much worse than we thought," I said.

"We got a bunch a dead bodies, Jake. And we're next, " Charlie said. "How's it worse than that?"

"When Minimura stole P.E.T. technology, it was an industrial theft. Maybe that was Kano's initial objective. But then OC-X got involved. The Japanese see computers as key for national power and economic strength. Then Deng and Madison's NASA launch got thrown in the pot, raising the stakes to national survival. According to K, this Shin thinks in geopolitical terms. He's used his gangster skills to wage clandestine international battles, ever since Manchuria. He's the one who saw the connection between optical computing, Sato's discovery of the electrical flaw in space, and Deng's visit to Houston."

"All that goes away if we stop the launch, doesn't it?" Madison asked.

"Depends which level you're thinking on. Deng's death is Shin's most important objective. But if the OC-X theft is suppressed, Japan also could claim an advance over the U. S. in computing, and Minimura might claim independent invention of optical computing to contest or defeat Madison's claims. All that's riding on getting Sato's information out and believed, as well as protecting Deng."

"Gol-*ee*," Charlie registered his shock. "They got ever reason to keep after us ta cover up the source a their technology."

I said, "Shin is driven to protect Japan from this new Chinese threat. The rest is important, too. He'll do anything, use any resource, coopt anyone, to stop us and destroy Sato's information." K's warning hit me with full force now. "Shin needs us dead."

We needed help, but we were alone. Except for Nico and Tom O'Hanlon.

Chapter 108
SEATTLE AREA, LATE SUNDAY, JANUARY 28

Madison and I had taken a cab from the base guardhouse. The taxi driver was waiting for us in a parking lot. I was paying for two soft drinks at a Seven-Eleven near the base to get change to call Nico when Madison showed me the evening paper.

"He's already here." Her voice sounded like it was coming from the end of the world.

The front page featured a picture of Deng Xiaoping smiling and waving heartily as he stepped out of his Boeing 707 at Andrews Air Force Base near Washington, D.C. that morning.

"We're here, too, Madison. We'll get to someone who'll listen."

When we landed at McCord, a sergeant with no name had whisked us through arrivals and took us to a room in the officers' quarters to clean up. Whatever alerts might have been issued for us at US airports, Henry Baik had found a way around them: another military installation. But, as he had warned Charlie, we couldn't assume our covers would last. Madison and I had left the base to call Nico. We hadn't wanted to leave Charlie, but he insisted. "I'm plum tuckered out. Ain't done this in over twenty years."

The easy part was over. K and his remarkable friends had taken care of everything in Japan and Korea. Now, assuming K was right, and Shin was working his U.S. network, we had to learn the lay of the land on our own before we disclosed our presence in the U.S.

I handed the cashier a five.

"Can you give me the change in quarters?"

We went outside to the pay phone. It was a risk calling Nico directly, but we had to give him ammunition for his inquiry right away. I fished out the card I'd kept in my wallet, the one he'd written his home number on at Cameron what seemed like a decade ago.

"Hello?"

" Nico. It's Steve White from U.Va. law. How are you?" Everyone knew White at the law school. He was head of fund raising. He also made Tom O'Hanlon look thin.

"Huh?" Nico hesitated, then he seemed to recognize my voice. "This is quite a surprise. It's been a long time. How are you?"

"I'm great, Nico. You wouldn't know me. Lost about a hundred pounds. I'm calling because we need your help. You know the Commonwealth of Virginia only supports the Law School about twenty-five percent, so we need your contribution to annual giving. Can we count on you?"

Nico took some time before he replied.

"To tell you the truth, I'm in government service so things are always a bit tight. Plus, we're undergoing a shakeup of responsibilities here and I'm not sure I can really contribute much."

He was in trouble. I couldn't risk giving him details over the phone. We had to meet somehow. But not in Washington, D.C., headquarters of all the agencies who might be looking for us. There was only one other possibility.

"You might want to join us for the class dinner. It's a good way to catch up on what's been happening. I'd love for you to meet the little woman." Madison punched me in the arm. "And who knows. You might enjoy it enough to become a contributor. Besides, our big donor will be there speaking about intellectual property law."

"Now that's more interesting, Steve. When's the dinner?"

That was enough.

"Hello? Nico? Hello? Can't hear a word."

"Steve, I'm right here," Nico yelled.

"Nope. Bad connection. Must have lost him. I'll have to call him back later, honey." I pushed the receiver cradle down, cutting Nico off.

"What was all that about?" Madison asked. "The little woman? That wasn't a panic attack at Cameron. You *are* a macho pig!"

"Something's going on at Nico's office. It doesn't sound good. We've got to try to get to him through Tom O'Hanlon."

"We'd better warn Charlie before we call Tom."

I punched in Charlie's number and extension at the base.

He answered. "I just saw yesterday's paper. Madison's picture's inside. The whole story put together by Shin. You better not come back to the base. We're all wanted over here now, too."

"But . . . ." I started to respond when I heard a loud hammering on the other end of the line.

"You better git, Jake. Sounds like I got company." The line went dead.

I leaned over and laid my head against the pay phone. Now we'd lost Charlie. For the first time since I met him, I was going to be without him. That night at the U-Stor-It, I thought he'd trapped me, put my career at risk. He had, but it had been the right thing to do, and I hadn't seen it. Charlie had known all along how to handle this kind of unpredictable, off the radar investigation. He'd been getting us out of jams ever since, always with good humor. I turned to Madison. She was staring at me with concern.

"Your picture was in the papers yesterday here in the US," I said. "All of us are in the story. As criminals, following Shin's script. Someone just banged on Charlie's door and he hung up. We're on our own."

"Then we'd better get out of here."

We had nothing but the clothes on our backs, the remaining false IDs, a few credit cards, Baik's cash, and Sato's documents that Madison had stuffed into a military duffle sack on the plane. She had not let them out of her sight since Tokyo. We got in the cab.

"Airport please."

"We call it an air base here, son."

We had to be careful not to leave a trail. The MPs were probably after us now, too. They could find this cabbie. I had to think like Charlie.

"Wait. Sure. What was I thinking? We need a hotel in Tacoma." We had to ditch this cabbie, I had to call Tom O'Hanlon, then we had to figure out how to get to New York without being arrested in our own country.

Chapter 109

MCLEAN, VIRGINIA, 6:30PM, THE SAME DAY

After Jake cut off the call, Nico was left standing in his front hall, perplexed. Jake and Madison had somehow made it back to the U.S. So Nico had driven to the 2010 Convenience Store on Corporate Ridge Road, about two miles from home, to make another call.

He put the milk he'd bought down on the pavement under the pay phone outside the store. As he waited for Tom to answer his home phone, Nico hoped Jake had gotten to him.

"Hello?"

"Tom, it's Nico."

"Where are you?"

"Public phone."

"Okay. I'll keep it brief. Jake called. They've got the goods. The Japs stole OC-X. Madison and Jake are back over here. Charlie's probably under arrest. Did you see Sunday's paper? Jake and Madison are absolutely cut off."

"They're not the only ones. I'm off the case."

"*What*?

"Someone's bringing down a lot of pressure from the top."

“Can you get up here mid-morning tomorrow? We have to get them cleared by Friday. I’ll fill you in when you get here.”

“I’ll try.” He should take the train. It would be harder to trace him than on the Eastern Airlines shuttle.

“Call me at the office when you get in.”

It wasn’t just a matter of avoiding the people pursuing Madison and Jake. They had to strike at the roots of the wider conspiracy seeking to destroy them. Nico had to get his friend back on Untermeyer as soon as possible. They had to come up with a way to get to the man running him. And Nico had to save his own career, if it wasn’t too late. He picked the phone back up and called the unlisted number he kept with him all the time now.

Chapter 110
THE UNIVERSITY CLUB, MANHATTAN, 4PM, MONDAY, JANUARY 29

Our taxi pulled up to One West Fifty-Fourth Street. I got out and held the door for Madison as she emerged from the back seat. She was still carrying the duffle sack with Sato's documents, but her hair was now a striking brunette. She had on dark glasses and a wide brimmed black hat, clearly back in her element.

She smiled radiantly as we walked into the elegant lobby. "It's so good to be out of those Podunk airports and back in New York."

"It was Pullayap, Washington, not Podunk," I said. Baik's cash had been enough to charter a small plane from Washington state to Utah. "At least you're smiling again,"

"What's got me smiling is your costume."

I was wearing a too large buckskin jacket with long fringe and a black Stetson hat I'd bought at the airport in Salt Lake City. Using two more of Baik's precious IDs, we'd bought our disguises and caught a flight that morning to JFK.

Nico had made it to New York as Tom requested. He and Tom were in a private room upstairs at the University Club. Nico listened with dismay to Tom's review of his meeting with Bob Langston an hour earlier.

"Madison's suspended from any Consolidated activity and Bob has called in the FBI and been cautioned by some guy Stancill at DARPA to report any contact from the team."

The plot went deeper than Nico could have imagined. The trap was closed, all the way from Japan, and Nico's boss had helped.

Madison and I approached the receptionist who viewed our outfits with dismay.

"We're with Mr. O'Hanlon's party." He directed us with ill-concealed contempt to the private dining room where Nico and Tom were waiting. They leapt up to greet us.

"I've booked rooms in case you need to rest and clean up," Tom offered.

"Thank you," Madison replied. "We slept a little at a motel near the Salt Lake City airport. A few shops were open before our flight. Too few, as you can see." She did a turn, curtsied, and framed me with her hands. "Jake lost."

Tom ordered sandwiches for four, over which we recounted what we'd been through. Madison explained the failure of the OC-X computer at Kagoshima and the devastation it had caused. It took time for Nico and Tom to absorb the technical issues. Then I laid out how this was the basis of the plot against Deng's life. I'd only told Tom on the phone that Friday was critical, not what was really at stake. They were understandably shocked.

"Let's get going," I said. "Who do we need to contact to stop this thing?"

Tom and Nico exchanged worried looks.

"The plan you've uncovered is incredible, unbelievable. Even in normal circumstances it would be hard to take seriously," Nico admitted. "But you need to know what's been going on here."

"Here's the latest," Tom said. "Felix Untermeyer was in Cameron over the weekend, auditing the OC-X security system at R&D. He concluded this morning that there had been massive copying of OC-X data from at least four years ago."

He paused. I knew what this meant, but I could see it hadn't hit Madison yet.

"He says you did it, Madison. You gave away OC-X. And he's got computer records to back it up."

She jumped up from her chair and started pacing. "They're faked. He's altered them. He's got cover from McElwain." She stopped, then nearly whispered. "*He can do anything.*"

She stared at Tom.

"No one believes him, right? Tell me that, Tom."

"Madison, Nico and I don't. But we carry no weight in our organizations right now. You've been suspended from your duties at Consolidated and reported by Bob Langston for theft to the FBI. DARPA's warned CT against giving you any support. DARPA doesn't mean Nico, either. He's been pulled from the case as of Saturday night."

She dropped to her chair and held her head in her hands. I stared blankly at the table.

"You can't imagine what we've been through," I said. "Madison almost died in a mass slaying in Tokyo. A maniac ultranationalist with unlimited resources needs us dead. We've evaded arrest halfway across the globe only to lose Charlie, fly halfway across the country to get here, just to find out we're totally alone. And we still have to try to prevent an international disaster. We're exhausted. We need rest, we need help, we need hope. We don't have . . . . " I had nothing left to say.

No one said a word for what seemed like forever.

Then Tom said softly, "Take a rest. Then we'll talk."

"Okay. We'd better meet back here in, say, an hour and a half?"

Madison broke her silence. "An hour."

"Jake. Jake." Madison held my wrist softly between her fingers, an airline stewardess trick for waking passengers. I opened my eyes, smiling, until I recognized the room.

"How long have I been out?"

"About a half-hour."

"You sound better." But she looked like hell.

"I don't think so. I . . . I've never given up, Jake." Her voice trembled. "But this is too much." We were trapped, me and this strong, smart woman, standing at the edge of an abyss. I didn't see anything to prevent us both from falling in and disappearing.

We held each other, sitting on the side of the bed, and rocked slowly, sharing what little energy we had left, trying to ignore what we were facing. Our respite lasted a few peaceful minutes. There was no past, no present. Just us, now, together. It was enough. It had to be. It was all we had.

Charlie's amazing smile suddenly filled my brain. There was always a way. I averted my mind's eye from the chasm and looked at Madison.

"We can do this. You can do this. I think you can do anything you put your mind to. I'll do whatever it takes to make this work."

She held my face and smiled a tired smile, then jumped up. "Phone books. Where are the phone books?"

"How romantic."

We called all over checking train, bus, and rental car options. We had reception send up a road map of the eastern U. S. Flights were out of the question. Each method of transportation had problems: the trains were too easy to monitor. Busses were harder, but slower, enclosed, and subject to checks and phone calls to and from drivers at stops. A rental car, the most tiring, provided the least risk of discovery.

New York to Houston was over sixteen hundred miles. We plotted it out. At sixty miles an hour on Interstates, we could reach Dandridge, Tennessee, and I-40, by morning. We'd never heard of it. That sounded perfect. We'd get a motel for a few hours, change rental cars, and head to Baton Rouge, another ten and a half hours. Another car, another motel, if we needed it. With two stretches of reasonable sleep, we could still get to Houston by 10 am Thursday. And have twenty-four hours to improvise. More than enough time for Charlie if he were with us and not in jail, we agreed. Enough, we hoped, for us.

"Shouldn't we have Tom make a copy of Sato's documents?" I asked.

"I thought about that. I don't want them in anyone else's hands unless I know I can be there to explain them."

We tried our travel plans out on Tom and Nico.

"Frenchie's," Nico said. "Best Italian in Houston. Two miles from Mission Control. Meet you there at noon for lunch, Thursday. That gives you two hours for traffic delays. Any changes, I'll be at the Clear Lake Hilton."

He still had his DARPA badge to get into Mission Control for the launch.

"They won't take that away, too?" I asked.

"They need me. It's like the Super Bowl for space junkies. All business. I have meetings with contractors. Lots of deals get made at the Hilton around launches."

"CT uses it," Madison said. "We can't. It's too risky."

"There are plenty of cheap motels near Hobby Airport," Nico said, studying our costumes. "You will fit right in."

We'd lost Charlie and gained another comedian. But we weren't complaining about a little humor, no matter how bad, at that point.

"Do you need money?" Tom asked,

"We're pretty sure the U. S. Government is paying for us." I explained Henry Baik's many ventures. We had to hurry and rent a car.

Shin's man had to call Tokyo and report and his boss might explode. Swinton had assured him that the CIA, through DARPA, had cut their DARPA asset off from the CT team. But Shin's man, who had been trained by and worked with the American intelligence services during and after the war, did not trust them. His calls had confirmed that DARPA considered the link severed but discovered that the DARPA person in charge had been seconded by the CIA. Removing him from the case wasn't enough.

Shin had added a huge bonus if his man had to invervene personally. Not that the man considered that a burden. He understood from what Shin said that this operation could weaken the fabric of American foreign policy and alliances in Asia. He would have done it for free to undermine the country that had treated him like a dog.

He'd picked up Amalfitano in DC, followed him on the train to New York, and surveilled him until he entered the University Club. The man had found the service entrance and bribed a waiter who had served guests in a private room. So now Shin's man knew Amalfitano had met with a Mr. O'Hanlon from CT who had reserved the meeting room, a room to which the waiter had delivered four meals. A man and a woman had used a bedroom O'Hanlon had also reserved.

It had to be Whitmire and Payne. The man did not know how they had gotten from Korea to New York. Their entry into the U. S. had not shown up on any immigration records. But they were no longer in the club. He had missed them by minutes. His only link to them was Amalfitano. And one other piece of information from the waiter: the couple had ordered maps and transportation brochures, train and bus schedules from the concierge. He could not know the route but he knew what their destination must be.

He gave the international operator the number in Tokyo and waited for the call to go through. When the call was answered, the man said, in near perfect Japanese, "This is New York reporting."

Shin came on the line and the man explained the situation. Silence.

The man knew better than to interrupt. Finally, Shin spoke.

"You have access to flight information. Check on rail passages, too. There cannot be many connections. What about bus transportation?"

"It is possible. But I cannot cover the bus stations here in time. After New York, there are many routes. In three days, they can change busses, too. The surest way is to cover the bus depots in Houston. I will arrange it."

"Is that everything? They have proved resourceful. You must cover every possibility. They cannot approach the facility in Houston. And, you must understand, they have information that cannot become known. Use the most extreme measures to make sure they do not communicate it, even after Friday. Do you understand?"

"Yes, sir." Shin had just imposed a death sentence on the couple, invoking the bonus arrangement. There was an additional benefit of the bonus. It would allow him to disappear after he eliminated the targets.

He would arrange for others to cover the public means of transportation. He would tail Amalfitano himself. But what if the fugitives rented a car? He would call California, then check nearby rental agencies for a one way contract to be dropped off between Atlanta and Houston.

Chapter 111
NEAR STAUNTON, VIRGINIA, MIDDLE OF THE NIGHT, WEDNESDAY, JANUARY 31

"I can't get comfortable." Madison was squirming. Cruising down I-95 in New Jersey escaping New York, we were headed to Houston shoehorned into a midnight-blue convertible Chevy Camaro Z28. It was the only rental available for drop-off in the South, at New Orleans. Which was okay. We didn't want a trail directly to Houston.

"No wonder it was available," Madison said. "No one in New York would get near one of these things. What did they call it?"

"A muscle car. At least we're making great time. What kind of car do you drive?" She said nothing. I turned to look at her. "You don't have a car, do you? You must drive. You gave the rental agent a license."

"I got one when I was in prep school. I haven't driven since."

We took I-95 to northern Virginia, I-66 west to the Shenandoah Valley, and I-81 south. By the time we hit Staunton, Virginia, it was 3:30 in the morning and we were both awake, headed into a desolate stretch of the Blue Ridge mountains. There was nothing we could do to prepare until we arrived, so we tried to relax and take our minds off Houston.

"Is it alive?" Madison asked.

"It was once. Nineteen left."

“Was it alive before the Cambrian Radiation?”
“What?”
“The explosion of life forms 540 million years ago. If your thing was alive before then the classifications of life were much simpler. I would ask the questions completely differently.”
I was nonplussed by her approach to a child’s road trip game. “Have you ever actually played Twenty Questions, Madison?”
“Not since before I went to Harvard.”
“Maybe we should try a different game.”
“How about Botticelli?”
“I like his work.”
“No. It’s a . . . . Jake! Be serious.”
“About a game?”
“*Look out!*” I had to swerve to miss a pick-up truck with one taillight out.
“Where did this fog come from?” I said.
“London?”
Was that a joke, from Madison? I liked it, or at least I liked her trying to tell one.

The mountain fog turned into dense patches of swirling cotton. I slowed down, but still almost hit a deer, it’s glowing eyes only revealing its presence when it turned its head to us in the middle of the Interstate. I slowed down more and put the flashers on. “I don’t want to get hit by that guy’s cousin in another pickup truck.”
“What are the odds it would be a cousin?”
“Statistically? You’d be amazed. I need to introduce you to Frank Brazeale.” That required an explanation. “So, see? It could be a cousin. This used to be a wagon trail from Pennsylvania to the Carolinas.”
Madison snorted.
“What was that?”
“I laughed.”
That wasn’t a laugh. “It was . . . endearing.”

“That’s why I never laugh. I’ve been kidded about it since junior high school.”

“I . . . .” I realized how little time we might have left together. “I like it.”

Chapter 112
INTERSTATE 10, EAST OF ORANGE, TEXAS, THURSDAY MORNING, FEBRUARY 1

"Bodhi, we've come over a hundred miles since Houston, man." Cody was riding shotgun, complaining again, as his partner drove the Mustang II King Cobra they'd rented in Houston. It had been hard to find, but they wanted the speed and the handling. "This gig's a bummer." Cody was a daring driver. And a damn good bass player. But not good for much else.

"Just keep your eyes on the oncoming traffic." They were looking for a midnight blue 1979 Camaro Z28 with Louisiana plates. "Calm down and focus, man. The guy said we should go all the way to New Orleans if we have to. I'm not gonna tell you again. We'll make more dough off this gig than three years of stunt driving."

Bodhi had demanded triple the price they'd gotten for running the big German off the road in Dallas. It was only worth taking this job if they could lay low and do what they really wanted to for a while, pick up some gigs playing back-up. The California beach sound was making a comeback after the Beatles had limited its appeal.

Cody and Bodhi had drifted from beach music into driving on stock car circuits, then in chase scenes for the movies. They only knew their contact as a voice over the phone, but they knew he was in Houston to pay them the rest of their money when they completed this gig.

"Bodhi! There it is. Far left lane, cruisin' sixty. Cross over! Bootleg, man. Bootleg!"

Bodhi spotted a dirt track through the median ahead, chained off by the State Police to prevent motorists from using it. He checked the rear-view mirror. No problem. He floored the King Cobra, then, just past the chain, braked hard, and spun the wheel to the left, executing a perfect bootleg one-eighty. They bottomed out on the median grass, scraped a door on the chain post, hit the dirt track and spun the wheels in the cushion of dirt churned up by the state police cars, losing speed. Then they hit the grass again and shot into the westbound lanes of I-10, racing after the Camaro, which had a coupla minutes lead on them. They blew by an Interstate sign showing the Orange exit coming up in two miles.

Chapter 113
INTERSTATE 10, EAST OF ORANGE, TEXAS, HEADED WEST

I was driving. Madison had finally drifted off, balled up in the cramped bucket seat of the Camaro. The weather had stayed bad all through the mountains into Georgia with sleet, fog, and occasional snow. Then driving rain forced us to crawl most the way across the deep South: Georgia. Alabama, Mississippi. We had to stop under overpasses when visibility shrank to zero until the weather began to clear halfway across Louisiana. Madison's nap was the first sleep either of us had caught since leaving New York.

The Interstate signs said we were coming up on Orange, Texas. Normally that would mean nothing to me except for one thing. We were within thirty miles of the pulp mill construction site in Newton County where I'd baited Boyden, then escaped his men, the local sheriff, and the local judge, a lifetime ago.

Ever since we'd come out of the mountains in Georgia, I'd warned Madison to keep an eye out for any suspicious cars on the road. We'd chosen the hardest path for anyone to follow, but as we got closer to Houston, the alternatives narrowed, making it easier for anyone working for Shin to look for us. The stakes for him—and his resources—were sky high. Memories of the massacre in Tokyo came flooding back, the knives, the blood, the bodies of our brave companions, Madison in shock. And what? I was running toward her. And a realization. I hadn't panicked.

A sudden anomalous movement behind us caught my eye. Some deep recess of my mind recalled Charlie picking up the tail at the Cotton Fields. There was a car doing a hundred. In our lane. I juked into the ramp for Orange, Exit 880, that dumped into the middle of town.

Madison jarred awake. "Where are we?" she asked. I was taking the exit ramp at over seventy. We began to skid. She yelled, "Jake, are you crazy?"

I was fighting hard to wrestle the Camaro's speed down, but said "Look behind us."

She turned and saw a low, sleek car on the Interstate, running flat out as it neared the Orange exit ramp.

"Are they after us?

"I don't know, but I don't want to stop and ask them."

"Jake! For God's sake!" She was suddenly alert. "What do we do now?"

The Mustang screamed onto the exit ramp. Bodhi gripped the wheel and feathered the gas, downshifting to use engine braking and bring the Mustang from a hundred and twenty to sixty as they hit the sharp part of the ramp curve. Unlike the stock Camaro they were chasing, the Mustang King Cobra's suspension held the line under the powerful centrifugal force. And unlike whoever they were following, Bodhi was a skilled race pilot. His dad, a professor at Cal Tech in Pasadena, had taught him all about the physics of cars. Bodhi pulled the Mustang up to the stop sign. The small-town center was on the left.

"Which way did they go, Bodhi?"

“Gotta be toward the center of town. They turned off in a hurry. Must have spotted us racing. They’re looking for cover.”

I’d turned left on Texas Route 87. “Let’s head for that big green domed building, only tall one in town. Could be the Court House. Sheriff’s department has to be close by.” I didn’t want to ask for help. We couldn’t face a lot of questions. I just wanted cover, and time to make a plan.

“That’s smart, Bodhi.”

“Had to be to the left where that big green dome is. It’s a small place. Only one big building. Nowhere to hide. We got ‘em.”

Jake’s hope faded. The domed building turned out to be a church, not a courthouse.

“There’s a sign,” Madison shouted, pointing ahead. “Straight ahead. Texas Police Department.” In two blocks, I turned right and pulled up to the curb beside a low granite building’s parking lot with at least five squad cars sitting in it. Officers in uniform were sauntering between them and the back entrance of the police department.

“There’s a pay phone on the corner.” I asked, “You have any quarters left?” Madison scrounged through her purse and came up with two.

I got out, locked the car door, and walked quickly to the phone. As I got there, the low, sleek Mustang slid by on the main street. The passenger looked down the side street both ways, spied our Camaro, and started gesturing at it. There was a car behind them, so they sped up. They’d be around the block in no time.

I plunked in a quarter, called information, and was put through to the Newton County Sheriff's office some fifty miles away.

"Sheriff's office. How may I direct your call?"

"Give me the sheriff."

"May I say who's—"

"Now, ma'am." I shouted. "This is an emergency!"

They patched me through to the sheriff in his car. "This is Sheriff Tibbets. What's all the ruckus?"

"Sheriff. This is the foreman at the paper mill outside Forest Heights. Mr. Boyden's out of town, but he asked me to call you."

"Well, glad to help Newton County's largest tax pa— uh, employer. What's the hurry?

"You remember a couple of months back we called you to come after those guys stealin' documents?"

"Hmppff," the sheriff sniffed. "Not gonna forget them sumbitches soon!"

"Well they're back," I said, "Nearby."

"Nothin' I can do. That's all tied up in a Federal lawsuit."

"But that lawyer's heading to a meeting at the paper mill, down near Forest Heights," I explained.

"So what?"

Chapter 114
DOWNTOWN ORANGE

Bodhi finished driving the third leg of a rectangle, pulled up to a stop sign on West Front Street and peered right. "See anything?"

"Camaro's on the right side of the street now, facing away from us."

"How many in it?"

"Can't see."

Bodhi pulled onto West Front Street and stopped by the curb, a block behind the Camaro. "What's his game?" Bodhi asked the dashboard.

"Don't know," Cody answered.

A big black and white Crown Vic police cruiser eased out of the lot behind the parking lot, turned left toward the street that ran back to the Interstate, and pulled up to the stop sign. Its left blinker winked on. The Camaro's blinker did, too, then it slid away from the curb and stopped behind the patrol car. As the black and white slowly rolled left, the Camaro followed.

Cody said. "You think they hooked up with the police?"

"Nah. Man said they're all kinds of national bulletins out on 'em. If that's them, they can't take a chance. They gotta get to Houston. If they get back on I-10, we got 'em. It's flat. We can run 'em off the road at high speed, less risk than that overpass in Dallas." Bodhi moved the Mustang out to follow the Camaro. This gig was almost over.

As we trailed the police car, I filled Madison in on my conversation with the Newton County Sheriff.

"He's still mad at you?"

"Hopping. I just hope this patrol car's headed north into the county."

"If not, can't we get back on I-10 and outrun that . . . what did you say, Mustang?

"That's our worst option. That's a King Cobra Mustang. A real muscle car tuned better than this one. Did you see how it took that exit ramp? Those guys know how to use it."

The cruiser passed the green domed church at a sedate pace and continued north. I stuck close to our black and white lifesaver. In the rearview mirror, the Mustang hung back, but not far. The patrol car took a left, then a right. I followed it and could see I-10 ahead, running right through town. The patrol car eased into a left turn. Our two main options lay straight ahead: the on ramp, and this road into the rural part of the county.

I began to pick up speed. A sign said this was still a thirty-five mile an hour zone. I hit forty-five as we passed under I-10 and flew by the on-ramp. There were no commercial buildings after that, just a run-down subdivision on the left and a plain store-front church on the right. The terrain began to roll as we headed away from the coastal plain. Clear sailing straight ahead on Texas Route 87, all the way to the Newton county seat, fifty miles away.

"Hold on, Madison," I warned. I mashed the gas and the Camaro's four-hundred and forty cubes responded, pressing both of us deep into the leather bucket seats.

"They're running for it, "Cody shouted.

"I see," Bodhi yelled. "We got 'em now. Just like Colorado Boulevard back home." The Mustang had a smaller engine that was entirely designed for speed, not just a hunk of steel dropped in a standard convertible passenger car frame. The surfers were heating up like the engine block of the Mustang, stoked by the thrill of the chase, their main occupation since high school. Their Mustang began to close with the Camaro.

Madison was keeping lookout behind us. "How far do we have to get, Jake?"

"Sheriff just said, 'Not too far.'" But we were into rolling countryside. As the road began to rise, I worried that the Mustang might have an advantage.

"How far is the paper mill?"

"About fifteen miles from Orange, in the next county."

She turned and looked through the rear window. The Mustang was only three or four hundred yards back, and gaining. She whispered, "We're not going to make it,"

Bodhi kept his foot slammed to the floor. The Mustang's speedometer needle blew past ninety. The road was two-lane but narrow and rough. He fought to keep straight as they closed the gap.

Cody yelled again and pounded the dashboard with both hands. "It's them. There's two people inside. The passenger looks like a woman."

Bodhi shook his head. "Who else would be trying to outrun us? Of course it's them." He checked the odometer. They'd covered three miles since I-10 and were eating up another mile every forty-five seconds. There was nothing out here but pine trees, closely lining each side of the road, the road rising with occasional down slopes. The Mustang would have an advantage on hills. It leapt off the pavement at the crests, allowing the Camaro to surge ahead briefly, but their prey couldn't pull away. The gap between the howling cars narrowed.

Bodhi was running close now. He'd perfected his next move pulling bump and runs on the stock tracks around L. A. before he even had a license. His Mustang nudged the Camaro's back bumper. He let up just a hair, so he could generate a stronger hit. If the other driver panicked, or swerved the least bit, he'd lose control, run off the road, and hit a wall of sixty-foot pine tree fifteen feet away, doing ninety. Good enough.

Sheriff Tibbetts was in his patrol car on the side of Texas Road 87 facing north as he'd told Boyden's man he would be, just over the county line. And just over the crest of a hill on the road from Orange, out of sight from anyone coming from there. A favorite speed trap location since speeding cars leaving Orange felt free on the open road, not noticing they were entering another county.

Deputy Ebson was in a car on the other side of the road, next to the controller for the portable traffic restrictor, called a "stringer", they had bought to control cars at the county fairgrounds. Sheriff Tibbetts heard the whining engines before he could see anything. They were loud. Real loud. Two cars, he knew. Let the Camaro go by and stop the Mustang for speeding, Boyden's man had said. Tibbetts was looking forward to getting even.

He slipped his prowler into gear, ready to give chase to the Mustang if need be. He would let the Camaro go like he told the foreman from the paper mill. Tibbetts, eager to catch the smart-ass lawyer, gave a thumbs up to Deputy Ebson across the road. "Only one way out, this time, you shyster."

Then he spied the top of a car in his rearview mirror, running way too fast. The stringer was too dangerous at that speed. He waved for Ebson to back off.

Bodhi saw the two patrol cars too late. Surprised, he let off the gas and the Camaro shot ahead. He banged the steering wheel and bellowed. "God dammit!"

I recognized the sheriff's cars I'd seen from my client's King Air as we climbed above the paper mill airstrip back in November. A thick black chain like the sheriff had described ran across the road between the sheriff's cars. I stomped the pedal, as if it would do any good. The Camaro's engine was straining full out. There was a thump, and a jump, as our Camaro raced over the black chain.

Deputy Ebson had set the stringer up perfectly. Proud of the highest tech weapon in the Newton County Sheriff's department's arsenal, he'd pounded the stakes through the chain on either side of the road and deep into the ground, just like the manual showed, leaving a little slack so the teeth lay flat on the pavement. The stringer needed to be real tight to work right. It had a small explosive cartridge that tensioned it better than two men could. He'd tried it a couple of times at the fairgrounds, though they really didn't need it there.

They would here, though, with the cars moving at top speed. The timing would be a challenge. But he could do it. He focused his vision and readied his hand. As the Camaro shot by, Deputy Ebson mashed the red button. The cartridge fired tightening the chain, lifting the jagged teeth of the stringer, canting them toward the King Cobra.

At first, Ebson didn't notice any difference. Then all hell broke loose. The Mustang's tires began to smoke. The stringer's sharp teeth had punctured all four. Deflated rubber shredded between the chromed rims and the asphalt pavement and started to burn. Then sparks flew as the bare rims ground against the pavement. The Mustang began to wobble, careened to the left, then veered sharply to the right, and went airborne.

It slammed into the wall of dense pine trees lining Route 87. Clumps of metal and glass shot into the air, dug into the grassy shoulder, and spewed across the road. Just over the Newton County Line, six-point-four miles north of the City of Orange.

Horrified by the disaster, Sheriff Tibbetts jumped out of his car and grabbed his service hat. Him and Ebson were in deep shit. He slammed his hat on the pavement and jumped up and down on it. He'd just wanted to scare the damned lawyer, not kill hm.

In the Camaro, I took my foot off the gas, but avoided braking until we slowed down to about fifty. I didn't want us to lose control sideways. But we still had to get out of there.

Madison turned and stared out the back window. "There's a plume of smoke above the trees."

Chapter 115
NEAR BEAUMONT, TEXAS, 10:00AM, THE SAME DAY

Madison and I looked at each other wide eyed, as we sped along Texas Highway 12 toward the small town of Vador.

Finally, she broke the silence. "How could they find us? This isn't Japan."

"They're smart, Madison. They can cover most of it with calls, just as we figured. And they have Shin's resources. K said he may be the wealthiest man in Japan."

"Then what chance have we got? They found us on a 1,600-mile trip!"

"Those guys looked like expert race car drivers, Madison. I bet so were the ones that ran Stefan Weidl off the road in Dallas. It's Shin, again, reaching out all the way from Tokyo."

We were exhausted, worried, taking turns at being scared.

"We're not far from Houston, on the shortest route. There was only one southern rental drop off. They got the descriptions just like we did, I guess. It's not rocket science, and it's certainly not polymer chemistry." I didn't get a laugh. "But Madison . . ." She turned to me, her red-rimmed eyes filled with worry. "We got away! Charlie would be proud We improvised and beat them with all their money. We'll be fine." I reached over and stroked her cheek. She took my hand and held it there.

At Vador, we took the entrance ramp onto I-10 toward Houston, nearly a hundred miles away. We were going to be late. As the adrenaline from the high-speed chase drained away, fatigue caught up with us again. The flat, dull miles rolled on. There was almost no traffic. Madison drifted off again. I looked over at her from time to time to keep from nodding off. She looked peaceful.

We were about forty miles from Frenchie's when she shifted in the passenger seat, stretched, then sat up.

"Where are we?"

"Past Beaumont, almost to Houston We'll be at Nico's restaurant in less than an hour. You got some sleep. Good."

"I feel better. How about you?

"I can gut it out. We need to get there."

She looked at her watch. "My turn. Pull over when you can."

"Thanks. You looked peaceful." And beautiful. "There's a rest stop ahead."

She was silent for a while, then said, "Jake, we're on the run, headed right toward the one place people are willing to do anything to keep us away from." She paused. Then in a voice heartbreakingly weak for such a strong woman, she said, "We may not make it."

"I know. K said Shin could do anything. I believe it now."

"I'm not afraid, Jake. Don't think that."

"Madison, you're the most accomplished person I've ever known. I know you're not scared. I'm not sure I can say the same thing."

"Come on. I'm not worried about you. Nico and the top people at CT weren't either. That's why they kept you on the case and they were right." I turned. She was looking down. "It's just that . . . what could happen concentrates your attention. We're headed as fast as we can to a place no sane person would want to go."

Ever since the massacre in Tokyo, we knew we could be caught and arrested any minute. The attack by the Mustang had confirmed that Shin was determined to kill us. As the flat southern coastal plain slid by beneath a now blue unchanging, infinite skies, the danger hadn't seemed real. But we'd just experienced how close, sudden, and fatal it really was.

I stared ahead, blinking to clear my misting eyes. It helped to think of our situation as another puzzle to solve, like a trial, where you were an actor, not really a participant unlike the parties to the case. I tried looking at our predicament as if I were floating, looking down, seeing actors on a stage. That had always helped at trial. I started to suggest it when Madison spoke.

"This is my life's work," she said in her strong executive voice. "I have no choice. You can still get out, Jake. Just get me to Nico."

She couldn't know. " Nico gave me an out. I turned him down." She looked up sharply. I caught it out of the corner of my eye. "That day we met with the team, the day I told you about my family. And my . . . the attacks. I'd never told anyone about that except my doctors in Charlottesville."

She put a hand on my shoulder. "Have you had an attack since then? We've been together every day. I haven't seen one."

"No."

"Jake, in Tokyo I saw you running toward me and the assassin with the knife before I blacked out. We were in the middle of a massacre and you were racing toward me. Maybe the panics are gone!"

" Nico knows about them. That may be the reason he offered me an out."

"How could he know?"

"He knew about my family at law school. Everyone knew."

"But you said you hid the attacks. What did Nico say?"

"Nothing, but he didn't have to. My security clearance. The FBI talks to everyone, finds out everything. Even from doctors. That day we met the team at Cameron, he offered to bring in CIA law firms from DC. In the time we had left, I didn't think they could help. The legal part of this is simple. I figured it was more a case of Nico concerned that I might screw up." I remembered Nico staring at me at Cameron, waiting for my decision. "I didn't like that. So I'm in this with you to the end."

I was fully back in the car, not an actor anymore. We drove on in silence as the last miles slipped away.

Then she said, "I don't think he or anyone else thought you couldn't do this." After a moment, she continued. "Maybe the law is simple. For you. But that's not all you do. It's not even the most important thing you do."

"I'm a lawyer, Madison. A trial lawyer. A small-town trial lawyer."

"No, you're not."

"What?" I shot her a glance but had to turn back to watch the road.

"Charlie calls you *Counselor*!"

"It's just an inflated title, like a TV series, 'Counselor at Law.' Charlie and I kid each other."

"I've seen you in action, Jake. Even while people are getting killed all around you. Look, when Tom O'Hanlon told me how you rescued Charlie in Dallas, I was shocked. I couldn't function in that kind of chaos. I saw you differently."

"What are you talking about? He told me you didn't want me leading this thing, that you wanted the Gordon firm to take over." She could have had CT kick me off the case.

"Yes, I was still mad at you."

"That was clear. You almost knocked me down in the lobby at Cameron." She laughed. "But you didn't tell anyone. Why?"

"You did the other thing . . . . the counseling thing."

I'd only told her about me, about my sister, about my panic attacks. "I didn't say a thing about you . . . except I guessed you might have been a dancer."

She snorted, then turned serious again. "When you explained why you reacted to me the way you did, I changed. In a split second, I saw you better but I saw my life differently, too."

Where was all this coming from? "Madison, you're kind. But this isn't a date. You don't have to flatter me."

"Stop it." Then her voice changed completely, becoming a soft whisper. "I'm serious. I haven't been this close to anyone since I lost my parents. And I couldn't be, until you showed me how to trust someone. In the lobby at Cameron. I have to tell you this. We don't have any time left."

Her nearly inaudible message was straining to be heard, understood, valued, sheltered . . . and loved. I started blinking again, blew out a troubled breath, cleared my throat and managed a husky, "We'll be okay. Together."

No time. The urgency, the pressure, the danger were still all around us, first waiting, now stalking, drawing close. We might not survive. What would I leave behind? My family was gone. She had been brave and resolute forging a plan in New York. And beautiful. Every minute. Even angry, exhausted, dazed, covered with blood, squeezing my hand in that freezing, dusty Hikone dining room. And tender, in Tokyo, in Shin's apartment after the massacre.

The massacre. She was right, I hadn't panicked. Maybe we would survive. Maybe we'd succeed in Houston. And after.

No time left. I had to tell her. "Madison—"

"Jake! The exit!"

I swerved and regained shaky control just in time to squeeze onto the off ramp for the rest stop, cutting off a string of cars and launching a barrage of angry horn blasts and rude gestures.

I skidded to a stop in the parking lot. Madison was laughing so hard, truly laughing, not snorting, that tears streamed down her cheeks. All she had said stuck in my mind and I was grateful. I watched her as her laughter gave way to silence. She looked relaxed, happy, strong. Then something changed.

She turned to me, looked deep into my eyes, and smiled that thousand-watt smile. She reached over, put her hands around my neck, pulled me gently toward her, and we kissed. And held each other. Across the rental car console. It could have lasted forever. Her tears wet my face, but not tears of laughter now. Something warm.

Chapter 116
HOUSTON, NOON, FEBRUARY 1, T-MINUS ONE DAY

We walked into Frenchie's on East NASA Parkway and spotted Nico in a booth under a wall covered with astronauts' autographed photos. He rose and led us to a private room in the back.

"How was your trip?"

"The spy can't tell by looking?" Madison asked. "Nearly sixty hours driving a cramped rental hot rod through mountains, rain, fog, sleet, and snow. No stops. We need to find one of your cheap motels as soon as we're done here and get some rest."

"How about you?" I asked.

"Got in last night. I've talked to Grover Walker and Jim Cernak. Security was already tight, but it's been beefed up. Bull Halsey is on a rampage, cursing at Madison every few minutes. He's heard from CT, DARPA, and NASA. His ass is on the line."

Madison said, "No way we can count on him."

Nico continued. "There's a pre-launch briefing at seven tonight. Let's meet again after that. The launch crew takes over at Mission Control tomorrow morning at five AM. VIPs arrive at nine. Liftoff's scheduled for ten." The waiter arrived and we ordered.

Shin's man sat in his car in the parking lot. He saw Amalfitano greet the couple and lead them into the back of the restaurant. There was no sign of the drivers from California. It had been a long shot, worth trying to take out the couple as far from Houston as possible. It hadn't worked. But Shin's instructions were clear. It still had to be done.

Nico went over the layout of Mission Control. He could get two contractor passes using his DARPA connections, but our appearances would be a problem. We would be on a watch list, but Madison was a celebrity, even before Tokyo. She was the only one who knew how to prevent the disaster, and she would be the primary target of all the security thanks to Untermeyer and, now, Halsey. Even in disguise, she would stand out in the control room, where she had to be. Nico had his DARPA pass, but that would only get the holder into the observers' gallery for a tour, not onto the Mission Control room floor for the launch. Neither would the contractors' passes. Getting Madison there was the real problem.

Madison spelled out the technical aspects of a launch, including the events in the control room before and after liftoff. She emphasized the short time it would take the rocket to enter the dangerous zone of the ionosphere that Sato had identified. Grover and Jim Cernak would have worked out the mission protocols while she was away so she couldn't know the details, but she knew the essential steps leading up to the OC-X module activation and, thanks to Sato's notes, the instrumentation warning signs.

Then Nico went through his expected movements until lift off. We dissected every one, considered alternatives, suggested options. We came up with a bunch, none of them good. There were so many variables, so many obstacles. We couldn't see a way in. Protecting Madison's identity was still the biggest problem.

"The odds were always bad. Now they're getting worse," I said.

Madison, head down, said nothing. We were out of time, energy, resources, and everything else. Something Nico had said about his movements at the Hilton gave me an idea. I made one last stab at how to get Madison in.

"But, Nico," I said, "this means you'll have to be in the building through the launch. If we can't stop the activation, you risk being caught in the explosion."

"I know that," he said with some difficulty. "Look at the risks you two have been taking ever since you arrived in Tokyo. Let's not talk about any of that now."

My plan was complicated. I was still a lawyer. But Madison and Nico liked it. Besides, none of us could come up with a simpler way to meet our objectives and cover the risks. The clincher, we all agreed, was that Charlie would have loved it.

Nico took Madison to the EconoLodge near Hobby Airport and I went downtown to do some shopping.

Shin's man saw the threesome split up in the parking lot. He had to get to the couple, take them both out. She was the biggest danger. She was the scientist. According to Shin, her knowledge and credibility were the real problems. She was the primary target. But Payne was a witness. He had get to them both, away from Mission Control, in a quiet, isolated place. They were splitting up now.

He started his rental car and eased out of the parking lot at Frenchie's to follow Amalfitano and the woman.

Chapter 117
HOUSTON, 8:00PM, THURSDAY, FEBRUARY 1,

T-MINUS FOURTEEN HOURS

Nico returned to the Clear Lake Hilton. The lobby bar was buzzing as usual before a launch, full of military, contractors, and space fanatics.

The launch briefing had provided Nico with a useful update on contractor security measures. He'd reported to Jake and Madison at the EconoLodge. Now he had critical tasks to perform. Madison had written two notes, then handed them to Nico, one in a large manila envelope to deliver tonight, and one in a smaller letter sized envelope for tomorrow.

Madison's Consolidated team was at The Hilton, too. First, Nico went over to the reception desk. There was no clerk. He reached over the counter and put the manila envelope on the work surface where a manager would be sure to see it. A note on the outside said: "URGENT. Please deliver to Grover Walker of Consolidated Technologies IMMEDIATELY."

Nico rang the call bell, left the front desk, and walked toward the cocktail lounge to meet an Air Force contact for a drink. The major was ostensibly here for the launch, but really wanted to discuss his advanced fighter guidance technology idea and get Nico's help with DARPA funding.

Shin's man had backed into a space in the EconoLodge parking lot. He watched the stairs at the back of the motel that the woman had taken up to room 212. He had seen her open the door with the key and go in, then Amalfitano left. The lot was still full of cars coming and going. The lawyer had come by, dropped off a garment bag, then left.

Around 7:30, Shin's man saw the midnight blue Camaro Z28, pull into the parking lot and drive around to the back stairway. The lawyer got out holding a fast-food bag, climbed the stairs, and knocked. As the door to the room opened, the light shone on his face. Shin's man saw a weary smile and the lawyer went in.

Shin's man relaxed deep into the seat of his rental car, watching cars come and go in the parking lot. The time to take them would be the dead of night after the parking lot was full and quiet. When his prey were asleep, or at least in bed. They would be out cold or distracted and off guard. He had a couple of hours to wait.

If the parking lot stayed busy, as some did at these cheap motels, he could wait until early morning. But it was riskier, more chance of being observed. This was the right place, two-thirty was the right time.

Chapter 118
PARKING LOT, ECONOLODGE, HOUSTON, 2:45AM, FRIDAY, FEBRUARY 2

The silence and the absence of people were right. But the lights were not. The parking lot was brightly lit. The nearby airport shut down at night, but its security lights were like a night football game at half-time. Some of the lights outside the rooms were burnt out. At least the lot was full. No one else would be pulling in.

He got out of the car, opened the trunk, and took a Beretta 71 semi-automatic pistol fitted with a cartridge suppressor out of his tool bag, the assassin's weapon the Mossad preferred. There were more lethal guns for a single shot, but nothing compared to the silence, accuracy, and negligible recoil of the Beretta 71. With its eight-shot magazine, he had plenty of rounds to incapacitate, then finish off both targets. He had fixed his backup mechanism to his left arm while he waited in the car. It might be overkill, but he had learned a process and followed it. Be prepared. No mistakes.

After scanning the parking lot one last time, he closed the trunk, and started up the outside staircase toward Room 212. As he approached the room, he confirmed the curtains were drawn and no light shone through the gaps. He'd surveyed an identical room layout with the night receptionist around 10pm. The receptionist was still in that vacant room and would not rent it out that night or any other night ever again. No witnesses. A process. Be prepared. No mistakes.

He visualized his prey, gauged his movements, adapted his focus to the light, calmed his nerves, slowed his breathing, readied to sense, and integrate the targets' least movement into his aim. Kick in the door, empty the suppressed bullets into the two sleeping bodies, walk back to the car. He squared off, his eyes and brain glued to the door, then rocked back to add momentum to his kick.

"Uh uh, Wolf." Albert Wolf was stunned to hear his name. He'd had all the time in the world to prepare for the kill but on hearing words spoken by a person, his synapses suffered a small part of a second delay in reorienting his attention to a new object to his left, in the dark where a bulb had burnt out. That slowed by a longer fraction of a second his effort to raise his left arm and turn his head to release the spring-loaded dagger strapped to his arm.

He heard the quiet "pfftt, pfftt, pfftt" of three suppressed .22 rounds and felt them hit his upper left shoulder, making it impossible to effectively deploy the knife loaded in the backup spring mechanism. The assailant had known about the knife. It was an old CIA trick, part of the process. Wolf's eyes widened in surprise at the dark shadow standing sideways to minimize his profile, arm extended, only the barrel suppressor of a Beretta 71 in view. Contemplating all those facts, Wolf's brain slowed further now as he realized the assailant was CIA trained, too.

Wolf started to bring his right shoulder forward so he could swing his right hand around to unload his Beretta at the man. "Pfftt, pfftt" Two rounds caught his right arm. Wolf's Berretta clattered to the walkway as he pitched back onto the cement, wounded on both sides.

The shooter walked slowly up to him and pointed his identical Beretta at Wolf's head.

"How did you know?" Wolf managed to whisper, getting dizzy and faint as his blood pooled on the walkway.

"I've been shadowing you for weeks in New York. From a distance you could never imagine possible. New tech, Wolf. You're out of the loop. We needed to know what you were up to. But you'll have time to add words to the pictures." The other advantage of the Beretta 71 .22 was you could incapacitate targets without killing them. And keep them alive for interrogation.

Wolf gasped. "My name . . . how?"

"The Agency never forgets a face, Albert." The man clubbed Wolf with the butt of his Beretta, hefted him onto his shoulder, leaving Wolf's legs and custom-made oxfords dangling, and carried the wounded man down the stairs.

Chapter 119
MISSION CONTROL, 8:00AM, FRIDAY, FEBRUARY 2

T-MINUS TWO HOURS

Nico's tasks this morning were more difficult. He had to get his material into place, then position Madison's white envelope. At NASA, even with tight security, many contractors would be there for this launch. There would be two entrances.

Nico left the Hilton early to be at Mission Control when the doors opened. Now there was nothing else he could do. According to Jake's plan, Jake and Madison would arrive at the last minute, after Nico was in.

As Nico waited in line, he looked around. Security personnel were inspecting briefcases. In the contractor's world, personal luggage was a status symbol. There were silver aluminum Halliburtons of every size and description, big document bags, leather satchels, and squared off plastic vinyl covered Samsonites. He'd looked over the groups milling as the doors opened at 7:30 and had lined up behind one well-equipped group of engineers whose baggage would take time to inspect, tag, and put on mobile racks. "You'll get them back on the way out," the inspector informed each person in line. That had been part of the security briefing so Nico was prepared.

The lines bogged down. Nico's was on the left, closest to the contractors' assembly point inside Mission Control. Their plan counted on that. By the time he got to the front of the line and opened his document case to expose nothing but paper, the inspector was relieved. Nico was DARPA, government—defense, not a private contractor. "I need this inside. Those are DARPA papers NASA needs for the launch." The guard shuffled through the top layer of files, confirmed Nico's badge number against his list, and waved him through with his case. A tired bureaucrat lulled into a violation of Halsey's security directives.

Inside, Nico was directed to the observation gallery, gathering point for contractors authorized for the control room tour. The gallery was separated from the control room by a bank of large windows. This next bit would be more difficult. They were split into groups of six with a guide. Each group would start the control room tour at one of six prescribed stations, like a shotgun start at a golf tournament, so they could all get through quickly.

Between Madison's knowledge and the security briefing last night, Nico knew a lot about the layout and the players. The heart of the control room was in the center of the top bank of desks where Jim Cernak, the Flight Operations Officer—the FOO—held sway. While he deferred to Bull Halsey on security generally, Cernak managed all technical aspects of the mission, so in that room, according to procedure, he was the ultimate authority, not Halsey.

When it was time for Nico's tour, his group was led into the amphitheater. At their last station, they crowded around their guide to listen to the most interesting explanation of the morning. Nico edged over to the desk with Cernak's name engraved on a plastic plate. Cernak was with the ops crew by the back wall, making room for the tour.

A row of thick manuals stood neatly on Cernak's work surface, but no loose papers. Nico leaned as the guide droned on and quickly slipped Madison's white letter-size envelope between two thick binders, sticking out just enough to appear to be in place, but still catch the eye of the FOO. Madison had summarized the technical explanations from Sato's documents in the manila envelope for Grover. For Cernak, she had boiled her message down to one sheet of paper.

Nico's group exited the control room floor. Additional guards took up places by the doors behind them.

Nico located the men's and women's restrooms near the observation gallery.

If the warnings to Grover and Cernak didn't work, Madison would have to intervene physically. Nico checked his watch. It was 8:45. He had one more task.

Chapter 120
MISSION CONTROL, 8:45PM

T-MINUS SEVENTY-FIVE MINUTES

Fully exposed, Madison and I stepped up to the ends of the two contractors' lines. If Shin had another surprise for us, now was his last chance. I kept glancing around for anyone loitering or looking out of place. Like a Mustang doing a hundred. It was all I had left to do. Unless Madison needed me.

I looked over at her standing in line on the left, where Nico should have entered. We had timed it so there were only a few people left in the lines. The sirens of the approaching VIP motorcade filled the air. As Nico had explained, Deng and his entourage were arriving at the front entrance about now. As he predicted, a thrill went through the people still in line at the contractors' entrances.

I managed to get up to the official checking IDs in my line and present my badge just as Madison was stepping up to the official at the other door. The man in front of me read the name off my badge and leafed through the list on a clipboard.

Madison spotted Jake in the line to her right. He seemed nervous, but maybe just vigilant. She couldn't tell.

She hadn't been nervous during her dissertation defense, or the months of DARPA review of OC-X, but she had been before DARPA awarded her invention the launch opportunity. And she was now. Each place she moved up in line increased her fear of discovery and the risk of failure of their mission.

The guard at the door behind the official lifted a paper on his clipboard, looked down, then looked back up at her. There were so few women. Halsey had to have handed out her photo. At this close range, the massive red hair teased high above her head, thick makeup and cat-eye, rhinestone-covered glasses frames might not be enough to get her in, even though she and Jake had inserted updated photo booth pictures into the badges Nico had given them.

As the official looked closely at her badge, she felt the most exposed she'd been since the Egmont Hotel. Suddenly Madison was staring at poor Sato, wild eyed, screaming as the assailant drew blood from a shallow cut in his neck.

Like a film in slow motion, she saw gashes open wide in Sato's and Harry's throats, bright red streams of blood pumped as the assailant's knife sliced through their tendons, muscles, and flesh like ripe tomatoes. She felt the crush of Park's and his assailant's bodies falling on her, her breath exploding from her lungs. She felt Harry's lifeless body beneath her, smelled blood as it flowed over her, soaking into her clothes.

Her knees started to buckle. She was close to blacking out, like she had in front of the Egmont, and again in K's apartment. This must be what Jake experienced during one of his attacks. It was horrible.

As the official looked at her badge, the nearby guard looked up from his clipboard and began to move toward her. He must have her photo. The disguise wasn't working.

Out of the corner of my eye, I caught Madison stepping up to the official in the other line. The one in front of me spoke.

"You're not on this list. I can't let you in. Please step aside."

Hearing him challenge me, the armed guard standing in front of the door for my line stared at me. He lifted a clipboard and leafed through some papers, looked at one, then back at me.

I glanced to my left. Madison was not in yet. A guard started moving toward her. I glared at the official in front of me and went into action.

"You must be wrong," I protested loudly. "J. Randolph, of the Simons, Randolph firm. We're the lawyers for the Center. It was a last-minute thing, but I have a special invitation."

The official looked back at his list. The armed guard looked down at his clipboard. If it was my photo, my hair color was wrong, and I had a fresh crewcut and thick, dark rimmed glasses.

The official at the door looked at his list again. "No sir. Please move out of the line and clear the area."

Madison was showing her badge at the other door. The guard near her had stopped and was staring in my direction, at the uproar. Even with her disguise, she might need a diversion. That's why I was here. I raised my voice again, nearly yelling, "There's been a mistake. *I want to talk to your supervisor.* ***You can't treat me like this***." Heads all around the entrances snapped in my direction to see what was going on.

The guard shifted the clipboard to one hand, put his other hand on his pistol grip, and moved toward me. "Lower your briefcase to the ground, sir. Put your hands in the air."

I raised my briefcase to my chest. The armed guard dropped the clipboard, drew his pistol, and grabbed his radio from his belt with his other hand. I screamed as loud as I could,

"**This is outrageous. I won't stand for it.**"

The guard raised his gun, aimed it at me and spoke into the radio. I glanced at the door on my left. Madison was still standing there. The official in front of her had turned to look toward the disturbance I was creating, but he was still blocking Madison's path.

I closed my eyes and pushed my briefcase into the official checking IDs.

The guard shouted. "Down on the ground. *Now.*"

I pushed the briefcase harder into the official's chest with one hand on the handle and grabbed a lapel with my other hand to get closer to him, blocking the officer's aim.

I heard running footsteps. There were other guards in the area. I turned to my left. Madison was still not in. It wasn't going to work. I gave the official another push that sent him sprawling. I turned and started to run.

Madison saw the official in front of her turn his gaze to his left. She followed and saw the guard at the other door pull his gun on Jake. The armed guard at her door took off to help. The official checking Madison's ID remained fixed on the disturbance.

Thank you, Jake, she said to herself, pulled her badge from the official's hand, and walked fast through the door. Before it had time to close behind her, a shot rang out.

Chapter 121
MISSION CONTROL, 8:55PM

T-MINUS SIXTY-FIVE MINUTES

As Madison entered Mission Control, she was almost knocked over by a pack of Halsey's security officers rushing toward the shot. The guard had been within point blank range of Jake. Without him, she would have been arrested. Madison wanted to run to him.

A piercing alarm whipped her attention back to her objective. She turned and walked quickly to the staircase Nico had described. When she got to the landing, she slowed down to avoid attention, walked up the stairs to the observation gallery level, and turned right. In a few strides, she opened the door and went into the women's restroom.

Nico came out of a toilet stall. "The case is in there." He hadn't heard the pistol crack.

" Nico, hurry. It's Jake. I'm afraid he's been shot."

He bolted out of the restroom. Madison went into the stall and changed into the clothes Nico had hidden under the papers in his document case. She wadded up her own clothes around her contractor's badge and stuffed them with her wig into the case. Then she grabbed the lanyard of the special badge Nico had left for her and put it over her head.

She went to the sink and wiped off her thick makeup with moist paper towels. She looked in the mirror, then at the new badge, then back at her face. It would have to do. She put the last accessory of her new outfit on her head, picked up Nico's document bag, and peered out the women's restroom door.

The observers were all in the gallery and no officials were in sight. They were probably all outside where the shot had come from. Madison walked briskly by the doors to the gallery, across to the other side of the landing, and into the men's room.

She checked her new aviator's wristwatch, a fitting gift from Jake last night. It was 9:10.

Chapter 122
MISSION CONTROL, 9:15PM,

T-MINUS FORTY-FIVE MINUTES

The VIP observers stood in line to wait for their special tour of the Control Room to begin. Madison did not stand out. She was dressed in a male Air Force captain's uniform that Jake had picked up at Redmon's Military Tailors yesterday afternoon using the measurements she had given him. She, too, now wore thick black rimmed glasses. Her own hair, died dark dull brown, was trimmed in a military crew cut under a black billed service hat.

She had waited in a stall in the men's room for ten minutes while the crisis Jake had created subsided. That helped avoid having to mingle with the real military officers, Then she had gone into the observer's gallery, taken a few papers out of Nico's bag, and focused on them intently to avoid any small talk. Now she waited for the military observers to be called to go into Mission Control.

Why had Jake run? The plan was just for him to provide a distraction. She had no idea what had happened. They'd both known the risks that had hovered over their conversation in the car like a vulture. But to think that someone she loved . . . .

That word was a surprise. Her feelings for Jake had a name now. She might never get to tell him. At least she had admitted it to herself.

There was renewed buzz in the air as Deng and his group entered the building. An officer ordered the military observers to line up.

Madison's special military badge survived the security check and she entered Mission Control. The Air Force major who owned the badge was sick in bed at the Hilton after a bad reaction to a drink Nico had doctored last night, a suggestion from Jake that Nico had finally accepted, risking his career again. The medals and insignia from the officer's uniform looked official on her brand new one.

After she entered the control room with the other guests, Madison jostled into place behind and between the seats of Grover Walker and Jim Cernak, directly behind the OC-X activation switch.

The electrical systems panel in front of the engineer who sat on the other side of Jim Cernak included the External Electrical Charge scope. If Sato's information was correct, the cosmic radiation would cause spiking on this instrument as the mission capsule entered the upper ionosphere. If human intervention failed before that, this ExEl Scope would be the only warning of imminent danger in the room, but an objective one that a flight engineer couldn't ignore, unless they were distracted or overcome by fear.

Would Grover act? Madison had more confidence in Jim Cernak, even without the detailed calculations that Nico had left for Grover last night. Jim Cernak was tough, used to evaluating hard data in a split second under high stress. If he failed, Madison was the last line of defense.

Bull Halsey entered Mission Control and headed straight for Madison's location, trailing two NASA security guards. They were trained to respond with all force necessary in this sensitive room if anyone made a false move.

She thought about Jake again. Fear that he was dead gripped her. Her heart sank. Harry, Sato and the two Koreans had lost their lives. Nakamura was missing. Charlie was in custody. Tom O'Hanlon and Nico had put their careers, and Nico his life, in jeopardy to help. Now Jake.

Chapter 123
MISSION CONTROL, 9:47AM

Madison eyed Grover closely. His hands were twitching, his eyes darting around the room. As the project manager in charge of OC-X, he was responsible for its performance. It was clear to her that he had received and read the documents Nico had left for him at the Hilton. He was not reacting well.

Suddenly, Halsey came up behind him, leaned in and pinned Grover to his desk.

"Walker, I want you to make sure this goes off without a hitch. Deng goddamned Xiaoping will be up here in a few minutes and it's your job to make sure your OC-X startup goes smooth as a baby's butt. Got it?"

Halsey turned to his armed NASA Security Guards and pointed to the OC-X activation lever. "No one, I mean no one, stops the little Chinese guy from throwing that switch."

"Yes, sir," they barked.

Grover cowered and turned to look at Cernak. Madison saw the white envelope was sticking out from between two binders, unopened. If he even read it,

Cernak might have little time to react, so her message was factual and blunt:

Jim-

Japanese stole OC-X from Cameron and built a system they put in their I.M.S. launch last September. Unexpected massive cosmic radiation during that mission caused electrical energy spikes, overloading the OC-X copy in their satellite and ground links, blowing up Kagoshima mission control, killing forty.

They covered it up. For confirmation, watch for spikes on the ExEl scope.

A reading of thirty-five is already dangerous. If it goes above fifty you will all die.

I went over Bull's head to DC once. I'm counting on you now. Remember I backed Bull down when he wanted to remove OC-X from the flight. Now you must back him down to do just that.

Madison Whitmire

The last part of the message was the only way she could think of to authenticate her authorship. Jim was dedicated to facts, a man of action. She prayed that he would see the spike on the scope, that he would believe the note, and that he would abort the OC-X activation.

But he wasn't looking at the scope. He hadn't read her note. He was busy talking into his headset, probably to Cape Kennedy. They were coming up on the go-live for Mission Control.

As Madison watched Cernak closely, the Chinese delegation took their place. The Chinese and their Secret Service agents closed in and blocked her view of the control desks.

At a minute to liftoff, a cheer went up in Mission Control. The crowd between Madison and the control desk thinned as the visitors spread out to get a better view of the massive telemetry and video screens at the front of the room.

Madison's line of sight to the activation switch was still partially obstructed. The big NASA security guards flanked Grover, carefully watching anyone near his desk. There was no way she could get through them to prevent the initiation. But if Cernak didn't, she would have to try.

The audio feed from Cape Kennedy came over the control room speakers. "T minus ten, nine, eight seven, six, five, four, three . . . ." The roar of the giant Athena rocket drowned out the final words as it rose majestically from the launch pad on the video screens. The sound was so loud, her body shook and her vision blurred.

The men lining the back wall surged forward as if pulled by the energy of the rocket engines. Madison pressed forward with them to get closer to the OC-X activation switch. There were less than ten minutes to OC-X initiation.

She saw Jim Cernak clap his neighbor on the shoulder and heard him say, "Hot dog, Sam. I love a launch."

Now that Mission Control tracking was locked on, Cernak had a few minutes to savor the thrill. His real job would start as soon as the missile reached the upper ionosphere. He looked down to check the critical event sheet positioned beneath the glass cover on the top of his desk. Madison saw him stare at the out of place white envelope between his mission binders. He pulled it out, saw his handwritten name and the words "URGENT. MISSION CRITICAL. OPEN IMMEDIATELY."

He looked up. Everywhere around him, there were strange faces. He tore open the envelope and started to read it.

A hush fell over the room as everyone watched the video screens and saw the streaking rocket become smaller and smaller. In the eerie silence, for a moment, the only sounds were the soft clicks from digital readouts.

Then Bull Halsey barked instructions. “Clear out. Make room.”

The men in front of her moved aside and there was a short man in a Mao jacket standing by Grover. Madison was now two just steps away from Deng Xiaoping.

Three dark suited Americans with radio earpieces hovered around him. Halsey was speaking to Deng’s interpreter and pointing to the OC-X button, gesturing to show how it worked.

Grover lifted the security cover that prevented an accidental activation of the OC-X system. Madison knew then that he wasn’t going to abort. She watched intently as the huge digital readout on the front wall passed T plus four minutes. She could see the ExEl Charge scope. It wasn’t moving. Had she read Sato’s data correctly? Then the scope needle began to rise. She stared at Cernak, trying to will his attention to the scope.

Her eyes jumped back to the scope. The needle crawled by ten, then started to speed up as the capsule rose in the ionosphere. It was up to twenty and moving faster now. She looked back at Cernak. He was staring at her note.

Oh God, Jim. Do something. He looked up at Halsey. She followed his shifting gaze, as he scrutinized Grover and scanned around Deng. The three Secret Service agents were scanning, too. Halsey’s two NASA guards had their hands on their holstered pistols.

The needle passed thirty, accelerating. Cernak would be too late. Madison had to cover two steps, then pull the security lid over the switch without activating the system. She shifted her gaze from the holstered guns to the OC-X switch and gauged the distance. Like initiating the run up to a high jump, she rocked once to create muscle tension. Time slowed to a crawl.

The Secret Service agents caught her movement. They began to collapse on Deng. Halsey’s NASA Guards saw it, too. They drew their guns. They were trained to assess the risks of a shot near critical systems that could ignite something that might explode.

The readout spiked above thirty-five and Cernak shouted, "Abort OC-X. *Don't throw the lever, Grover.* ***Lock it down.***"

His shout distracted Halsey's NASA agents. Cernak was the supreme authority in the room, the only person there who outranked their boss. As they turned to look at Cernak, they took their eyes off Madison's Air Force uniform. Cernak was right next to Grover who was now completely paralyzed.

Cernak reached over to shut the OC-X initiation switch cover, but Halsey, gun drawn, was in maximum protection mode. He pushed Cernak out of the way. That cleared Madison's access to the switch. She lunged.

Halsey, off balance after pushing Cernak, turned and fired as she snapped the cover shut, aborting the OC-X activation.

That's all she remembered.

Chapter 124
HOUSTON, SUNDAY, FEBRUARY 4

I heard metal scrape against metal. A blinding light hit my eyelids. I strained to lift my hand to cover them, but it didn't move. With difficulty, I tried to turn my head away from the light. No luck. I sensed I was in a hospital bed and saw a woman with an odd buzz-cut but an exceedingly pretty face sitting beside me. What a weird dream, I thought. She looks a lot like Madison.

As I opened my eyes slightly, the image resolved into Nico's concerned face.

"What are you looking so worried about?" I said. "Where's Madison? She was just here."

"Jake," Nico said with some difficulty. "She's not here."

I tried to sit up but fell back. "Where are we? What happened? What do you mean, not here?"

"This is a Level Four trauma center. She stopped the madness, Jake. Deng is safe. But she was shot in the process."

Though I couldn't move a muscle, my mind went wild. Nico, looking into my eyes, saw it. "She's nearby, in intensive care."

Adrenaline pumping, I tried to sit up and managed to raise up an inch or so, then fell back. "I've got to see her."

Nico put his hand on my shoulder. "Not now. She's under heavy sedation. Give her a chance to recover."

"No." I was frantic, not thinking. "If she's in any danger, I need to see her right away."

"Doctors won't let you, Jake. It's intensive care. They're in control. Settle down and rest so you'll be strong when she comes out of it."

"What happened?" I was having trouble clearing the cobwebs out of my brain and separating what was real from what was not. It felt a lot like most of the last month.

"You don't remember?" Nico asked. "You got shot. That wasn't in the plan."

Now it was coming back. "I . . . I didn't think Madison would get through. I needed to make a bigger distraction."

"Don't worry. It was plenty," Nico assured me. "You got shot in the back, running away. Damned lucky nothing vital was hit, but you lost a lot of blood. It took a sewing machine to stitch it all up. You'll be back to work in no time."

"What about K? Where's Charlie?"

Nico's weak smile couldn't hide the bleak reality. "No one has seen Nakamura since he left you seven days ago." He brightened slightly. "Charlie will be here any minute. Tom's picking him up at the airport. It took a fair amount of lobbying to spring him from the brig at McCord. A lot has happened in the last forty-eight hours. We've been working while you've been napping."

Charlie burst into the hospital room followed by Tom O'Hanlon. "Dang it all, Jake. I take a little time off and all hell breaks loose. Is the little Chinese guy in here, too?"

Nico responded. "Went to a rodeo down the road then off to Seattle, wearing a huge ten-gallon hat. Looked like a buffoon in the pictures, but it worked like a PR flak's dream. The American public is now officially in love with Communist China."

"Are we under arrest?" I wondered, "I don't see any cops."

Tom stepped over to my bedside. "It's complicated. Nico may have rescued us all."

"It's a huge mess, Jake," Nico offered. "The guy we found when we tailed Untermeyer, remember?"

"Yeah," I recalled, "something about a hamburger joint near Wall Street."

"Well," Nico explained, "He was found by the FBI yesterday afternoon in a Houston motel after an anonymous tip. He was tied up in a chair next to a dead body and a box of audio tapes laying out the whole scheme, it seems." Nico paused. "A lot of agencies are fighting over who gets him. But no one knows quite what to do with him. Don't worry, they'll think of something."

"Which you know nothing about, of course," I started to laugh, but stopped and clutched my chest as the pain flared.

"No details." Nico watched me recover, then looked around, leaned in close, and whispered in my ear, "Well, just a few. He was the key to Shin's network in the US. Got hooked up with Shin as a result of his intelligence work in Japan. Fluent in Japanese. Talented guy. Shin had a great deal of experience sniffing out personal weaknesses and turning them to his advantage."

Tom chimed in. "The guy paid Felix Untermeyer money to steal OC-X. A lot of money. In Switzerland."

"Untermeyer did it for the money?"

Tom added, "And a misplaced sense of his own importance. He knew he wouldn't rise any higher at CT, but he felt he was better than all the other execs, including McElwain. Untermeyer managed Staley's access to McElwain."

"Ego. Frustrated ambition. Sounds like Malinkrodt. Who does your hiring, Tom?" I started to sit up again, but still couldn't make it. "What about Untermeyer's accusations against Madison? His proof she was the thief?"

"Untermeyer used his top security clearance to bring two IT professionals into Cameron R & D. They inserted the faked files in the IT system. Charlie, tell him the best part."

"Remember I told Jerry Suddeth to go in and check some document references? While he'as there that Saturday, he saw old Felix and his two partners go into R & D. Then checked the security log. The two others weren't signed in. Jerry smelled a rat, a bamboo rat . . . whatever. He went into R & D and saw them go into the computer center with bags. Come Monday he got Preston's name from Frank Brazeale and gave an affidavit while ya'll was creating a commotion down here. Helped the IT guys trace the faked files this weekend."

Despite the good story, I only had one thing on my mind now. "I need to see Madison."

Tom spoke. "She's been unconscious or sedated since she got here. The doctors have to ease her back to consciousness."

"Why?" I demanded.

Tom lowered his voice, "Jake, there's a bad risk of an embolism from internal bleeding. If one got loose—"

Nico jumped in to reassure me. "You're in the Texas Trauma Center. These are the best emergency docs in the world, Jake. She'll pull through."

"Tom just got a message from Preston Lawton at your firm," Charlie added to the distraction. "You and me gotta be in Greenville soon as you can travel to git ready to try the case against Malinkrodt. It's set for the middle a March. I'm bringing the spit and the charcoal. Frank'll get the barbecue sauce, some a them torta-rilla chips, and that green stuff."

"What else did Shin's guy give up, Tom?" Their efforts to distract me from Madison's condition were working.

Tom laid it out. "Kano wanted OC-X *and* P.E.T. technology. He asked Mueller to get Malinkrodt to go after both at Cameron, even rented a photocopier for

Malinkrodt's home. That's how OC-X showed up in the handwritten note Stefan had taken by mistake. But Malinkrodt got scared and wouldn't go after OC-X. So, Shin put his man to work."

"They went after Felix. But they didn't let up on P.E.T. Kano, diligent negotiator that he is, used Malinkrodt's refusal on OC-X to demand more and better P.E.T disclosures. Malinkrodt signed a separate consulting agreement with Minimura, cutting out Mueller. That's what Minimura and Garrett, the Swinton associate, tried to hide from you: the second contract directly with Malinkrodt, his lecture notes, and all the notebooks of the engineers who attended Malinkrodt's second set of lectures that you found during the second Nagahama factory visit. They almost succeeded. That's where the technology for Line Four came from: Malinkrodt screwing Mueller to get Minimura to pay him directly."

I managed a weak smile. "Preston would proclaim *No honor among thieves!* And a jury would eat it up."

"One more thing," Tom added. "We're in settlement negotiations with Minimura. It'll be at least ten million dollars, maybe more."

A nurse approached. "That's enough, gentleman. He needs to rest."

"One more thing," I insisted. "What the hell was Morgan's involvement, and the Gordan law firm?'

"Morgan was truly a rogue, recruited by Shin's man, too. He used the prestige of the Gordon firm to keep others from checking behind him: Beau Stoner from your firm was easy. He never read Mueller's deposition because the Gordon firm took it."

"He got me, too," Tom admitted. "I accepted Morgan's explanation about his agreement with InterTech about disclosing names. I remember you challenged me on that, Jake. I'm sorry."

I didn't need sorry. Morgan was in jail.

The nurse stepped in and shooed them all away, leaving me alone. I laid back, worried, and brooded. I had to see Madison as soon as the doctors would let me.

Chapter 125
HERMAN DUKE TRAUMA CENTER, 10:30AM, TWO DAYS LATER

I learned that Bull Halsey shot Madison with a .357 Magnum loaded Smith and Wesson Model 19 revolver. A beast of a gun for a beast of a man. The damaged blood vessels caused an extreme amount of internal bleeding. In all the confusion in the control room, it had taken too long to get Madison through the security at NASA, into the ambulance, and rushed to the trauma facility at the Texas Medical Center, twenty-eight miles away.

The operation had taken six hours. The danger of an embolism remained severe. The doctors had to keep her sedated, on a respirator, to avoid unnecessary motion. They had to feather her off the meds to see if she could safely regain consciousness. But that took four days. She was off the respirator but severely weakened by the ordeal.

The doctors finally let me in to see her on the fifth day. They warned me she was still at-risk from blood clots. She couldn't take blood thinners in case there was one and it got loose.

I was the first one from the team to see her after the shootings.

As a doctor and some administrator were leaving Madison's intensive care bay, the nurse rolled my wheelchair in and locked it beside her bed. Madison lay quietly, her eyes closed. I listened a moment to her soft breathing amid the hums and low beeps from her support systems. I didn't say a word, just reached over and held her hand.

She opened her eyes, turned to me, and smiled. It wasn't the thousand-watt version, but it was way up there. And I lit up like a Christmas tree.

"You look like hell, Jake." Her voice was very weak. "Does your last name finally apply to you, not just to all the people you interrogate?"

I laughed, really laughed, at another of her terrible jokes.

"I'm fine." I gave her a soft kiss on her cheek." You, on the other hand, look beautiful."

"You're a liar, lawyer, but thanks."

"You did it, Madison, you saved the Chairman. He was sorry not to see you in person. But he told Tom to thank you for allowing him to make the rodeo over near Fort Worth. And for saving his life. The pictures of him in a ten-gallon hat are on every front page in the country, maybe the world. Next to yours."

"We did it, Jake, you and me, with help from all the others. How are they?"

"Charlie got released and just arrived. No word about K, yet. I'm afraid there won't be any."

"I'm so sorry." The intensive care nurse was still hovering nearby, but Madison wanted to talk to me, alone. "Would you mind giving us a bit of privacy?" she asked.

"I'll be right outside, Doctor. But no movement, none. And no excitement, understand?" She shot me a withering glare.

Madison lifted her arms weakly, pierced with intravenous drips. "What trouble could I get into, skewered like this?" She smiled again, making the nurse's day.

After the nurse left, Madison turned to me. "I lashed out at you, Jake." She tried to laugh but gasped and clutched the bed rails. "Oooh, I was mad at you after you grilled me that first day." She stopped and held my hand to her cheek. "Then you reached out to me."

Her smile brightened as tears ran down her face. "It was like a key opening up my heart."

Those words touched off a silent shock wave within me. I could barely see. I couldn't speak.

"Thank you for that, Jake."

"Madison." I leaned over and kissed her once more. "I won't leave you again."

The nurse was rustling now. Our time was short.

"You won't have to, Jake. I have a plan."

I sat up and looked into her eyes. They were sparkling and bright. The nurse was on the move now. "Sir, she has to rest. This is too much for her."

Madison gently pulled me to her and whispered, "I'm coming to you. I'll work on OC-X from Cameron. We can . . . ." Her eyes fluttered.

"It will work, Madison. It's a great plan." I was overcome. "But if we have to, we'll *impervise*."

"We can have a real date. Lots of them to make up for lost time. We've never had one." I smiled and kissed her again. "Jake, be here in case I . . . ."

Don't make it? She was scared. I was scared.

"I will, Madison. Don't worry. Sleep now. I'll see you soon." It was a hope, and a prayer.

She closed her eyes.

Chapter 126
KITA CITY, TOKYO, DAWN, SUNDAY, FEBRUARY 17

Shin, kneeling on the *tatami* mat laid incongruously on the polished wooden floor in the thoroughly western oak paneled study of the *kyu-Fujiwara,* stared at the implements for the ceremony: the *wakizashi* blade and the *choku* filled with *saké* before him. He must concentrate, but one thing haunted him. The news had been like the kick of a horse to his gut.

Deng had survived, due to the monk and the three Americans the monk helped escape. Deng was now untouchable. And Shin's worst fears about the looming threat of China would become reality.

In his shame, Shin had to admit the worthiness of his opponents. He had hated them too much. He had not respected them. But they did not understand. They would come to regret unleashing the Chinese dragon. Shin's thinking was correct. He was grateful that he would not live to be proven right.

There was a knock at the door. Shin's *kaishakunin* had arrived. It was not such a surprise when the man had contacted Shin. His assessment of the man had changed. In fact, Shin considered it an honor to meet him now.

When Shin learned that K Nakamura was a master *samurai*-trained swordsman, he had accepted K's offer to be Shin's second for the *seppuku*. It was fitting that one's enemy assured that the ritual suicide would succeed.

Chapter 127
GREENVILLE, 9:10AM, TUESDAY, MARCH 13, 1979

I was in the courthouse on a wooden bench in the hall outside the big courtroom. Malinkrodt was inside, awaiting his fate in CT's civil trial. By agreement it would be a trial without a jury. We hoped a judge would understand the complex facts and protect the trade secrets better than a jury. Malinkrodt's lawyer, Tinsdale, was hoping a judge, unlike a jury, could set aside the emotional impact of facts like the 957-foot factory elevation and the secret tour of Minimura engineers at Cameron and give credit to Malinkrodt's personal expertise. The Consolidated team were all there to testify. Charlie, Jerry, and a raft of experts would explain over thirteen trade secrets.

The courthouse is across the street from the Lawton firm where this all started. It seemed like years and a world away. My first day on the case, I'd been dead wrong about all three of my partners: Tom, Charlie, and Madison. And while I'd been wary of John Morgan, there was no way I could have imagined he would send private investigators to break into Stefan's apartment and threaten him or send them after Charlie to beat him up, or worse..

I could not have imagined the depths to which the best lawyers from the best firms in the world could sink. Morgan was in jail charged with conspiring to and abetting breaking, entering, assault, and witness intimidation. Austen Swinton was disgraced and charged with income tax evasion for the millions he had been paid under the table by Shin. I couldn't see how Garrett could make partner. But then maybe his scheming in Tokyo assured that he would.

In fact, nothing was as it seemed. The massive Minimura *keiretsu* turned out to be a shield for Shin's machinations. The industrial trade secrets case hid an international assassination plot. I would never view the world the same again. I started out knowing that in court the truth was what you made it. It turned out the world wasn't much different.

State court was not the only legal venue that would be pressed into service to resolve the legal consequences of Kano's ambition and Shin's mania. As soon as Consolidated received the large settlement payment from Minimura, Tom O'Hanlon instructed me to turn all the evidence over to the Federal District Attorney. The FBI was preparing a trip to Tokyo to add what it could to my files. They really didn't need to. There was enough in my files to support Federal charges of interstate theft against Minimura and Malinkrodt.

Japanese defendants could not risk a trial in the U.S., especially in South Carolina. I was certain the corporation would plead guilty. Kano would not. The US-Japan extradition treaty did not allow it for white-collar crime. That was too bad. At least Kano could never return to the US or he would face arrest and Federal prison.

I had learned all about Shin from a translation of his personal diary that K Nakamura had sent me and from K's accompanying letter. Shin had given K the diary at their last meeting, instructing him to share it with me and no one else. After reading Shin's life story and K's explanation of how Shin died, I could almost sympathize with Shin, except for the fact that he was a raving psychopath.

The bizarre circumstances of Shin's ritual suicide were unfathomable to a Westerner, at least to me. K had offered to assist Shin and he had accepted. In my mind that made K as enigmatic as Shin. Apparently by granting that grisly yet respected role to an adversary, Shin increased the dignity of his personal sacrifice. Go figure.

The U.S. national security espionage situation was opaque. Nico had quit the CIA he really worked for. Privately lauded by many of his colleagues, he was officially a pariah in the twisted post-FISA world for helping thwart Deng's assassination. We'd developed some kind of ongoing relationship. No one was saying what happened to Shin's man after he was found, shot, bound, and gagged next to the tapes with his confession. But Nico knew. He told me his version of the whole story, including how close Madison and I had been to death in room 212 at the EconoLodge. Were we friends or was he manipulating me for some other reason? I couldn't tell.

Not only was the truth difficult to pin down, secrets made it harder. Shin used his massive resources to keep theft of P.E.T. and the OC-X technology secret. I tried to hide my panics, my guilt, my shame. Madison kept the effects of her parents' deaths, of sexual harassment, and an erosive anger secret even from herself. We traded secrets, sometimes for the better, sometimes for the worse. Madison and I had shared our deepest secrets that night at Cameron and during our extended ride to Houston. We'd discovered a relationship that freed us from our pasts and opened up our future.

As the clock ticked down to the start of the trial, I thought of those who wouldn't be there, ever. George and Stefan. K's Korean guards. The stalwart Japanese: Harry and Sato. Tom O'Hanlon had Sato's handwritten notebook from his red knapsack translated and sent me a copy. It told his story of struggle and sacrifice.

Confronting and escaping death. In front of the hotel in Tokyo, I was afraid Madison had died. But she survived the massacre. In trying to save her, in putting her life before mine, I discovered I had conquered my panic, at least for now.

She was in terrible shape when I saw her in intensive care in Houston. The administrator I saw leaving her was in fact another lawyer. In a selfless act of kindness, ever the objective scientist, she had known the danger to her life and made a will. Under it, I would receive any royalties from her patents and the assets from her trust fund if she died.

Now that we had validated Sato's documents, her technology was safe. Developing it could fill a long, fruitful career.

If Madison hadn't intervened, Deng would have died, and her invention would have been discredited. That would have left the door open for the Japanese to trumpet their system as "independent and superior" and muddied the water over the rights to her patents. Thanks to Sato's revelations and Madison's courage, the theft and use of OC-X were known by the right people. Minimura would not risk making any claim.

Warned by Madison, Consolidated designed their own shielding solution to protect the launch tracking system, NASA had given Madison's payload a place of honor on an I.M.S. launch two days ago. By all accounts, her invention was a success.

Our race across the Pacific and fight against the odds had dominated the international press. Was it worth it? Who could say if Shin's geopolitical fears were misplaced? Maybe the Japanese with their perspective of millennia across the sea from China understood that nation and its people more clearly than naïve, impatient Americans. Perhaps one day China would prove to be a powerful and dangerous adversary to us all. But the thought that such fine people had sacrificed their lives in error to save Deng was too much for me to contemplate.

These were deep currents carrying possible truths that would never surface in the trial. They were causing me difficulties in making sense of our ordeal, the power of the forces that had emerged from the darkness to fight against us, or that our eclectic and slightly eccentric gang had so narrowly defeated them. My reverence for big time law practice was blunted, thanks to the illegal and unethical actions of some of the most respected lawyers and law firms in the world.

And Shin's cultural analyses were troubling. Was the materialism and unbridled individualism of America a systemic flaw? Did the timeless, selfless values attributed to Japanese culture grow out of a more basic understanding of human nature, of all nature? I didn't like philosophy in college, or constitutional law the way it was taught in law school: lots of angels dancing on heads of pins. But these questions grew out of real life.

For now, I tended to view it all pragmatically: Morgan, Garrett, and Swinton were unethical crooks, and Shin was a psychopath. We won. But the jury in my mind was still out on the larger questions.

My future was uncertain. I knew I had to move on, but where? Hell, Beau had moved on. Preston had to take over the Texas paper mill case. Beau had to move on to a face-saving appointment in a magistrate in small claims court, arranged by Preston.

I had learned so much in a few short months. The larger legal stage I had wanted to play on was eclipsed by the real world. Could I spend untold hours rehashing clients' mistakes? Did I really want to risk expending time and energy preparing only to end up at the quixotic beck and call of venal, self-serving executives like Untermeyer and McElwain?

The smug self-confidence that I'd picked up from watching Preston work cases was half-right, a misreading of his true strength. Courage was needed to confront adversity, but not fool-hardiness. Charlie and his friends, and Nico, and Madison had all taught me to listen to and respect others' opinions. I hoped I wouldn't forget that.

Having burned his bridges with the CIA, Nico joined a group of seasoned international troubleshooters to start a law and consulting firm. His version of the real story of Shin's man was a test. He'd asked me to join his firm, working on international matters "making real money." I hadn't decided.

It was too soon. I couldn't solve all the puzzles or make sense of the real story. Not yet. For now, there was only the story of the case, the one that I would begin telling in a few minutes.

I turned these thoughts over and over in my mind. Not to resolve them. I couldn't. But I didn't want too. They were a distraction. From the worst thing. The worst thing in my life. The thing that should have killed me. I wished it had.

Madison died in intensive care. We were on the threshold of something new, something extraordinary and exciting. We had almost no time to talk about it, but there was no doubt. We had a future together, somehow. Now there was none, together, or for me, without her.

The pain I suffered each night overwhelmed me as I sat there on the hard-wooden bench. Sobs shook my body and tears soaked my shirt. I was helpless. She was the strong one. She knew what would happen, yet she used her last breaths to give me hope. Her love and generosity were beyond value. The thought of having to start a new life without her crushed my soul.

I couldn't move for a long time. Finally, I began to breathe without gasping. The bailiff stuck his head out the courtroom door and called to me from down the hall. "Judge's coming, Jake. Better hurry."

Struggling to my feet, I trudged down the hall. Somehow, I arrived at the heavy polished mahogany door and tugged it open. Heads turned. Standing at the threshold of the wood paneled chamber, I wavered, clutched the door, and leaned on it for support. It took a moment before I could summon the strength to take the first step.

As I shuffled along the bar that separated the legal actors from the real world, head down trying to hide my swollen face, I nodded at Tom O'Hanlon and Charlie seated at the plaintiff's table. I slumped down in the "first chair" for the lead counsel that Preston had left unoccupied next to him. He clasped my shoulder.

A door at the side of the raised dais opened. The bailiff cried, "All rise." I did, barely.

The judge strode in, black robes swirling as he crossed to the bench, and took command. "Be seated," the bailiff intoned. I slumped down again. The closest I'd been to judges and courtrooms in months had been running from them in Texas. A thousand years ago.

If I could just start, I thought, I could weave the story of the case, even though it was too close to the real one that was now a part of me. But with my body emptied by grief, I couldn't stand. Avoiding the judge's expectant stare, I turned my face away.

And then I saw her. Madison. Seated alone. Not burned or wounded. Not damaged. Miraculously whole again. Strong, eager. She smiled her thousand watt-smile and urged me on. I straightened in the first chair and we held each other across the distance. I felt her hot, warm tears on my face again. Tears of joy.

"Counselor?" The judge shuffled papers, impatient. The room was silent, wondering. As I turned back, Preston's fierce eyebrows shot up in a question. I rose to plead a case for the last time.

"May it please the Court."

ACKNOWLEDGMENTS

Listing my indebtedness and gratitude to all those who contributed directly and indirectly to this work over forty years would be an convoluted journey and a bewildering one for the reader. So I'll refer here to the groups from which inspiration and support have come. More particulars are available through extended material that can be found at www.paynethrillers.com. Any bright spots in this book are due in many respects to these people. Any errors are mine alone.

-teachers and learners from: New Trier Township High School, Princeton University, and The University of Virginia School of Law;

-colleagues and students at: Haynsworth, Perry, Bryant, Marion & Johnstone; Groupe Michelin; ESC Clermont Graduate School of Management; George Washington University Graduate School of Business; Holy Spirit University of Kaslik, Beirut; The Mahler Company; Cairn Consulting LLC; Processes and Procedures LLC.

-gracious and supportive editor and literary agent the late Loretta Barrett; generous authors Gayle Lynds, Diane Burke, and Jo Watson Hackl; and writing instructors, authors, and students at OLLI at Furman University and International Thriller Writers Inc.

-patient and thoughtful readers Curt Fitzgerald, Brian and Marian Hays, Susan Humphreys, Susan Morton, James Roy, Tom and Jamie Shuler, and Charlotte Cecil Raymond.

ABOUT THE AUTHOR

Thomson Roy has worked in over forty countries as a trial and corporate lawyer, international executive, professor/instructor, and consultant. He has lived outside the U. S. with his family in France, Brazil, Hong Kong, and Singapore. And for extended stays—missing his family terribly—in Japan, South Korea, Thailand, the Philippines, India, and China.

He and his wife of forty-seven fantastic years, Janeice, now live in Greenville, South Carolina and have three great children and three wonderful grandchildren spread around the world.

THOMSON ROY'S NEXT NOVEL
A JAKE PAYNE INTERNATIONAL THRILLER
COMING SOON

THE CRESCENT AND THE DOUBLE CROSS

Jake is on his own and hurting when Tom O'Hanlon calls to send Jake and Charlie are off again, this time to Paris. To see if the same industrial trade secrets have been stolen, again. How hard can that be?

Full workdays, sure. But the food! Walks along the Seine and through storied *arrondissements.* Visits to cultural treasures. And trips for the client to Lyon, a *bijou* in the French gastronomic crown.

Until an incident in a restaurant owned by the Lebanese family of a friend of Charlie exposes a world of modern and ancient feuds.

In the midst of political and religious upheaval in France, Beirut—the Paris of the Middle East—and beyond. On the brink of the Iranian Revolution.

You are cordially invited to visit paynethrillers.com to discover what's behind Jake Payne thrillers. There you'll find true stories, even a few puzzling challenges, just for you.

Why should Jake and Charlie have all the fun?

Made in the USA
Middletown, DE
27 December 2020